THE FORTY-NINERS

THE FORTY-NINERS

WILLIAM W. JOHNSTONE
AND J. A. JOHNSTONE

THORNDIKE PRESS
A part of Gale, a Cengage Company

Then shalt thou lay up gold as dust,
and the gold of Ophir as the stones of
the brooks.

— Job 22:24

He that trusteth in his riches shall fall;
but the righteous shall flourish as a
branch.

— Proverbs 11:28

■ ■ ■ ■

BOOK I

■ ■ ■ ■

CHAPTER 1

The Ozark Mountains, Arkansas, 1848
Cord Bennett laid his cheek against the smooth wood of the rifle stock, peered over the barrel at his target, held his breath, and squeezed the trigger.

The old flintlock boomed and kicked hard against his shoulder. Gray smoke gushed from the barrel. For a moment, Cord couldn't see what he'd just shot at.

Then the smoke cleared, and he spotted the small, furry shape lying on the ground at the base of the tree. A moment earlier, the squirrel had been standing on a branch, chattering away.

The critter was dead now, head clipped clean off by the ball from Cord's rifle. That left the body intact for skinning, cleaning, and plunking in the stewpot.

Along with the other three squirrels Cord had shot earlier during his tramp through the woods, they would make a nice mess of vittles. Enough to feed Cord, his pa, and his two brothers for a couple of meals, anyway.

Cord walked over to the trees to pick up the squirrel he'd just shot and add it to the bounty in the sack slung over his shoulder. He was glad it had been a productive jaunt and he wouldn't come home empty-handed.

Whistling a little tune, Cord started to walk off, but then he stopped. Even though there was nothing all that dangerous in these woods, a smart man reloaded his rifle as soon as he got a chance after using it. An empty rifle wasn't worth a blamed thing unless the threat got close enough to use it as a club. It was just a burden.

Once the flintlock was ready to fire again, Cord started home. In his early twenties, he was of medium height but appeared slightly stocky because of the heavy muscles he had developed working on the farm. His back and shoulders stretched the fabric of the homespun shirt he wore.

He had no hat, so the sun beat down on the thick shock of light brown hair on his head. His face was open and friendly, often smiling, an indicator of his stubborn determination to make the best of things, no matter how bad they got.

And here lately, they had gotten pretty bad.

He emerged from the trees and came out at the top of a bare slope overlooking the little mountain valley where the Bennett family farm was located. Smoke curled from the stone chimney at one end of the log cabin.

Beyond it was the shed where the milk cow and the two mules were kept, and past that was the hog pen. Chickens pecked futilely at the bare ground between the cabin and the shed and pen. Maybe they thought they saw some bugs, but Cord was pretty sure they were mistaken.

The fields stretched off to the left, toward the head of the valley. They looked pretty pathetic. The corn was dying from the hot, dry weather. The fruit trees in the little orchard had produced what looked, earlier in the summer, like it might be a pretty good crop.

But now the fruit was shriveling up, too. Nothing could grow worth a lick in weather like this. Even the hog pen had just about dried up, and the hogs were covered with crusted dirt instead of mud. They looked miserable.

And the worst part of it was, this was the second summer in a row with such prevailing conditions. The relief the area had gotten during the previous fall and winter hadn't been enough to allow things to recover.

Cord shook his head and told himself not to dwell on such things. You had to take the world and do what you could with it. You sure couldn't reach up to the sky and *shake* the rain out of it, no matter how much you might feel like doing that.

He saw no sign of his older brothers Flint and Steve and didn't know if they were inside the cabin or off somewhere else. Not that it mattered. Cord couldn't blame them for not working. What could they do . . . what could anybody do . . . in weather like this.

A moment later, his pa come out of the cabin and walked around toward the shed and hog pen. Verne Bennett was tall and rake-thin, with white hair under his shapeless old hat and a white beard. Cord saw the sun flash off something his pa was holding and realized Verne had a knife.

He was going to butcher one of the hogs, Cord thought, thinning the bunch even more. Eventually the hogs would all be gone.

That wasn't necessary today, not with the bounty Cord was bringing in. Cord leaned the rifle against a nearby tree and cupped his hands around his mouth to shout, "Pa, wait!" The words echoed from the hills that surrounded the valley.

Verne halted and looked around toward the hill where Cord stood. At that moment, Cord caught a flash of movement from the corner of his eye and turned his head to the left to look along the valley.

Dust rose in that direction. After a second, he spotted the buggy heading toward the farm. He waved his arm so his pa could see and then pointed in that direction.

"Company comin'!"

That was a stroke of luck. Verne turned away from the hog pen so he could greet the visitor, whoever that might be. Mountain hospitality wouldn't allow him to do any less. That would give Cord time to get down the hill and let his pa know about the squirrels in his sack.

It rankled a little, knowing Pa hadn't had any confidence that he'd bring back some game.

By the time Cord reached the bottom of the hill, the buggy had stopped in front of the cabin. He saw sunlight flash again, this time on fair hair, not the blade of a butcher knife. His heart gave a little jump in his chest as he recognized Caroline Stockton on the buggy seat.

Cord had been sweet on Caroline for

almost as far back as he could remember. Her pa had a much more successful farm than the Bennett place in the next valley over, and Hiram Stockton also owned several businesses in the nearby settlement of Wilbur. He was rich, at least according to Boston Mountain standards.

And he wasn't fond of the idea of his daughter getting mixed up with a hardscrabble farmer like Cord.

Luckily for Cord, Caroline didn't seem to feel the same way. She'd been friendly ever since they were kids, and as they got older, that friendship showed signs of maturing into something deeper.

Cord sure hoped so, anyway.

As he walked up, his father was standing beside the buggy horse, holding the animal's headstall while Caroline sat on the seat. She turned to Cord with an excited smile and said, "There you are! I was hoping you'd be here."

"Where else would I be?" Cord asked, then immediately felt like an idiot for saying that.

"Why, off tramping around in the woods, of course. You like to do that better than anything else, don't you?" She gestured toward the sack slung from his shoulder.

14

"And I see that's exactly what you've been doing."

Cord glanced down at his side. Blood from the squirrels had soaked through the cloth and was dripping slowly from the bottom of the sack. He was embarrassed that somebody as refined as Caroline had to witness such a crude spectacle.

He muttered, "Let me do something with these," and started to turn away, but his pa stopped him.

"What you got there, boy?" Verne asked. "Squirrel or possum?"

"Squirrel. Four of 'em."

"Well, give 'em here. I'll tend to 'em whilst you talk to Miss Caroline. I expect it's you she come to see, more'n me."

She said, "I always enjoy visiting with you, Mr. Bennett. You know that."

"Mebbe so, but I'm a better hand at cleanin' critters than Cord is, so I'll handle that chore." Verne took the sack that Cord handed him and added, "Boy's a better shot than me, though, I'll sure give him that."

Still feeling a little awkward and embarrassed, Cord watched his father walk around toward the back of the cabin and then said, "Pa's the one who taught me how to shoot, so if I'm any good at it, he deserves the credit."

"Along with your natural talent," Caroline said. She waved a slim hand. "But I didn't come here to talk about shooting squirrels. I came to see if you'd heard the news."

Cord didn't care about any news Caroline might have brought. He would have been content just to stand there and look at her, with her curly blond hair under a blue sun bonnet. She wore a matching blue dress that was store-bought, not homemade, and tight enough to reveal the appealing curves of her figure. Her blue eyes twinkled, and her red lips curved.

Cord had never seen a prettier girl.

Things might have gotten even more awkward if he hadn't realized that she was waiting for a response from him. He tried to look like he was interested as he said, "What news? We don't hear much of anything out here unless somebody comes by, and you're the first one in days."

"Joe Dalrymple, you know, the man who has the freight wagon, he delivered a load of goods to my father's store this morning. He'd been up in Springfield and heard all about it there."

"Heard all about what?" Cord asked, shaking his head a little in confusion.

"Why, the gold, of course." Caroline's voice held a note of awe and excitement as

16

she went on, "They've found gold in California. Tons and tons of gold!"

CHAPTER 2

The tavern on the settlement's outskirts didn't have a sign or even a name, officially. Folks just called it Abijah's Place, after the owner, Abijah Spencer. A squat building constructed of logs and stone, it had several tiny log huts behind it where Abijah's brood of daughters worked.

From time to time, the pastors of the two churches in Wilbur — Baptist and Methodist — tried to rouse the righteous fury of the townsfolk against the sordid enterprise Abijah ran, but they never got very far with the effort. Too many of the settlement's upright male citizens liked to slip out to Abijah's place of a night and pay an occasional visit to his girls.

The tavern wasn't very busy in the middle of the afternoon like this, but it was a hot day, and half a dozen customers were in the place, seeking refuge from the sun. The heat was like a fist in the face to any man foolish enough to step outside.

Flint Bennett picked up the big cup of beer in front of him and swallowed some of the bitter, brackish stuff. It wasn't good, but it was wet, and if a man drank enough of it, it dulled the desperation somewhat.

On the other side of the table, Steve Bennett reached out with his empty cup to scoop more beer from the bucket the brothers had bought earlier with the last of their coins. Flint curled his lip in a snarl. Steve pulled his hand back without filling the cup.

"Sorry, Flint," he said.

"Don't go gettin' more than your share," Flint said.

"Didn't mean to, I swear. Reckon I, uh, just forgot how much I'd had."

"Never lose track of how much you've had to drink." As the oldest Bennett brother, Flint regarded it as his job to dispense such bits of wisdom. "You want to get just drunk enough to take the edge off, but never so drunk that anybody can take advantage of you."

Steve nodded. "Yeah, I'll remember that."

He probably wouldn't, though, Flint brooded. Steve had never been very bright. He had gotten the size in the family, towering over Flint and the youngest brother, Cord, but not the brains. Flint was the one who had gotten the smarts, and Cord had gotten the shooting eye, along with a stubborn, annoying sense of right and wrong.

Cord didn't know how to look at things from a practical standpoint. Flint did.

Life just hadn't given him enough chances yet to demonstrate that ability. But sooner or later it would, Flint believed, and then he would show everybody how much a man with ruthless drive and determination could achieve.

Until then, he thought wryly, he would sit here and drink beer in this squalid tavern and whorehouse.

"You reckon all of Abijah's girls are asleep?"

Flint didn't realize at first that his brother had asked him a question. He gave a little shake of his head to break out of his reverie and then said disgustedly, "It's the middle of the day. Besides, those cabins don't have any windows. Shut the door and it'd be like an oven in there."

"I don't care if the door's open."

"No, you wouldn't. But we spent the last of our money on the beer, remember? Anyway, we have other things to do."

"Like what?"

Flint's eyes narrowed as he looked at the table where four men sat playing cards. He

20

recognized three of them: a farmer from up in the hills foolishly losing what little bit of money he'd saved up, and two store clerks from here in Wilbur. They were losing steadily, too.

The fourth man, the stranger, was the only one who appeared to be winning regularly. He'd built up a nice pile of coins in front of him. He was dressed well enough in a suit and beaver hat that Flint took him to be a traveling gambler. Those other fellas at the table never really had a chance. They should've had more sense than to play with him.

But if everybody had good sense, the world would be a tougher place for a smart man to survive in.

"I'm out," the farmer announced as he threw in his cards. The sigh he let out held all the weariness in the world. "I'm plumb busted. My wife ain't gonna be happy."

"My condolences, friend," the stranger said, not sounding the least bit sincere. "How about you other two gentlemen?"

Both clerks folded. One of them said, "That's the last money you'll take from me today, mister. I'm done."

The second clerk nodded.

The stranger began stacking up the coins from the pile. "Well, then, better luck next time," he said. "I've enjoyed our game and will gladly give you a chance to win back some of your funds any time you'd like."

The other men just stood up, shook their heads, and started toward the open door.

From behind the crude bar, Abijah called, "You gents want me to go wake up the gals?"

One of the clerks said, "I'm sorry, Mr. Spencer. I don't have any more money." He waved toward the gambler. "This fella done took it all."

The gambler spun one of the coins on the table and said, "I'd be willing to stand you to a bit of female companionship, lad. As a gesture of goodwill, let's say."

The young clerk just shook his head, muttered, "Too blasted hot," and followed the other two out into the sunlight.

Behind the bar, Abijah sighed in regret at the missed business. But the day was far from over.

The gambler packed his winnings away in a leather poke and slipped it inside his frock coat. Abijah asked hopefully, "Want some whiskey or beer, mister?"

"No, the best thing to do in weather like this is to sleep it away," the gambler said as he got to his feet. "I have a room at Mrs. Kent's boarding house. I believe I'll see if I can catch a breeze, and a few winks, there. But I'll be back later." He glanced across the room at the table where Flint and Steve sat. "Unless you gentlemen would be interested in a game . . . ?"

"We're broke, mister," Flint said in a flat voice.

The gambler shrugged and went out.

Flint and Steve had continued to drink. The bucket was empty now except for the dregs. Flint picked it up, drained the last of the beer, and wiped the back of his hand across his mouth. He stood up. Steve did likewise, because Steve always followed Flint's lead.

Abijah didn't even try to talk them into staying. He knew he'd gotten all he was going to get from the Bennett brothers today.

Flint picked up the pace as he turned and followed a path that ran behind the buildings along Wilbur's main street. Even though Flint was almost trotting, Steve's height and long legs allowed him to keep up with ease.

"Where are we goin'?" Steve asked. "It's kinda hot to be runnin'."

"You'll see," Flint said, panting a little from the heat.

They reached the back of a house with a number of trees around and behind it that provided some shade, anyway. Flint hurried through the side yard. He came up to the corner just as the beaver-hatted gambler turned off the road and started toward the house's front door.

"Hey, mister," Flint called softly.

With a surprised frown on his lean face, the man looked toward Flint. A look of recognition appeared. He recalled seeing Flint at Abijah's place a few minutes earlier.

"Change your mind about that game? Perhaps Mrs. Kent would allow us to use her parlor —"

Flint let out a bark of laughter that interrupted the suggestion. "That old biddy don't hold with gambling. If she knew you make your living with a deck of cards, she never would've rented you a room. What'd you tell her you do?"

The gambler strolled closer and grinned. "I told the lady that I'm a traveling salesman, which happens to be the truth."

"Oh? What do you sell?"

"Hope."

Flint chuckled. "I get it. The hope of winning at cards against you. But there ain't much chance of that, is there?"

"There's always a chance. Anything can happen in this world."

"Yes, indeed, it can." Flint glanced at the

street. Nobody was in sight. No surprise there. Nobody moved around much in weather like this. "You want to make some real money?"

The gambler looked suspicious, of course. "How would I go about doing that?"

"My brother and I have a horse, a race-horse. Mighty fast, but the thing of it is, just to look at him, you wouldn't think he could run a lick. We've been going around the state, matching him against horses that the locals think are fast, and of course they always bet on their own nags. We've been cleanin' up."

The gambler nodded. "Sounds like a lucrative enterprise, all right . . . but one that's necessarily limited, too. Word's bound to get around about what you're doing, and then you won't get any takers."

"I know," Flint said. "In fact, that's already started to happen. That's why we're lookin' to take on a partner, somebody who can front for us while we lie low for a spell. It's worth a third of the take, if you're interested."

The gambler stroked his chin and frowned in thought. "It seems that I'd be running all the risk," he said after a moment. "I believe I should have two thirds."

"Two thirds!" Flint repeated. "But the

horse belongs to us." He considered for a moment, then went on, "Half. And my brother and I will split the other half."

"We have a deal . . . potentially. However, I have to see the horse first and make sure I believe the scheme is feasible."

"Well, of course," Flint said. He jerked a thumb toward the rear of the property. "He's in the trees back there. You can take a look at him right now."

The gambler hesitated, then shrugged. "All right. Show me."

"Come on." As the three men started toward the trees, Flint added, "This is my brother, by the way."

"Howdy," Steve said.

The gambler just nodded.

As they entered the trees, Flint glanced over his shoulder toward the house. The windows were empty. Nobody was watching. The heat had dulled everybody's senses, including the gambler's. Flint had made up the story as he went along, spinning it out of whole cloth, but the stranger had accepted it, even though Flint thought it wasn't one of his better efforts.

The trees grew thicker and closed around them. Flint said, "The horse is right up here —"

He fell silent as the gambler stopped short

26

and then took a quick step back so that Flint and Steve went on ahead a few feet before coming to a halt. When Flint looked around, he saw that the gambler had produced a gun from somewhere.

It was a short-barreled revolver, the sort where the trigger dropped down into sight when the hammer was pulled back, as happened now when the gambler cocked the weapon.

"How stupid do you think I am?" he demanded. "Did you honestly believe I would fall for that ridiculous story? Obviously, you made it up on the spot so you could lure me back here and rob me of the money you saw me win in that squalid tavern. And in broad daylight, no less! The only reason I played along with you was to see how far you'd push this farce."

"You've got it all wrong, mister," Flint said. "We really have this racehorse —"

"Bah! Don't heap insults atop more insults. I should just shoot you both and be done with it."

"Mister," Steve spoke up, taking both the gambler and Flint by surprise, "what kind of gun is that? I don't reckon I ever saw one like it before."

"What? Why do you . . . This is what they call a Baby Paterson. It's a five-shot revolver, so I have plenty of rounds for both of you, if you force me to use it."

"What caliber is it?"

The gambler looked even more confused. "It's a twenty-eight caliber —"

"Mister," Steve said, "you could shoot me with all five rounds from that little bitty gun, and it wouldn't come close to stoppin' me before I got my hands on you."

Hope jumped up in Flint again. He said, "And once my brother gets his hands on you, he can twist your head right off your shoulders in the blink of an eye. So just go ahead and shoot, if you want to be sure of dying."

The gambler looked a little scared now, and a lot less confident that the gun would protect him.

"How . . . how about if I shoot *you* instead?"

"Oh, well, then you'd die for sure," Flint said with a grin. "My brother would see to that. Wouldn't you?"

"Yeah," Steve said, "I'd kind of have to."

"Well, then . . . then . . . what in blazes do you want from me?" the gambler asked as he started to back away.

"Don't run," Flint warned him. "That'll just get my brother worked up even more. Somebody runs away from him, and he can't help but chase 'em. As for what we want . . . we're not unreasonable men. How much did you win in that poker game?"

"I . . . I'm not sure. Around sixty dollars, I think?"

"All right. Give us forty of it. A three-way split, just like I first suggested about the racehorse."

Steve said, "I thought we agreed to half and half."

"That was before this man pulled a gun on us," Flint said.

"Oh. Yeah. That was kind of a mean thing to do, mister."

"You want me to just give you forty dollars —"

"You still get to keep twenty," Flint said. "That's a good day's work. And you're alive to move on and fleece some more gents somewhere else."

"But that's robbery!"

"I call it a good deal."

"What's to stop me from giving you the money and then reporting your crime to the law?"

"First of all, the town marshal is sixty years old and don't take kindly to being disturbed. And you don't know who we are."

"I don't know your names, but I know

29

you're brothers, and how many men around here will fit your descriptions?"

"You're still thinkin' that folks in these parts will cooperate with you," Flint said. "These are the Ozarks, friend, and you're an outsider. Nobody's gonna care about you. We could kill you and take all the money and leave you in these woods, and nobody would raise a fuss. So . . ." Flint extended a hand in front of him. "Do the smart thing. Hand over that poke."

"You said you'd take forty dollars!"

"And that's what I intend to do. I'll count it out so you can see." Flint grinned. "What, don't you trust me?"

The gambler sighed, lowered the gun just a little, and fished the leather poke from his coat with his other hand. He tossed it to Flint, who caught it deftly and laughed.

Five minutes later and forty dollars richer — Flint had kept his word — the brothers walked through the woods toward the valley where the Bennett farm was located.

Steve asked, "You reckon that fella will try to make trouble anyway?"

"No, he'll consider himself lucky and clear out of Wilbur as fast as he can."

"You're sure smart, Flint. You always know what folks will do."

"Most of the time," Flint said. It bothered

30

him that the gambler had managed to pull a gun on them like that. He had believed he'd fooled the man. But Steve, bless his heart, had played things just right. All he'd done was tell the truth, of course — that little gun wouldn't have stopped him — but it was the right moment to do so.

A few minutes later, Steve said, "Flint . . . ?"

"What?"

"We don't really have a racehorse, do we?"

Flint laughed and reached up to clap a hand on his brother's broad shoulder. "No, we don't, Steve. But maybe one of these days we will. One of these days."

CHAPTER 3

"Gold?" Cord echoed as he looked up at Caroline. "In California?"

"That's right." She held out a hand to him. "Help me down, so we can get out of this sun, and I'll tell you all about it."

He wasn't going to pass up the opportunity to hold her hand, even if it was only for long enough to assist her from the buggy. When she was on the ground, he risked continuing to grasp her hand as he led her toward the big shade tree at the far end of the cabin.

"I can get you a dipper of water from the bucket if you'd like," he offered.

"No, I'm fine. I just wanted to see you, Cord."

He glanced toward the cabin. His pa was nowhere in sight. Probably still around on the other side, messing with those squirrels.

"You don't know how happy I am to hear you say that, Caroline."

"Oh, I think I can make a good guess," she said, the sparkle in her eyes growing more mischievous.

He knew she was friendly and flirtatious; that was just her nature, not prim and proper and stiff-necked like most girls. But there was something special in the way she acted around him, like it wasn't just a pose but rather her genuine feelings.

"I suspect you'll be even happier to hear this," she went on, as she turned toward him in the shade of the leafy branches and rested a hand on his chest. "I'd very much like for you to kiss me right now."

Cord had to grin for a second, but then he got serious and obliged her.

Nothing tasted sweeter than Caroline Stockton's lips, and the heat of the sun paled next to their warmth. Cord put his arms around her, reveling in the feel of that lithe, slim body in his arms, and kissed her until his heart was pounding so hard it felt like it was about to bust clean out of his chest.

Both of them were a little breathless when they finally pulled away from each other.

"I really shouldn't allow you to be so forward," she said in a mock-scolding voice.

"I seem to recollect that it was you who suggested doing that," he reminded her.

"Well, one of these days I'm liable to suggest something else, and what are you going to do then, Cord Bennett?"

He wouldn't have thought it was possible for his heart to slug any harder in his chest, but sure enough, it did. He cleared his throat and said, "I, uh, I reckon we'll find out."

Caroline laughed. "Yes, I reckon we will. But for now, I want to tell you about the gold!"

"Go ahead."

"It was found several months ago, at a place called Sutter's Mill. As I understand from what Mr. Dalrymple said, a man was building a sawmill on the American River, wherever that is, and he found gold nuggets in the stream. Big chunks of gold, fabulously valuable! When people started looking around, they were able to dig more nuggets right out of the ground. Except for the places where they were just sitting out in the open!"

"Chunks of gold, sitting out in the open," Cord said.

"That's right."

"Sounds pretty far-fetched to me." He didn't want to throw cold water on Caroline's enthusiasm, but what she was saying didn't seem like it could be real.

34

"Well, I haven't seen them with my own eyes, of course," she said, her tone a little cooler now, "but Mr. Dalrymple said that he'd read numerous accounts in the newspapers, and they all claimed the same thing. It's the most fabulous discovery of wealth in history."

"If that's true, I bet there'll be a heap of people flocking to California, all of them hoping to lay their hands on some of that gold."

"Of course there will be. Why, if I wasn't a girl, I'd be tempted to go myself!" She shook her head. "Not that my father would ever allow such a thing. But it sounds like a grand adventure, doesn't it?"

"If you're the sort who likes grand adventures," Cord allowed.

She stared at him in amazement and said, "But who doesn't?"

Well, him, for one, he thought. He'd never been the sort to want to go off gallivanting across the country. That was all well and good for other people, but he'd always been content to live right here in the mountains and work on the farm.

Of course, life had been a mite less satisfying after his ma passed away from a fever several years earlier. That had taken a toll on his pa and his brother Steve, too, although Flint seemed to bear up under the loss just fine. Flint wasn't much for sentiment. Even so, Cord had enjoyed his existence here.

At least until the rains stopped coming and the farm started to look like it was going to dry up and blow away.

Those thoughts went through his head in a heartbeat, but he wasn't going to express them to Caroline. She wouldn't understand. A girl like her, who had never really wanted for anything, was always going to want more and more.

That was why the idea of the gold discovery in California intrigued her so much. But she had no idea of the hardships that would be involved in a trip all the way out there.

Instead, he asked, "What else do you know about the gold?"

She shrugged and said, "Not much, really. The men who don't dig for it in the ground search for it in the streams. Evidently, they use some sort of technique that involves a pan . . ." She shook her head. "I don't know the details. All I know is that a lot of people are becoming very wealthy because of it."

"Your pa does right well for himself, between his farm and the businesses he owns in town."

"I know, we're comfortable enough, I suppose. But we'll never be rich."

Compared to nearly everybody else in these parts, they already were, Cord thought, but again he didn't voice the sentiment.

"If we didn't have the farm to take care of, my brothers and I might have to think about it," he said. "Pa needs all of us here, though. So I reckon we'll stay around."

Caroline smiled. "I didn't really expect anything else."

Cord couldn't tell if she sounded a little disappointed or not. He hoped she wasn't.

Verne came around the cabin, the skinned, dressed-out squirrel carcasses dangling from one bloody hand. "Would you like to join us for supper, Miss Caroline?" he asked. "I reckon we'll have us a good mess o' squirrel stew. It's mighty tasty the way I fix it."

Her smile didn't falter as she said, "No, thank you, Mr. Bennett, although I appreciate the invitation. I have to get back home."

"Well, you're welcome to visit any time. I know Cord's always mighty glad to see you."

"Are you?" she asked Cord as she put a hand on his chest again. "Glad to see me?"

He wanted to grab her, pull her into his arms, and kiss her again to show her just how glad he was to see her. But instead he said in a slightly husky voice, "You know I am."

"And I hope you always will be." She grew more businesslike. "Now, help me back onto the buggy, please."

Cord did so, taking her hand again before they reached the vehicle, which was actually sooner than he had to. Once she was on the seat, she handled the reins with practiced ease and swung the buggy around, calling, "Goodbye!" as she drove off, then adding, "Don't forget about that gold!"

"Gold?" Verne said. "What in blazes is she talkin' about?"

"Best get those squirrels in the stewpot, Pa, and then I'll tell you all about it."

CHAPTER 4

Verne Bennett hadn't been lying when he said that his squirrel stew was mighty tasty. He cooked it with wild onions, chunks of potatoes from the few they had left in the root cellar, and herbs that he'd gathered in the woods.

Cord could have eaten more than one bowl of the stuff, but he forced himself to stop with that, because they needed to have enough left over for at least one more meal. Anyway, Steve ate enough for two men, and you couldn't fault him for that because of his size.

Flint and Steve had walked up in the late afternoon, returning from a jaunt into town. They brought some supplies with them. Cord wondered where they had gotten the money to buy anything, but he decided he wouldn't ask any questions.

Sometimes it was better not to know all the details of what was going on, especially where Flint was concerned.

While they were eating, Verne said, "Tell the boys what Miss Caroline told you this afternoon, Cord."

"Caroline Stockton was here?" Flint asked, his interest visibly quickening.

"She just stopped by for a few minutes," Cord said. He hadn't liked the look he had seen in his eldest brother's eyes the times they had run into Caroline together in town.

Of course, she was a beautiful young woman, he reminded himself. Any man with eyes in his head was going to look at her and acknowledge that fact. It wasn't like Caroline had any interest in Flint.

"She brought some news she'd heard," he went on. "About somebody finding gold in California."

"Gold!" Steve repeated. "Gold's worth a lot of money. In fact . . . uh . . . gold *is* money, ain't it?"

"They make coins out of it," Flint said, adding dryly, "you know that, Steve. You've seen a few of them in your life." He turned to Cord. "Did she say how much gold they've found?"

"A lot, to hear her tell it." Cord filled them in on what Caroline had heard from the freighter, Joe Dalrymple. "Of course, I don't know how much of it is true. Dalrymple could have been making up the whole thing."

"I don't figure that's right," Verne said. "I've knowed Joe Dalrymple for a long time. He's an honest man." Verne snorted. "And he ain't smart enough to make up somethin' like that, neither. If he said it, he actually heard it. But that still don't mean it really happened."

Flint leaned back in his chair and frowned. "If it is true, if there's really that much gold just laying around on the ground, a man could make a fortune by going out there and getting some of it for himself."

"You reckon we ought to do that, Flint?" Steve asked, always eager to do whatever his older brother thought was best.

"It's a long way to California," Cord said before Flint could answer. "You'd need a wagon and a team and plenty of supplies. It would cost a lot of money and might not make you anything. Not to mention, there's a lot of wild country between here and there, from what I've heard. It would be a long, hard trip."

"Yes, and it would mean taking a chance, too, and we can't have that, can we?"

Cord felt a surge of anger at the contemptuous tone in Flint's voice. It wasn't that he was against taking chances, but he didn't see any point in taking foolish ones.

He was about to say as much when his father sighed and said, "The way things are goin', we may have to do somethin' like that whether we want to or not."

"What are you talking about, Pa?" Cord asked.

Verne made a vague gesture and said, "Oh, nothin', nothin'. Just that if it don't start rainin' soon, and give us some mighty good rain, too, we ain't gonna have a crop to speak of this year. Without a crop, I don't see how we can afford to stay here and keep the farm goin'."

Cord stared at him for a moment and then said, "But this is our land. It was Grandpappy's land before that, and his pa's before that. This is where we belong, Pa. Nothing else would be right."

Flint said, "You think the world gives a damn about what's right, Cord? Grow up! What's right doesn't mean a blasted thing. The only thing that matters is what you're willing to do to get what you want. That's what the world pays attention to."

That seemed like a mighty harsh way of looking at things to Cord, but he wasn't going to waste time and breath arguing with Flint. He knew he wouldn't change his brother's mind.

"I think the weather is going to change and the drought will break soon," he said instead.

"Why do you reckon that, Cord?" Steve asked.

"Well . . . because it's got to."

The look on Flint's face told Cord just how little stock his brother put in that sentiment.

Over the next couple of weeks, Flint's pessimism proved to be much more accurate than Cord's hopeful prediction. The weather remained hot and dry, although there were a few days when clouds bulked in the distance and looked like they might have rain in them. A couple of times, Cord even thought he could *smell* the moisture in the air.

But if there actually was any rain, it never approached the valley where the Bennett farm was located. It just teased relief, turned around, and went the other way.

Cord watched the crops burn and shrivel and felt despair at his powerlessness to do anything. The nearby creek, which furnished water for the farm, dwindled to a trickle. Even if it had been flowing at its normal rate, he couldn't carry enough water in buckets from the stream to keep the plants in the fields alive. For that, they needed rain . . . and there was no rain.

Flint and Steve were hardly ever around these days. Cord didn't know where they went or what they did, but it didn't matter. There wasn't enough work here to keep one man busy, let alone three.

He was standing on the cabin's sagging porch, gazing at the rows of dead cornstalks in the field, when his father came up behind him and said, "We're beat, son."

"I know it, Pa. I wish it wasn't true. I wish there was something I could do about it. But there just isn't. I can't think of a thing." Cord shook his head. "We'll try again next year, I reckon."

"How are we gonna live until then? What are we gonna eat?"

"We still have hogs and chickens —"

"The hogs are wastin' away, and the chickens are gonna stop layin'. We can eat them, too, I reckon, but how long is that gonna last? Even if we don't starve to death, we'd have to buy seed corn to start over, and we sure can't afford to do that."

Verne put a scrawny, clawlike hand on Cord's shoulder.

"No, son, there just ain't no way out. We got to leave this place and start over some-wheres else. We're gonna lose it anyway,

44

soon as the taxes come due on it."

Cord turned toward his father with a rare burst of anger. "Blast it, Pa, we can't just give up! Maybe . . . maybe . . ." As his brain searched desperately for an answer, inspiration came to him. "Maybe we can borrow the money to see us through until next year."

"Borrow it from who?"

"I'll bet Hiram Stockton would loan us what we need —"

Cord stopped short as his father began to laugh. It wasn't a sound of genuine amusement, though. It was hollow, aching despair wearing a mask of laughter.

"How do you reckon we made it through *last* winter?" Verne asked.

Cord blinked in confusion. "You said you had some money saved up —"

"That was a lie, boy, because I was too ashamed to tell you and your brothers the truth! I went to Hiram Stockton last year and begged him for the loan of enough to get by and try again this year."

Just hearing the bitter note in his father's voice was enough to put a bad taste in Cord's mouth.

"I had to crawl to that man and swallow ever' bit of pride I got, just to try to save this here farm," Verne went on. He raised a trembling hand and scrubbed it over his weathered face, then sighed. "Hiram made it mighty plain that was just a one-time deal, too. He ain't a-gonna loan us more money this time, when there ain't no way for us to pay back what we borrowed last time. Shoot, you can forget what I said about losin' the farm for taxes! Hiram'll just take it when the note comes due in the fall."

Cord clutched the railing along the front of the porch. He felt like he had to hang on to it to keep from flying off into space, because the world had been turned upside down around him.

"You never said anything —"

"Because I was ashamed to, I told you!"

"Flint and Steve don't know?"

Verne snorted. "No, I never told them, neither. It was my shame, my burden to bear."

"It wasn't anything to be ashamed of, Pa. You can't control the weather —"

"That don't matter. As the head o' the family, the responsibility falls on me. And it's me who let you boys down, to say nothin' of your grandpappy and your great-grandpappy. They passed this place on down to me, and after all these years, I'm gonna be the one to lose it."

Cord stood there in awkward silence. He

couldn't think of any words to say that would make his pa feel better.

But then something occurred to him, and he said, "I could talk to Caroline, and she could talk to her father —"

Verne stopped him with a sharp, slashing motion. "No! One Bennett beggin' for help is enough. More than enough! Whatever's between you and Miss Caroline ain't got nothin' to do with this farm." The old-timer drew in a deep breath. "Anyway, if you think anything she could say to her pa would make a difference, then you don't know Hiram Stockton like I do. That man's got a ledger book where his heart oughta be. No, sir, you just put that idea outta your head, Cord. If you was to go crawlin' to that gal, I . . . I'd be plumb hurt, I tell you. Cut to the quick."

Cord swallowed hard. "All right, Pa. If that's the way you feel about it, I'll do what you want, of course."

Maybe he would and maybe he wouldn't, he thought, but he didn't have to argue with Verne about it right now.

Instead, he said, "But if we have to leave here, where are we gonna go?"

His father's eyes lit up with the first sign of life Cord had seen in them for a while. Verne licked his lips and said, "I've been ponderin' what Miss Caroline said about all that gold in Californy . . ."

CHAPTER 5

At supper that night, which was just poke-weed boiled with a little hamhock, Verne laid out the dire situation for his other two sons.

Steve looked dismayed to hear how bad things were, but Flint listened with a flat, unreadable expression on his face. Finally, when Verne was finished, Flint said, "Pa, anybody with a lick of sense could see a long time ago that we don't stand a chance. Even if it started raining tomorrow and didn't let up for a month, it's too late. It's too late to get a crop in and pay what you owe."

"Maybe Mr. Stockton would be willin' to wait for his money," Steve said.

Flint shook his head. "You know better than that, little brother. Stockton's a hard-headed businessman. Not only that, somebody like him, who already owns more than anybody else around here, well, he's always going to want to own more and more.

There's never enough to satisfy somebody like that."

Although Cord didn't know Hiram Stockton well, he suspected that Flint was right about the man. Stockton had a reputation for being canny in all his dealings.

It wasn't that he was ruthless, exactly . . . he would even extend credit at his store to folks who needed a hand, for example . . . but he always made sure that he got paid back one way or another, too.

And Stockton had all the personal warmth of a fish. His wife was much the same way. Cord had wondered more than once how two such dour people could have produced a girl as sweet and vivacious as Caroline.

"Cord thinks the idea of us goin' to Californy to look for gold is loco," Verne went on.

Flint glanced at his youngest brother. "Does he, now?"

"Like I said before, we can't afford a journey like that," Cord said. He gestured at the skimpy, unappetizing fare on the table in front of them. "We can't even afford decent food. How can we buy a wagon and team and the supplies we'd need?"

"We might not have to have a wagon," Flint said. "We could ride horseback. Use the mules we already have as pack animals."

"You mean load them down with supplies we don't have money to buy? And nobody's going to just give us good saddle mounts, either."

"Blast it, Cord," Flint burst out, "you're nothing but a damned old woman! Always whining and complaining and talking about what can't be done, instead of what might be."

Anger flared up inside Cord, too, but at the same time, he felt the flush of shame. Flint's statement contained some truth, he had to admit, if he was being honest with himself.

Sure, the thought of going to California, finding gold, and becoming rich had some appeal to it. It had *plenty* of appeal. But as far as Cord could see, it was a hopeless dream.

Maybe he shouldn't say that, though. Giving up accomplished nothing.

Flint slapped a hand down on the table. "What'll we do if we stay?" he demanded. "The drought has hurt everybody. You reckon we could get jobs working on somebody else's farm? Somebody like Hiram Stockton, maybe? Or you could be a clerk at his store. Steve and me could be clerks, too."

The sneer on Flint's face made it clear

51

just how unlikely he considered that possibility.

"What about Pa?" Steve asked, not really grasping Flint's meaning. He was so straightforward in his thinking that sarcasm generally eluded him. "What could he do?"

"Nothing," Flint said, with brutal honesty that made Verne wince. "Not a blamed thing except sit in a rocking chair somewhere and wait to die."

Cord put his hands on the table and started to push himself to his feet. "Flint, you've no call to talk like that —"

Flint came up out of his chair and glared defiantly at his brother. "What are you gonna do about it, Cord?" he challenged.

The two men were roughly the same size. Cord was an inch taller, Flint ten to fifteen pounds heavier. But Flint had a reputation as a brawler. He had been in dozens of tavern fights, and he'd never been whipped, as far as Cord knew. And from roughhousing when they were kids, he also knew that Flint would go to any lengths to avoid losing, even if it meant fighting dirty.

"I don't want to fight you," he said.

Flint smirked. "No, I didn't figure you did."

"But I still think it's a crazy idea to go to California and look for gold. I mean, what do we know about searching for gold?"

"If it's just laying on the ground, like folks say, then you wouldn't have to know anything, would you?" Steve asked.

"I don't figure it'd be quite that easy," Flint said, "but we can learn. That's the easy part. What's hard is figuring out how to get there."

"I'll bet you can think of somethin', Flint," Verne said. "You always was a determined cuss, even when you was little. Your ma said you was the stubbornest baby she ever saw."

"Let me mull it over, Pa. I'll come up with something. I'll find a way for us to get there. And when I do . . ." Flint threw another challenging look at Cord. "When I do, then whoever wants to come along and get rich is welcome to join in. And whoever's scared to take a chance . . . well, he can just squat right here where he is, like a toad in a dried-up pond."

A few days later, under a sky dotted with fluffy white clouds that held no rain, Flint and Steve brought the mules they were riding to a stop in a dense grove of trees.

Neither their pa nor Cord had asked them where they were going when they rode off earlier in the afternoon. The mules weren't needed for plowing right now — or ever again, more than likely — so it didn't matter if Flint and Steve wanted to go for a ride.

Steve was as much in the dark as his brother and pa. He was willing to go wherever Flint wanted to go, of course, but he was curious what they were doing here, several valleys away from home.

When Flint motioned for them to stop, Steve finally gave in to that curiosity. "Are we goin' to visit somebody, Flint?" he asked. "I don't recollect knowin' anybody over in these parts."

"Yeah, you could say we're gonna pay somebody a visit," Flint replied. He pointed through the trees and down a slope. "You see that building down there?"

Steve looked where his brother was pointing. "Yeah, I reckon. What is it?"

"That's a store owned by a fella named Ike Plemmons."

Steve shook his head and said, "I don't know him."

"That's all right. I don't really know him, either, but I know who he is. You won't be going down there. You'll wait right here."

"Why's that?" Steve asked with a frown.

"Because I've got to do a little business with Mr. Plemmons, and I shouldn't need your help. If I do, though, I'll holler for you, so you listen close while I'm gone, you hear?"

"I reckon." Steve sighed and shook his head. "But I sure am confused, Flint."

"You won't be when I tell you about it later."

"You promise?"

"Sure."

That was enough to satisfy Steve. He nodded and said, "I'll wait right here, then."

"Thanks, Steve. I knew I could count on you."

Flint nudged the mule into motion again. He had to jab the critter in the flanks twice before the mule started plodding down the hill toward the store, which was the only building around here. The only one in sight, anyway. Chimney smoke rose here and there around the hills.

Ike Plemmons did a decent business from folks who didn't want to make the five-mile trip into Wilbur. Flint was aware of that from things he had heard over the years. He'd had this idea stirring around in the back of his head for a while now, and the time had come to put it into action.

Dry grass crunched like broken glass under the mule's hooves as the animal plodded down the hill toward the log, stone, and plank building that sprawled next to the road between the villages of Wilbur and Abernathy.

The store had grown as Plemmons's business did, but he had added on to it haphazardly, with whatever materials he could come up with at the time. A tin stovepipe stuck up through the roof.

Flint rode around the corner of the building to the front, where Steve couldn't see him anymore. No horses or wagon teams were tied up at the hitch rail.

That was a stroke of luck. Flint would have waited until the store was empty except for Plemmons if he'd had to, but he was glad that wasn't necessary. He wanted to get this over with. He wasn't worried that he would lose his nerve, but there was no point in delaying things.

He brought the mule to a stop and swung down from the saddle, dropping the reins. The stolid beast wasn't going to wander off.

He reached inside his shirt and drew out a canvas sack, then pulled it over his head. He had cut holes in it for his eyes, so he could see where he was going. As he strode toward the door, he slid a hand inside his shirt again and withdrew the single-shot percussion pistol he had stuck inside his waistband earlier.

He had a good reason for leaving Steve

up on the hill, even though his brother might have come in handy on this risky venture. The makeshift hood would conceal his identity, but Steve was so big that nobody in this part of the state could fail to recognize him by his size, whether his face was covered or not.

And if folks knew that Steve Bennett had robbed Plemmons's store, they would also know that Flint had been in on it with him, because the brothers were seldom apart.

Gripping the pistol's curved grip tightly in one hand, Flint used the other to grab the door's latch string and jerk it open. As he stalked into the building, he thrust the pistol in front of him. The eyeholes in the mask actually made it easier somehow, going from sunlight outside to relative dimness inside.

He saw Ike Plemmons, a scrawny, middle-aged man with thinning hair, spectacles perched on his beak of a nose, and an enormous Adam's apple, standing behind the counter at the back of the room.

"Put your hands up!" Flint rasped, making his voice sound as different from his regular tone as he could. "Put your hands up and bring out your money box!"

Plemmons, a bachelor, was alone in the store, just as Flint had hoped. The man's eyes widened so much they looked like they were about to pop out of their sockets. He lifted his hands and backed up against the shelves on the wall behind the counter.

"Land's sakes, mister, put that gun down!" he bleated. "It's liable to go off!"

"You're damn right it's liable to go off," Flint growled. "It'll go off and blow a hole right in your stupid face if you don't hand over all the money in this place and any other valuables you got."

"You're robbin' me?"

Flint jabbed the gun at him and said, "What does this look like, you crazy old coot?"

Plemmons's eyes were drawn to the gun, and when he looked closer at it, so did Flint. They realized the same thing at the same time.

In working himself up to do this, Flint had forgotten to cock the pistol's hammer.

Plemmons launched himself across the counter and grabbed for the gun. Flint jerked it back out of reach, then instead of trying to cock it belatedly, he lashed out with it instead, slamming the barrel against the side of the storekeeper's head.

The spectacles flew off of Plemmons's nose. He cried out in pain as blood started to run down through his thin hair onto his face.

Snarling under the hood, Flint hit him again.

Plemmons went down this time, sprawling loosely on the floor behind the counter. Flint hurried around the end of it and checked on the man. Plemmons's breath rasped in his throat. He was alive but out cold, and he didn't look like he'd be regaining consciousness any time soon.

Keeping one eye on Plemmons the whole time, Flint started searching for the box or poke or whatever the man kept his money in. He found it a few minutes later on one of the shelves under the counter, a wooden box with some heft to it that jingled nicely when he shook it.

For good measure, he took Plemmons's watch, too, and a couple more watches he found in a display case. That was all he came across that appeared to be of any value.

Leaving the storekeeper there, Flint went to the door and looked out to make sure nobody was around before stepping out. He yanked the hood off and stuffed it back inside his shirt, along with the gun and the money box.

Then he climbed onto the mule and rode back up the hill to rejoin Steve, who asked him, "Did you get your business done?"

"Yeah," Flint said, a little breathless from the unexpected excitement that lingered inside him. He felt more alive than he had in quite a while. "Yeah, I did."

Steve pointed at the lump the money box formed. "What's that under your shirt?"

Flint hadn't wanted to tell his brother what he was doing, just in case anything went wrong. He'd done some pretty shady things in the past, but never anything like this. He didn't want to look like a failure in his brother's eyes, although he wouldn't have admitted that, even under torture.

Sure enough, his inexperience had almost betrayed him into a potentially fatal error. Forgetting to cock the pistol was a mistake he'd never make again.

Now that he knew he could pull off these jobs successfully, though, it was all right to tell Steve. In the long run, he'd have to know what Flint was doing.

"Come on, let's go home," Flint said with a cocky grin on his face. "I'll tell you all about it on the way."

CHAPTER 6

Cord lifted his head when he heard something he hadn't heard in a long time. So long he could barely remember it.

A rumble of thunder in the distance.

He knew the air was heavier today. Instead of the pretty but empty white clouds, the sky was streaked with lower clouds. Cord didn't expect that it would come to anything, which was why he'd gone out hunting. He was all but absolutely certain that he wouldn't get caught in the rain.

He wouldn't mind being proven wrong, though. In fact, he'd happily admit his error if it meant he got soaked to the skin.

He had one possum in his game bag. That was all he had seen, other than a few small lizards, snakes, and birds. The woods were almost empty of animal life, at least any that would provide any sustenance for the Bennetts. The creatures had moved on, no doubt in search of more welcoming surroundings. Cord felt lucky to have bagged the possum.

He turned and headed for home, grinning as he heard another rolling peal of thunder. He didn't see any lightning in the gathering clouds, but it had to be there or else there wouldn't be thunder.

By the time he came in sight of the cabin, he had felt two or three small drops of rain on his face. The clouds had swallowed the sun. The sky was more overcast than it had been for months.

Maybe it was too late, maybe it wouldn't be enough, but Cord still felt a surge of gratitude for whatever blessing they were about to receive.

He broke into a run, shouting, "Pa! Pa!" By the time he reached the cabin, the rain was falling steadily and getting his face wet. His clothes started to grow damp. Sheer exuberance made him dance a little jig.

That's what he was doing when his father stepped out on the porch, stared at him, and said, "Boy, what's wrong with you? You done lost your mind?"

"No, Pa, it's raining!" Cord cried. He held out his arms and tilted his head back so the drops could hit him in his face, which wore a broad grin. "It's —"

But it wasn't.

Cord's feet shuffled to a halt. He peered up at the gray clouds with an intense expression, as if he could compel them by sheer force of will to release more of their moisture. It had been raining only a moment earlier. He *knew* it had. He could see the wet spots on his homespun shirt where the drops had landed. He could see the circles they'd made in the dust . . .

But nothing was coming down now.

"You say it was rainin'?" Verne asked, his tone skeptical.

"It was," Cord insisted. "You can see my shirt's wet, and my hair, and look here at the ground." He pointed at the tiny starbursts in the dust.

Verne shook his head. "Well, if it did rain, it weren't even enough to get the top o' the ground wet. And it's over now."

"It'll start up again in a minute . . ."

Cord's voice trailed off as he realized that no, the rain wouldn't start up again. He'd never been one to assign human qualities to things that weren't human, but what the clouds had just done . . .

Well, that was just downright cruel.

"I don't know about you, son," Verne said from the porch, "but Californy is lookin' better all the time."

■ ■ ■ ■

That day was the closest the valley came to breaking the drought as the hot, dry weather continued. The crops were gone now, nothing but dry, brittle husks littering the fields.

Flint and Steve were gone most of the time, too, but they were physically absent, off doing who knows what. Cord didn't care anymore what his brothers were up to. Probably no good, knowing Flint, but there was nothing he could do about it.

Verne had made up his mind and had his heart set on heading for California to hunt for gold. In the weeks that had passed since Caroline first brought the news, Cord had heard more about it every time he ventured into the settlement.

The Gold Rush, as people had started calling it, seemed to be all that folks talked about. Everybody liked to dream about getting rich, even those who would never actually take any steps to accomplish that dream.

Leaving still seemed like a foolish idea to Cord. Arkansas was the Bennett family's home. He wasn't going to allow his father and brothers to give up and abandon the farm as long as there was any chance of saving it.

But summer turned into fall, and even though the temperature cooled off a mite, the drought continued in full force.

Cord thought it was worth making one last-ditch effort to find a solution, so on a day when Flint and Steve had gone off somewhere, as usual, he left his pa brooding in the cabin and walked across the ridge to the next valley, where Hiram Stockton's farm was located.

Even though the blistering heat of summer was over, the day was warm enough to make beads of sweat pop out on Cord's face and dampen his shirt under his arms and down his back.

He didn't hold out much hope that he could change Stockton's mind, assuming he even caught the man at home. Stockton split his time between the farm and tending to his business interests in the settlement, so there was a good chance he wouldn't be there.

But Cord had to try, anyway, and if Stockton wasn't home, maybe he could at least see Caroline for a few minutes. They hadn't spent much time together in recent weeks, to Cord's disappointment. She hadn't come back to the farm, and he had only run into her on a couple of occasions in her father's mercantile.

After what seemed like a longer walk than it really was, the Stock ton farm finally came into view. The farmhouse was no ramshackle log cabin. It was an actual house, two stories constructed of actual lumber, whitewashed so that it gleamed in the sun, with a slate roof and a large veranda supported by columns, giving it a look vaguely similar to the plantation houses down in the southern part of the state.

Shade trees surrounded the house. They hadn't started losing their leaves yet; none of the nights had been cold enough for that, so far. But many of those leaves had turned yellow and brown from the drought.

Off to one side stood a large barn with a couple of corrals, a hog pen, and a chicken house arranged around it. Everything was in good repair.

Cord could see the fields in the distance. The drought hadn't spared Stockton any more than it had the Bennetts. The crops were dead. The difference was that Hiram Stockton could withstand a few bad years and carry on, while the drought had ruined the Bennetts.

But all he and his family needed was a stake, Cord told himself. Surely it was impossible the weather would be so dry three years in a row.

He would make that argument to Stockton, if the man was at home. There was only one way to find out. He was headed for the front door when movement from the direction of the barn caught his eye.

Someone had just pulled one of the big double doors open slightly. Cord stopped as he watched Caroline slip through the gap and disappear into the barn. He could tell she was intent on what she was doing and hadn't noticed him. The door swung closed behind her.

He wondered what she was doing out there. Maybe he would wait to talk to Stockton, he decided on the spur of the moment. He wasn't going to pass up an opportunity to see Caroline.

If nobody else was in the barn, maybe she would even allow him to steal a kiss.

He changed course and headed in that direction.

Caroline paused just inside the barn. Flint knew she was letting her eyes adjust from the bright sunshine outside to the shadowy dimness inside.

He'd been waiting beside the door, knowing that she would be here. He moved up behind her and, without warning, grasped her shoulders with both hands.

She jumped in surprise at his touch, but she didn't struggle as he turned her around and jerked her close to him.

Nor did she try to pull away as he brought his mouth down on hers in a kiss urgent with savagery.

In fact, she raised her arms, twined them around his neck, and returned the kiss with just as much passion, pressing her body tightly against his as she did so.

The kiss lasted a long moment. Finally, Flint lifted his head. His hands left her shoulders to drift down her slender shape, fondling and probing. His caresses made Caroline moan deep in her throat and sag against him. Her head rested on his chest.

"You're a terribly incorrigible man, Flint Bennett," she whispered.

"And you love me for it, don't you?"

That audacious question made her lift her head and look up at him.

"I wouldn't use that word," she said with a slight frown.

"But you're fascinated by me. You're drawn to me. Don't bother denying it."

"I . . . the good Lord help me . . . Yes! Yes, I am . . ."

She kissed him this time. It was as long and passionate as the first kiss.

When it ended, she asked, "Are you alone today?"

"Yeah. I left Steve at this old, abandoned cabin we found up on Claussen Mountain. We've been spending quite a bit of time there lately. It's a good place to get away from all the hectoring on the farm."

"When I got your signal, I hoped it would be just you. I mean, Steve is a sweet man, and gentle in his way, and I didn't really mind what you asked me to do, but I prefer it when it's just you and me."

"So do I, darling," Flint said.

They had worked out a set of signals so that he would know when her father wasn't at the farm and no one else was around. The curtains in the window of her bedroom upstairs would be arranged in a certain way.

When he saw that, he could send a signal of his own by hanging a long piece of bright red cloth from a low branch of a particular tree that stood by itself atop a hill in plain view from her window. That meant he would meet her in the barn as soon as he could get there.

So far, the system had worked quite well. They had rendezvoused numerous times in the barn without ever being discovered.

They met there, rather than in the house, just in case her father showed up unexpectedly. Flint could hide in the loft until he got a chance to slip away unnoticed.

Now Caroline angled her head toward one of the stalls with a thick pile of clean straw he had prepared as soon as he got here. He had even spread a blanket over the straw. She smiled at him in a way he knew quite well.

Flint growled a little as he pulled Caroline to him again, scooped her off her feet, and carried her toward the stall.

Cord didn't know whether to go on in the barn or wait for Caroline to come out when she'd finished whatever she was doing in there.

Probably checking on one of the animals, he thought. A cow or a horse might be sick. Caroline was a soft-hearted girl who would want to make sure all the creatures on the farm were well cared for.

He had just reached for the door, unable to stay away from her any longer, when he heard voices coming from inside. He couldn't make out the words, but he recognized the tone of Caroline's voice and could tell that she was talking to a man. Her father, more than likely.

Well, that was good, Cord told himself. That way, he could speak to Hiram Stockton and see Caroline at the same time.

Then he hesitated. He wasn't sure he wanted Caroline to witness him begging her father for money so that the Bennett family could hang on to their farm for another year.

Even if the effort was successful, he hadn't figured that he could keep it a secret from her. But to do it right in front of her that way . . .

Cord's hand dropped away from the door. Better to wait, he decided. If they both came out of the barn in a few minutes, he could claim that he was there to see Caroline — which was true, at least in part — and try to catch her father alone before he went back to the farm.

As he listened to the soft voices, however, a frown began to crease his forehead. Something about the sound of them wasn't right. They weren't exchanging casual words like a father and daughter normally would. There was something more urgent about them. Something . . . intimate.

Cord's jaw tightened. What in blazes was going on in there? Obviously, Caroline wasn't talking to Hiram Stockton.

But who *was* in there with her?

Cord tensed even more when he heard a cry from inside the barn. Whoever was with

Caroline was hurting her! He lunged forward, reached for the door —

But stopped short of jerking it open as he heard more exclamations from her. She blurted out, "Yes! Yes!", followed by more words he understood, though he had never heard them coming from Caroline's lips before and never dreamed that he would.

His face flamed with a heat that had nothing to do with the temperature as his hand dropped away from the barn door and he stepped back. A deep feeling of shame washed through him as the wanton words made him realize what Caroline was doing in there.

In unguarded moments, thoughts of her . . . like that . . . had come to him and always left him uncomfortable and frustrated. He knew he had no right to be thinking such improper things, no matter how stealthily they crept into his mind. Time enough for that if he was ever fortunate enough to make her his wife.

Clearly, Caroline didn't feel the same way about postponing the joys of the flesh until marriage. Her enthusiastic cries made it clear that she was experiencing a great deal of joy, right this very minute.

Cord continued backing away from the barn. He could no longer hear what was going on inside the cavernous structure, but that didn't matter. The sounds played over and over in his head until he turned and started to run.

That exertion finally forced them out. He ran until he couldn't hear anything over the wild hammering of blood in his brain . . .

He couldn't run fast enough to escape the question of who had been in there with her, but it didn't matter. It wasn't him. And now nothing would ever be the same again.

Suddenly, the thought of staying in these parts made him sick. The bitter, sour taste of defeat was under his tongue. The hope of hanging onto the farm meant nothing. He wanted to get as far away from Caroline Stockton as he could.

Somewhere as far away as, say, California.

Where fortunes in gold lay on the ground, just waiting for strong men to come along and claim them.

CHAPTER 7

"What in the world made you change your mind?" Flint asked that evening as he looked across the rough-hewn table at the sullen face of his youngest brother.

"Does it matter?" Cord snapped. "You're getting what you want. I won't stand in the way of your plans. Isn't that all you care about?"

"By you agreeing to come along with us to California, you mean?" Flint laughed. "Don't rate yourself too highly, little brother. I would have gone without you, and so would Pa and Steve. Isn't that right?"

Steve nodded and said, "You ain't never steered me wrong, Flint. I'll always listen to you."

Verne Bennett's weathered, bearded face looked a lot more reluctant, but he nodded, too.

"Don't reckon we would've had any other choice, Cord," he said. "But I'll say this. It gladdens my heart and lightens my burden to know that you're comin' with us. There just ain't nothin' left for us around here no more."

"I guess it just took me until today to figure that out for myself," Cord said in a dull, heavy voice.

"I don't know what happened to change your mind," Flint said, "but I'm glad to know that you're finally showing some sense, Cord."

"I still don't know how we're going to pay for the journey, though."

"Don't worry about that. Steve and I have been working and saving up some money."

Cord and Verne both stared at Flint. When Cord found his voice, he asked, "Working at what?"

"A little of this and a little of that," Flint replied with a shrug. "Hauling freight, mucking out stalls, slaughtering hogs . . . We've ridden up and down every valley in this part of the country, taking whatever odd jobs we could find. You didn't think we were just lazing around somewhere, all that time we weren't here, did you?"

That was exactly what Cord had thought, but he didn't see any point in saying that. Instead he commented, "Sounds like you've been pretty industrious."

Flint snorted. "I've taken this whole Gold Rush business serious from the start. I knew as soon as I heard tell of it that that was our way out of this disaster. So Steve and I set out to make it possible."

"Yeah, we've been workin' hard," Steve put in. "All over this part of the country."

He grinned and chuckled. Cord didn't see what was so funny about that, but evidently, Steve did.

"We have nearly enough cash saved up for what we'll need," Flint went on. "Give us a few more days, and we'll have a good stake."

"I can start coming with you and helping," Cord offered. "After all, there's really nothing more to do around here, especially if we're leaving."

Flint gave a curt shake of his head and said, "No, that's not necessary. Steve and I have a regular routine down and work well together. We can handle it. What you need to do, Cord, is start getting ready for us to pull out when the time comes. Figure out what we're gonna take with us and what we're gonna leave behind. Maybe make a list of the supplies we'll need. You've always been smart when it comes to things like that."

"And you write good," Steve added. "A whole heap better than me, that's for sure!"

Cord nodded as he mulled over what had been said. He was thinking about the upcoming journey, not what he had almost walked in on at the Stockton farm earlier that day, and that was a relief.

In fact, now that he turned his mind to the task at hand, it felt good to be thinking once again of problems and possible solutions. For too long, there had been only one real problem facing the Bennetts — the lack of rain — and not one blasted thing they could do about it.

"California's a long way off," he mused, "and there are mountains between here and there. It's fall already. I'm not sure we can make it before winter sets in, and we sure don't want to get caught up in the Rockies during a blizzard."

"Maybe it'd be better to wait until spring to leave," Verne suggested. Then he shook his head. "No, I don't reckon we can do that. This place will belong to Hiram Stockton afore then, and I ain't of a mind to ask his leave to stay once it don't belong to us no more."

Cord felt the same way. He had nothing against Stockton. It was Caroline who had turned out to be so much different than he expected. But even so, it would be too galling to hang around once they'd lost the farm.

Flint said, "Pa's right, it's best that we get started as soon as we can. We don't know how fast we'll be able to travel. If we see that we can't make it the whole way before winter, we'll stop somewhere along the way and wait it out. If everything we've heard about California is true, there'll still be plenty of gold there waiting for us next spring!"

The half-dozen robberies Flint had carried out since holding up Ike Plemmons's store had gone off without a hitch. He had picked isolated taverns and stores, and in one case, a blacksmith shop. None of the hauls were very large, but they added up.

The hood had worked perfectly to conceal his identity. None of his victims had any idea who he was.

Nor had he been forced to resort to further violence. Each time, just the threat of the gun had been enough to insure co-operation.

But just in case, Steve was always close by, out of sight but ready to spring into action if Flint needed his help.

Flint was beginning to think that his plan would continue to work all the way to the end of this campaign to raise money for the trip to California. One more job ought to do it . . .

He settled on Jethro Kilroy's Hole in the Rock tavern and trading post as the target. It was several valleys to the north, not far from the Missouri border, a lucrative enterprise built into the side of a mountain, under a beetling bluff that loomed over the trail.

As busy as Kilroy's was, it might be difficult to find a time when only one or two people were in the place. But nothing had happened so far, and by now, Flint was confident in his ability to deal with whatever came up.

So he wasn't worried about that. As long as the trading post wasn't too crowded when he and Steve got there, he was going through with his plan.

The trail that ran past Kilroy's curved around the side of the mountain, climbing at a relatively easy slope until it reached the long, level stretch where the trading post was located. Flint and Steve rode the mules to that point and then reined in.

"Where am I gonna hide, Flint?" Steve asked. "There ain't no good place."

Flint scowled as he realized that was true. With a steep, tree-dotted rocky slope falling away on their right and a bulging rock face rising on their left, there was no cover between here and the trading post, which lay about a hundred yards away.

The trail followed a twenty-foot-wide ledge. Except for a few rocks too small to hide anything Steve's size, the trail was bare. It had been a while since Flint had been here, and he hadn't recalled all the details exactly correctly.

"You're just gonna have to come with me this time," he said to Steve. "But you can wait right outside with the mules, out of sight. When we ride away, hunch over in the saddle as much as you can, to make yourself look smaller."

"I'll try, but makin' me look small ain't gonna be easy!"

Flint knew that was true. He thought about sending Steve back down the trail to wait farther away from the trading post. He was hesitant to do that. Even though he hadn't needed his brother's help in any of the robberies so far, all it would take to ruin their plans was for things to go wrong once.

"There are only a couple of horses tied up out front," Flint said. "I don't reckon we're likely to get a better chance. Come on."

They rode slowly toward their destination. Flint tensed in the saddle as a man came out of the stone building.

The fellow barely glanced toward them, though, before he untied one of the horses at the hitch rail, swung up into the saddle, and rode off in the other direction without looking back. By the time Flint and Steve reached the trading post, the rider had gone out of sight around the curve of the mountain.

"Look at that," Flint said. "Luck's with us, boy! Now there's only one customer in there with old Kilroy."

"You still want me to wait outside?"

"Yeah, I think that'll be best."

Flint eased the pistol a little inside his waistband.

When they were close enough, he motioned for Steve to stop and wait. He handed his mule's reins to his brother and dismounted.

Flint paused for a moment to draw in a deep breath and settle his nerves. Then he took the hood from inside his shirt, pulled it over his head, drew the gun, and stalked into the trading post.

The tavern area was to the left, shelves of trade goods to the right. Directly ahead was a counter behind which stood Jethro Kilroy, a heavyset man with graying, rust-colored hair and a jowly face like a bulldog.

81

Flint locked eyes with Kilroy for a split second, then glanced to the left and saw a well-dressed man sitting at a table with a bottle and glass in front of him, as well as a deck of cards spread out in a solitaire hand.

At the sight of the hooded man entering his trading post, Kilroy started to reach for something under the counter, but Flint thrust the pistol toward him and said, "Don't do it! I'll kill you!"

Kilroy stopped the motion, lifted both hands a little, and moved back a step.

Flint snapped the gun toward the man at the table and ordered, "Don't you move, mister! I'll put a bullet in you, too."

The man lifted his hands and spread them, as if to assure Flint that he wouldn't try anything.

Flint turned slightly so that he could watch both men. He pointed the pistol somewhere between them. He needed another pistol, he realized. This single-shot weapon could put him at a distinct disadvantage.

He should have thought of that before now, he told himself bitterly.

The good thing was that neither man appeared inclined to put up any sort of a fight.

The air was cool and a little clammy in here, not surprising since the ceiling and

three walls had been hacked out of the bluff's face and were pure stone. The ground underfoot was rock, as well. Despite that coolness, Flint felt sweat on his face under the hood.

"I want all the money and any other valuables you've got here, mister," he said to Kilroy. He didn't call the man by name, figuring it would be best if Kilroy thought he was a stranger.

"Just be careful with that pistol you're wavin' around," Kilroy rumbled around the stub of a cigar he had clenched between his teeth. "You don't want to go shootin' nobody."

"No, I don't, but I will if I have to."

"Money's under the counter in a poke. I got to reach for it. Don't shoot me."

"Just get it," Flint growled. "Slow and easy-like."

Since he was talking to Kilroy, his attention naturally drifted more in that direction. He could still see the other man from the corner of his eye. He was aware of it when the man suddenly leaned forward.

"You're the man with the racehorse."

"What?" Flint said.

"You and your brother. You claimed to have a racehorse and wanted me to help you swindle people. But what you really wanted to do was rob me." With a note of satisfaction, the man added, "I recognize your voice."

Two things happened at once. Kilroy dropped a leather poke on the counter so that it landed with a loud clink. At the same time, the man at the table thrust out his arm, and a two-barrel derringer appeared in his hand from up his sleeve. The little gun went off with a loud popping sound as Flint swung his pistol in that direction.

The ball from the derringer hummed past Flint's ear like a lead hornet, and a fraction of a second later, the pistol in his hand roared and bucked against his palm. The man at the table flung both arms in the air as he went over backward with the bullet from Flint's gun in his chest.

The derringer flew upward and landed on the table among the cards, its second barrel unfired.

Kilroy grabbed at something under the counter and brought up a sawed-off, double-barreled shotgun.

Flint knew he didn't have time to reload. He flung the empty pistol at Kilroy as hard as he could. The gun whirled through the air.

Either Flint's aim was good, or he was the luckiest son of a gun around, because the pistol walloped Kilroy in the face, breaking his nose and causing him to reel backward as he jerked the scattergun's triggers.

The double boom was like an enormous clap of thunder in the low-ceilinged stone room. With the sound ringing in his ears, Flint ran at the counter, put one hand on it, and vaulted over, while grabbing a bowie knife from a display of them with the other hand.

He didn't think about what he was doing. He just rammed the bowie into Kilroy's thickset body as hard as he could.

Kilroy groaned, and his eyes rolled up in their sockets. His knees buckled. Flint jerked the blade free and stabbed Kilroy again. This time he left the bowie in Kilroy's chest as the man collapsed onto the stone floor behind the counter.

Instinct warned Flint that somebody else was close by. He whirled around and saw Steve charging into the trading post, drawn by the gunfire. Steve stopped just inside the door and looked around. His mouth moved, but Flint couldn't hear what he was saying.

That was because the gunshots had deafened him. Only temporarily, he hoped.

He scooped up his gun from where it had landed on the floor after hitting Kilroy in the face, grabbed the poke full of money, and rolled back over the counter. Even though he couldn't hear himself, he yelled to Steve, "Let's get out of here!"

Steve jerked his eyes away from the sprawled body of the man Flint had shot. He nodded and said something else Flint couldn't hear. Flint waved for him to move.

Steve looked mighty confused, but he moved. He hurried out of the trading post with Flint right behind him.

A few moments later, they were mounted and driving the mules back down the trail as fast as the stubborn beasts would go.

Flint heard, "— roy?" and realized his hearing was coming back. He looked over at Steve, who repeated, "Wha — appened — ister — Kilroy?"

Flint deciphered the question and said, "I had to knock him out. He was behind the counter."

That was a lie, of course. It was better if he was the only one who knew the truth about what had happened here, Flint decided.

"— other fella?"

"He had a gun and tried to kill me. I didn't have any choice but to shoot him."

"Are you all right, Flint?"

Flint heard all of that question. His ears were working again.

"I'm fine. That shot the fella took at me missed."

"Did you get the money?"

Flint patted his shirt where he had stuffed the poke, along with the hood and pistol.

"I got it," he said. "We ought to have enough now to get us to California."

And he had learned a lesson, too, a lesson that might prove to be as valuable as the coins in that poke. He wouldn't have had any problem back there if fate hadn't sent that gambler across his path again.

So from now on, he decided, he wasn't going to leave anyone alive behind him who might cause trouble for him in the future.

CHAPTER 8

Fort Childs, Unorganized Territory

This area had started off as part of the Louisiana Purchase, Cord knew. Later it had been regarded as part of Missouri Territory.

These days, although still belonging to the United States, the Great Plains found themselves in a region known as Unorganized Territory.

Maybe nobody wanted the plains, Cord thought as he gazed westward from the encampment just outside Fort Childs and saw nothing but mile after empty mile of level, treeless grassland.

He'd heard folks refer to the area between here and the Rocky Mountains as the Great American Desert, but the plains weren't actually a desert. Plenty of vegetation grew here, but it was all short, coarse grass.

Cord looked at the landscape with a farmer's eye. As flat as the terrain was, it would be easy enough to plow, but would the soil grow crops? He hunkered on his heels, picked up a handful of dirt, and rubbed it between his fingers.

"What in blue blazes are you doing?" his brother Flint asked from behind him.

"Trying to figure out if this would make good farmland."

"Why would you do that?" Flint said as he stepped up alongside Cord. "We're not staying here. None of these folks are."

He swept his hand from side to side behind him to indicate the two dozen wagons parked in an irregular circle approximately two hundred yards from the buildings of the military outpost.

Flint was right about that. All the people who had stopped and camped near Fort Childs had their eyes on a much bigger prize than some potential farmland.

They were after gold . . . gold in the Promised Land. California . . .

And the Great Plains were nothing but a way for them to get there, one more stretch of ground to be covered in the Great American Exodus.

Cord tossed the dirt down and straightened to his full height.

"You're right," he told Flint. "I'm just in the habit of checking the soil."

"Well, you'd better get in the habit of checking it for gold nuggets. That's what we're after now."

A gust of chilly wind blew from the north and tugged at the brown hat on Cord's head. The heat of summer back in Arkansas seemed a long way gone now, both in distance and time. Recently, every night on the trail had been colder than the one before, and now that brisk feeling was creeping into the days, as well.

Among the pilgrims in the camp were several old-timers who had spent considerable time on the plains. According to them, winter's true arrival was still several weeks away. A traveler would have time to cross the plains before the snow and bone-chilling temperatures began to roll in.

But that would take them only as far as the mountains, and if a blizzard came crashing down at that point, it would spell doom for whomever it caught there, sure as anything.

That was why so many people had decided to stop here at Fort Childs and wait out the bad weather before continuing on the journey. This was the last outpost of civilization for more than a thousand miles.

The delay was maddening, of course. Every day they weren't in California was a day somebody else was finding gold and they weren't. But nothing could be done about it. Nobody could change the course of the seasons.

That hadn't stopped Flint from arguing about it when they first got here. He wanted to keep moving on.

"After we hurried to get away from the Ozarks as fast as we did, now you want to just stop?" he'd asked incredulously when Cord and Verne suggested they ought to stay here at the fort until spring.

"I don't like it any more'n you do, son," Verne had said. "But freezin' or starvin' to death when winter catches us somewhere betwixt here and there ain't gonna put any gold in our pockets."

Flint had complained profanely and at length about it, but eventually he had come around to their way of thinking . . . or at least he pretended to, for the sake of keeping the peace.

Cord knew that giving in bothered his oldest brother a great deal, though. Once the decision had been made to leave the farm and head west, Flint had been like a man possessed, wanting to get out of there and on the trail as quickly as possible. He had worked long hours rounding up supplies and saddle mounts and everything else they'd need for the trip, using the money he and Steve had made.

He had cast a lot of nervous glances over his shoulder, like a man worried that something bad was coming up behind him. That had puzzled Cord, but once they had put some distance between them and their former home, Flint had relaxed some. He was just anxious to reach their destination and start the search for wealth, Cord supposed.

He and Flint turned and walked back toward the wagons, two big, broadshouldered young men, each wearing holstered revolvers that Flint had picked up as part of their outfitting for the journey. They were new Colt Dragoons, massive .44 caliber weapons that each carried six rounds in its cylinder.

The Colts were expensive, but Flint insisted they might come in handy when danger arose on the trip, as it inevitably would. They had also brought along their rifles, shotguns, and several single-shot pistols.

A well-armed group was more likely to reach its destination safely.

The same was true of a large group. Although the wagons had arrived at the fort at different times, already the men who had brought them in had begun talking about banding together for the rest of the trip. Safety in numbers, as the old saying went.

As Cord and Flint approached the encampment, the older brother pointed to the east.

"Somebody else coming in. More gold-seekers."

"Looks like it," Cord agreed. He shaded his eyes with a hand to get a better look at the wagon rolling toward them.

It was a sturdy, good-sized vehicle, probably used as a farm wagon at one time, as most of the others in camp had been. Wooden ribs and a canvas cover stretched over them had been added to the back to provide protection against the elements.

A man perched on the driver's seat, handling the reins attached to a team of four mules. He had a fairly short, salt-and-pepper beard. Mostly white hair stuck out from under the battered old hat he wore with its brim pushed up in front. He had a flannel shirt on under a cowhide vest trimmed with fringe.

Flint grunted. "Stovall's appointed himself a welcoming committee, I see."

A man in high black boots, whipcord trousers, a store-bought shirt, and a fine, broad-brimmed black hat strode toward the newcomer. From where Cord was, he couldn't see the man's face, but he knew what it looked like.

Lean, handsome, with a haughty expression and a black mustache. As a former military man, Matthew Stovall was accustomed to command, and he didn't hesitate to let people know that. Stovall had started the talk about everybody traveling on to California together, come spring, and naturally, when they did, he would be in charge.

"Let's go see what he has to say," Flint suggested.

"I don't care what Stovall has to say. The man's a blowhard."

A grin creased Flint's face. "Maybe somebody ought to take him down a notch. Let that new fella know Stovall's not actually in charge around here, no matter what he says."

With that, Flint stalked toward the newly arrived wagon. The driver had just brought it to a halt and sat there with the reins in his hands as Stovall came toward him.

Flint was going to try to stir up trouble, Cord realized. Actually, he was a little surprised that Flint had waited this long. Flint enjoyed starting ruckuses. Life in this camp would be boring for him.

Sometimes even he got in too deep, though, despite his reputation as a brawler. Cord hurried after his brother, just in case. He glanced around but didn't see Steve anywhere. Steve's sheer size sometimes was needed to get Flint out of trouble.

Cord supposed that job — if the need for it came up — fell to him this time.

As Flint walked up with Cord about ten feet behind him, Matthew Stovall, who had reached the vehicle first, rested his left hand possessively on its sideboard and said, "You have a fine wagon here, my friend. Welcome to Fort Childs."

The bearded driver frowned at Stovall's hand, turned his head to spit off to the other side, and said, "You ain't the commanding officer, are you?"

"Not exactly. I'm Major Matthew Stovall. Retired." Stovall smiled. "These days, a simple pilgrim such as yourself, sir."

The bearded man nodded and introduced himself.

"Abraham Olmsted's my name. The army don't mind folks campin' here, do they?"

"Not at all. In fact, they encourage travelers to do so instead of attempting to start out onto the plains at this time of year."

"Too dangerous because of winter comin' on, eh?"

"Indeed. That's why I'd suggest you remain right here with our friendly little group."

"All the folks with these wagons are travelin' together? This here's a reg'lar wagon train?"

"That's right —" Stovall began.

"That hasn't actually been decided yet," Flint interrupted as he stepped closer. Stovall turned his head to give him a quick scowl.

Flint went on, "We're all camped here for the moment, but nobody's made up their mind what's going to happen in the spring . . . except maybe Stovall here."

"Major Stovall," the former officer said tightly.

"*Major* Stovall," Flint corrected himself, but the disdain he put in the word negated any apology about it.

With his lips a taut, angry line under the mustache, Stovall turned toward Flint. Cord thought Stovall might throw a punch, or at least say something else, but before that could happen, the canvas flaps at the entrance to the wagon bed parted, and a dark-haired head was thrust out.

"Where are we?" a striking young woman asked.

Another head, this one covered with flaming red curls, appeared as well, and a second, equally lovely young woman said, "Are we going to be staying here?"

If they did, thought the small part of Cord's brain that wasn't struck dumb by their beauty, there was bound to be trouble.

CHAPTER 9

The group camped at Fort Childs included a few women, but not surprisingly, almost all of the pilgrims bound for California were men. Not many men bent on making a long, dangerous journey across the country and then searching for gold would subject their wives or daughters to the hardships of such an enterprise.

The handful of women in the bunch were tough, middle-aged females who had refused to allow their husbands to head for California alone . . . probably because they thought their men might never come back. Indians or road agents or some other mishap might claim their lives.

Or the more likely possibility, the men might strike it rich and decide there was nothing waiting for them at home any better than what they had in California.

Certainly, none of the ladies in the group were anywhere near as young and pretty as these two.

Abraham Olmsted snatched his old hat off his head and swatted at them without actually hitting them.

"Get back in there, dadgum it! Didn't I tell you gals not to poke your heads out until I said it was all right?"

"You can't keep us cooped up in here, Pa," the brunette said.

"That's right," the redhead added. "We need sunshine and fresh air, too, you know."

A group of about a dozen men had gathered not far away, their attention drawn by the arrival of newcomers. A wave of excited, interested murmuring came from them now. They had spotted the two young women, and even if the brunette and the redhead ducked back into the wagon bed, nobody was going to forget they were there.

This could stir up a considerable amount of trouble, Cord thought again. More than Flint could have hoped to cause by baiting Matthew Stovall.

The former officer swept off his hat and bowed. "Ladies!" he said. "When I greeted your father and told him he was welcome to join our little group, I was unaware of your presence. But that invitation extends to you as well, of course."

"Why, thank you, Major," the brunette

said. She pushed the canvas back even more and swung a leg over the driver's seat, revealing a beguiling flash of ankle in a high-buttoned shoe.

Abraham Olmsted rolled his eyes and shook his head, indicating that he was accustomed to his daughters defying his wishes.

The redhead followed her sister out of the wagon as the brunette started to climb down the wagon wheel on the other side. Several men from the assembled bystanders rushed forward, intent on helping her, but she dropped to the ground with lithe ease before any of them could circle around the mule team.

They got there in time to assist the redhead, who bestowed a bright smile on them. Cord looked away, a little sickened. All women were like that, he supposed, smiling at every man who crossed their path so they'd be assured of always having someone around to do their bidding.

"My, it feels good to get out and stretch our, um, limbs, doesn't it, Glory?" the brunette said.

"It does," the redhead replied. "That wagon bed gets awfully cramped after a while."

Stovall stepped around the mules, too, and

bulled his way through the small crowd, still holding his hat clasped against his chest.

"Major Matthew Stovall, at your service, ladies," he said.

"I'm Katherine," the brunette said. "But you can call me Kat."

"And I'm Gloriana," the redhead added. "I generally go by Glory, though, since the other is a little on the highfalutin' side."

"Your mama set great store by that name, gal," Olmsted snapped. "It was her grandma's name."

Glory Olmsted dropped her green-eyed gaze to the ground. "I know that, Pa," she said. "I'm sorry. I didn't mean to make fun of it."

Stovall said, "It's a lovely name for a lovely young woman, Miss Olmsted." He smiled quickly at Kat. "As is yours, Miss Katherine."

"Did I hear you say you and these other men are spending the winter here?" Kat asked.

"That's right."

Glory said, "You see, Pa, Kat and I were right when we told you we couldn't make it all the way to California before winter sets in."

"You're going to California?" Stovall said.

"That's right. We're going to find gold and

101

get rich!"

From the wagon seat, Olmsted grumbled, "We made it this far, didn't we? We got that much of a lead on all the folks who ain't even started yet."

"That's true, my friend," Flint said as he stepped forward and held up a hand. "Flint Bennett's my name. I'll be glad to give you a hand with these mules."

"I'm obliged to you, son," Olmsted said as he stuck out a leathery paw and clasped Flint's hand.

On the other side of the wagon, Stovall glared, obviously wishing he had thought of offering to help the old-timer first. That might have gained him some favor in the eyes of Olmsted's daughters.

Cord didn't care what the Olmsted girls thought of him, but he shook hands with the older man and introduced himself, too, out of sheer friendliness and hospitality.

"There's plenty of room for you to park and make camp over by where our tents are pitched," Cord said. "We're traveling on horseback, so we brought tents with us to get in out of the weather when we need to."

"You got no wagon?"

"We're traveling pretty light," Cord explained. He grinned. "We've got picks and shovels and pans. Once we make it to

California, those ought to be just about all we need."

Olmsted laughed. "I like the way you think, son. A fella who's confident in what he can do is gonna be right more often than he is wrong. You boys can show me which way to steer these jugheads."

"What about your daughters?" Flint asked.

Olmsted looked at Kat and Glory, who were surrounded by Stovall and the other men as they smiled and chatted and laughed.

"Oh, I reckon they'll be all right," Olmsted drawled dryly. "Those two gals know how to take care o' theirselves. They've had to learn, bein' raised up by an old pelican like me. Their ma passed on when they was mighty young. I don't reckon either of 'em even remember her."

"That's a shame," Cord said. "But it looks like you've done a good job."

Olmsted just rolled his eyes again. Cord had a feeling that Kat and Glory did pretty much whatever they wanted and got away with it.

He and Flint walked next to the wagon and pointed out the area near their tents where there was plenty of room to park the vehicle and unhitch and picket the mules.

Actually, almost anywhere would have done as well as another place, Cord thought. There wasn't much out here other than wide open spaces. The nearby Platte River provided water, although at times it had to be strained through cheesecloth to get some of the mud out.

As the wagon creaked to a halt, Verne crawled out of one of the two tents. He stood up, yawned, and rubbed his eyes, indicating that he'd been napping. His thinning hair stuck out wildly from his head.

"Who's this?" he asked.

"Another gold-seeker on his way to California," Flint said. "Mr. Olmsted, this is our pa, Verne Bennett."

Olmsted climbed down quickly, demonstrating that he was still pretty spry despite his age. He shook hands with Verne and said, "Abraham Olmsted. You can call me Abe. Mighty pleased to make your acquaintance, Verne."

"Likewise," Verne said.

Olmsted chuckled. "I'm glad to see I ain't the only old geezer loco enough to run off in search of gold."

"Old geezer, is it?" Verne's grin showed that he wasn't actually offended by the term. "Well, I reckon that's what I am, when you get right down to it. Are you travelin' alone, Abe?"

"Nope. I've got my daughters with me."

"Daughters? You're takin' gals with you to California?"

Flint said, "Mighty good-looking young women they are, too, Pa."

Olmsted cleared his throat and said, "I know I'm a mite long in the tooth to have gals that young, but their ma and me got hitched later than most folks. That's prob'ly why she weren't never too healthy again after havin' two young'uns. Birthin' Kat and Glory just took too big a toll on her, may she rest in peace."

"May she rest in peace," Verne repeated. "Sorry for your loss, Abe."

"It was a long time ago," Olmsted said with a slight shrug. He changed the subject. "Your boys said it'd be all right for me to camp here."

"Oh, sure, sure. We ain't got no say in such things. This is all gov'ment land, I reckon, and the army don't care. They're used to folks campin' here. This is the spot where a bunch of different trails come together. Ever since immigrants started passin' through these parts on their way west, there's been a heap of traffic. Not much at this time of year, though. All the reg'lar immigrant trains went through earlier."

105

"Now it's just people on their way to California to look for gold," Flint added. "Say, Pa, where's Steve?"

"I think he wandered off toward the fort a while ago. He likes to watch the blacksmith work."

Cord and Flint helped Olmsted unhitch his mules and picket them where they could graze on a decent patch of grass. Since the Bennetts had two buckets of water at their camp, Verne emptied one of them into a bucket Olmsted fetched from the back of the wagon, and they put that out for the mules, as well.

"No need in makin' you trudge down to the river until you have to," Verne said. "Whereabouts are you from, if you don't mind my askin', Abe?"

"Kentucky," Olmsted replied. "Mighty pretty place, and we had a decent farm there, but I just couldn't pass up the chance to make some real money by findin' gold."

"Same for my boys and me. A man don't get many chances to strike it rich."

That wasn't exactly how things had happened, Cord mused, but he wasn't going to contradict his pa. It seemed like Verne and Olmsted had hit it off immediately and were getting along well so far. It would be good for Verne to have a friend closer to his own age, especially if they were going to be stuck here at Fort Childs all winter, as seemed likely.

Olmsted lowered the wagon's tailgate so he and Verne could sit on it and talk. The two old-timers pulled out their pipes and began to pack them.

"Reckon I'll go over to the fort and find Steve," Flint said to Cord.

"I'll come with you," Cord said, even though Flint hadn't invited him. Flint didn't object, so they strolled together toward the numerous buildings laid out in a rectangle around a central parade ground. That was all Fort Childs amounted to.

But even though the outpost didn't have a stockade wall, the Indians had left it alone so far. They respected the soldiers, their rifles, and especially the artillery with which the post was equipped.

As Cord and Flint walked along, they passed the spot where Kat and Glory Olmsted were still surrounded. The number of their admirers had grown as word spread through the encampment that a couple of pretty girls had arrived.

Cord noticed several men standing beside their wagons and gazing wistfully toward the crowd, obviously eager to join in. But their wives were standing nearby with arms crossed and stern looks on their faces. Any husband ignoring those warning frowns would do so at his own risk.

Flint let out a harsh laugh. "That old man's going to be rich long before he makes it to California."

"You mean Mr. Olmsted?" Cord asked.

"Yeah. He's already struck gold."

Cord shook his head. "I don't know what you mean."

"Don't be a fool, Cord," Flint said. "Those girls aren't his daughters. It's as plain as the nose on your face. They're whores, and he's going to make a small fortune selling them before they even get to the gold fields. And once they *do* get there . . ." Flint laughed again. "That'll be the real bonanza!"

CHAPTER 10

Cord stopped short and said, "Wait a minute. Those girls don't strike me as being that type."

Flint came to a stop and regarded his brother with an amused expression. "Because you know so much about whores that you can recognize one right away?"

"Well, I never said that . . ."

"Take it from me, little brother. I have a lot more experience with the world than you do."

"You're only a few years older than me," Cord pointed out.

"Maybe, but I was *born* a lot older than you were."

Cord looked back toward Kat and Glory and said, "You can see the resemblance between the two of them. I think they really are sisters."

"I never said they weren't sisters. I just said they lay down with fellas for money.

And I didn't see any family resemblance to that old man who brought them here, did you?"

"Well . . . I'm not much of a judge of such things. Maybe they got their looks from their ma and don't take after their pa much. That happens sometimes."

Flint clapped a hand on Cord's shoulder. "Don't worry about it," he said. "Anyway, what does it matter whether he's really their pa? Either way, we might be able to scrounge up enough coins for you to pay a visit to them, once they get set up and start entertaining gentleman callers. Which one do you think you'd want? Kat or Glory?"

"I'm not even going to talk about it, because I still think you're wrong."

"Suit yourself. Come on."

Flint started toward the fort again. Cord walked alongside, mulling over what his brother had said. He supposed it was possible Flint was right about the Olmsted sisters. From what Cord had heard, the frontier was notorious for its lack of women, especially respectable women. Most of the females to be found out here were indeed prostitutes.

But that didn't mean Kat and Glory were like that. High-spirited and flirtatious, maybe, but not . . . soiled doves.

Although he didn't intend to consider it, Flint's question lingered in his mind. If it were up to him . . . and if Flint actually was right about the Olmsted sisters, or whatever their names really were . . . which one *would* he pick?

Kat was the prettier of the two, he decided, with her raven hair, slightly olive skin, and intriguing, heart-shaped face, but there was something about Glory that drew him to her. Maybe it was that red hair, brighter than any he had ever seen, or the deep green eyes that reminded him of pools of water with untold secrets in their depths.

If he had to choose . . .

But he didn't, thank goodness. No matter what sort of women they turned out to be, he didn't have any intention of treating them with anything other than polite but distant friendliness.

As they neared the fort, Cord heard the blacksmith's hammer ringing against the anvil. Steve liked to stand in the shop's doorway and watch the sparks fly. He would have made a good blacksmith himself, Cord had thought more than once. Steve certainly had the size and strength for it.

Some small cottonwood trees were planted along the edges of the parade ground. They were the only trees visible in the vast sweep

111

of flat landscape, except for a few stunted examples on an island formed by shifting channels in the broad, turgid Platte River. With no lumber for construction, the fort's buildings were all made of sod or adobe.

More than a dozen three-inch cannon were arranged around the parade ground, as well, all of them pointing outward to be used in defense of the fort if the Indians ever attacked. At the far end of the open space were several larger field pieces on carriages that could be hauled around by mule teams to provide more firepower where necessary.

Even though those defenses hadn't been tested so far, Fort Childs had a reputation as a tough nut to crack, the old-timers said.

Cord had overheard some of the soldiers talking about Indians attacking wagon trains west of here, however. More than one massacre had taken place in the past.

That was a good reason for the gold-seekers to set out together in the spring, despite Flint's reluctance to go along with the idea. The only reason Flint didn't like it was because Matthew Stovall had come up with it.

Stovall rubbed Flint the wrong way. Otherwise, Flint would see how practical it was.

Before they reached the blacksmith shop,

Cord noticed an officer striding toward them. The man raised a hand and called, "A moment, please, you two."

Cord knew the man to be Daniel Woodbury, the commanding officer here at Fort Childs despite the fact that he was only in his mid-thirties and a lieutenant in the Corps of Engineers. Woodbury was an imposing individual with a dark, close-cropped beard and keen eyes.

"What can we do for you, Lieutenant?" Flint asked as he and Cord came to a stop.

"I've heard that there are new arrivals at the encampment outside the fort."

Flint smiled. "Word travels fast when there are pretty girls involved, doesn't it?"

"Then it's true?"

"It's true," Cord confirmed. "A fella named Abraham Olmsted drove up in a wagon a little while ago. He has his two daughters with him."

"Or at least he *says* they're his daughters," Flint added. "Personally, I've got my doubts."

"You believe them to be, ah, ladies of a certain persuasion . . . ?" Woodbury asked.

"Why else would they be out here where there are plenty of men but hardly any women?"

Cord's voice was sharp with annoyance as

he said, "Maybe because they're on their way to California to look for gold with their father, just like they claimed?"

"You believe what they told you, then, Mr. Bennett?" Woodbury asked.

Cord shrugged. "I don't have any reason to believe or disbelieve their story, Lieutenant. But I like to give folks the benefit of the doubt until they prove to me that they're not telling the truth."

"A good policy, in general," Woodbury said, nodding slowly. "I take it these two young ladies are attractive?"

"You're right about that," Flint said with a grin. "One with hair as dark as a raven's wing, and the other with such red curls that you'd think the sun was coming up."

"But they haven't given any overt indication of, ah, selling their wares, so to speak?"

"Not so far," Flint admitted. "But give 'em time."

"Time is exactly what I shall give them, gentlemen. So far, relations between the garrison here and the men in your group have been fairly peaceful. As long as that state of affairs continues, I won't place the fort off limits to you and your companions, nor will I declare your encampment off limits to my men."

Woodbury frowned and went on, "But if

114

there should happen to be any trouble, I might be less inclined to extend the fort's hospitality to you and your friends." Woodbury nodded curtly. "You might pass that information along to the others, if you'd be so kind."

"Sure, we'll spread the word," Flint said. "But it's not our responsibility what some old-timer and his girls do."

Woodbury just nodded again and went on his way.

Flint's affable pose vanished as soon as Woodbury was gone. He glared after the lieutenant and muttered, "Stuffed shirt's got a rifle ramrod stuck up his —"

"Let's just go find Steve," Cord interrupted.

They followed the clanging sounds to the squat, adobe blacksmith shop. Steve lounged in the entrance, where the door was propped wide open to allow the cool air in. He had a shoulder propped against the side of the opening as he watched the smith hammer out some bit of harness hardware and use tongs to plunge it into a bucket of water. Steam rose as the water hissed on the hot metal.

Steve looked over his shoulder at his brothers and asked, "What are you boys doin' here?"

"Just making sure you're all right," Cord said.

"Why wouldn't I be? Rufus don't mind me bein' here and watchin' him, do you, Rufus?"

The blacksmith, a burly, black-bearded civilian named Rufus Russell who worked for the army, shook his head.

"No, you're generally pretty good company, Steve," Russell said. "You're welcome any time I'm workin' out here."

"See?" Steve said, as if he had won an argument, although neither Cord nor Flint had disputed Russell's tolerance of Steve's presence.

Steve continued, "Heard tell some pretty girls have showed up in the camp. Some of the soldiers were talkin' about them. Is that true?"

"It's true," Flint said.

"I'll bet you'll be goin' after 'em mighty quick-like, won't you, Flint?" Steve asked with a chuckle. "Just like you went after —"

"Never you mind what I'm going to do," Flint said sharply. "That's not really anybody's business but mine, is it?"

Steve looked embarrassed as he nodded. "Yeah, I reckon I did speak outta turn, didn't I? Sorry, Flint."

He glanced at Cord, then looked at the

116

ground and shuffled his feet.

Cord wondered what in the world that was about. Flint usually bragged about his conquests to anybody who would listen. It wasn't like him to practice a little discretion and propriety.

And what did that glance Steve had thrown his way mean? Cord didn't care what Flint did. It was none of his business, and to tell the truth, he'd rather not know.

The blacksmith paused in his work to wipe sweat off his face with the sleeve of the long underwear he wore under his overalls and heavy canvas apron. Despite the cool crispness of the outside air, heat always built up inside a blacksmith shop from the fire underneath the forge.

"Is the lieutenant gonna put your camp off limits?" he asked. "I noticed you talkin' to him a few minutes ago."

"It's not really our camp more than it is anybody else's," Flint said. "That popinjay Stovall is the one who acts like he's running things."

"But Lieutenant Woodbury said he wouldn't put the camp off limits to the soldiers unless there was trouble," Cord added.

"Oh, there'll be trouble, all right," Russell said, with a grin wreathing his bearded face.

"What makes you say that?"

"I never saw a time when pretty girls showed up that trouble didn't follow 'em."

Cord couldn't very well argue with that, since the exact same thought had crossed his mind a short time earlier. More than once, in fact.

The only real question was how long it would take.

CHAPTER 11

As it turned out, a fight didn't erupt until that evening, after supper, and it was between gold-seekers and didn't involve any soldiers from the fort.

Three brothers named Klingberg, originally from Sweden, approached the Olmsted wagon intent on asking Kat and Glory to go for a walk with them.

Two other fellows, an Irishman from New York City and a backwoodsman from the Smoky Mountains in Tennessee, showed up at the wagon at the same time, for the same purpose. Harsh words were exchanged, and then blows.

With the Swedes outnumbering the other two, they soon emerged triumphant . . . but then, caught up in the heat of battle, the brothers turned on each other. It was quite a spectacle to watch those tall, rawboned blonds whaling away at each other.

With the Bennetts' camp being so close

by, they had front-row seats to the ruckus. At one point, Cord started to stand up from the crate he was using as a seat.

"We ought to put a stop to this," he said. "Somebody's liable to get hurt —"

Flint reached out and caught hold of Cord's arm.

"Have you lost your mind, little brother? The one who'll get hurt is you. If you stick your nose into that, those dumb Svens will bust it for you. You ought to know by now that nobody fights harder than brothers, but if an outsider tries to horn in, they'll all stick together again and turn on you."

Cord sighed. He supposed Flint was right. He sat down again and resumed watching the brawl, which took on a new dimension when a couple of the Irishman's friends from the Ould Sod showed up, drawn by the commotion, and pitched in to avenge his defeat.

Over by the Bennett campfire, Verne chuckled and declared, "Best scrap I've seen in a coon's age."

Cord looked past the mass of angrily flailing arms and legs at the Olmsted wagon. Old Abraham was trying to hustle his girls back into the wagon bed, under the canvas cover, evidently to keep the brutal sight away from their delicate eyes.

He wasn't having much luck, though. Kat stood there watching, her eyes bright, seemingly enthralled by the violent display.

Glory was beside her, equally rapt, but she appeared to be more horrified than entertained.

Olmsted finally gave up on trying to get them to listen to him. He threw his hands in the air, and his lips moved in the white beard. Cord figured he was muttering frustrated curses.

Eventually, the battle came down to one of the Klingberg brothers and one of the Irishmen. All the other combatants were down, either unconscious or in no shape to continue. The two men battered each other until they simultaneously launched desperate punches that missed badly.

Thrown off balance by those misses, both men stumbled and pitched forward onto their faces. They tried to rise but then slumped back down and groaned. All the fight had been knocked out of them.

The brawl had drawn quite a bit of attention. More than a dozen men had gathered around to look on eagerly.

Now, with the conflict over, some of the spectators turned to each other and began exchanging coins. From the looks of it, considerable betting had gone on.

Into the relative quiet, Abraham Olmsted said to his daughters, "Now, blast it, will you two get in the wagon like I told you, or am I gonna have to paddle you both?"

"You're not going to paddle us, and you know it, Pa," Kat said with a smile. "Anyway, it was just a fight. Boys have fought over us plenty of times before, you know."

"Yeah, I know it, but that don't mean I have to like it."

Olmsted snatched his battered old hat off his head and raked his fingers through his hair. He looked completely exasperated, Cord thought . . . which was probably a pretty common expression for fathers of pretty, headstrong girls.

Flint was the one who stood up this time and started toward the wagon. Cord got to his feet and hurried after him, saying, "I thought you said we should stay out of it."

"The fight's over," Flint said, waving a hand toward the limp figures scattered on the ground. "I want to talk to Kat."

The two girls were still standing by the lowered tailgate at the rear of the wagon when Cord and Flint walked up to them. Glory had a shawl wrapped around her shoulders to protect her from the chilly wind, but Kat stood with no wrap or hat, her dark hair blowing around her face.

She pushed it back, looked boldly at the Bennett brothers, and asked, "Are you two boys going to fight now?"

"No, ma'am," Flint said with a grin. "We're peaceable men, aren't we, Cord?"

"We try to be," Cord allowed.

"I just hope you ladies weren't too upset by that barbaric display." Flint nodded toward the brawlers, who were beginning to groan and stir around more.

"Like I told my father, we've had men fight over us before. It's nothing new." Kat laughed softly. "This *was* one of the more entertaining battles, though."

Glory said, "I don't see why they had to start fighting. We would have been happy to sit and talk with all of them, wouldn't we, Kat?"

"Of course. I always enjoy some stimulating conversation."

"In that case," Flint said, "maybe the two of you would like to take a stroll around the camp with me and my brother, perhaps even over to the fort —"

"Ain't nobody takin' no gol-dang stroll," Olmsted interrupted as he came up to them. "It's nighttime, blast it. You girls ain't goin' gallivantin' around in the dark, especially with two fellas you just met. Not to mention, we're on the dang frontier, a long ways

123

from civilization! Why, there could be Injuns just a-lurkin' out there in the shadows, or mountain lions —"

"There aren't any mountain lions," Kat broke in. "Because there aren't any mountains for hundreds of miles. Is there such a thing as a plains lion?"

"I dunno, I never heard tell of such a — dadgum it! That ain't the point. It's dangerous to go walkin' around in the dark. And you young fellas . . ."

Olmsted turned a baleful glare on Cord and Flint.

"You go on back to your campfire," the old-timer went on, "before I fetch my shotgun."

"Take it easy," Flint said, sounding annoyed. "There's no need for threats."

Verne and Steve had walked up in time to hear the last part of the conversation. Verne said, "Flint, you mind what Abe says. I raised you to respect your elders, and you'd best do it."

Flint looked like he wanted to argue, but then he shrugged and chuckled.

"Sure, Pa. We didn't mean to cause any trouble, did we, Cord?"

Cord started to say, *I didn't.* He wasn't sure about Flint. But instead he said, "No, we were just visiting with the young ladies for a minute. That's all. Come on, Flint."

Not to be denied one last chance to flirt, Flint pinched the brim of his hat, nodded to Kat, and said, "Have a pleasant evening, Miss Kat. You, too, Miss Glory."

"Good night, Mr. Bennett," Kat said. "Maybe we can take that walk during the day sometime."

"I'll hold you to that," Flint said.

" 'Night, miss," Cord said to Glory, touching a finger to his own hat brim.

"Mr. Bennett," she said.

The short response could have been cool and curt from another woman, but Cord thought he detected a hint of warmth in Glory's voice. Or maybe he was just imagining it, he told himself.

As the four Bennetts walked back to their campsite with Verne and Steve in the lead and Flint and Cord following a few steps behind, Flint said quietly, "That gal Glory likes you, little brother."

"You're loco," Cord muttered.

"I don't think so."

"She was just upset about the fight. She was nice to me because I didn't start throwing punches at anybody."

"Maybe. The only one who can find out for sure is you." Flint laughed. "I already know Kat likes me."

"According to what you said earlier, they're girls who like any man who has the right price."

Flint came to an abrupt stop. Cord halted, too. In the faint light that reached them from the campfire, Flint actually looked serious as he said, "Maybe I was wrong about that. Could be I jumped to the wrong conclusion for once. We'll have to wait and see, I suppose."

It was very rare for Flint to ever admit that he was wrong about anything. For him to do so now told Cord that brief conversation with Kat might have meant more to Flint than he would let on. And Flint was certainly right about one thing.

They'd have to wait and see.

Not surprisingly, that wasn't the last fight over the Olmsted sisters, and as was inevitable, soldiers from Fort Childs were involved in several of them, leading Lieutenant Woodbury to order his troops to stay away from the gold-seekers' camp.

The lieutenant didn't forbid the civilians from coming to the fort, but he made it clear that if any of them started any trouble while they were there, he would deal with them just as harshly as he would with his own men. He wouldn't hesitate to lock them up in the guardhouse.

Since the commanding officer was the only thing resembling the law for hundreds of miles, both sides took him seriously, leading to an uneasy truce between the gold-seekers and the soldiers.

Then, a couple of weeks later, winter came roaring down the plains a little early, and nobody was concerned with much of anything except not freezing to death.

A few of the men who had some experience with winters out here had already started erecting sod shelters. Wagons and tents weren't going to be enough. After a few bone-chilling nights, everybody joined in that effort.

Steve's great strength came in handy again, as he proved quite capable at carving out the thick blocks of sod and stacking them up to form walls. Cord and Flint helped, too, but Steve did the lion's share of the work erecting their shelter.

Then, when they were finished and had a small, square hut with a canvas roof and a single opening for a door, Flint surprised everybody by saying, "We need to let Mr. Olmsted and his daughters use this one. Now that we know what we're doing, we can build another one for us pretty quickly."

"That's a mighty generous thought, boy,"

Verne said. "Abe and them gals are still tryin' to get by in their wagon. They can't build nothin' like this."

"You never said anything about that to me," Steve said.

"The idea just occurred to me," Flint responded.

Cord wasn't sure he was telling the truth, though. Flint might have had this in mind all along, because of his interest in Kat Olmsted.

It was obvious by now that Flint's initial judgment about the sisters had been wrong. There had been no sign that they were interested in selling themselves.

In fact, from the conversations he'd had with Glory, Cord had found her to be friendly but rather shy when she was away from Kat. She could act brash around her sister at times, but Cord supposed she felt she had to be like that, in order to keep up with the much bolder brunette.

By herself, though, she was as sweet as could be, and Cord found himself more and more in agreement with Matthew Stovall's idea that the entire group should travel on to California together when the time came.

If indeed spring ever returned to the Great Plains, which, after weeks of frequent snow

and bone-chilling winds, Cord was beginning to doubt would ever happen . . .

CHAPTER 12

Of course, despite Cord's doubts, by the spring of 1849, winter had loosened its grip. Warm winds from the south melted the snow and turned the plains into a sea of mud.

The ground would have to dry quite a bit before the wagons could leave. If they attempted that now, they would bog down before they had gone a mile.

Fort Childs was now Fort Kearny. Official word had arrived from the War Department in December, informing Lieutenant Woodbury of the name change. The post had been renamed to honor General Stephen W. Kearny, one of the heroes of the recent Mexican War.

Woodbury, who had been in charge of the party that established the post, had called the place Fort Childs in honor of another Mexican War leader, Colonel Thomas Childs, who also happened to be Woodbury's father-in-law.

No doubt Woodbury would have preferred to keep that name, for the sake of his marriage if nothing else, but as a good officer, he had no choice but to go along with the War Department's decision.

Fort Kearny it was.

Flint had abandoned his opposition to Matthew Stovall's plan for all of them to travel on to California together. Doing so would allow him to continue spending time with Kat.

Staying with the group was fine with Cord, too. He and Glory had become friends and often went for walks together when the weather would allow it. They had even held hands on a few of those walks, and once, feeling extremely daring, Cord had leaned over and planted a kiss on Glory's cheek.

She didn't pull away when he did that. In fact, she smiled at him and squeezed his hand. With that encouragement, Cord might have tried to go even further, but he got control of himself. Pushing too far, too fast, could lead to disaster.

Besides, the memory of Caroline Stockton lurked in the back of his mind and made him hesitate to give his emotions free rein. Glory seemed trustworthy . . . but so had

Caroline.

Now that the weather was better, a sense of impatience grew stronger among the gold-seekers with every passing day. While standing beside the sod hut with Cord one morning, Flint stared westward over the plains, frowned, and muttered, "We've got to get on the trail. All the gold's going to be gone before we ever make it to California."

"If what they were saying last year is true, there'll still be plenty of gold for everybody," Cord said. "The stories in the newspapers talked like the gold strike would last a hundred years or more!"

Flint slashed at the air with a hand. "Just because a newspaper says it, that doesn't mean it's true. Those journalists will say anything to get people to read their drivel."

"It wasn't just the papers. People said it, too."

"After reading it in the newspaper." Flint shook his head. "You need to learn something, Cord. If you sit around waiting, you're going to come up short, every time. Success goes to the man who reaches out and grabs what he wants first, no matter who he has to run over to get there." He grunted contemptuously. "Everybody else just takes the leavings and has to be satisfied with them."

"Well, we won't be first, no matter what we do," Cord pointed out. "All the folks who got there last year were first. We'll just have to be satisfied with getting there in '49 instead of '48."

Steve had come up behind them and listened to the conversation. He said, "That means we'll be Forty-Niners instead of Forty-Eighters. That sounds better anyway. And there'll still be plenty of gold for everybody."

Flint half-turned and said, "How in the world do you know that?"

"Because if there ain't, there's no reason for us goin' all that way, is there?" Steve's smile showed that he absolutely believed that simple yet logical statement.

Cord chuckled and said, "He's got a point."

Steve grinned, pleased that Cord had agreed with him. Flint just shook his head, blew out a frustrated breath, and said, "All I know is, that mud had better dry up pretty soon. I'm ready to get out of here."

They all were, Cord knew.

The warm, steady wind from the south did a good job of drying the mud. After a couple more days, Matthew Stovall walked out a good distance from the camp, then came back and declared, "I think the ground's in good enough shape for the wagons to travel."

Stovall didn't know that Cord and Flint had already walked along the Platte for a ways, checking the same thing, and come back to camp to start getting ready to depart. Stovall noticed that they were loading supplies on their mules and frowned.

"You Bennetts are jumping the gun a little, aren't you?" he asked. "I just said —"

"We know what you just said," Flint interrupted him. "And we don't have to wait for you to give us the word about this or anything else, Stovall. You're not in charge of this bunch."

"Well, if we're all going to make it to California safely, somebody needs to be in command," Stovall insisted. "In fact . . ." He raised his voice. "I think we should call a meeting of everyone right now and elect a captain."

Mutters of agreement came from some of the gold-seekers as they gathered around, while others looked more dubious.

That didn't deter Stovall, who strode around loudly proclaiming that he was the best choice to lead the group to California because of his military experience. Those who agreed with him began calling out their support.

Flint raised his own voice. "Wait just a minute here!"

Stovall swung around to face him. "Do you want to stand against me, Bennett?" he challenged. "You've never wanted to admit that I'm the better man. Why don't we put it to a vote? Unless you're afraid . . . ?"

Flint surprised Cord by not taking a swing at the arrogant former officer. "I never said I wanted to be in charge of this bunch. I'm responsible for me and my family, that's all. But we've got a man here I'd put my trust in more than I would in you, any day of the week."

Flint turned and pointed.

"I'm talking about Colonel Abraham Olmsted."

"Colonel . . . ?" Cord repeated, taken by surprise at his brother's bold declaration.

Abraham Olmsted, who was standing nearby with Kat and Glory, glared at him for a moment before saying, "Dadblast it, boy, there ain't no need for you to go bringin' up ancient history —"

"But it's true, isn't it, Mr. Olmsted?" Flint said. "You served under Andy Jackson and were there with him at New Orleans and then later, during the Creek Wars."

"I was a whole heap younger then." Olm-

135

sted looked over at his daughters. "One o' you gals has been talkin' outta turn about your old pa, ain't you?"

It had to have been Kat who told Flint about her father's military history, Cord thought. He knew Glory had never mentioned it to him.

Kat confirmed that by saying, "Well, why shouldn't we talk about it, Pa? We're proud of you. You served with honor and distinction and led plenty of men into battle. I think it's a good idea for you to take over this group. You can get us all safely to California."

Now the murmurs of agreement came from men who supported that idea, rather than Stovall's suggestion that he take over.

"All that was a long time ago," Olmsted said. "And I ain't done nothin' since then 'cept farm and horse-trade and raise you two gals."

Stovall had looked surprised and confused at first when Flint suggested Olmsted was better suited to lead them, but now his confidence was coming back. He said, "With all due respect, Mr. Olmsted is right. His experiences were a long time ago, and you need a younger, more vital man to take charge —"

"Now hold on," Olmsted broke in. "I

reckon I ain't quite ready for the rockin' chair just yet. I'm still plenty vital, if that's how you want to put it."

"I'm sure that's true, but in this case —"

One of the men called, "How many battles have you been in, Stovall?"

Stovall's head snapped around toward the man who'd asked the question. "That doesn't matter. The point is, I'm much younger —"

Again, he wasn't allowed to finish before another man said, "I'd like to know about that, too. If Abe was at the Battle of New Orleans with Old Hickory, that's pretty impressive."

"A lot of men were involved in that battle," Stovall said, clearly struggling to maintain his composure and hang on to his temper.

"Maybe so, but Abe was a colonel."

"Not then, I wasn't," Olmsted said. "I was a major. Didn't get promoted to colonel until we were fightin' the Creeks down in Alabama."

The man who had spoken up first said, "You never answered that question about how many battles you've been in, Stovall."

"What does that matter?" Stovall said, flinging his hands out to the sides in exasperation. "I know about wagons and mules. I was in charge of transporting supplies all over New Jersey —"

"So you were a supply officer . . . in New Jersey."

"That's right. And I'll have you know that I did an excellent job!"

The man pointed a finger at him. "But if the Injuns attack us while we're crossin' the plains, you won't have any damned idea what to do, will you?"

"I've thoroughly studied the tactics of engagement —"

"And Abe Olmsted has lived through engagements like that." The man turned to face the crowd and raised his voice. "I vote that we declare Abe our captain for the rest of the trip to California!"

Shouts of agreement rose, including ones from Flint and Steve and Verne. Cord went along with that, although he could tell that Olmsted didn't really want the job.

It was likely, though, that the old-timer actually was the most qualified among them to hold the position.

The support for Olmsted quickly overwhelmed that for Stovall, who, to be honest, wasn't that well-liked among the goldseekers. Men gathered around the old-timer to slap him on the back and congratulate him on being picked to lead them.

Olmsted nodded and thanked his well-wishers, but Cord was standing close enough to hear him mutter, "Lord help us all!"

CHAPTER 13

Once it was decided that the ground was fit for travel, the gold-seekers wasted no time packing up their gear and getting ready to depart.

The Bennetts were ready before any of the others, since they had only to fold up their tents and load what they could carry on their saddle horses and pack mules.

As he stood holding his horse's reins, Cord looked at the sod hut that had been their home for the past few months. Riding away from the farm back in Arkansas had been gut-wrenching, because of so many fond memories of growing up there.

He couldn't summon up any good memories about the sod hut. Even though it had been better than being out in the open, it had been damp and cold and a generally miserable place to live. Cord was glad to be leaving it behind at last.

Flint saw where Cord was looking and

140

said in a slightly jeering tone, "Don't tell me . . . you're so damned sentimental that you're going to miss the place."

"Not hardly," Cord said. "If I never lay eyes on it again, that'll be just fine with me."

"We're in agreement on that, little brother. I'd just as soon forget the time we've spent here." Flint glanced toward the Olmsted wagon, where Kat and Glory were helping their father get ready to depart. "Well, I'd just as soon forget most of it, anyway. Some parts of it weren't too bad."

Cord didn't ask Flint to elaborate. Instead, he nodded toward the fort and said, "Here comes Lieutenant Woodbury."

The young officer strode toward the encampment with a solemn look on his face. Abraham Olmsted saw him coming and, befitting his new position as the group's leader, walked out to meet him.

Cord and Flint followed the old-timer, curious what the lieutenant wanted.

Woodbury nodded as he came up to them and then said, "Mr. Olmsted, it appears that you and the rest of the group are preparing to leave."

"That's right, Lieutenant. We figure the ground's dry enough now that the wagons won't bog down."

Flint added, "He's too modest to tell you

141

about it, Lieutenant, but Mr. Olmsted's been picked to lead this bunch the rest of the way to California."

"Is that so?" Woodbury smiled. "Well, I wish you the best of luck, sir. Command has its privileges, but it brings with it a great deal of responsibility, as well."

"Reckon I know that," Olmsted said. "I was in the army, a ways back."

"He was a colonel," Flint said with a grin. "Under Andrew Jackson."

"Really?" Woodbury looked at the old-timer with a new respect. "In that case, sir, I'm sure you know what I'm talking about, and you'll understand when I tell you that you may be going into a situation fraught with danger."

"Pretty much knowed startin' out that travelin' across the country in a wagon wasn't gonna be quite safe. I didn't want to bring those gals o' mine with me, but there wasn't nowhere else to leave 'em, and besides, they was bound and determined to come along and hunt for gold, too." Olmsted scratched at his white beard. "When you say danger, are you talkin' about Injuns?"

"Yes, the Pawnee and the Cheyenne roam freely to the west of here, all the way to the mountains. Some bands are hostile, some

142

aren't, at least most of the time . . . but even the ones who are normally peaceful can decide not to be, practically on a moment's notice."

Olmsted nodded and said, "I fought the Creeks with Andy Jackson. I know what you mean."

"But they're not the only threat," Woodbury went on. "I've had reports about gangs of white renegades who prey on the wagon trains bound for Oregon. I can't help but believe that such outlaws would attack a group of travelers headed for California, as well."

"Yeah, thieves'll go after any target they think is temptin' enough."

"And the elements themselves can be quite treacherous," the lieutenant continued. "I've seen terrible storms come boiling up almost out of nowhere at this time of year. Fierce winds, blinding rain, hail the size of a man's fist, vicious lightning, even cyclones . . . all of those things are possible out on the plains. You can't even rule out a late blizzard."

Flint said, "You make it sound like we ought to just squat here from now on if we want to stay safe, Lieutenant."

"Not at all. I just want to make sure you gentlemen know what you're getting into."

"I know what I want to get into," Flint said. "Those gold fields out in California! And any Indian or outlaw or cyclone that gets in my way will be sorry!"

By mid-morning, the group of gold-seekers was ready to depart. Quite a few of the soldiers gathered outside the fort to watch the wagons roll away. Some waved their hats and shouted encouragement.

Quite a few looked like they wished *they* were on their way to the rumored Promised Land, too.

Since Olmsted had been selected as the leader, Flint had suggested that his wagon go first. Olmsted insisted that wasn't necessary, but several other men spoke up in support of the idea, and the old-timer finally agreed to go along with it. So his wagon rocked along in the lead, with more than a dozen other vehicles lined up behind it.

Matthew Stovall's wagon was in the very back of the group, Cord noted, as if the former officer was pouting about not being put in charge and wanted to be as far away from Olmsted as possible.

That was all right. Stovall could be as sullen as he wanted to, as long as he didn't try to cause trouble.

Cord and Verne rode at a deliberate pace

about halfway along the line of wagons. Flint and Steve rode with them at first, but they hadn't been underway for long when Flint said, "Come on, Steve. Let's ride up front and offer Colonel Olmsted our services as scouts."

Verne said, "What do you know about scoutin' for a wagon train, boy?"

"I've gone hunting, haven't I? It's just a matter of keeping your eyes open."

"Cord's done more huntin' and is better at it than you are. I ain't meanin' to insult you, son, but that's the truth."

Flint glared for a second, then said, "How about it, Cord? Want to come along and be a scout, too?"

"No, I'm perfectly fine riding right here with Pa," Cord said. "If Mr. Olmsted needs me to help out along the way, I'll be happy to do what I can, but I don't reckon I'll volunteer."

Flint grunted, seeming surprised. "I figured that's exactly what you'd do." He nudged his mount ahead and added over his shoulder, "Come on, Steve."

Steve followed closely behind him, as usual.

Verne watched them go and mused, "You know, Cord, it seems to me that Flint's right. You're the one who usually steps up to help folks out."

"I'll help out anybody who needs it and deserves it, Pa. But I think Flint's just hoping to run into trouble somewhere along the way, so he can get a little excitement. This trip hasn't been all he was hoping it would be, so far."

"The trip ain't the reason for what we're doin'. The gold is the reason."

Cord nodded. "That's true. But Flint wouldn't mind some action along the way."

Verne sighed and said, "It does seem like the boy's always been naturally attracted to trouble."

If Cord was right about his brother wanting some action, Flint was disappointed that day, and for several days afterward. The wagons rolled peacefully across the prairie under wide blue skies decorated by towering white clouds. The nights were still on the chilly side, but other than that, the weather was perfect, with just enough of a hint of coolness in the air that the temperature during the day was comfortable.

The gold-seekers didn't see another human being during that time. They spotted plenty of rabbits, as well as fat, ungainly, and apparently flightless birds that Cord supposed were prairie chickens. It was too early in the season for snakes to be crawl-ing.

A couple of times, they saw herds of antelope grazing in the distance. The wagons didn't come close enough to spook the animals.

"I wonder if you could sneak up on those antelope and bag a couple," Flint speculated one evening as they sat around the campfire. "Some fresh meat would be good."

"I might give it a try," Cord said. "I'll bet they spook pretty easy, though."

The next day, they saw something more impressive than antelope.

Flint and Steve were somewhere out in front of the group, searching for any signs of trouble, when Cord spotted a rider returning in a hurry.

The man's size made his identity plain as day. "Here comes Steve, Pa," Cord said to Verne, "and he's riding like something might be wrong."

"Well, you'd better go see what it is," Verne told him. "Your brothers might need help."

Cord nodded and heeled his horse to a faster pace. He arrived at Abraham Olm-sted's wagon at the same time Steve did.

"What's wrong, young fella?" Olmsted called as Steve reined in. The old-timer hauled back on his team's reins, bringing the wagon to a halt. Behind them, the other wagons had no choice but to stop, too.

"Flint and me found somethin'," Steve replied. He sounded excited, Cord thought, but not scared, so maybe it wasn't anything too bad.

Steve half-turned in the saddle to wave an arm back in the direction he'd come from and went on, "There's a whole herd of buffalo up yonder about a mile!"

"Buffalo!"

"That's what Flint says they are. I never seen nothin' like 'em before. Big, shaggy critters. There must be thousands of 'em. Maybe even millions!"

Kat was riding on the driver's seat next to her father. She asked, "Can we go see them, Pa? I've read about buffalo in books, but I've never seen any!"

"Neither have I," Glory added as she poked her head through the opening in the canvas cover behind them.

"Hold on now," Olmsted said. "We don't want to go chargin' up on a herd of buffalo. I've heard they're critters that are easy to spook, and if ever they start a stampede, you don't want to be nowhere around it." He looked over and saw Cord sitting there in his saddle. "Cord, you go and take a look, too, will you, then come back and tell me what you see."

Cord nodded. "I reckon I can do that."

"And tell that brother o' yours not to start shootin'! A buffalo or two would give us plenty of fresh meat for a spell, but we got to do it the right way; otherwise, we may be askin' for trouble."

Trouble was something that Flint had never been shy about asking for, so Cord knew what Olmsted meant. He nodded and heeled his horse into motion again, saying, "Come on, Steve, show me these buffalo."

CHAPTER 14

The landscape might look as flat as a tabletop from a distance, but a man riding across it was aware of all the long, gentle swells and dips. Cord knew that was why he and Steve couldn't see the buffalo herd until they were about a quarter of a mile from it.

Cord spotted Flint sitting horseback atop a small rise first. He and Steve rode up alongside their brother and reined in.

Flint sat with his hands resting on the saddle pommel and leaned forward as he squinted into the distance. He spared Cord barely a glance, as if he couldn't stand to tear his gaze away from the huge, dark mass spread out on the prairie in front of them.

"You ever see anything like that before in all your borned days, Cord?" Flint asked with awe in his voice.

"No, I sure haven't," Cord admitted. He felt more than a little awe himself as he stared at the buffalo herd.

The herd was like a dark brown sea flowing slowly across the plains. The massive creatures eased along, stopping every few feet to crop at another tuft of grass. Their coats were thick and shaggy. Some had short but wicked-looking horns curving up from their massive heads.

Cord couldn't even venture a guess as to how many of them were in the herd. As Steve had said, thousands, certainly. Probably not millions. They stretched as far as the eye could see to the north and south, but some small ridges were visible in the west, beyond the herd.

Those ridges and this rise where Cord, Flint, and Steve sat watching formed a broad, shallow valley, a natural route for the buffalo to follow as they traveled either north or south.

Flint leaned forward, grasped his rifle, and pulled it from the leather scabbard in which it rode.

"Those dumb brutes aren't paying the least bit of attention to us," he said. "I'll bet I can get within a hundred yards of the ones at the outside edge of the herd. That's plenty close enough to drop a nice fat one." He laughed. "We'll be having buffalo steaks tonight, boys!"

"Mr. Olmsted said not to start shooting,"

151

Cord told his brother. "He doesn't want us to cause a stampede."

"A stampede? They don't look like they'd know it even if we shot down a dozen of them. And if they did stampede, they'd just keep going south, the way they're already going. The wagons won't be in any danger."

"You can't be sure about that. Are you willing to risk Kat's life on you being right, Flint?"

"A man's got to take some risks, or he's not a man," Flint snapped.

"Might be smarter to wait until the herd passes and then take a straggler or two," Cord suggested.

"Wait?" Flint swept his hand from side to side to indicate the size of the herd. "How long should we wait, Cord? All day? Because it may take that long for this bunch to pass."

"We're going to have to wait anyway," Cord pointed out. "That's the direction we're going, and we can't get through until the buffalo are gone."

Flint scowled. He couldn't refute Cord's logic.

"We could still shoot a couple of them and get started dressing them out," he said instead.

"All I know is that Mr. Olmsted said not to shoot any of them until I'd ridden back and reported the situation to him."

"Well, then, go ahead," Flint said, clearly exasperated by Cord's caution. "The sooner you do that, the sooner you'll get back and we can get some fresh meat for the group."

Cord nodded. "All right. You coming, Steve?"

"Naw, I'll stay here with Flint," Steve replied. "I want to watch those critters some more. I never saw anything like 'em back in Arkansas."

Flint grinned. "Before we're done, boy, you'll see plenty of things you never saw the like of back in Arkansas."

Cord turned his horse to ride back to the wagons. He hadn't gone very far, a couple of hundred yards, maybe, when he heard the boom of a rifle shot.

"Damn it, Flint," he said. "You just couldn't wait, could you?"

He jerked his mount to a halt and twisted in the saddle to look back. He didn't see Flint or Steve on top of the rise where they had been sitting when he rode off.

Pulling his horse around, he booted the animal into a run. When he topped the rise, he looked around, trying to locate his brothers against the vast swath of brown and tan formed by the buffalo herd.

He spotted Flint to the left, riding toward

a dark heap on the ground that looked like a shaggy, fur-covered boulder. That had to be the buffalo he'd shot.

Steve was off to the right, also closing in on the edge of the herd and holding his rifle. He was after a shot of his own.

"Steve!" Cord shouted toward him. "Steve, come back! Stay away from those buffalo!"

Steve either didn't hear him or ignored him.

Biting back another curse, Cord swung toward Flint again. Flint had reached the fallen buffalo, which lay by itself because the other beasts that came along veered away from it, perhaps spooked by the smell of blood.

The other buffalo didn't appear to be upset, though. They moved at the same plodding pace and didn't seem to be on the verge of stampeding.

Flint put his rifle back in its scabbard and swung down from the saddle. Cord saw sunlight glint on something in his brother's hand. Flint had his knife out and was going to start gutting and skinning the buffalo right there where it had fallen.

There was nothing else he could do. The buffalo was too big to move. They would have to dress it where it was and haul the meat back to the wagons.

Cord hated to admit it, but it looked like Flint had been right. They would get some good meals out of that buffalo . . .

Another shot roared. That would be Steve trying to bring down one of the beasts.

But this time, instead of the rifle's echoes rolling harmlessly over the prairie and then dying away, they were swallowed by a rumbling noise that welled up like thunder.

Cord's head jerked toward the racket. Some of the buffalo had started running. The first shot hadn't set them off, but evidently, the second one had.

Right now, the stampede was confined to only a tiny sliver of the herd. But the herd was so large, that tiny sliver still had at least two hundred buffalo in it.

And they were all headed straight toward Flint, Cord realized, as a feeling of cold horror washed over him.

"Flint!" Cord bellowed at his brother. "Flint, get out of there!"

Flint straightened from where he'd been sawing at the fallen buffalo's hide with his knife. He looked toward the stampede. The creatures had such a lumbering gait that it didn't seem like they were moving very fast, but they were swallowing up the ground as they charged.

They wouldn't be turned aside by the smell of blood, either. Cord knew that in his bones, and Flint seemed to, as well, because he made a desperate lunge for his horse's dangling reins.

The horse, already skittish from the blood and the noise, panicked and jerked out of reach of Flint's grasping hand. Whirling around, the horse raced toward the rise where Cord sat his mount.

Flint ran a couple of steps after the animal and then stopped, realizing the chase was futile.

So was any hope of him being able to dash out of the way of the stampede on foot.

Cord didn't stop to think. He kicked his horse into a run and leaned forward in the saddle.

"Flint!" he yelled as he waved an arm at his brother. "Flint, come on! Toward me!"

Flint hesitated, but only for a second. Any shred of a chance was better than none. He put his head down and ran straight toward Cord, his arms pumping and his legs flashing.

Like all kids, the Bennett brothers had run races against each other when they were young. Steve won most of the time, because he had the longest legs and could cover the most ground with each stride. Cord was the second fastest. Flint had never really had much speed.

But he still won some races, because he figured out ways to trip his brothers or gain some other advantage, and he just laughed at their cries of "No fair!"

That wasn't going to work with a couple of hundred stampeding buffalo.

Still, Flint ran for his life.

Cord urged his horse on, closing the gap between them and his brother. At the same time, the buffalo were closing the gap, too. Cord fought down the impulse to look toward the charging beasts. He didn't want to know how close they were.

If he did, the instinct for self-preservation might make him turn back, no matter how much he tried to overcome it.

He wasn't going to abandon Flint. Blood didn't abandon blood.

The sound was so loud now that it washed over Cord like an ocean. Or maybe that was the blood pounding in his veins. Either way, he ignored that, too, and thrust out his right hand as he hauled back on the reins with the left.

Flint made one last lunge and reached up. His hand slapped Cord's wrist and closed around it as Cord caught hold of his wrist.

Momentum made Flint's feet come off the

ground as Cord swung him up. Flint kicked out, throwing a leg over the back of Cord's horse as he landed behind the saddle.

"Hold on!" Cord shouted. He didn't know if Flint could hear him over the unholy racket, but Flint's arms locked around his waist. The horse reared a little as Cord yanked it around. It had to be terrified of the onrushing buffalo.

As Cord turned, he couldn't help but see the stampede practically on top of them.

Fear gave the horse extra speed, even carrying double. It spurted forward like a seed out of a watermelon. With both Bennetts hanging on for dear life, the horse raced at an angle to the stampede, getting every second and every foot out of its effort. A cloud of dust raised by the churning hooves of the herd billowed around them, blinding them . . .

Then they burst out of the dust, and the buffalo thundered on behind them. Cord looked around wildly to see if they were actually in the clear.

They had escaped the stampede with only a few feet to spare. The closest buffalo's shoulder must have brushed against the horse's tail as it streamed out behind.

Cord kept moving until they were well out of the stampede's path and then slowed gradually to a stop. Still breathing hard from the sheer terror of that close shave, he said to Flint, "Are you . . . are you all right back there?"

"Yeah, I . . . I think so." Flint let go of Cord's waist and slid off the horse's back. He stumbled when his feet hit the ground and reeled a couple of steps before his legs gave out from under him.

Flint sat down hard and stayed there, sitting on the ground and breathing hard like his brother. His eyes were huge. He sounded amazed as he went on, "I . . . I'm alive. I'm still alive."

Cord dismounted. He was pretty shaky, too, so he hung on to the saddle with one hand while he extended the other to Flint.

"That was a mighty close call," he said. "As close as I ever want to have."

Flint clasped his wrist again. Cord pulled him to his feet. Both brothers turned to look at the buffalo.

Not surprisingly, the stampede had spread to the rest of the herd. All the shaggy beasts they could see were running now. Dust was thick in the air, but through gaps in those churning clouds, they saw the buffalo, a fast-moving river of hair and flesh, bone and sinew, instead of the gently flowing sea they had resembled earlier.

And there was still no end to them.

Maybe there really were millions of the creatures, Cord thought.

"Where's Steve?" Flint asked abruptly. He caught hold of Cord's arm. "Where's Steve? Did he get caught in it?"

Cord pointed and said, "No, here he comes now."

Steve was riding hard toward them, using the reins to whip the horse. He pounded up to them, and his mount skidded to a stop.

"Flint! Cord! Are you all right?"

"We're in one piece," Cord said. "Just a mite shaken up."

"We're in one piece, thanks to you," Flint said. "I wouldn't have had a chance if not for what you did. You saved my life, Cord."

"You'd have done the same for me," Cord said.

But even as the words came out of his mouth, he wasn't sure if what he said was true. Not one hundred percent.

Steve dismounted, threw his arms around Flint in a bear hug, and pounded him on the back.

"I thought you was a goner," he said. "When I shot that buffalo and all them others took off runnin' straight at you, I didn't figure you had a chance in hell of gettin' outta the way."

"Wait a minute," Flint said as he pulled loose from Steve's hug and stepped back. "You started that stampede?"

Steve frowned in confusion. "Well, it started when I shot that buffalo, like I said, but that's what I was supposed to do, wasn't it? You said we'd shoot a couple of them critters, and the whole bunch would have plenty to eat —"

Cord saw Flint's right hand clench into a fist and knew Flint was about to punch Steve, even though the middle brother didn't deserve it. He stepped forward quickly and rested a hand on Flint's shoulder, feeling the tension in the muscles there.

"Steve didn't mean to cause trouble," he said. "It was an accident, pure and simple."

Punching Steve would be like kicking a dog. He wouldn't understand what was going on. He'd just be hurt for no good reason.

Slowly, the stiffness in Flint eased. Steve started to say something else, but Cord lifted a hand and motioned for him to be quiet for the moment.

All three of them were all right. Flint's horse had even escaped the stampede. Better to just let it go.

"I'm all right," Flint said curtly. Cord took his hand off his brother's shoulder. "What

161

happened to that buffalo I shot?"

"It was right in the path of the stampede like you were," Cord said. "After all that trampling, I don't reckon there'll be much of it left."

"Just like there wouldn't have been much of me left," Flint muttered. "Not enough to bury, even. I owe you, kid."

"You don't owe me a thing."

Steve said, "The one I shot is all right. Well, other than bein' dead. Since the others started runnin' from that spot, I don't think any of them trampled over it."

"Let's go and see. Cord, can you catch my horse?"

"I'll be right back with it," Cord said.

He had already spotted Flint's horse grazing about a hundred yards away. He mounted up and rode over to the animal. The horse was still a little spooked but allowed him to lean over and catch hold of the reins.

Cord had just done that when he saw the Olmsted wagon rolling toward him with the rest of the wagons in the group strung out behind it.

Cord waved to let them know that everything was all right, then rode back to Flint leading the other horse.

"Here comes the rest of the bunch," he

said as he handed Flint the reins.

"That old pelican will probably have some things to say," Flint replied.

"What in blue blazes happened?" Olmsted demanded as he brought the wagon to a halt a moment later. Kat was still beside him, with Glory looking eagerly over his shoulder from the wagon bed. "I thought for a minute it sounded like a dadgum earthquake, but I see now it was a buffalo stampede."

"They got a mite worked up," Flint acknowledged, "but we have fresh meat from the one Steve shot."

He didn't mention the one he had downed, only to lose to the thundering, slashing hooves of the herd.

Omsted glared at Cord. "I thought I told you to tell your brothers not to do any shootin'."

"Don't blame Cord," Steve spoke up. "I'm the one who fired my rifle. The whole thing's my fault."

"You fellas have got to learn how to take orders if you want to make it to California alive."

Kat said, "Stop fussing at the boys, Pa. You're no expert on buffalo. You're like the rest of us. You never even saw one until just now."

Olmsted cleared his throat and admitted, "I reckon you're right about that. I've heard old frontier hands talkin' about them, though, and from the looks of what I'm seein', ever'thing they said was right."

"Still, fresh meat will be good," Glory put in.

"That's true. You say you got one of the varmints, Steve?"

A proud grin spread across Steve's face at Olmsted's question. "I sure did!" he said. He pointed. "It's back yonder a ways."

"Well, let's go dress it out and see how much meat we can get from it."

The stampede lasted for another hour before the last of the herd finally vanished to the south, leaving the stink of dust and dung in the air and a churned-up strip of ground nearly half a mile wide.

Cord and Steve were still working on butchering the dead buffalo. When they were finished, and the cuts of meat had been wrapped in canvas and loaded into several of the wagons, the group started across that stretch of torn-up ground.

That made for a rough ride, but there was no way around it.

Besides, it lay between these pilgrims and the golden dreams waiting for them in California, so there was no chance they would allow such an obstacle to stop them.

The wagons and riders reached the ridges on the other side of the valley and moved into them, leaving behind the stampede's path.

None of the gold-seekers saw the four mounted figures that appeared on the rise where the Bennett brothers had first viewed the buffalo. These men rode bareback on unshod ponies, and feathers decorated their long, black hair. Impassive, copper-hued faces watched the travelers disappear into the west.

CHAPTER 15

The buffalo steaks roasted over campfires were tough and had a strong, slightly gamy flavor, but the meat was fresh, and everyone in the group enjoyed it that night.

The rest of the meat was salted to preserve it as long as possible. If they hadn't been on the move, Cord would have smoked and dried some of it into jerky.

As it was, some were bound to go to waste, but in all likelihood, they would encounter more buffalo farther on. The plains were supposed to be teeming with the creatures.

And next time, Cord thought as he chewed on a bite of meat, they would have a much better idea of how to go about hunting the shaggy brutes.

No stampedes next time, Cord vowed . . . even if he had to hogtie his brothers.

That would make for an interesting tussle, he thought with a slight smile.

Before leaving Arkansas, Cord had studied maps in the newspapers and the illustrated weeklies, which had many articles about what they were now calling the Gold Rush.

Like the Oregon Trail, the route to California followed the North Platte River. The Oregon and California Trails were the same until they extended beyond South Pass, in the Rocky Mountains.

A short distance west of that landmark, they split, the California Trail leading on across the Sierra Nevadas and ultimately to Sacramento and San Francisco.

Cord knew that some of the gold-seekers — the Forty-Niners, as Steve had dubbed them — had traveled by ship, leaving the East Coast and sailing past South America to circle Cape Horn and head north again, ultimately arriving in San Francisco.

Starting out from the middle of the country, as he and his father and brothers had done, it would have made no sense to go that way. Not to mention, they couldn't have afforded the passage. It would have taken all their money just to reach some port on the eastern seaboard.

Besides, being a confirmed landlubber, Cord couldn't imagine making such a long journey by sea. He was sure he would have been hanging over the railing and heaving up his guts the whole way.

But at least folks traveling by ship didn't have to worry about buffalo stampedes . . .

For two more days, the miles slowly unraveled behind the wagons. On the afternoon of that second day, Cord was riding beside the Olmsted wagon when Glory, who was perched on the driver's seat beside her father at the moment, said, "Pa, is it all right if I go for a ride with Cord?"

"A ride?" Abraham Olmsted repeated. "You ain't got no horse. What're you gonna ride?"

"Cord's horse is big and strong. It can carry double, can't it, Cord?"

"Well, it carried me and Flint the other day, when we were trying to get out of the way of that buffalo stampede," Cord admitted. "We didn't really have very far to go, though, or any real choice in the matter."

"But you wouldn't have to go fast today. Just a nice, easy ride. And I weigh a lot less than your brother."

Cord knew that was true. It was unusual for Glory to be this bold, but he could tell by looking at her that she had been working up her courage to make the suggestion.

The idea of holding her on horseback in front of him was very appealing, too. He couldn't deny that.

Olmsted frowned, cleared his throat, and said, "I ain't sure that's a good idea. Seems a mite . . . improper."

"Why? I thought maybe we could ride a little ahead of the wagons, but we'd still be in plain sight. Nothing improper would happen, Pa. I can promise you that."

"Well . . . I reckon if Cord don't mind you bein' such a little pest . . ."

"Oh!" Glory exclaimed in mock outrage.

Cord grinned and extended a hand to her as he brought his horse closer to the wagon seat.

"Come on. Just be careful stepping over here."

"Of course." Glory grasped his hand, put one foot at the edge of the floorboard, and stepped out with the other. Cord had his other arm ready to wrap around her and guide her onto the horse's back in front of him.

She settled down astride, right in front of the saddle. She didn't have a riding skirt, which meant her dress rode up quite a bit, exposing most of her calves in thick woolen stockings above the high-laced shoes.

"Plumb scandalous," Olmsted muttered under his breath as he shook his head.

Glory just laughed and didn't seem to mind.

"This feels wonderful," she said over her shoulder to Cord. "I haven't been on a horse in so long. I loved to ride when I was a little girl. We always had horses around our farm, since Pa was a horse trader, too." She laughed. "Let's go faster."

Cord nudged the horse's flanks with his bootheels. It picked up the pace, and they drew a little ahead of the wagon.

Glory's bright red hair was loose. It blew back and tickled Cord's face, as well as filling his senses with its clean, intriguing smell.

"Kat's going to be jealous," Glory went on. "You watch. She'll demand that Flint take her for a ride."

"She and Flint get along pretty well, don't they?"

"She's fond of him." Glory turned her head to look at Cord. "Is there anything wrong with that?"

"Not as far as I'm concerned," Cord said, even though Flint had a reputation as quite a ladies' man back home. He didn't seem overly concerned about staying true to any one girl for very long, either.

And there had been those ugly rumors about girls who had turned up in the family way and claimed that Flint had something to do with it, claims that Flint vehemently denied. Cord wanted to give his brother the benefit of the doubt, but sometimes that wasn't easy.

However, none of that was anything he was going to say to Glory Olmsted. Kat was a full-grown woman, and judging by her attitude, had at least a little experience with the ways of the world. More so than Glory, anyway. She would have to look out for herself where Flint Bennett was concerned.

Flint and Steve were somewhere out in front, scouting the trail, but weren't anywhere in sight. It wasn't Cord's intention to get too far ahead of the wagons, but that was what happened, anyway. The wagons gradually fell farther and farther behind as Cord's horse loped easily over the plains.

With each stride the horse took, Glory rocked forward and back, which meant she was pressed against Cord's chest a lot of the time. He enjoyed having his arm around her trim waist.

She laughed when they scared up a small flock of prairie chickens. The ungainly birds burst out of a brush thicket, flapping their wings as they scurried away, as if they were trying to fly. Other than a few short-lived hops, though, they couldn't make it into the air.

"I ought to shoot a few of them," Cord

said. "I'll bet they'd roast up pretty good."

"Oh, no! That wouldn't be fair. Look at them, Cord. They wouldn't even have a chance of getting away."

"That's what you want when you're hunting for meat."

"Well, we're not out of buffalo steaks yet, so just leave those funny little birds alone."

Cord chuckled. "All right, Glory. Whatever you say."

He glanced over his shoulder, thinking that he ought to see how far ahead they had gotten, and was surprised to realize that the wagons were no longer in sight. He and Glory had gone over a few small rises, but he wouldn't have guessed that the terrain was irregular enough to hide the rest of the group from view.

While he was doing that and figuring that they'd better turn back, Glory suddenly said, "Cord."

Her tone of voice and the way she stiffened inside the circle of his arm told him something was wrong. He looked and saw several riders sitting on ponies at the top of a swell of ground a hundred yards ahead of them.

"Are those Indians?" Glory asked as Cord reined his mount to a stop.

"I think they are."

He didn't know what else they could be.

At this distance, he couldn't make out details, but he could tell that a couple of the men were bare-chested while the other two wore buckskin shirts. Feathers stuck up from their hair. They carried long poles. Lances, Cord thought, even though he couldn't see the sharp flint tips from where he was.

"Are . . . are they hostile?" Glory's voice quivered a little with fear.

"I don't know. Maybe not —"

Cord's answer was abruptly cut short when the four warriors leaned forward, banged their heels against their ponies' flanks, and uttered shrill, yipping war cries as they charged toward Cord and Glory.

Cord couldn't hold back the curse that escaped from his lips as he hauled hard on the reins and pulled the horse around. He had a lot more important things to worry about right now than whether Glory would think he was crude and vulgar.

"Hang on!" he told her as he tightened his grip around her waist.

"What are we going to do?" she cried.

"Ride as hard as we can and get away from those Indians!"

It couldn't be too far back to the wagons, he thought. He and Glory hadn't gotten ahead by *that* much. And when the Indians

173

saw the rest of the party and realized they were greatly outnumbered, they would call off the attack and turn around.

The problem with that idea, Cord realized as he glanced over his shoulder at their pursuers, was that the Indians *weren't* outnumbered.

At least twenty more riders had appeared behind the four that were giving chase to Cord and Glory.

Those riders weren't coming as fast as the four in the lead, but they weren't wasting any time, either. Were they planning to attack the group of Forty-Niners?

The Indians could have been watching them for days, Cord thought bitterly. Just biding their time until they were ready to ambush the white men.

And today, that time had come.

But the others would have more of a chance with some warning, so Cord transferred the reins to his left hand while keeping that arm clamped around Glory, then used his right hand to pull the Colt Dragoon from the holster on his hip.

"Get ready for some loud noises!" he told her.

"What are you —" she began, but before she could finish the question, he thrust the revolver behind him, aimed in the general direction of the pursuers, cocked the revolver's hammer, and squeezed the trigger.

Even with the swift rataplan of hoofbeats from the horse beneath them, the Colt's roar was thunderous. As quickly as he could ear back the hammer and pull the trigger, Cord fired two more shots.

He had thought about firing three shots into the air, since that was a universal signal for trouble, but then he'd decided to throw the lead toward the Indians instead.

He didn't expect to hit any of them. It would be just blind luck if he did. But at least there was a chance of the shots doing some good that way, and Abraham Olmsted and the other men would still be able to hear them and realize that trouble was headed toward them.

Cord had felt Glory flinch with each blast of the Dragoon.

"It's all right," he told her as he leaned close to her ear. "I was just trying to discourage them!"

"Did it work?" she asked.

Cord looked back and made a face. All four warriors were still mounted and closing in, their fleet ponies gaining steadily on his heavily burdened horse.

"I'm afraid not!"

"They're going to kill us, aren't they?"

"I won't let that happen! I give you my word!"

Cord knew that was a promise he might not be able to honor. But only death would prevent him from keeping his word.

With a valiant effort, the horse surged up another rise and topped it. Just like that, Cord saw the wagons. He and Glory were practically among them.

The vehicles had been pulled into a rough circle. Olmsted's command experience must have come to the forefront when he heard the warning shots. He had taken quick action, and obviously, the other men had obeyed his orders.

Cord aimed the horse for a gap between wagons and darted through it. He hauled back on the reins and brought the lathered mount to a skidding, stumbling halt. In the blink of an eye, he was out of the saddle and on the ground, reaching up for Glory.

He plucked her off the horse's back and held her for a second, then looked around.

"There are your father and Kat," he told her, pointing to a nearby wagon. "Get over there with them!"

"What are you going to do?" she asked as she clutched at his left arm with both hands.

"I'm coming with you," he said. He holstered the Dragoon, then reached for his rifle and pulled it out of the saddle scabbard.

Holding one of Glory's arms, Cord hustled her over to her father's wagon. Abraham Olmsted waited at the front of the vehicle with a rifle in his hands. Kat stood next to him, sheltered by the wagon bed and the canvas cover. She had a rifle, too, ready to hand to him.

"Gloriana!" Olmsted exclaimed as Cord and Glory ran up. "Are you all right?"

"I'm fine, Pa," she said. "Cord got us away from those Indians."

Olmsted looked at Cord. "Injuns, is it?"

"Four of them coming pretty quickly behind us," Cord said, "and about twenty more behind them."

"We got our hands full, then." A grim smile appeared on the old-timer's bearded, weathered face. "But they'll be in for a surprise when they come a-boilin' over that little hill in a second. I told the boys to cut loose as soon as whoever was chasin' you two came in sight."

At that moment, a flurry of gunfire erupted, but not from the side of the circle where Cord and the Olmsteds waited. It came from behind them, and as Cord swung around, his heart slugged harder in his chest at what he saw through the gaps between the wagons back there.

More than a dozen mounted warriors were closing in, firing arrows and throwing lances as they came. They had almost reached the wagons. The Forty-Niners were caught between two forces.

"Looks like the surprise is on us," Cord said.

CHAPTER 16

There was no time to waste feeling sorry for themselves. Olmsted yelled, "Here they come this way!" and threw his rifle to his shoulder. The weapon boomed.

Cord moved to Olmsted's side in time to see one of the four warriors who had just topped the rise throw his arms to the sides and topple backward off his pony.

The man next to him screeched angrily and hurled his lance. The flinthead thudded into the far side of the driver's box and embedded there. The shaft quivered from the force of the impact.

Cord cocked his rifle, drew a bead on the Indian, and pulled the trigger. The man jerked back as the rifle ball slammed into him, but he managed to stay mounted and veer his pony away.

"Here, Pa," Kat said as she handed Olmsted the loaded rifle. She sounded cool and calm, but her eyes were wide.

Cord pushed his rifle into Glory's hands. "You know how to load this?"

She jerked her head in a nod.

He drew his Colt again and turned to let her get on with reloading. Two rounds still remained in the revolver, and he intended to put them to good use.

Another loaded cylinder was in his saddlebags, but his horse was somewhere in the confusion inside the circle of wagons, and he didn't have time to find it. Instead he cocked, aimed, and fired at one of the remaining two Indians who had chased him and Glory back here.

The warrior's arm was drawn back to throw his lance, but Cord's shot blasted first. Blood and bone exploded in a pink mist from the Indian's arm as the .44 caliber ball smashed through his elbow and nearly blew it clean off. Howling in agony, the man clutched his ruined arm and rode off.

Olmsted fired again, then glanced over at Cord and asked, "How you holdin' up, son?"

Cord just nodded. This was the first time he had ever shot at another human being. Maybe later, he would think about how he had killed men today, and it would bother him.

But for now, he didn't have time to worry about that. The air was full of gun-thunder and rolling clouds of powdersmoke that stung the eyes and nose and left a man half-blind. Chaos surrounded him. He clutched the Dragoon's grips and looked for another target.

A buckskin-clad warrior suddenly appeared on the other side of the wagon. He leaped off his pony, planted a foot on the floorboard of the driver's box, and dived at Cord, ramming a shoulder into his chest.

The collision drove him backward off his feet. He was vaguely aware of someone screaming close by and thought it might be Glory, but he couldn't be sure. The Indian perched on top of him, cruelly digging a knee into his belly and pinning him to the ground.

The man's face, streaked with war paint, contorted in rage and hate as he clamped his left hand around Cord's throat. With his right hand, he raised a tomahawk and poised it over his head, ready to bring it sweeping down in a blow that would smash Cord's skull.

Instead, the Indian jolted forward as a rifle butt slammed into the back of his head. He lost his grip on Cord's throat. Cord jammed the Colt's muzzle under the man's chin and pulled the trigger. His face turned into a gruesome red smear as the bullet crashed upward through his head.

Cord shoved the dead warrior off him and looked up to see Glory standing there holding his rifle. The butt plate had a little blood on it from where she had hit the Indian. Her face was pale, and she looked a bit stunned, like she might be on the verge of fainting.

But then she drew in a deep breath, thrust the rifle toward him, and said, "Here. It's reloaded."

Cord scrambled up, pouched the empty iron he still held, and said, "Thanks," as he took the rifle from her.

He meant that gratitude for more than her reloading the rifle, but he didn't have time to explain that. Anyway, he had a feeling she understood.

By now the Indians who had been following the ones giving chase had arrived. Instead of charging the wagons, though, they sat off a short distance and sent arrows whistling through the air from their bows.

The men using the wagons for cover kept up a steady return fire with their rifles and pistols. Several of the Indians fell, and Cord began to hope they would give up the attack.

Then he saw a commotion atop the rise. Two new figures on horseback appeared as Flint and Steve attacked the Indians from behind.

Flint was right there among them, twisting in the saddle as he fired right and left at almost point-blank range. A warrior fell every time he pulled the trigger.

A few yards away, Steve caught hold of a lance as an Indian thrust it at him. He ripped it out of the man's hands and slammed it through his body with such force that the flinthead, now dripping blood, stood out a full foot behind the man's back.

That was enough. Yipping furiously, the surviving Indians wheeled their ponies and fled.

Flint and Steve let them go.

Cord swung around toward the other side of the circle and saw that the warriors had broken off their attack back there, too. At least half of their number were sprawled limp and lifeless on the ground. The others were racing away.

The Indian force has been larger, but their arrows, lances, and tomahawks hadn't been able to stand up against the rifles and pistols of the Forty-Niners.

"Anybody hurt?" Olmsted shouted as he

walked around the wagons. "Anybody killed?"

As it turned out, a couple of men had suffered arrow wounds, but almost miraculously, no one in their party had been killed.

Such luck on the entire journey would be too much to hope for, Cord thought . . . but even so, it never hurt to hope.

By the time Flint and Steve rode in, Cord had found his horse, retrieved the loaded cylinder from the saddlebags, and replaced the empty one in his Colt. As his brothers dismounted, he grinned at them and said, "I sure was glad to see you boys show up when you did."

"Are you all right, kid?" Flint asked.

"Yeah. Got banged up a little tussling with one of those Indians, but I'm fine."

Steve said, "You mean you took him on hand to hand?"

"He didn't give me much choice in the matter. But Glory pitched in and gave me a hand, so I was able to stop him before he bashed my brains out."

Flint grinned. "So a girl had to save your life."

"Believe you me, right then I'd have taken all the help I could get from anybody."

Flint looked around and said, "Where's Pa?"

That reminded Cord that he hadn't seen Verne since he and Glory rode in. "I don't know. Let's see if we can find him."

He should have checked on his pa already, he scolded himself. But this was the first aftermath of an Indian battle he had experienced, so he couldn't blame himself too much for not thinking of it until now.

They located Verne Bennett on the other side of the circle, evidently unharmed by the looks of him. And excited, too, judging by the way he was waving his hands around and talking animatedly to Abraham Olmsted.

"— saw such a fight in my life," Verne was saying as his three sons walked up. "Screamin' Injuns all over the place and guns goin' off and smoke thick in the air . . . I never been in a war like you, Abe. Are battles always like this?"

"No, some of 'em you don't survive," the other old-timer said dourly. Olmsted shrugged. "But they're all loud and confusin' and make your insides feel like you got to make a dash for the outhouse. To make it through, you've got to put all that aside and just think about the job that's in front of you, right that second. No point in worryin' about anything past that."

185

"Because you might not make it past that."

Olmsted nodded. "Yep. But your odds are better if you keep a clear head."

"Your daughters certainly kept clear heads," Cord told him. "Both of them. Glory saved my life."

"I ain't surprised. Taught 'em both to stay calm when trouble comes up. Of course, they never saw trouble like this before today."

One of the men came up and asked, "Colonel, do you think those Indians will come back?"

"I don't know," Olmsted answered. "I ain't no expert on Injuns. But it'd be a good idea for us to get movin' and put some distance between us and this place. I figure they'll come back for their dead . . . and we don't want to be here when they do."

CHAPTER 17

Everyone agreed with that sentiment, even Matthew Stovall, who didn't seem to have much to say these days. Abraham Olmsted had done a good job of leading the group so far.

They didn't waste any time getting the wagons rolling. The two wounded men weren't able to drive, so Cord and Steve volunteered to take the reins of those teams.

Cord would have preferred staying closer to Glory, but it was more important for the group to get away from here. Flint was scouting ahead, looking for a good place for them to camp that night.

If possible, it needed to be a spot that could be easily defended, since it seemed likely the Indians might try another attack.

Flint rode in late that afternoon and led the wagons to a broad, flat knoll overlooking a small creek about fifty yards from the wide, hard-packed trail left by the thousands of immigrant wagons that had rolled this way.

The remains of numerous campfires made it evident that other wagon trains had stopped here in the past. Cord could see why. It was higher ground than the surrounding terrain, although not by much; water was handy, and it had a clear field of fire around it in case of attack.

"We won't find no better campsite than this," Olmsted said. "Good job, Flint." He raised his voice to address the whole group. "We're gonna double the guard tonight, so some of you folks may wind up a mite short on sleep. Better that than to wind up short on hair, though."

They all knew what he meant. They'd heard about the horrifying practice in which Indians scalped their victims, and no one wanted to fall prey to that atrocity.

The night passed quietly, however, except for some wolves howling in the distance. Cord, who heard them while he was standing guard, wondered if they actually were wolves, or if they might be Indians using those cries to communicate.

Either way, nothing happened, and a tired but relieved group got underway again the next morning.

For two more days, the wagons rolled on

with no signs of trouble. Olmsted warned the others not to relax. It was hard to stay alert, though, as the long, wearying miles lulled the Forty-Niners into something of a stupor.

The man whose wagon Cord was driving had been gashed on the leg by an arrow during the fight. He had recovered enough after a couple of days to take over the reins again. Cord was glad to get back on horseback. He enjoyed ranging ahead of and behind the group, helping keep an eye out for potential threats.

The best part about getting back in the saddle, though, was being able to ride alongside the Olmsted wagon and enjoy Glory's company when she was taking her turn on the driver's seat next to her father.

The friendship that had grown up between them before the encounter with the Indians had been strengthened even more by that shared danger. Cord would never forget how she had saved him when that warrior was about to split his head open with a tomahawk.

She hadn't suggested that they ride together again. Maybe she thought that would be tempting fate, he mused.

Instead, one day while Cord was riding beside the wagon, Glory's adventurous nature came out again when she said, "You need to let me handle the team for a while, Pa."

"You mean you want to drive the wagon?" Olmsted said in obvious surprise.

"Well, why not? You know I can do it. Kat and I both drove wagons back on the farm, plenty of times."

"That's right," Kat said from where she was riding in the wagon bed behind the seat.

Olmsted shook his head. "Drivin' a light wagon hitched to a couple of jennies around the farm ain't the same thing. This team's harder to handle, and the wagon's a heap bigger. What if a bunch of savages jumped us again and we had to make a run for it?"

"You'd still be right here with me," Glory pointed out. "I could give the reins to you. Anyway, I'll bet I could handle something like that."

Olmsted snorted and said, "Reckon I'd just as soon not find out." But he shrugged and handed the reins to Glory. "All right, there you go, if you're bound and determined to do it. Just keep 'em movin' slow and easy. We don't want the team runnin' unless there's a good reason for it."

Kat stuck her head through the opening and said, "Pa, why don't you come back here and stretch out? Get a little extra rest. You've been pushing yourself awful hard, and you're not a young man."

"Well, thank you 'most to death for pointin' that out. I'm fine right here where I am."

"I just thought you might like a break," Kat said.

Olmsted scratched at his beard and said slowly, "These ol' bones o' mine are gettin' a mite weary . . ."

"See? I told you it was a good idea."

"All right, all right. I should'a knowed it wouldn't do no good to argue with you gals. It never has, and I reckon it never will."

Kat laughed as she and her father traded places. Olmsted climbed over the seat and disappeared into the back of the wagon. Kat sat down next to Glory with a pleased expression on her lovely face.

"Where's your brother, Cord?" she asked.

"Flint? He's up ahead somewhere with Steve."

"Why don't you go find him and tell him to come back here and ride with us?"

"Wait a minute," Glory protested. "I like having Cord here."

"I'm sure you do, after you went riding off with him that day like he was Ivanhoe or somebody."

Cord wasn't exactly sure who Ivanhoe was. A character in a book, maybe.

"I just wonder what the two of you had gotten up to before you ran into those Indians," Kat continued.

"Why, nothing except riding!" Glory responded. "Nothing improper happened, did it, Cord?"

"I gave your pa my word that it wouldn't," he said, "and I try to keep my word."

"Maybe so," Kat said, smiling, "but I'll bet if you'd gotten the chance —"

She stopped short as a gust of cool wind struck them. The air had been pretty still most of the day, so the sudden gust caught their attention.

Cord had been keeping his eye on a bank of low clouds to the northwest, thinking that they might bring some rain later that night. The weather had been very good so far on this journey, but he knew better than to expect it would stay like that the whole way.

Now it appeared that the clouds might arrive sooner than he'd thought. As the wind began to blow even harder, it seemed as if the dark gray, shelf-like formation was rushing toward them, swallowing up the sky.

"What's goin' on?" Olmsted asked as he stuck his head out through the opening flap in the canvas. "I heard this canvas pop just now."

"The wind picked up," Kat told him over her shoulder. "Nothing to worry about."

Cord wasn't so sure about that. The way the clouds were hurrying across the landscape, they would soon blot out the sun. And the air was starting to have a damp, heavy feel to it.

"I think there's a storm on the way," he said. "Maybe we'd better stop."

"My bones feel the same way," Olmsted agreed. "Glory, you haul in on them reins."

The horses hitched to the wagon had gotten more skittish in the past couple of minutes. Glory had to work harder to keep them under control. She glanced back at her father and said, "I don't think this is a good place, Pa. We're right out in the open."

"Blast it, folks call this place the Great American Desert," Olmsted replied. "There ain't hardly any place that *ain't* right out in the open."

Cord stood up in his stirrups, peered off to the right, and pointed in that direction at a dark line meandering across the prairie.

"I think there's a little gully over there," he said. "I'll go check. It might give us some shelter, at least."

He rode around the wagon and headed

for what he hoped was a gully. As he came closer, he saw that it was indeed a dry wash, no more than six feet deep and maybe twenty wide. The banks were gentle enough that the wagons could get down there.

The wind was behind him and getting still chillier as he hurried back to the wagons. He waved them away from the trail.

"Over there!" he called to the Olmsteds. "We can take cover in that wash!"

"Do what he says," Olmsted told Glory, who was still struggling with the reins.

Kat said, "Here, give me those!" and snatched the reins out of her sister's hands. She grabbed the whip from its holder and slashed at the rumps of the team. "Hyaaah! Get moving there! Move!"

The mules turned and lunged ahead as Kat continued tugging on the reins as she yelled at them. Glory hung on to the seat, and their father toppled over backward in the wagon bed as the vehicle lurched and picked up speed.

Cord waved for all the others to follow the Olmsted wagon. He wished Flint and Steve were here, but unless they returned pretty soon, they might be caught out in the open when the storm hit.

And it was going to hit, there was no doubt about that now. The sun was gone, vanished behind the clouds. Cord saw fingers of lightning clawing through the dark sky and heard thunder rumble.

"Tater wagon's rollin' over." That was what Cord's mother had said whenever it thundered when he was a boy. To him, that was exactly what it sounded like.

Kat reached the wash and guided the team down into it. She turned the wagon and brought it to a stop against the northern bank, which Cord thought was a good idea. That would break the force of the wind somewhat and protect them from the rain. The others followed suit.

Cord was sitting in his saddle on the southern bank, watching the wagons line up against the other bank, when his father rode up, leading the two pack mules.

"Have you seen your brothers?" the old-timer asked with a worried look on his face.

"Not since they rode off earlier today to scout ahead of us," Cord said. "I thought maybe they'd come back when they saw the weather turning bad."

"Dang it, they're gonna get caught in this, and it's gonna be a bad one. I can feel it in my bones."

"Mr. Olmsted said the same thing."

"Well, o' course he did! Abe's been around, like I have." Verne frowned. "I ain't sure it's such a good idea hunkerin' down in that wash. It's liable to flood. There's a reason some folks call bad storms gully-washers!"

Cord bit back a groan. His father was right. But staying out in the open had its dangers, too, as was proven dramatically a second later when a bolt of lightning lanced down out of the clouds and slammed into the earth with a deafening clap of thunder, no more than a mile or so away.

"We're the tallest things out here on these hosses," Verne said. "Like it or not, we'd best get down there before that lightnin' comes a-lookin' for us."

Cord agreed with that. He took the reins of one of the pack horses from his father, and they rode down into the wash with the animals.

They headed for the Olmsted wagon, but before they could get there, the rain hit.

It was like somebody dumped a giant bucket on them. The drops were huge and slashed down with such force that Cord felt almost like a fist had struck him. The rain fell so thickly that in the blink of an eye, he could no longer see the wagons that were no more than twenty feet away. His horse stopped dead under him, lowered its head, and hunched its back against the downpour.

Cord reached out blindly toward where his father had been. His fingers brushed against Verne Bennett's skinny arm. He closed his hand around it, knowing that it wouldn't be a good idea for them to get separated.

He was close enough to make out Verne as a vague shape in the rain. Leaning closer, he shouted, "We need to get under cover!"

"All right, boy!" Verne's reedy voice came back. "You lead the way!"

Clinging tightly to his father's arm and the pack mule's lead rope, Cord urged his mount forward, in what he hoped was the right direction. The horse didn't want to move, but Cord prodded it into one step and then another and another.

It seemed to take longer to cross the wash than it actually did, but finally the wagon loomed up in front of them, visible even through the pouring rain.

"We're here, Pa!" Cord shouted to his father. "Stay on your horse while I get the animals tied up!"

He dismounted, tied his reins and the pack mule's lead rope to one of the wagon wheels, and then tied his father's mount and the other pack mule. Lightning flashed almost constantly now, blinding streaks that ripped the gloom open, followed instantly by booming peals of thunder that shook the earth.

Cord helped his father down from the saddle, and then they ducked under the wagon to get some blessed relief from the rain's pounding. In the garish glare of another lightning flash, Cord saw Abraham Olmsted, Glory, and Kat huddled underneath the vehicle. The ground on which they sat had already turned to mud, but at least they were out of the rain.

Glory caught hold of Cord's sleeve. "I don't think I've ever seen a storm this bad!"

"They can be pretty rough out here on the plains, from what I've heard about them," he replied.

Olmsted said, "I'm a mite worried about a flood comin' along. The water ain't risin' yet, but it could, if this downpour keeps up long enough."

"I told the boy the same thing," Verne said. "Sometimes these toad-stranglers move on pretty quick-like. I reckon that's what we got to hope for."

Kat leaned closer to Cord and asked, "Did you see Flint anywhere out there after the storm hit?"

He shook his head. "No, he and Steve didn't make it back in time."

"Then they're out in it. They'll be struck

by lightning, or washed away."

"Flint's mighty good at looking out for himself," Cord told her. "He'll be all right, and he'll take care of Steve, too."

He hoped that was true, but right now, hoping was all he could do.

He sat with his back propped against one of the wheels. Glory sat beside him, getting as close as she could, and without thinking about it, Cord slipped his arm around her shoulders and pulled her closer. He realized that her father was right there beside them, but he didn't care and, under the circumstances, he doubted that Abraham Olmsted did.

It was almost as black as night under the wagon now. Even as miserable and uncomfortable as he was, Cord enjoyed having Glory so close to him.

Too bad that every time they got to be this close, something dangerous happened . . .

"Sounds like it's lettin' up," Verne said suddenly.

Cord lifted his head and listened. His father was right. The rain wasn't coming down as hard now. When he looked out, he could even see the bank on the other side of the wash. A few trickles of water ran here and there, but no flood. Maybe they had been lucky.

Then he heard something else, a low, rumbling roar. He had seen a train once, during a visit up into Missouri, and he realized that was what this sound reminded him of: a locomotive approaching in the distance.

Cord caught his breath as he visualized a wall of water crashing along the wash toward them. Maybe that was what he was hearing. He let go of Glory and said, "Stay here."

She clutched at his sleeve again. "Where are you going?"

"Got to take a look around." He didn't offer any other explanation. Better to be sure what they were dealing with first.

"Boy, what are you —" Verne began as Cord crawled out from under the wagon, but then Cord was out in the rain again and it was still falling hard enough to obscure his father's words. He listened intently and heard the roar again.

But as far as he could tell, it wasn't coming from either direction along the wash. It was farther to the north, he decided, although under the circumstances, it was difficult to be sure about anything. Cord walked around the wagon and climbed the bank, slipping and sliding some but eventually reaching a spot where he could thrust his head up and gaze over the plains in that direction.

What he saw turned his blood to ice in his veins.

A tall, funnel-shaped cloud that had to be at least a mile wide at its base was coming toward them, weaving a little from side to side but never deviating much from the path on which nature had placed it.

That monster cyclone was bearing down on them, and it would hit within seconds.

CHAPTER 18

Cord slid down the bank. He saw Glory crawling out from under the wagon and told her, "Get back under there! Cyclone coming!"

For a heartbeat, she didn't seem to comprehend what he'd said. She gasped as she stared up at him. The rain pelted her face and plastered her bright red hair to her head.

She hesitated only a second, though, before scrambling back under the vehicle.

Cord saw other members of the group starting to emerge from shelter, now that the rain wasn't falling as hard. He ran along the line of wagons, shouting and waving.

"Get back under cover! Cyclone coming! Cyclone!"

Matthew Stovall, as usual, had the last wagon in line. He was standing up beside it when Cord reached him.

"Bennett, what in blazes are you yelling

about? The storm's going to be over soon . . ."

Stovall's voice trailed away as the roar coming from the onrushing cyclone penetrated his dismissive attitude. His eyes widened in horror as he turned around and looked to the north.

The cyclone was close enough now that it was in plain sight, looming over them. The towering funnel looked like it was about to fall on them, as if a giant tree were toppling toward them. Stovall yelled incoherently and dived back under his wagon.

Cord's head jerked toward the other end of the line. He wanted to be with his father and Glory. But he didn't have time to get there. If he tried, the huge twister might pick him up right off the ground and whirl him around and around, as limp and helpless as some child's discarded rag doll . . .

Those thoughts flashed through Cord's brain in less than a second. Then, with the cyclone's roar so loud that he felt like it was about to crush his eardrums, he threw himself to the ground and crawled desperately under Matthew Stovall's wagon.

The horses in Stovall's team whinnied in fear and tried to rear up so they could paw at the air, but the harness prevented them from doing so. Stovall had set the brake firmly; otherwise, the animals might have bolted.

As it was, they were as terrified as the human beings huddled in this gully. Cord and Stovall hugged the ground. They could hear the wagon shaking a few feet over their heads.

The cyclone's roar was so loud now it seemed to fill the entire universe. Cord knew it had to be right over them. A perverse part of his brain wanted him to stick his head out so he could peer up into the very heart of the terrible funnel. What wonders might he see there?

His own death, that was what he'd see, he told himself. Some things man wasn't meant to witness firsthand.

Cord expected the cyclone to lift all the wagons into the air and whirl them away before doing the same thing to the hapless Forty-Niners. The wagon continued to shake, but somehow its wheels stayed on the ground.

Cord could only pray that the same thing was true of the other wagons.

After a minute or two that seemed more like an hour, the terrible, moaning roar began to subside. It was still deafening, but no longer so loud that Cord felt as if it were about to crush his skull like an eggshell.

He lifted his head and peered out from under the wagon. The rain had continued to slack off. It still fell, steady but not nearly as heavy now. He saw the drops hitting the puddles that had formed on the bed of the formerly dry wash.

"Is . . . is it over?"

It took Cord a minute to realize that Stovall had asked him something, raising his voice to a near-shout to do so. Cord looked over at the man, whose face was drawn and haggard from tension, and said, "What?"

"The cyclone . . . is it gone?"

"I think so."

Using his elbows and toes, Cord dragged himself through the mud until his head was clear. He turned onto his right shoulder and craned his neck to peer upward.

Rain washed mud from his face and obscured his vision until he blinked some of the moisture away. Once he could see again, he could tell the air wasn't revolving above the gully. The clouds were still thick, but the cyclone appeared to have moved on.

He pulled himself clear and climbed wearily to his feet. Once he was standing, he looked to the south and saw the cyclone, now several hundred yards beyond the gully and moving away. For a moment, it turned into a waterspout as it crossed the North Platte and sucked water from the broad stream, and then it was past the river.

"Well?" Stovall called from underneath the wagon. "Is it gone?"

"It's gone," Cord confirmed. "You can come out."

The rain had soaked his clothes and glued them to his body, but he didn't mind too much, because it continued washing the mud from him, as well.

He looked around, saw that some of the other Forty-Niners were once again crawling from under their wagons. He trotted along the line, asking if anyone was hurt. Everybody appeared to be all right, although shaken from the close brush with the cyclone.

Cord reached the lead wagon. Kat was already out, leaning against the vehicle's sideboards. Cord grasped her shoulder and asked, "You're all right?"

She nodded without saying anything. He looked down, saw Glory's arm reaching from under the wagon, and hunkered down to help her. When she was clear enough, he lifted her to her feet. He was so relieved to see her that it seemed as if she were almost weightless.

"Oh, Cord," she said as she wrapped her

arms around his neck and hugged him. "When you didn't come back, I was so afraid that cyclone got you!"

"I'm fine," he assured her. He put his arms around her, too, and patted her on the back. "I just didn't have time to get back here before the worst of the storm hit. I rode it out under Matthew Stovall's wagon."

"Stovall make it through all right?" That question came from Abraham Olmsted, who had crawled out to join them. Verne Bennett emerged last. The two old-timers were so covered with mud that they were almost indistinguishable from each other, but they didn't seem to be hurt.

"He was fine the last I saw of him," Cord said.

Olmsted nodded. "Good. He can be a pain in the rear end, but I don't want to lose nobody. How about all the other folks?"

"They came through it all right."

"I'm mighty glad to hear it." Olmsted looked around. "You know, it'd be a good idea for us to get out o' this wash. There could still come a flash flood, especially if it keeps rainin'."

"I was just thinking the same thing," Cord agreed. He cupped his hands around his mouth and shouted along the line, "Get back in your wagons! We've moving out of here, right now!"

The Forty-Niners hurried to follow the order. The lightning and thunder had followed the cyclone off to the south, and Cord didn't figure there was much chance of the storm backtracking. They ought to be fairly safe out on the plains again. The steady rain was an annoyance, but not an actual threat as long as they got out of the wash.

While people were getting ready to move, Kat came up to Cord and asked, "You still haven't seen Flint, have you?"

Cord shook his head. "He and Steve didn't make it back. But that doesn't mean that they're not out there somewhere, doing fine. They could have found a place to ride out the storm, just like we did."

"What do you think the chances of that are?" Kat asked with a bleak expression on her face.

"I don't know the odds," Cord answered honestly, "but as long as there's reason to hope, I'm going to hang on to it."

She sighed and nodded. "That's all we can do, isn't it?"

"For now. Once we get out of here, if they haven't showed up, I'll go and look for them."

"Thank you, Cord. I know he's your

brother . . ."

"Both of them are."

"Of course. I'll pray they're both all right."

Cord squeezed her shoulder and then turned his attention to the task of getting the wagons out of the wash. The banks were muddy now, so the wheels were more likely to slip. Cord and Verne mounted up and rode on either side of the first team to make the attempt. They grasped the harness and tugged, forcing the horses to keep pulling.

It was a hard chore. Cord thought that for every foot of progress they made, they slid back a couple of feet. Actually, it just seemed that way; the reality was the other way around. But it was still enough to wear out humans and horses and mules alike.

By the time they were finished, and all the wagons were out of the gully, everyone was exhausted. The rain had diminished to a light drizzle. The cyclone was long since out of sight, although a few flashes of lightning were still visible in the distance, along with a few barely heard rumbles of thunder.

"I reckon we'll camp right here tonight," Abraham Olmsted announced. "We're all too tired to move on today, and this is as good a place as any."

That decision was greeted with stolid acceptance. No one had enough energy to demonstrate any enthusiasm, but that didn't mean they disagreed.

Only a few minutes had passed since the last wagon — Matthew Stovall's — made it out of the wash when a new sound caught Cord's attention. He was still with the Olmsteds and his father, so he said, "Do you folks hear that?"

"That rumblin' sound?" Verne asked; then a look of alarm crossed his face. "By grab, that sounds kinda like that cyclone did before it got here!"

"Is there another one coming?" Glory asked.

Cord shook his head. "I don't think so. It's not as loud, and it's coming from the west . . . Look!"

He pointed at the wash. Around a bend about a hundred yards along it to the west, a low wall of water appeared, surging steadily toward them. It came about halfway up the banks, which meant the water was approximately three feet deep. Cord could tell it was flowing with a strong current.

"I ain't surprised," Olmsted said. "I knew there was a chance that gully would flood. It's deep enough, and movin' fast enough, that it likely would've washed some of the wagons away, as well as draggin' the teams along and drownin' 'em. No tellin' how many of us would've drowned, too."

Verne said, "Reckon that's the first flash flood I've ever seen. Figured it'd be, I don't know, more powerful than that."

"Don't underestimate its strength, Pa," Cord said. "It's running hard. You just can't really tell it."

They got a better idea a few minutes later when several pieces of brush floated by. The brush was moving fast and bobbing along the muddy surface.

"We been mighty lucky again," Olmsted commented as he raked his fingers through his beard. "That worries me."

"Why would it worry you?" Verne asked.

"Because when a run of good luck breaks, it usually turns mighty bad in a hurry."

"That's just superstition, Pa," Glory said. "We don't know that's going to happen."

Kat said, "I'm already worried about Flint coming back. I have this terrible feeling that something's happened to him."

Cord would feel better if his brothers showed up, too, and as if that thought gave birth to the reality, one of the men called, "Riders comin' in!"

Cord and the others hurried to the edge of the campsite and gazed to the west. It was late enough in the day, and the overcast was thick enough, that the light was beginning to fade.

But it was still bright enough for Cord to make out the two men on horseback loping toward the camp. He knew both of them instantly by the way they rode, as well as by Steve's hulking presence in the saddle.

"Oh!" Kat cried. She ran forward to meet them, lifting her skirts as she hurried so they wouldn't drag in the mud. That was just habit; the garment was already filthy, like all the clothes on the others.

Flint swung down from the saddle before Kat got there and was ready to gather her into his arms. As far as Cord could tell, both of his brothers appeared to be unharmed.

"See?" Verne said. "They made it through the storm all right. Looks like our luck is holdin'."

A frown creased Abraham Olmsted's forehead, and Cord felt some of that same unease stirring in him.

If their luck eventually *did* turn bad . . . how bad would it get?

CHAPTER 19

"When we saw that cyclone," Flint explained around the campfire that evening, "we started looking for a low place in the ground. It didn't take us long to find one, thank goodness."

"It was a little buffalo wallow," Steve added. "That's what Flint called it, anyway."

Flint nodded. "That's what it looked like to me. All I really cared about was finding a place low enough that that twister would go over us, the way you did here."

"That has to be what happened," Cord said. "The cyclone lifted up a little as it went over the wash. None of us dared to look, but there's not any other explanation that makes sense."

"We got into that wallow, pulled our horses down, and made them stay down," Flint went on. "I never heard anything as loud as that cyclone."

"It was so loud it just about rattled the

teeth right outta my head," Steve said. "I was sure scared. Flint said we'd be all right if we kept our heads down, though, and sure enough, we were." He grinned. "You ain't steered me wrong yet, Flint."

"And I never will, brother." Flint took a drink from the cup of coffee he held and went on, "As soon as the storm was past, we got back here as fast as we could. I was mighty relieved to see that everybody was all right."

He smiled over at Kat, making it clear that he was talking about her more than anyone else.

Abraham Olmsted said, "I give Cord a lot of credit for us makin' it through. He's the one who found that gully where we took cover, and he kept a clear head through the whole thing. Verne, you raised a good bunch of boys."

Verne grinned and nodded. "Thanks, Abe. I've always thought they turned out all right. They're hard workers, and I reckon they'll all find gold in California and get rich."

"Don't you want to get rich, Pa?" Steve asked.

"Aw, shoot, I'm too old to worry much about that. It ain't like I'll need that much in the time I got left. But I truly would like to see you boys do well for yourselves, so

I'd know I don't have to worry about you further on down the line."

"That's the way I feel about these girls o' mine," Olmsted said. "What I'm doin', I'm doin' for them."

"You don't have to worry about us, Pa," Glory said. "We'll be all right, won't we, Kat?"

"Sure," Kat replied as she hugged Flint's arm. "Everything's going to work out just fine when we get to California."

"But we still have to get there," Olmsted pointed out. "And I reckon we ain't seen the last of trouble along the way."

That cast a little pall over the atmosphere around the campfire, but everyone was too tired, and too relieved to have survived this day, to concern themselves too much with what the next day might bring.

What it brought was several more miles of slow, monotonous progress across the plains. The storm had left the ground muddy, but it began to dry out by midday, and the wagons were rolling on firm ground by nightfall, when the Forty-Niners made camp again.

Four more days passed with no sign of bad weather, Indians, or any other threat. Then, on the fifth day, something happened,

215

but it was a positive development, not a dangerous one.

Steve came riding back to the wagons, alone and obviously excited. Cord saw him coming and hurried out on horseback to meet him.

"What is it, Steve?" he asked as he reined in. "Is something wrong? Where's Flint?"

"He's still up ahead," Steve replied. "He sent me back to tell you that we saw the mountains! The Rocky Mountains!"

The Olmsted wagon, in the lead as usual, was close enough for Abraham Olmsted and Glory, who was riding beside him, to hear what Steve said. Glory called, "Is it really true?"

"Yes'm, it sure is," Steve told her. "That means we'll be at South Pass before much longer, and then make the turn for California and the gold fields!"

The wagon reached Cord and Steve and kept moving. The brothers swung their horses around to ride beside the vehicle.

"Best not get too excited," Abraham Olmsted advised. "As flat as this country is, I reckon you can see the mountains from a long way off. Might still take us a week or more to get there. And makin' it to South Pass is just part of the trip. The easy part, at that!"

216

Kat stuck her head through the opening behind the driver's seat. "I don't think it's been all that easy so far," she said. "Maybe we'll be lucky, and the second part of the journey won't be as much trouble as the first."

"Wouldn't that be something?" Glory said.

Cord said, "It sure would, and I hope it turns out that way."

He doubted that would be the case, but he didn't see any reason to throw cold water on their excitement.

Olmsted said, "Cord, ride back along the line and tell folks to keep their eyes open, that we'll be comin' in sight of the mountains soon. If nothin' else, it'll be nice to have somethin' in front of us besides nothin' but mile after empty mile of these plains. That'll give 'em somethin' to get their spirits up again."

"Sure thing, Mr. Olmsted."

Excitement grew among the group as Cord passed the word. When he was finished, he returned to the lead wagon and rode next to it. Steve had already galloped back ahead to find Flint.

Cord kept his gaze trained on the western horizon. The change was so subtle, though, that he missed it at first. Finally he realized that the dark, irregular line he was seeing wasn't the horizon itself, but rather the mountains that rose in the distance.

He turned in the saddle, called, "There they are!" to Olmsted, Glory, and Kat, and pointed at the barely visible peaks.

Olmsted said, "My old eyes ain't good enough to see 'em yet. How about you gals?"

"I see them, Pa," Glory said. "They're out there ahead, just calling to us!"

Kat said, "It's not the mountains I hear calling to me. It's the gold on the other side of them!"

Cord heard that call, too, and felt something stirring inside him. So far during the trip across the Great Plains, most of his thoughts had concerned simply staying alive from one day to the next.

But now, with the first visible sign of their progress in a long time lying in front of them, maybe he needed to start devoting some thought to what lay at the end of the journey . . .

And whether he wanted to share that destiny with Gloriana Olmsted.

Abraham Olmsted's prediction proved to be accurate. Days crept past as the wagons seemed to never get any closer to the mountains. The peaks just lurked there in the distance, tantalizing the gold-seekers.

More rain moved in one night and remained through the next day. This wasn't a destructive storm like the previous one, just a steady rain that was still enough to make the ground muddy and slow their progress.

But they kept moving, and eventually Cord was able to tell that they actually were closer to the mountains. Things seemed to speed up after that. It wasn't long before they could see the foothills that rose in front of the snow-capped peaks.

Ranges of smaller mountains appeared off to the sides of the trail they were following. It had been so long since they left the Ozarks that a part of Cord wanted to ride over and explore them, but he wasn't going to waste time doing that.

He would see plenty of mountains before this journey was over, he told himself. They still had to cross the Rockies and the High Sierras.

It was a relief when the group reached the foothills and saw some actual trees again. Instead of using buffalo dung as fuel for their fires when they made camp that night, they were able to use broken branches from the scrubby pines that grew on the slopes. The dung didn't really smell bad, but the pine smelled better and made little popping sounds as the pockets of resin trapped in the wood exploded from the heat.

"This country is beautiful," Glory commented that evening when she and Cord were taking a walk around the outskirts of the campsite. "I almost wouldn't mind staying here."

"You'd have a hard time making a living," Cord said. "You might be able to farm some, out on the flats, and you could graze cattle among these hills, but you'd be so far away from everything else that it would be a pretty lonely life."

"I suppose that would depend on who you were with."

He looked over at her and saw that she was giving him a shy smile. That was about as close as Glory ever came to flirting, and Cord wasn't overly comfortable with that himself.

He cleared his throat and said, "Maybe we could come back here someday for a visit. You know, after we've found gold and gotten rich in California."

"That sounds like a good idea. Assuming, of course, that we actually do find gold and get rich."

"Well, of course we will." Cord chuckled. "As my brother Steve says, if we don't, then what's the point of going to all this trouble?"

That brought a laugh from Glory. It sounded good, and Cord liked it even better when she linked her arm with his and her shoulder bumped him a little as they walked along. That gave him a nice, companionable feeling.

South Pass was visible when they started out the next morning. Cord thought they would reach it in another couple of days. The long, gradual ascent would take the travelers higher in elevation than they had been for a long time.

The approach was flanked by sparsely wooded hills on both sides. Those slopes were also covered with clusters of boulders left there by some geologic cataclysm in the dim past. Cord found himself looking from side to side, especially at those boulders, as he rode with the Olmsted wagon.

Something was bothering him, but he couldn't say what it was. Just a feeling of uneasiness that made the skin on the back of his neck prickle.

He looked up ahead. Flint and Steve were closer today, riding a couple of hundred yards ahead of the wagons instead of being out of sight.

Maybe Flint was uneasy, too, and that was why he and Steve were staying closer.

Cord had a hunch he would have disapproved of many of the things Flint had done in the past, had he been aware of them, but one thing he trusted was Flint's instinct for trouble. Flint always seemed to know when something was going to happen.

Maybe some of that had rubbed off on him, Cord thought. With the horse's reins in his left hand, he moved his right to the butt of the Colt Dragoon on his hip. He gripped the revolver and moved it a little, making sure nothing was binding it in the holster.

Abraham Olmsted's eyes might not be as good as they once were when it came to distances, but they were still keen close up. The old-timer was alone on the driver's box at the moment. Glory and Kat were both in the back of the wagon. Olmsted squinted at Cord and asked, "Somethin' wrong, son?"

"I don't know, sir," Cord answered honestly. "I just have an uneasy feeling . . . but I've looked all around, and I don't see a thing out of the ordinary. Flint and Steve must not, either, or else they would have ridden back to warn us."

"Maybe you're just a mite spooked because we're back in country where folks could hide if they had mischief on their minds. Out yonder on the plains, you can see trouble comin' from a long ways off. Easy to get used to that."

"Maybe," Cord allowed, although he wasn't convinced that was the explanation for the tension he felt.

"If you want, you can ride on ahead and ask your brothers if they've seen anything suspicious."

"If they had, they would have let us know," Cord said, echoing the thought he'd had a moment earlier. "I'm sure everything's all right."

Olmsted chuckled, but he didn't sound genuinely amused. "You're just worried that it's about time for our luck to turn again," he said quietly, clearly not wanting his daughters to overhear the conversation. "To tell you the truth, son, I've been feelin' the same way. It's almost like trouble's overdue —"

As if on cue, a gunshot suddenly blasted through the clear air. Up ahead, Steve's horse reared, and Steve toppled loosely out of the saddle. Fear for his brother exploded inside Cord.

But he didn't have time to worry about Steve, because that shot was the signal for a thunderous volley of more gunfire to erupt from the hills on both sides of the trail.

CHAPTER 20

Lead howled savagely through the air and raked the wagons with deadly claws. Cord yanked his Colt from its holster and raised the revolver, then grimaced and lowered it as he realized the range was too far for a handgun.

Abraham Olmsted hauled back on the reins and brought the team to a stop. Behind him, Kat swept the canvas flap aside. She and Glory peered out through the opening.

"Pa!" Kat said. "What —"

"Get down!" Olmsted interrupted her as he dropped the reins and twisted on the seat. "Down in the bottom of the wagon bed!"

He dived over the back of the seat to join them.

Cord hoped the girls did as their father told them. The wagon's thick sideboards ought to stop most rifle balls.

He heard one of those balls hum past his head as he jerked his mount around and rode along the line of wagons.

"Take cover!" he shouted to the other members of the group. "Everybody get down and take cover!"

He didn't have to tell them twice. Men were already scrambling under the canvas covers of their wagons. A few poked heads and rifle barrels back out and began returning the fire from the hills.

As Cord reached Matthew Stovall's wagon, he saw that the former major had retrieved a rifle from the back of the vehicle and was kneeling on the driver's box as he drew a bead with the weapon.

The rifle cracked, and Stovall let out an exultant shout. Cord glanced toward the nearest cluster of boulders and saw a man toppling out from behind them. From the loose-limbed way he slid down the slope, Cord figured Stovall had drilled the man fatally.

"Good shooting, Major!" Cord called to him. "Now hunt some cover!"

A few yards away, Verne Bennett rode up leading the two pack mules.

"Cord!" he called. "What in blazes is goin' on?"

Cord wasn't sure, although he had a pretty

225

good idea. He waved and said, "Get down, Pa! Get under the wagon!"

Since they were caught in a crossfire, the wheels wouldn't offer complete protection from the ambush, but any cover was a lot better than none. Cord leaped from the saddle, grabbed the lead ropes from his father, and wrapped them around one of the wheels on Stovall's wagon.

With all the lead flying around, there was a good chance the mules would be hit, but there was nothing else Cord could do.

As soon as his father's feet were on the ground, Cord grabbed his arm and hustled him underneath the vehicle. They heard rifle balls thudding into the sideboards, and a couple of bullets chewed splinters from the wheel spokes and sprayed them with the flying slivers.

Cord had pulled his rifle from its saddle sheath as he dismounted. He threw himself down on the ground and thrust the barrel past one of the wheels. He aimed at the hillside to the north. A puff of smoke from behind a boulder told him one of the ambushers was hiding there. He waited and watched, and a moment later he saw a brief movement, probably the man lifting his head slightly as he reloaded his rifle.

Cord squeezed the trigger.

The same skill that allowed him to knock a squirrel off a branch at a hundred yards sent the rifle bullet speeding on its way. Cord saw another flicker of motion but didn't know if his shot found its mark until he spotted a man's arm lying motionless on the ground next to the boulder.

The ambusher had fallen and wasn't moving, so Cord was going to count that as good. He began reloading.

Above him, inside the wagon, Stovall's rifle cracked again. Fire rippled up and down the line of wagons. The Forty-Niners were putting up a good fight, as Cord expected they would. He knew that many of them came from hardscrabble backgrounds. Some had fought in the Mexican War.

Cord was a little surprised he didn't hear horses screaming in pain from being shot. When he thought about it, though, that made sense. He believed their attackers were a gang of white renegades like the ones Lieutenant Woodbury had mentioned back at Fort Kearny.

Outlaws, pure and simple, bent on stealing anything valuable they could get their hands on, and willing to kill in order to do so. Those horses and mules would be worth money to them, so the raiders would try to preserve their lives.

Unlike the men and women of this group, who just represented obstacles to be killed!

Although the women might be valuable to the renegades, too, Cord realized — a thought that sent cold horror through his veins. They couldn't allow Glory, Kat, and the other women to be captured. A terrible fate awaited them if that happened.

Verne had his rifle with him, too. It blasted as the old-timer fired a shot toward the ambushers on the south.

"Dadgum it!" Verne exclaimed. "I never was as good a shot as you, Cord. I think I missed that varmint I just aimed at."

"Well, keep fighting, Pa," Cord said as he nestled his rifle's stock against his shoulder again and squinted over its barrel, searching for a target. "You'll get another chance."

From above him in the wagon, Stovall called, "Riders coming in from the east, Bennett!"

Cord bit back a curse and squirmed around to look in that direction. Stovall was right. At least a dozen mounted men were attacking from the rear, firing pistols as they charged. Clouds of powdersmoke billowed in the air.

It was a vicious trap: ambush the Forty-Niners from both sides to pin them down and do some damage, then sweep in from behind on horseback to finish them off.

Cord couldn't fight the riders from under the wagon. He told his father, "Stay here, Pa!" and then rolled out into the open. As he sprang to his feet, Matthew Stovall leaped down from the vehicle and landed nearby. Stovall had a pistol in his hand now.

Cord drew his Dragoon. The attackers were almost on top of him and Stovall. The Colt roared and bucked in his hand as he cocked and fired again and again. Bullets whistled around them, ripped through the wagon's canvas cover, and smashed into its sideboards.

Verne didn't do as Cord had told him. Instead, he crawled out from under the back of the wagon, reached up to grab hold of it, and pulled himself to his feet. He yelled blistering curses, uncommon in such a mild-mannered man, as he raised his rifle and fired.

One of the raiders flipped backward, smashed out of the saddle by Verne's lead.

A split second later, Verne dropped his rifle and reeled back against the tailgate. He pressed both hands to his chest. Crimson welled between the splayed fingers as he began to slide downward.

"Pa!" Cord bellowed. From the corner of his eye, he had seen his father hit. His gun's

229

hammer clicked on an empty chamber. He didn't try to reload. He sprang to Verne's side instead as the old man collapsed.

One of the renegades veered his horse toward Cord and Verne and thrust a long-barreled pistol at them. Before he could fire, Stovall leaped forward and triggered a shot that caught the man under the chin and bored up through his brain, killing him instantly.

Then Stovall jerked and fell against the wagon's sideboards but managed to stay on his feet.

"Pa, damn it," Cord rasped as he knelt beside his father. "Why didn't you stay under cover?"

Verne's eyes were open. He gasped for air as he looked up at Cord and managed to say, "Ain't no place . . . safe . . . if the world decides . . . your time's up . . . You go . . . find that gold . . . and look after . . . your brothers . . . They ain't . . . as strong as you . . ."

"I'll look after them, Pa," Cord promised.

But the long, rattling sigh that came from Verne Bennett's throat told him that his father probably never heard that vow.

The raiders had swept on past the rear wagon, so the rataplan of hoofbeats wasn't as thunderous now. Stovall's strained voice penetrated Cord's stunned grief, saying, "Bennett . . . they're breaking off the attack. I guess they figured out . . . they bit off more than they could chew."

Cord looked up, saw Stovall leaning on the wagon with blood on his shirt, too. He leaped to his feet and said, "You're hit!"

Stovall waved his free hand. "It's . . . nothing. Your father . . . ?"

Cord shook his head.

"I'm sorry. I wish I could have —"

Stovall didn't finish his sentence. He dropped to his knees and then fell over on his left side. The way his head lolled loosely on the ground told Cord that he was gone, too.

With a bitter, sour taste filling his mouth and the powdersmoke that was thick in the air stinging his eyes and nose, Cord looked around. The renegades who were still mounted had charged up the hill to the south and were now vanishing over its crest, fleeing from the bullets that still fanged through the air after them.

Men on foot were running away, too. Those would be the riflemen who had hidden behind the boulders, Cord knew. They were giving up, as well.

Would they regroup and try again? Cord had no way of knowing, but it was certainly possible. Although he hated to leave his father and Stovall where they had fallen, he had to check on the rest of the group, including Glory.

Especially Glory.

As he hurried forward, he remembered that Steve had fallen to the first shot of the attack. He didn't know how badly his brother was hurt. He might have lost a father and a brother today.

Cord pushed that pain down deep inside him. There would be time for mourning later.

Two more men had been killed in the attack, he discovered as he made his way along the line of wagons, and several had suffered bullet wounds, some minor, some appearing to be more serious.

When he reached the Olmsted wagon, a wave of relief went through him. Not only were Glory, Kat, and Abraham Olmsted standing next to the vehicle, apparently unharmed, but Flint and Steve had joined them.

Steve's right hand clutched his upper left arm, where blood showed on his sleeve. Cord came up to him and asked, "You're not badly wounded?"

"Naw," Steve answered. "That bullet knocked a chunk o' meat off my arm and made me fall off my dang horse, but it ain't a killin' matter. Hurts like blazes, though."

Kat said, "You should have seen the way Flint came galloping in, shooting so fast and accurately. He drove those men off almost single-handedly."

Cord knew that wasn't true, but if Kat wanted to think so, he wasn't going to argue with her.

Flint turned to Cord and said, "Where's Pa?"

Cord drew in a deep breath, looked from Flint to Steve and back again, and then said, "Boys . . . he didn't make it."

Steve's eyes widened. "No!" he boomed. "You're lyin'! Pa can't be dead!"

Flint, on the other hand, squinted icily at his youngest brother. "What happened?"

"We were fighting side by side with Stovall at the far end of the wagons when those riders came in. Pa blasted one of them out of the saddle, but the next moment, he got hit. A clean shot to the chest. He didn't last long."

Cord didn't repeat what Verne had said to him. Those things had been for his ears alone.

Tears started to roll down Steve's tanned cheeks. "Pa can't be dead," he said again. "He just can't!"

In a hard voice, Flint said, "With all that lead flying around, I'm surprised more people aren't dead."

Olmsted asked, "How many did we lose, do you know, Cord?"

"Four so far. Major Stovall didn't make it, either. Hal Bedford and Frank Stokes are dead, too, and maybe half a dozen more wounded."

Olmsted shook his head. "Matthew Stovall was a stiff-necked son of a gun, but I'm sorry to hear that he's dead."

"He may not have been in any battles when he was a soldier, but he fought like a demon today," Cord said. "He accounted for at least two of those renegades, maybe more."

"They were outlaws?" Flint said.

"Like the ones Lieutenant Woodbury told us about, back at the fort. Nothing else they could have been. I got a pretty good look at the ones on horseback. They were all white."

"Damn a man who'd stoop to such evil," Olmsted said. He sighed. "We'd best get the wounded patched up, reload all the guns, and move on outta here as soon as we can. We don't want that no-good bunch comin' back and makin' another try."

Flint said, "We'd better reload first and then tend to the wounded. And put the

234

dead in the wagons to be buried later."

Olmsted nodded in agreement. "You boys mind passin' the word?"

"We'll take care of it," Cord said.

He started to turn away but stopped, lingering a moment to say quietly to Glory, "You're all right, aren't you?"

"I'm fine," she assured him. "Cord, I . . . I'm sorry about your father."

Cord nodded. "He had a dream, but like he said, it was more for us than for him. I reckon we owe it to him to finish the journey . . . and find what's waiting for us in California."

The four casualties of the battle were laid to rest that evening on a hillside where the group camped. It was a nice, peaceful spot, and from here, Cord thought, his pa would be able to look down at the trail where thousands of immigrants would continue to pass, some bound for golden dreams in California, others for new lives in Oregon and Washington.

He hoped that Verne would be content resting here.

Glory, Kat, and the other women had been kept busy tending to the injured men, cleaning and bandaging wounds, assuring them that they would be all right. Cord was no doctor, but he felt that there was a good chance all the wounded would pull through.

He and Flint had been forced to take the reins and drive a couple of the wagons. They would have to make do without scouts for the time being. But everyone was alert, and loaded guns were always close at hand.

It was a very subdued camp that night, after the burials and the words that had to be said. Everyone was quiet. There were no sounds except for the crackle of flames from the campfire, the sighing of the wind, and an occasional moan from one of the wagons where a wounded man lay.

Glory sat on a rock beside Cord and held his hand. On the other side of the fire, Kat leaned against Flint's shoulder. Steve was nearby, sipping from a cup of coffee and sporting a bandage wrapped around his wounded arm.

Glory finally spoke up. "I don't know what to say, Cord."

"No need to say anything," he told her. "Pa was a good man, and he'll be missed." His mouth hardened into a grim line. "The worst of it is that he died for no reason other than senseless greed. Those men wanted what we have, and they were willing to kill to take it. There's no excuse for evil like that."

236

Flint said, "You don't know their stories, Cord. You don't know but what life drove them to be what they are."

Cord shook his head. "Nobody has to be a thief and a murderer. That was their choice . . . and I hope they all burn in hell for it."

"Lucky for them that's not your choice to make, isn't it?"

"They'll get what's coming to them," Cord said. "Sooner or later, somehow, they'll get what's coming to them. Knowing that is some comfort, even though we won't be around to see it."

"You just cling to that, then," Flint said. "They're gone, and all I care about is what happens to us from here on out."

Steve surprised his brothers by lifting his cup and saying, "To Pa. May he rest in peace."

The others raised their cups, as well, and echoed the sentiment.

In the morning, the wagons rolled on toward South Pass, and what lay beyond.

■ ■ ■ ■

BOOK II

■ ■ ■ ■

CHAPTER 21

Rio Oro City, California, three months later
"This don't look much like a city to me," Steve commented as he rode down the street with Cord and Flint.

For that matter, it wasn't much of a street, either, just a wide, unpaved stretch of mud and animal droppings, churned up into a reeking morass by thousands of hooves and wagon wheels.

Scores of tents bordered the so-called thoroughfare on both sides. Dotting the landscape and scattered among the tents were a few actual buildings, if you could dignify such hastily thrown together, ramshackle structures of wood, tin, and canvas with the word *buildings.*

Despite the name that somebody had burned into a board nailed to a tree at the edge of the settlement, this wasn't a city, and it wasn't even a town, Cord thought.

It was a gold camp, and a mighty raw

one, at that.

Cord looked over his shoulder. All the wagons that had left Fort Kearny together were there, still moving along in a ragged line, their wheels slipping and sliding through deep ruts in the mud, threatening to bog down at any moment.

It was nothing short of a miracle that they had made it here, he told himself, all the way across the Great Plains, the Rocky Mountains, and the Sierra Nevadas.

Of course, just because the wagons had made it didn't mean all the people had. Four men had been lost to violence, another man and a woman to sickness when a fever came on them. The wagons belonging to Matthew Stovall and the other two gold-seekers killed in the outlaws' ambush had been taken over by other members of the party. The married couple who'd succumbed to illness had been traveling with a cousin, and he carried on with their wagon.

But except for the fever that had caused half the group to be sick for several days and taken two of their number, the rest of the journey had been relatively uneventful after crossing the Continental Divide at South Pass. They had seen no more Indians or outlaws, and the few rainstorms had been mild compared to the savage weather they'd encountered out on the plains.

Maybe the fever had used up the last of their bad luck. Cord was going to allow himself to hope so.

"Is this where we're going to stake our claims?" Glory called from the wagon seat, where she perched beside her father.

"Not here in town," Cord said. "Up the canyon a ways." He pointed at an opening in the tree-covered heights beyond the settlement. "That's Rio Oro Canyon. Supposed to be plenty of good claims left up there, according to what we've been told."

They had heard that from several different men they'd run into since reaching California. Rio Oro Canyon was the site of the latest strike. Judging by the size of the camp that had sprung into existence here at the canyon's mouth, those claims had to have some truth to them.

Now it was a matter of whether or not all the good claims had been taken already, and there was only one way to find out about that.

Without warning, shots roared up ahead, causing Cord, Flint, and Steve to rein in sharply and Abraham Olmsted to bring his wagon to a halt.

Cord and Flint rested their hands on the holstered Colt Dragoons, and Steve pulled his rifle from its saddle scabbard, as they looked around to see what the trouble was.

Two men appeared from behind a tent, one of them running from the other. The fleeing man stopped and thrust a pistol toward the pursuer. Flame lanced from the muzzle as the gun roared.

Wherever the bullet went, it didn't hit the second man. He stopped, too, and fired back with the gun he held. No more than fifteen feet separated the two men as they blazed away at each other.

Cord expected both of them to fall, mortally wounded, but instead they stood there blasting away until the hammers of their guns fell on empty chambers. Neither man appeared to be injured.

Evidently, accuracy wasn't their strong suit.

The first man yelled a curse and then charged the man who'd been chasing him.

"I'll bash your brains in, Ed Newton!"

"Come and try, Benton!" the second man responded, as he met the charge with one of his own.

They came together and slashed and flailed at each other with the empty guns. None of the blows landed solidly. They didn't appear to be doing much more damage this way than they had by shooting at each other.

After a moment, their feet got tangled up as they lunged back and forth. Both men swayed and waved their arms as they tried to keep their balance, but they couldn't stay upright. With wild yells, they fell, landing face down in the mud and losing their guns, to boot.

"Oh, no!" Glory said as she lifted a hand to her mouth. She looked horrified.

Cord felt a little queasy himself as he thought about what was in the thick brown mixture into which the men had plunged. Their faces were covered with the stuff as they struggled up, not to mention the rest of their bodies and their clothes.

The mishap hadn't knocked the fight out of them, however. They reached their feet at the same time, and as soon as they were standing again, they charged at each other, swinging wild, roundhouse punches.

Abraham Olmsted chuckled. "If those boys ain't careful, they're liable to hurt theirselves, accidental-like."

"I'm just glad they're not shooting at each other anymore," Flint said. "If they were, I'd be more worried that they were going to hurt somebody else."

The battle ended when the two combatants took out-of-control swings at the same time, missed badly, and slipped in the muck and fell down again. This time, they were too worn out to get up and continue the fight, although they tried before sagging back into the mire.

A crowd had gathered to watch the fight and had gotten even larger once the shooting stopped and the bystanders weren't in danger of stopping a stray bullet. All of the onlookers were men, most dressed in the rough canvas trousers, flannel shirts, and felt hats of miners. They had been shouting encouragement to the brawlers.

The only females in sight, other than Glory and Kat, had emerged from one of the buildings and stood on its porch. From the fact that some of them wore gaudy, revealing dresses and others had on only their underclothes, Cord realized they were sporting gals.

He felt his face warming in embarrassment, because Glory and Kat were being exposed to those soiled doves, who had cheered on the battlers just as loudly and crudely as the miners.

Flint and Steve, on the other hand, were eyeing the "ladies" with interest.

Cord noted that the building they'd come from wasn't finished. It was still under construction, with some of the walls and roof not yet completed. Sheets of canvas served to enclose the rooms, instead. But the framework of what would be a substantial two-story building was in place.

The group of miners and soiled doves on the porch parted as a burly, barrel-chested figure pushed through them. The man came down the steps to the ground and started toward the two fallen fighters. The mud sucked loudly at his high-topped boots with every step he took.

He wore gray-striped trousers, a bright blue swallowtail coat, a white shirt under a dark red vest, a bright yellow cravat, and a black top hat. A gold watch chain looped across his ample belly from one vest pocket to the other.

The man stopped where he was looming over the two lying in the mud. He put his fists on his hips and bellowed in a gravelly voice, "Charley Benton! Ed Newton! What in blazes are you boys doin'? Tryin' to kill each other?"

One of the bystanders called, "That's exactly what they were doing, Harville! Didn't you hear the shooting?"

The big, fancy-dressed man called Harville reached down and closed ham-like paws on the collars of both men. He hauled them upright with apparent ease and shook them, causing their heads to wobble back and forth.

"Speak up, lads! What's this all about?"

Both men stayed upright when Harville let go of them. They started spitting and trying to wipe mud off their faces. One of them said, "He tried to steal my poke full o' dust!"

"That's a damned lie!" the other man responded. "Why would I do that? My claim's got a hell of a lot more color on it than yours does!"

"Check his pockets if you don't believe me, Teddy! He's got my poke!"

The other man spread his arms and said, "Go ahead. Search me. I don't have his blasted poke!"

Harville made a face, but he patted the man's pockets and then said, "Sorry, Ed, but he doesn't seem to have it."

"Well, then, he must'a dropped it while I was chasin' him . . ."

The man's voice trailed off as he slowly turned his head and looked back in the direction they'd come from. He suddenly broke into a run, but so did a dozen other men, all of them churning through the mud in eager hopes of maybe finding a poke full of gold dust.

That turned into a stampede in little more

than the blink of an eye.

Harville heaved a huge sigh, shook his head, and turned back toward the building. As he did, he saw the wagons and riders, apparently noticing them for the first time.

"Welcome, folks!" He threw his arms wide, too, although he probably wasn't inviting a search like the fellow called Benton had been. "Welcome to Rio Oro City!"

His eyes widened at the sight of Glory and Kat. Snatching the top hat off his head, he bowed deeply, although not so deeply that he got his head anywhere close to the muddy street.

"Ladies! I am stunned! It's like our dear Lord in heaven has sent angels to visit us unworthy sinners." He clapped the hat back on his head and stomped through the mud toward the Olmsted wagon. "Allow me to introduce myself. My name is Theodore Harville. I'm the mayor here in Rio Oro City."

"Mayor, my hind foot," one of the few remaining bystanders commented. "Nobody elected you mayor of anything, Teddy. If there was an election, you were the only one who voted."

Harville glared at the man. "Somebody's got to step up and take responsibility, don't he? Do you see anybody else around here who's tryin' to do things for the good of the whole community? No, ever'body's out for his own self, and devil take the hindmost!"

"You're just trying to do things for the good of your saloon. Don't think you're fooling anybody."

Harville sniffed in disdain and turned back to the newcomers. "If there's anything I can do to help you folks get settled here, you let me know."

Olmsted said, "Is there a place to stop that ain't quite so muddy? My name's Abraham Olmsted, by the way. These here are my daughters Katherine and Gloriana."

Harville tipped his hat again and said, "It's an honor and a privilege, ladies. And a pleasure to meet you, as well, Mr. Olmsted. If you'll just drive on toward the canyon, there's some open ground this side of it where you can park."

"We're obliged to you."

"You'll have to come back into town if you need any supplies, though. We've got a fine mercantile store right over yonder run by a fellow name of Higginbotham. It's in that big tent there. Prices ain't what you'd call cheap, but nothin' is, out here. Things are always high in the gold fields."

Olmsted nodded and said, "I reckon that makes sense."

Harville turned to Cord, Flint, and Steve and asked, "Who might you boys be? Are you related to Mr. Olmsted here? Is your group, by chance, a family? I think I see a resemblance between you lads."

"We're the Bennett brothers," Flint replied. "No relation to the Olmsteds, just friends." He waved toward the rest of the wagons. "All of us have traveled here together from Fort Kearny. I'm Flint, this big fella is Steve, and the boy there is Cord."

"Mighty pleased to make your acquaintance. I'm sure I'll get to know each and ever' one of you. And if you boys are ever hankerin' for a, uh, libation, I got the finest whiskey you'll find this side o' San Francisco right there in my establishment. I ain't had the sign painted yet, but when I do, it'll be up there for ever'body to see. The Golden Nugget Saloon! Best in the gold fields! First drink's always on the house!"

Flint smiled. "We might just take you up on that, Mr. Harville."

"Some might," Olmsted said. "I don't hold overmuch with drink-in', myself, but I don't begrudge others who might feel different."

"Well, that's the best way to be," Harville said with an emphatic nod. "Live and let live."

"Like those men who were shooting at each other a few minutes ago?" Kat asked with a smile.

"Life in a minin' camp can be high-spirited at times, I'll grant you that, miss. But that's one reason we're tryin' to make Rio Oro City more than that. One o' these days, it's gonna be one of the finest cities in California, you just wait and see. Mark my words on that!"

Harville stepped back and waved the wagons on. Once they had ridden past him, Flint said quietly to Cord, "Colorful varmint, isn't he?"

"Seems like it."

"I wouldn't mind paying a visit to that Golden Nugget Saloon of his, though."

"You want that free first drink?"

"And other things," Flint said. "Some of those ladies looked pretty nice."

"I don't reckon they're ladies," Cord said, "and I thought you and Kat were fond of each other."

"Maybe we are. You wouldn't want to eat the same thing for every meal, would you? Just because a fella likes one thing, that doesn't mean he can't ever have anything else."

Cord could have pointed out that where women were concerned, that was exactly what it meant, but he didn't figure it would do any good. He and Flint just looked at things differently, that's all, he told himself.

Steve, getting to the heart of the matter as he often did, said, "Right now, all I want to do is find me some gold."

Cord and Flint both nodded. That was why they were here, after all.

CHAPTER 22

The open ground that Harville had mentioned turned out to be a wide field that butted up against the steep, thickly wooded slope of the ridge just west of the settlement.

Close by, Rio Oro Canyon cut through that ridge, twisting and turning so that Cord couldn't venture a guess how far it penetrated. Since it was the center of the gold strike in this area, it had to be pretty deep in order to accommodate all the prospectors who had flocked here, he thought.

A creek meandered through the canyon, emerged to run past the open field toward the settlement, then took a sharp southward turn just before it reached Rio Oro City. The stream wasn't very wide, but it flowed swiftly, and when Cord dismounted to kneel beside it, cup his hand, and take a drink, he found the water to be cold and good.

"Careful," Flint advised him, grinning.

"You don't want to guzzle down some gold dust by accident."

"I reckon it's likely any gold in this creek has been panned out before it gets this far." Cord pointed up the canyon. "Claims as far as you can see."

It was true. The canyon was wide enough at its mouth that quite a bit of level ground lay between the creek and the canyon wall on both sides of the stream. That area was covered with tents and crude cabins.

Men knelt beside the creek and dipped flat pans into the water, scooping it up and swirling it around. Cord had read as much as he could find about searching for gold and knew they were panning for gold dust, the tiny flecks of bright color that lurked amidst the dirt and gravel of the streambeds.

Other men labored along the canyon walls, digging holes, chipping away at rocks with pickaxes, and gouging out tunnels, all in hopes of finding solid nuggets of the shiny stuff.

Everybody seemed to have a slightly different method of hunting for the elusive yellow metal.

"If these men live out here on their claims, then who were all those men in town?" Glory asked.

"These are probably the first claims,"

Cord said, with a nod toward the canyon mouth. "More than likely, the deeper up the canyon you go, the smaller the claims get. The ones farther up the canyon may not have room for the fellas to live on them. They probably walk up there and dig or pan for gold during the day and then come back to the settlement at night."

"Or some of them get tired and thirsty from all that work and head for town to get a drink," Flint added. "I imagine that accounts for a lot of the ones we saw."

Abraham Olmsted said, "Let's get these teams unhitched so they can rest. They've done their jobs, bringin' us all the way across the country to this place."

"I want to go look for gold!" Steve said.

Flint laughed and told him, "Time enough for that in the morning. It's too late in the day to venture up that canyon today."

That was good advice. Cord had figured Flint might want to get started on the hunt right away, like Steve, but Flint could be pragmatic at times, despite the streak of wildness that ran through him.

The newcomers weren't the only ones camping here near the canyon mouth. Far from it. A number of wagons were parked in the field, and tents were pitched beside many of them. The group that had just arrived, led by Abraham Olmsted, had to scatter to find suitable places.

It occurred to Cord as he helped Steve unhitch Olmsted's team that with their arrival at Rio Oro Canyon, they weren't really a group anymore. The journey was over. They had arrived at their destination.

Now the Forty-Niners were on their own, the married couples, the brothers, the cousins all working together, maybe, but for many of them, it was every man for himself.

That was kind of a bittersweet notion, he reflected, as he looked at Olmsted, Glory, and Kat. They might still be friends with the Bennett brothers . . .

But they were also rivals in the search for the golden dream.

Out of habit, the Bennetts pitched their tents near the Olmsted wagon. Cord wanted to stay close to Glory, and he knew Flint felt the same way about Kat.

After the sun had set, but while a reddish-gold arch still hung in the sky over the mountains, Cord saw Glory walking toward the creek with a bucket in each hand. He wasn't doing anything at the time, so he hurried to intercept her.

"Let me give you a hand there," he said.

"I can do this," she replied.

"I know you can, but there's nothing wrong with accepting a little help when it's freely offered."

Glory smiled. "No, I suppose not." She pulled back the bucket in her right hand when Cord tried to take both of them from her. "I'll carry one of them. That way we're sharing the work."

Cord considered that for a second and then nodded. "All right. Sounds like a good way to do it."

As they came up to the stream, they saw two men also filling buckets in it. Both wore canvas overalls and battered old hats, but the similarities ended there. One was tall and lanky, the other short and on the rounded side. Cord figured they were both around fifty years old.

"Howdy, folks," the shorter one greeted them. "Welcome to Rio Oro."

"The city or the canyon?" Glory asked with a smile.

The man made a circling motion with a pudgy hand. "Oh, all around hereabouts, I reckon. My name's Lew Spooner. This tall drink of water here beside me is Hamlin Erskine."

The tall, rawboned man grunted. "Just call me Ham. I ain't answered to Hamlin in a long time."

"I'm Cord Bennett," Cord introduced himself. "This young lady is Miss Gloriana Olmsted."

"And I answer to Glory," she told them.

"You two ain't married?" Lew Spooner asked.

"No," Glory said. "Why do you ask?"

"Oh, I dunno. Reckon you just got the look of folks who are hitched."

Cord felt his face warming and said, "Miss Glory and I are good friends, that's all."

Ham Erskine said, "Don't pay no mind to Lew. He likes stickin' that nose of his into things that ain't none of his concern. See how short and kinda pushed up it is?"

"Well . . ." Cord didn't particularly want to comment on someone else's appearance.

"That's 'cause folks keep pushin' it back when he sticks it into their business."

"Dadgummit, I was born with this nose, and you know it," Spooner objected. He looked at Cord and Glory and went on, "We been friends since we learned to walk, Ham and me. Growed up on neighborin' farms back in Pennsylvania."

"My brothers and I were farmers, too," Cord said.

Spooner chuckled. "Until you got the gold fever?"

"Until a drought ruined our crop two

259

years in a row. Couldn't make a go of it after that."

Spooner and Erskine both nodded solemnly, to show that they understood.

"Reckon we'd best be gettin' back to fillin' these water buckets," Erskine said.

He turned to the stream and was about to lower the bucket he held into the water when Spooner muttered, "Uh-oh."

Cord and Glory had moved to the edge of the water and were about to carry out the chore themselves when they heard Spooner's under-the-breath exclamation.

"Something wrong?" Cord asked.

"Here comes Rip Jordan and his pals."

Spooner said the name as if they ought to know who Rip Jordan was. Cord said, "We just got here, remember? Who's Rip Jordan?"

"I hear somebody with my name in their mouth?" a man asked as he strode along the creek bank, trailed by two other men.

Cord took a good look at Rip Jordan. The man was only medium height, but he seemed taller than that because of his lean, wolfish build. He wore high-topped black boots, gray trousers with suspenders, a dark red shirt, and a tan hat cocked at a jaunty angle on his head. Coarse black hair stuck out from under the hat, and equally dark beard stubble covered his chin, cheeks, and lantern jaw.

The handle of a Colt revolver stuck up from Jordan's waistband where he had shoved it, butt forward so he could pull it with a crossdraw.

The two men with him were also roughly dressed, like all the men Cord had seen out here so far with the exception of Teddy Harville. Both were burlier than Jordan, but of the three, he gave off the most distinct air of menace. The other two weren't armed as far as Cord could see, but that wasn't the only reason Jordan seemed more menacing.

He just had the look of trouble in the cool way he regarded Spooner and Erskine.

Then his gaze drifted over to Cord and Glory. His eyes lingered on Glory, and they heated up as he studied her. The moment stretched out long enough that Cord started to get angry.

He was about to say something when Jordan hooked his thumbs in his waistband and drawled, "You two came in with that new bunch, didn't you?"

"That's right," Cord said.

Jordan nodded toward Glory. "Bring any more doves with you, or is this the only one?" He grinned as he addressed her directly. "If you don't have any help, little gal, you're gonna be mighty busy."

Annoyance and instinctive dislike exploded into the heat of anger inside Cord. But before he could say or do anything, Glory spoke up.

"I beg your pardon, sir. You're quite mistaken about the sort of woman I am."

"Oh, I am, am I?" Jordan's smile turned into a leer. "I reckon you can tell some things about a person just by looking at them."

"That's right," Glory snapped. "I can recognize a boor and a lout when I see one."

The grin remained in place on Jordan's face, but his eyes grew colder. Cord moved so that he was between Jordan and Glory and told the man, "I think you've said enough, mister. You insulted the lady, and you need to apologize."

From the corner of his eye, Cord saw the worried looks on the faces of Spooner and Erskine, but he ignored the little warning shake of the head that Spooner gave him. He was furious, and he wasn't going to back down.

"It's an apology you want, is it?" Jordan rasped. His right hand drifted closer to the butt of the gun in his waistband.

Cord could tell by the confident look in the man's eyes that Jordan must be fairly fast with that Colt. Cord could haul the Dragoon out of the holster on his hip, cock, and fire it without much delay, but he didn't possess any real speed. In a fight, Jordan would get off the first shot, Cord was pretty sure of that.

But it was too late to head off the trouble now. He tensed as Jordan went on, "I'm not in the habit of apologizing to whores —"

A footstep sounded behind Cord, followed by a familiar voice asking, "Some sort of trouble here, Cord?"

Cord glanced back just long enough to see that Flint, Steve, and Abraham Olmsted had come up behind him. Steve carried his rifle, while Olmsted held his shotgun.

Flint just stood there with his hands hanging loose at his sides and a look of anticipation, almost eagerness, on his face as he locked eyes with Rip Jordan.

The taut moment lasted only a couple of heartbeats before Jordan said, "No trouble. I was just saying that I'm not in the habit of apologizing to whores. But since I made a mistake here, I don't mind saying I'm sorry." Slowly, he lifted his left hand to the brim of his hat and went on, "I apologize, ma'am. I spoke out of turn, and I regret it."

"Very well," Glory said. "I accept your apology, sir." She put a hand on Cord's arm. "There's no need for anything further."

"I suppose not," he said, "as long as it doesn't happen again."

Jordan eyed him for a few seconds, then said, "Be seeing you." He jerked his head at the men with him. "Come on."

The three of them turned and walked off. Cord could tell by the stiffness of Jordan's back that the man was still angry, but he hadn't wanted to buck the odds against him and his friends.

Lew Spooner heaved an exaggerated sigh. "That could've been pretty bad," he said.

Flint said, "That fella's some sort of bad-man?"

"He's killed a couple of men in gunfights since he came here." Spooner shrugged. "Fair fights, according to witnesses, so nothing's been done about it. If the other fella draws a gun, Jordan's got a right to defend himself, I reckon."

"Even if Jordan goads them into it," Flint said with a note of distaste in his voice. "I've seen his sort before. Brave enough if the odds are on his side or if he knows he's facing a man who isn't as good as he is, but otherwise, he's low as a snake."

Erskine said, "He won't forget what just happened here. You fellas had better watch your backs. Jordan's liable to try to get even."

"Let him," Flint said. "I'm not scared of the likes of him."

Olmsted said, "Well, I come out here to look for gold, not to get in a fight with some varmint. So you just steer clear of him and his friends, Glory, as much as you can."

"That's what I intend to do, Pa," she said. "I don't want to have anything to do with Mr. Rip Jordan." She forced a smile onto her face. "Now, let's get these water buckets filled up. That's why we came over here in the first place."

CHAPTER 23

Olmsted invited the two friendly old-timers, Lew Spooner and Ham Erskine, to have supper with them that night.

"Since Ham and I have been here a while, and you folks just arrived, it ought to be us invitin' you to join us," Spooner said. "But that would go against one of my rules: never say no to good food and fellowship."

"We'll drop these water buckets off at our camp and be right along," Erskine added. "Don't reckon we'll have too much trouble findin' you. The place ain't that big."

"And Miss Glory's the prettiest young lady in these parts."

Glory laughed. "You only say that because you haven't met my sister yet. She's much prettier than I am."

"Reckon I find that hard to believe, ma'am," Erskine said solemnly.

As far as Cord was concerned, Glory was the prettier of the sisters, all right. He was sure Flint felt just the opposite. There was a lot of truth in that old saying about beauty being in the eye of the beholder.

The Olmsteds still had some supplies left, as did Cord and his brothers, so they hadn't stocked up during their brief stop in Rio Oro City. They could do that sometime in the next day or two. Cord knew the prices of everything would be sky high, as Teddy Harville had warned them.

Because of that, after they and the guests had eaten that evening, Cord asked Spooner and Erskine, "How's the hunting around here?"

"Huntin'?" Spooner repeated. "You mean for huntin' for gold?"

"He's talkin' about huntin' game," Erskine said. "Ain't that right, Mr. Bennett?"

"Call me Cord. And yes, that's what I meant."

Abraham Olmsted said, "Cord's just about the best hunter I ever did see. Got a shootin' eye with a rifle the likes o' which you don't run into very often."

"I don't know if I'd go so far as to say that . . ."

"Yeah, but you're modest, little brother," Flint said. "Cord's a crack shot with a rifle, all right. But I'm better with a handgun."

He tapped the holster in which his Colt

267

Dragoon rode.

"What am I good at, Flint?" Steve asked.

"Well, just look at you," Flint responded. "Any time somebody needs a wagon lifted so they can change a wheel or work on an axle, who do they come to? Or when they need to load heavy bags of supplies, who's always there to help?"

Steve grinned. "I'm strong as an ox, ain't I?"

"Pretty much," Flint assured him.

Erskine said, "To answer your question about huntin', Cord, there are plenty of deer up in the hills. Bears, too, from what I've heard, but you want to stay away from them. I've seen fellas bring in deer carcasses and butcher 'em. They sell or trade for the meat they can't use. Get a pretty penny for it, too."

"And even at that, it ain't near as expensive as the meat you can get at Higginbotham's store, when he's got any," Spooner said. "A good hunter could do all right for himself, just hirin' out to provide venison for the fellas here in the camp."

"Maybe so," Cord said, "but he wouldn't get rich doing that, would he? Not like if he made a strike on his claim."

Spooner chuckled. "No, gold would make a man richer than meat."

Flint reached over, slapped Cord on the shoulder, and said, "But if the gold mining doesn't work out, you could always give that a try instead."

Cord chuckled, but it was something to think about, all right. A man couldn't count on finding gold. It was always good to have a second plan . . .

The rest of the evening passed pleasantly. They learned more about Spooner and Erskine, who had been best friends most of their lives and had farmed adjacent pieces of property back in Pennsylvania.

Then sickness had claimed the wives of both men less than a year apart, and with their children grown, they had decided to set off on an adventure. The gold strikes in California provided a perfect excuse for that. They had sold their farms, outfitted themselves, and set off to search for a fortune.

"We haven't found it yet," Erskine said. "In fact, we ain't found hardly a speck of color."

"But that don't mean we're plannin' to give up," Spooner added. "That gold's out there somewhere just waitin' for us. I can feel it in my bones."

"I'm the same way," Steve told them. "I just know we're gonna get rich. Ain't that right, Flint?"

Flint nodded. "I'll say we are, boy. One way or another."

He tightened his arm around Kat's shoulders, and she smiled encouragingly at him.

Spooner and Erskine mentioned that their claim was actually close to half a mile up Rio Oro Canyon.

"You'll have to go farther than that for your claims," Spooner explained to the Bennetts and Olmsteds. "It ain't exactly convenient, but it could work out for you in the long run. That's how it is out here. The gold could be anywhere. You just can't tell until you start lookin'."

According to the two old-timers, the canyon narrowed down, as Cord had suspected, until there was only enough room to pan in the stream or swing a pick at the canyon wall. Eventually, the claims would stretch to the very end of the canyon, where it petered out at the spot where the creek emerged from a spring at the base of a cliff.

"A fella's allowed to claim two hundred yards of ground along the creek," Erskine said. "The creek front's what counts. It don't matter how deep the claim is."

"Per man or per family?" Flint asked.

"Per man. So you boys can claim six hundred yards, all together if you can find a stretch that big. You probably can, if you're willin' to go far enough up the canyon."

Glory said, "Then that means we can claim six hundred yards, too."

Spooner cleared his throat and looked a little embarrassed as he said, "Well, uh, no, Miss Glory. Your pa's the only one who can file a claim. Wives and daughters don't count when it comes to things like that."

"What?" Kat said. "That's not fair! Who made that law?"

"It ain't a law, exactly, I suppose, since there ain't a town council to make laws nor a marshal to enforce 'em. There's a county sheriff somewhere, I suppose, but we ain't never seen hide nor hair of him. He don't come out here, even when there's a killin'."

"A killin'?" Olmsted repeated. "Are a lot of killin's in these parts?"

Spooner and Erskine exchanged a look. Erskine said, "There have been some. A few fellas have been too reckless about showin' around pokes full of gold dust and wound up dead, either with their throats cut or knife wounds in their backs. Claims have been jumped. Freight wagons have been held up and robbed."

"Good Lord," Olmsted muttered. "What kind of Sodom and Gomorrah have we come to?"

271

"Tell 'em about the Reapers," Spooner urged Erskine. "They're gonna hear about 'em sooner or later, anyway."

"Yeah, I reckon." Erskine gazed around the campfire at the Bennetts and Olmsteds. "There's a gang that showed up a few weeks ago. They wear masks and call themselves the Reapers. They're behind a lot of the lawlessness. Nobody knows who they are, whether they're new to these parts or if they're fellas who've been here for a while and decided to band together to become outlaws. But you got to watch out for them. Always keep a gun handy when you go up the canyon to work your claim."

"I'm beginnin' to wonder if we ought to just turn around and go home," Abraham Olmsted declared.

"Pa, we can't do that, and you know it," Kat said. "There's nothing to go back to. We put everything we own into this journey."

Glory said, "Kat's right. We know how much it meant to you to come out here. If you're worried about us, don't be. We'll be fine. We're always careful."

Olmsted scratched at his beard and frowned. "I don't know . . . there was already almost trouble with that Jordan fella and his friends."

"What you should do is try to get a claim next to ours, Mr. Olmsted," Flint suggested. "That way, the boys and I can help you look out for the girls. If we're all together or at least close by, Jordan won't try anything. He doesn't have the guts."

"You seem mighty sure of that."

"He's seen me," Flint said. "He knows I'm not scared of him. He counts on that when he goes up against another man. Being afraid makes a man nervous, slows him down when he needs to move fast."

Cord said, "I agree with Flint about getting the claims together. That'll be the safest thing."

Olmsted sighed. "The gals are right; we can't hardly go back. California's gonna be our home from here on out, so we'd best make the most of it." He looked at Kat and Glory. "You girls be mighty careful. Don't go wanderin' off by yourselves."

"We'll be fine, Pa, you'll see," Kat assured him. Glory smiled and nodded.

Cord didn't say anything else, but what they had heard from Spooner and Erskine, along with the encounter with Jordan, worried him, too.

Kat went on, "I'm still not happy about Glory and me not being able to file claims of our own. If there's no law out here, who's going to stop us from doing it?"

"The men won't honor it," Erskine said. "In a place where there ain't any law, it all comes down to what men will put up with. They'd be polite about it, and nobody's gonna disrespect an honorable lady, but they won't go along with females ownin' claims. That's just the way it is."

"Well, we don't have to like it."

"No, ma'am, nobody said you did."

Spooner and Erskine took their leave a short time later, heading back to the tent they shared near the base of the ridge. The others started getting ready to turn in for the night.

Glory picked up one of the water buckets, which had been emptied during the evening for cooking and drinking, and said, "I think I'll go fill this now, so it won't have to be done first thing in the morning."

Cord was on his feet before she finished getting the words out of her mouth. He took the bucket from her and said, "You're not going anywhere. I'll fetch the water. You just stay here."

"That's not your job," she argued. "I'm perfectly capable of doing it."

"I know that —"

Kat said, "Oh, let him fetch the water, Glory. He's trying to be a gentleman. A lot

274

of men don't go to that much bother."

Glory hesitated for a moment longer, then shrugged in acceptance.

"All right, but don't think you have to make a habit of taking care of me, Cord Bennett."

"I won't," Cord promised . . . even though taking care of Glory from now on seemed like a fairly pleasant prospect.

Hard on the heels of that thought, however, came memories of Caroline Stockton and what he had overheard in her father's barn that day, back in the Ozarks. Cord didn't believe that Glory would ever be as two-faced as Caroline had been.

But how could he know that for sure? Maybe she just hadn't had the chance yet.

Forcing that reaction out of his mind, he hefted the empty bucket and said, "I'll be back in a few minutes."

He headed for the creek. Enough light from the moon and stars washed over the rugged landscape for him to make his way through the camp. Most of the tents and wagons were dark. Men who had toiled on gold claims all day were exhausted and turned in early. A candle burned here and there, and embers still glowed in some of the campfires.

Cord heard faint music and laughter drifting through the air from the settlement, but it was quiet enough here in the miners' camp that even if he hadn't been able to see where he was going, Cord could have followed the sound of swiftly flowing water to the stream. When he reached it, he went down on one knee and bent forward to dip the bucket into the water.

That was when somebody hit him from behind, and he toppled forward into the creek with a big splash.

CHAPTER 24

Cord's head went under. Since he was caught by surprise, he swallowed enough water that he was choking and sputtering as he forced his head above the surface.

A heavy weight landed on his back. He was struck on the head again, a glancing blow because he was thrashing around. A hand on his neck shoved him back under the water.

This time, even partially stunned, he had the presence of mind to drag some air into his lungs just before the creek closed over his head. That gave him a chance to reach down with his hands and knees and find the rocky streambed. He was lucky that it wasn't any deeper than it was.

With that for leverage, he bucked up as hard as he could and then rolled to the side. That threw the man who was trying to drown him off his back. Cord got his feet under him and surged upright.

The creek came to his knees. He had dropped the bucket when he was hit the first time, but he spotted it floating on the surface nearby and took a long step that allowed him to grab it by the bail.

Behind him, the man he had thrown off was floundering around in the water, but Cord knew the attacker would regain his feet quickly. He whirled around as the man did so. The man was snarling curses and lunging toward Cord just as the bucket came around, swinging at the end of Cord's outstretched arm.

It slammed into the side of the attacker's head with a resounding *thump.*

The blow knocked the man sideways into the water. Cord turned to struggle, dripping, onto the bank. He intended to leave the attacker where he was, even if he was out cold.

But that meant the man might drown, and Cord grimaced as he realized he couldn't just walk off and let that happen, even to somebody who had tried to hurt or kill him.

He had just turned back toward the creek when another shape hurtled out of the shadows, crashed into him, and drove him to the ground.

That knocked the breath out of Cord, and after what had just happened, he had none to spare. The world spun crazily around him, and red explosions burst through the blackness that threatened to swallow him whole. After a second, he realized those fiery explosions were inside his head, and he was about to pass out.

He knew that if he lost consciousness, the attackers might well beat him to death. Forcing his muscles to work, he drove his knee up and felt it sink into something soft. Whether the knee landed in a man's groin or belly, Cord didn't know, but either way, it did the trick. The weight on top of him went away.

He rolled again and wound up on his belly. Lifting his head, he gulped down breath and tried to regain his strength along with his reason. He shook his head in an effort to clear some of the cobwebs from his brain, but that just made the world do insane things again.

Determined not to just lie here until his enemies came after him again, he willed himself to hands and knees, then pushed to his feet. Where there were two people who wanted to kill him, there could be more. He looked around, searching for a new threat.

Some of the tents were close enough that the men sleeping inside them must have been disturbed by all the splashing around.

A man crawled out of his tent, stood up, and called, "Hey, what's going on over there?"

More splashing caught Cord's attention. He swung around and saw a man clambering out of the creek a few yards away. That had to be the one he'd clouted with the bucket, he thought. The shape broke into a stumbling run along the bank, headed away from the spot where Cord stood.

Cord let him go. He was too weary to continue the fight, as well as still half-stunned and out of breath. He heard hurried footsteps and squinted into the shadows, barely able to make out that a second fleeing man had joined the first.

Rip Jordan had had two men with him during that earlier confrontation, Cord recalled. Both of his attackers just now were too big to be Jordan, but there was no reason the man couldn't have sent them after Cord.

The man who had called out to Cord came closer. Cord saw that he carried some kind of long gun, either a rifle or a shotgun.

"What's all the commotion?" he demanded. "Are you all right, mister?"

Cord was about to answer when he heard a branch snap in some brush about thirty feet away. His time spent prowling the woods back in Arkansas came in handy at that moment. He noticed such things, and he realized instantly what the sound might mean.

"Get down!" he cried as he threw himself to the ground.

A shot blasted as he dived forward. He saw muzzle flame bloom like a crimson flower in the darkness that cloaked the brush. Cord didn't know where the bullet went, but he was pretty sure he wasn't hit.

The booming report that instantly followed the pistol shot told him that the man who'd been questioning him had a shotgun. He heard the buckshot whip through the brush and set the branches to rattling.

The echoes rolled away over the hills. No more shots sounded.

Cord thought he heard someone moving rapidly through the brush, getting away from there as fast as possible, but he wasn't sure about that.

More men were headed this way now, some with lanterns. Cord decided it was almost certain the ambusher had fled, rather than hanging around and risking capture.

He called, "Hold your fire," before he climbed to his feet. He didn't know how trigger-happy the shotgunner might be, and the man had fired only one of the weapon's barrels.

Several men from the camp gathered around Cord. Lantern-light washed over him. A man said, "You're one of the bunch that just came in today, aren't you?"

"That's right. A couple of men jumped me while I was about to get water from the creek. I think they had it in mind to drown me."

"Drown you! Why, that would've been murder."

"That's been known to happen around here," another man put in with a tone of wry amusement in his voice.

"Cord, where are you?" The loud, angry voice belonged to Flint. He shouldered through the men from the camp.

"Here, Flint."

Flint stepped up and clamped his hands on Cord's shoulders. "Are you all right, kid? Hell, you're soaked!"

"Could've been a lot worse," Cord told him. He repeated what he'd just told the other men about being attacked.

"Two men, you say? And a third one took a shot at you?" Flint's hand dropped to the butt of his Colt. "Jordan! It had to be. He sent his friends after you, and when you whipped them, he took a shot at you himself."

"You're talking about Rip Jordan?" a man asked. "I don't know. Jordan's a killer, nobody's going to deny that, but I don't know that he'd ambush a man like that."

"Believe me, he would," Flint said. "I've run into his type before. His pride was wounded when he had to back down earlier, and he had to get back at somebody because of it." Flint looked at Cord. "And you played right into his hands, little brother, by coming over here by yourself. From here on out, none of us had better wander off alone."

That sounded like a pretty good idea to Cord.

"Let's get you in some dry clothes," Flint went on.

"I brought one of the Olmsteds' buckets over here. I've got to find it before I go back."

A man held it out to him. "Here go you, son. I saw it floating at the edge of the creek and picked it up. Went ahead and got water in it, too."

"I'm obliged to you," Cord told the man.

"Your brother's right. You need to watch out for Rip Jordan. He's a bad'un, sure enough."

"If everybody knows that, why doesn't somebody do something about it?"

"What can we do?" another man asked. "There's no law here, and even if there was, Jordan's never gunned down a man who didn't draw first. He's got as much right to look for gold as anybody else."

Cord shrugged. He supposed the man was right, but even so, it rankled him that Jordan was walking around loose.

The crowd scattered as Cord and Flint began walking back toward the Olmsted wagon. Flint took the water bucket from his brother, but he carried it in his left hand, keeping the right free and close to the gun on his hip.

"That last fella was wrong," Flint mused.

"About what?"

"About Jordan being here to look for gold. A man like that's not going to do any hard work unless he has to. Jordan's after something else. I'm sure he wants to get his hands on a fortune . . . but he'd rather take it from somebody else than work for it himself."

"You mean he's an outlaw just pretending to be a gold-seeker?"

"That would be my guess. One thing we know for sure after tonight. He's a dangerous man, and he'll come after us again."

Glory came running to meet them when

284

they walked up. She threw her arms around Cord and hugged him, heedless of his sodden clothing.

"Here now, you'll get yourself all wet," Cord said as he put his hands on her shoulders and moved her back.

"I don't care about that. Are you all right?"

"I'm fine. A mite shaken up maybe, but not hurt."

"What happened?"

He explained about the attack. Steve, Kat, and Olmsted listened, too, and when Cord was finished, Olmsted said, "You reckon it was that fella Jordan from earlier today who was behind it?"

"There's no doubt about it," Flint said.

"Too bad that fella with the scattergun didn't put him down like the mad dog he seems to be."

"I could hear him running through the brush. He was moving too fast to be hurt very badly," Cord said.

"Worse luck for us," Flint said.

The next day would be a busy day — the first of many while they were here, no doubt — so after Cord assured everyone again that he was unhurt, Glory and Kat climbed into the wagon to sleep while their father spread his bedroll underneath the vehicle.

Cord changed into dry clothes and crawled into the tent he shared with Steve. Flint, as the oldest brother, had the other tent to himself since the death of their father.

Cord was a little restless as he tried to go to sleep. He had expected plenty of hard work once they reached the gold fields, but he hadn't anticipated running into trouble almost as soon as they got here. The continuing threat from Rip Jordan cast a cloud over their plans.

But if they found gold, it would all be worth it, he told himself.

He was a little stiff and sore the next morning, but considering how things could have turned out, he was happy it wasn't worse than that.

"We're gonna need supplies," Olmsted said at breakfast, "so I reckon the gals and me will head into the settlement. You boys can go on up the canyon and start lookin' for promisin' claims."

"That's a good idea," Flint said, "with one change. Steve and I will go up the canyon. Cord, you need to head into Rio Oro City and pick up a few things for us."

Cord nodded, thinking that he knew what Flint had in mind. He didn't want Olmsted and the girls venturing into the raw boom-town by themselves. Cord didn't, either, so he was happy to agree.

"Sure, I can do that."

Olmsted looked like he was going to argue, then decided against it. More than likely, he would be happy to have Cord along, too.

The previous evening during supper, Spooner and Erskine had told them where to find the man in charge of registering claims. He would take a look around while they were in the settlement, Cord decided, just to be sure they knew where the place was. With any luck, they would be needing the land clerk's services before very long.

Soon after breakfast, Flint and Steve set off for the canyon. Cord saddled his horse to ride into Rio Oro City with the Olm-steds.

At this hour of the morning, the settle-ment was considerably calmer than it had been late in the afternoon the day before and then on into the evening. Not nearly as many men were moving on the boardwalks laid out along the edges of the muddy street.

Customers were coming and going at Teddy Harville's Golden Nugget Saloon, though, and as they passed the place, Cord noticed something he hadn't paid any attention to the day before.

There was another saloon almost directly across the street from the Golden Nugget. It was housed in a large tent with a flagpole in front of it. A colorful flag flapped on the pole in the morning breeze. The flag's field was mostly white, with a red stripe along the bottom, and above it, the figure of a bear on all four legs.

Cord vaguely remembered reading something about Californians flying a bear flag while they were trying to win their independence from Mexico several years earlier. Some folks even called that clash the Bear Flag Revolt.

Words had been painted on the tent's canvas wall next to the entrance: WHISKEY — GAMBLING — WOMEN.

You couldn't get much more straightforward than that, Cord thought with a smile. The Bear Flag Saloon — he was going to think of it that way, whether that was actually the name of the place or not — was also doing a pretty brisk business for this time of day.

Then a man pushed through the entrance flaps and stopped on the boardwalk, feet planted solidly and thumbs hooked in the pockets of the vest he wore under a dark brown suit. Sunlight glittered on the stickpin in his cravat. He had a cigar clenched between his teeth at a jaunty angle.

Cord took him for an older man at first, because his hair was white, but then he realized that the face under that hair was the relatively unlined visage of a man in his thirties. He didn't appear to have spent a great deal of time outdoors in his life.

The man met Cord's gaze and nodded as he returned the frank appraisal. Then his eyes turned toward the wagon, and Cord saw him take a deep breath.

That meant the man had seen Glory and Kat. They had that effect on fellows.

This one reached up with his left hand, took the cigar out of his mouth, and raised his right hand to sketch a leisurely salute to them. He smiled. The expression held the same sort of semi-mocking attitude as the gesture.

"I wonder who that is," Kat said from the driver's seat, where she rode next to her father.

"I reckon we'll probably find out," Cord said.

For some reason, the prospect didn't fill him with any pleasure.

CHAPTER 25

Higginbotham's store was housed in a big tent, too, but walls were going up on an empty lot next to it, and a sign painted on a board nailed to a post in front read FUTURE HOME — HIGGINBOTHAM'S EMPORIUM.

Abraham Olmsted parked the wagon in front of the tent. Since there were no hitch rails in Rio Oro City, Cord dismounted and tied his horse's reins to one of the wagon wheels. The muddy street sucked at his boots, but thankfully, he had to take only a few steps before reaching the boardwalk.

Glory and Kat waited on the driver's seat. Cord held out his hands toward them and said, "No need for you ladies to get your feet muddy. I can swing you over to the walk, one at a time."

"Oh, pshaw," Kat said. "I don't need any help. Just move over a little."

Frowning, Cord did so. Kat stood up, lifted her skirt, and jumped from the driver's seat to the boardwalk. She made the leap easily enough but stumbled a little on landing. Cord was there to grasp her upper arm and steady her.

"Thanks," she said, "but I would have been all right."

"I know that," Cord said. She had a stubborn, independent streak a mile wide, and he knew better than to argue with her about something like that.

"Well, I'll be happy to accept all the help I can get," Glory said from the wagon box. She could be stubborn and independent, too, but that tendency was tempered by practicalness.

Cord stood at the edge of the boardwalk, reached out as Glory leaned toward him, and caught hold of her under the arms. He lifted and swung and set her on the planks.

"Thank you," she said. "That was very chivalrous of you. You're like Sir Walter Raleigh, Cord."

He shook his head. "Don't reckon I know the fella."

Glory laughed and explained, "He was some old English nobleman. There's a legend about him taking off his coat and putting it on the ground so a lady wouldn't have to walk in a mud puddle."

"Why didn't she just go around?" Cord

asked with a puzzled frown.

Glory laughed and shook her head. "That's a good question. I don't know."

"Seems like the sensible thing to do."

Cord knew what Flint would say if he were here. Flint would make fun of him for always thinking about the sensible thing. But Cord couldn't help the way he was.

The four of them went into the tent. There was a puncheon floor inside, with shelves and barrels and crates and stacks of merchandise, from clothes to mining implements to food. Just about everything anybody would need for life in the gold fields.

But no luxuries, Cord noted. The prices for everything were so high that no one would be able to afford anything except the necessities.

Half a dozen customers were inside the mercantile, all of them male. A man wearing a canvas apron approached Cord and the Olmsteds. He was heavyset, with a jowly, bulldog-like face and thin, rusty hair that had started going gray.

"Howdy, folks," he greeted them. "New to Rio Oro City, ain't you?"

"That's right," Olmsted replied. "Just came in yesterday afternoon."

"And now you're here to stock up on everything you need. I'll be mighty happy to help you. My name's Orvie Higgin-botham."

"This is your place, then."

"You saw my name on the sign outside, didn't you? What can I get for you?"

Olmsted looked over at his daughters. "Girls?"

"We have a list," Glory said. She reached into the pocket of her dress and took out a folded piece of paper. "I wrote it all down."

Higginbotham looked a little surprised as he took the list from her, and Cord knew why. Most females weren't well-educated, especially if they didn't come from wealthy families. But Glory and Kat could both read and write and even do some ciphering. And they had learned most of it on their own, according to what Glory had told him. Their accomplishments were a tribute to their intelligence and persistence.

Higginbotham grunted and set about fill-ing the order on the list. Glory and Kat strolled around the store, browsing to see if they spotted anything else they needed.

Cord stood where he could see not only the entrance but also the other customers in the mercantile. Olmsted sidled up beside him and said, "Keepin' an eye out for trouble, ain't you?"

"That's why Flint suggested I come

along." Cord kept his voice as quiet as Olmsted had.

The old-timer nodded. "I figured as much. And you'll notice I didn't argue none, neither. I always knew life'd be hard and risky in the gold fields once we got here, but like I said before, I didn't expect to run into trouble so soon."

"Well, I don't see any signs of problems in here." All the customers were miners, Cord had decided, and none of them appeared threatening. The men looked at Glory and Kat with great interest — no man with eyes in his head could fail to be interested in them, Cord thought — but they didn't stare disrespectfully.

Movement at the store's entrance caught Cord's eye. The flaps were tied back to keep them out of the way, and a man had just strolled through the opening.

Cord recognized him as the gent he'd seen outside the Bear Flag Saloon a short time earlier. The man wore a brown beaver hat on his white hair now. The hat was a shade darker than the suit he wore. He didn't have a cigar clenched between his teeth anymore.

Cord could tell that his impression from earlier was correct. White hair or not, this man was relatively young. His jaw reflected strength, and his eyes, a surprisingly bright shade of blue, were deep-set and keen.

The man glanced around the store, then headed straight for Glory and Kat. Cord tensed and moved closer to them.

The white-haired man reached them first. He took off his hat, held it in front of him in his left hand, and smiled.

"Ladies," he said, "I'm sure I'm not the first to welcome you to our little community, but allow me to add my greetings. Just having your presence here in Rio Oro City improves the settlement immensely."

Kat looked him up and down and returned the smile. "Well, you're certainly the silver-tongued devil, aren't you?"

"Everywhere that has angels — and I'm looking at two of them right now — ought to have at least one devil, as well, shouldn't it? Just to balance things out, so to speak. My name is Patrick Elam, by the way."

"I'm Kat Olmsted. This is my sister, Glory."

"And I'm Cord Bennett," Cord said as he stepped past the girls and held out his hand.

A flicker of annoyance passed through Elam's eyes but was gone in an instant. He smiled at Cord and clasped his hand in a firm grip.

"Bennett, eh?" he said. "I took you at first for a protective older brother."

"Just a good friend of the ladies."

"Welcome to you as well, Bennett. And thank you for bringing these two with you."

"He didn't bring us," Kat said. "We just traveled out here to California together with some other folks."

"We came with our father," Glory added.

"I look forward to meeting him," Elam said.

Olmsted had come up behind Cord. He stepped around the younger man and said, "Well, then, you can do that right now, mister. Abraham Olmsted's my name."

Elam shook hands with Olmsted and said, "It's a pleasure, sir. You must be proud to have two such fine daughters."

"Oh, I'm right proud of 'em, all right." Olmsted changed the subject by asking, "What is it you do around here, Mr. Elam? You have a claim up the canyon where you hunt for gold?"

Elam chuckled and said, "No, I'm afraid I'm not cut out for swirling a pan or swinging a pick."

Cord could have answered that part of Olmsted's question just by looking at Elam. Clearly, the man spent most of his time indoors, and his hands lacked any calluses that would have come from hard physical labor.

Cord told himself not to be judgmental because of that, but it was hard not to, when he had worked hard all his life.

"I own one of the saloons here in town," Elam went on.

"The Bear Flag Saloon," Cord said.

Elam looked at him with new interest. "How did you know it's called that? We don't have a sign up yet."

"No, but you've got the bear flag flying out front. When I saw it, that's how I thought of the place. Are you saying that's actually the name?"

"That's right. You're very astute, Mr. Bennett."

"Call me Cord." Even though he didn't particularly like Patrick Elam, he didn't see any reason not to act friendly. That was the way he'd been brought up, after all. Verne Bennett had been the sort of man who never met a stranger.

"All right, Cord. You're welcome in the Bear Flag any time. First drink is on the house. The same offer applies to you as well, Mr. Olmsted."

"Ain't much of a drinkin' man," Olmsted said, "but I'll stop by and say howdy now and then, just to be sociable."

"Same goes for me," Cord said with a nod.

Smiling, Kat said, "You're not going to offer my sister and me a drink on the house, Mr. Elam?"

"You hush up," Olmsted said. "That wouldn't hardly be proper. Young girls don't go drinkin' in saloons." He glanced at Elam. "No offense intended."

"None taken," Elam said, as a grin stretched across his face. "Ladies, your father is absolutely correct. I intend to make the Bear Flag as nice a place as I can, under the circumstances, but it'll still be a saloon and no place for young ladies of such obvious refinement."

Kat arched an eyebrow. "You might be surprised." She saw her father about to react to that and added, "Oh, hush, Pa. I'm just joshing."

Olmsted muttered and grumbled but didn't say anything else Cord could make out.

Elam put on his hat, tipped it at a sporty angle, and said, "Now that I've introduced myself and welcomed you to Rio Oro City, I suppose I should get back to my business."

"Are you the official welcoming committee?" Cord asked. "Mr. Harville said yesterday that he's the mayor."

Elam continued to smile, but an icy glitter appeared in his eyes. "Teddy Harville can

298

say whatever he wants. That doesn't make it true, though."

Olmsted said, "One fella claimed there was never an election."

"That's right. Teddy just declared himself the mayor. Nobody else wants the job, especially since it's just a made-up one, without any power. Let him devote his time and effort to anything he wants. I'm more concerned with making my business a success."

"I'm sure you will," Cord said.

Elam touched a finger to his hat brim, said, "Ladies," and left the store.

"Funny-lookin' hombre with that white hair," Olmsted said. He raked his fingers through his beard. "I've earned mine, but he ain't hardly old enough to have it."

"I think his appearance is very striking," Kat said.

Glory shook her head. "I don't know. He seemed a little too smooth to me."

Kat didn't say anything to that, but it was obvious that Patrick Elam had impressed her.

He had made an impression on Cord, too, but not necessarily a good one.

The girls went back to looking around the store. Cord and Olmsted strolled to the entrance and looked out on Rio Oro City's single street, which was getting busier as the morning went on.

"What did you think of that fella, Cord?" Olmsted asked quietly.

Cord answered honestly. "I didn't like him much. Something about him rubbed me the wrong way."

"Yeah, I felt the same way." Olmsted paused, then added, "Kat seemed a mite taken with him, though."

"Yeah, I noticed that," Cord said. He hoped his brother Flint never had cause to notice the same thing.

Because that was bound to lead to more trouble.

CHAPTER 26

While Cord went to town with the Olmsteds, Flint and Steve headed up the canyon to look for a promising stretch of ground they could claim.

They went on foot, since Spooner and Erskine had advised them it was considered rude to ride across another man's claim. They'd been warned not to pick up any rocks without permission, too, since doing so could get a fella shot for attempted claim jumping.

Some of the prospectors had thrown up shacks hastily assembled of rough-hewn boards, tar paper, and tin, but most had pitched tents or stretched canvas between tree branches to provide primitive shelters.

The gold-seekers had devoted more time to the task of looking for the precious metal. Flint and Steve saw a lot of men standing or kneeling in the creek, dipping up water, sand, and gravel from the streambed in big, flat pans and swirling the water around in the hope of washing the lighter stuff away and leaving the heavier gold behind.

On several claims, they passed long flumes made from hollowed-out and halved logs. Those flumes were supported on posts so that one end was higher than the other. Men carried buckets of water, sand, and gravel to the higher end and dumped them so that the mixture ran back down toward the creek.

"What in blazes are those things?" Steve asked as he gestured toward one of the contraptions.

"They call 'em sluices," Flint said. "I read up on them. The fellas who use them carve little ridges on the bottom, so that any gold in the water sinks and gets caught on them as the whole mess flows back down to the creek."

"And it actually works?" Steve sounded dubious.

Flint shrugged. "Seems to. I don't think fellas would keep building and using them if they didn't. Cord and I have talked about building one, but it'll all depend on what sort of claim we have. There might not be room."

"You mean we might have to stand in the creek like those other fellas?"

"Yeah, we sure might."

Steve shook his head. "Sounds like a lot of hard work, stoopin' over and fillin' a pan with water that way."

"I suppose it's worth the effort if you find enough gold."

"We'd better, after comin' all this way out here."

Flint laughed and said, "I told you we'd get rich one way or another, didn't I?"

"Yeah, you did."

"I keep my promises."

The ringing impacts of pickaxes striking rock echoed back and forth between the walls of Rio Oro Canyon. As the Bennett brothers passed, Flint looked at the men swinging those pickaxes, many of them shirtless and streaming with sweat, even though the hour was relatively early and the air hadn't warmed up much yet.

When it did, such hard labor down here in this canyon would be well-nigh unbearable, Flint thought. Panning for gold or using a sluice struck him as better methods, although they had their drawbacks, too.

Flint found himself wondering what other ways a man could make money in a place like this, without actually searching for gold.

They were on the south bank of the creek. The steep canyon wall closed in on that side

303

until only about fifty feet separated it from the stream. The bank on the north side was wider, but not by much.

Most of the men working the claims had ignored them as they walked along, other than watching them warily. A few had nodded curtly. Flint had noticed that many of the gold-seekers wore holstered revolvers or had rifles or shotguns within easy reach. They were all willing to fight for what they considered theirs, even if they hadn't found a speck of color yet.

Flint understood that. He'd always felt the same way.

As they rounded a bend half a mile upstream, though, he heard a friendly voice hailing them.

"Howdy, Bennetts," Lou Spooner said as he straightened from the spot where he'd been hunkered down in the shallow water at the edge of the creek. He had a gold pan in his hands.

"Where's the rest of your bunch?" Spooner went on.

"Gone to the settlement for supplies," Flint said. "They sent us up here to take a look around and stake claims, if we can find some good ones."

"Hope you find somethin' better than we did," Ham Erskine said as he walked up carrying a pickax. His shirt was dark with sweat. Beads of it covered his face. He took off his hat and sleeved away some of the moisture.

"Not havin' any luck?" Steve asked.

"Not so far," Spooner replied. "But it's only a matter of time, ain't that right, Ham?"

Erskine just grunted, as if it was fine with him that his partner wanted to be optimistic, but he couldn't bring himself to give voice to such hopes anymore.

"How much farther up the canyon will we have to go to find some unclaimed land?" Flint asked.

Spooner rubbed his beard-stubbled jaw and frowned. "About a quarter of a mile, I'd say. Upwards from here, the claims start gettin' spread out more. You want some together, I recollect you sayin', and maybe one for the Olmsteds next to you."

"That'd be best," Flint said.

Steve spoke up, saying, "I've been thinkin' about something."

Flint looked at his brother in surprise. He resisted the impulse to tell Steve to leave the thinking to him. Figuring things out wasn't Steve's strong suit, but every so often, he was able to cut to the heart of a matter with his simplicity.

"Go ahead," Flint told him.

"Well . . . it seems to me the best claims would be higher upstream — the closer to where the creek starts, the better. That way, you could get all the gold before it floats on downstream."

Erskine said, "That makes sense, son, but it ain't necessarily the way things work. It all depends on where the gold is located underground, and how it gets exposed by the elements, and how it gets into the creek. You see, it takes a long, long time for all that to happen, and there ain't no way of tellin' what went on durin' all those centuries."

Steve frowned. "I think I follow what you're sayin'."

Spooner added, "And the fellas who dig in the ground, like Ham here, well, they can find color anywhere. There's no real rhyme nor reason to it, at least none that we can grasp."

"So what you're sayin' is . . . the whole thing comes down to luck."

Spooner laughed out loud, and even the dour Erskine smiled a little.

Flint clapped a hand on Steve's shoulder and said, "It's like everything else in life, boy, you need a little luck to go with your hard work. Come on, let's go see if we can find a good place for us to try our luck."

Flint and Steve didn't get back to camp until late that afternoon. Cord had started to worry a little about them and was thinking about venturing up the canyon to look for them, but then they strolled up to the Olmsted wagon with grins on their faces.

"Well, you two look like you found canaries to swallow," Cord told them.

"Why in the world would we want to eat canaries?" Steve asked.

"Never mind, Steve," Flint said. He looked at Cord and the Olmsteds, who had come to join them. "We found a good place and staked claims for all of us. Four claims, three-quarters of a mile up the canyon, at a spot where it widens out a little, so there'll be room to build one of those sluices we talked about, Cord, if we decide we want to. The claims are marked with little cairns of rock, the way everybody else does, and I've got all the landmarks in my head so I can describe the site to the land clerk in the settlement."

He tapped the side of his head to indicate where the information was stored.

"There won't be any doubt where they are, once the claims are registered," Flint concluded.

Kat said, "You just marked one claim for us?"

"That's what Spooner and Erskine said would be allowed."

"It's still not fair. I've got a good mind to go and talk to that clerk myself."

Olmsted said, "Now, girl, we don't want to go raisin' a ruckus right away and gettin' on the wrong side of folks to start with. Sometimes you just got to do the accustomed thing."

Kat snorted in disgust to show what she thought of that.

Flint said, "As far as I'm concerned, you can have your pick of the four claims. It doesn't really matter."

"You say that now," Glory said, "but what if we made a big strike on our claim and you didn't find anything?"

Flint grinned. "Then I'd be happy for you."

He probably meant it, too, Cord thought. Flint seemed genuinely fond of Kat. Of course, he hadn't seen the way she was smiling at Patrick Elam in the settlement this morning.

"Had we better go register those claims, now that you've marked them?" Cord asked.

"Can't it wait until morning?" Kat said.

Flint shook his head. "No, Cord's right. It

would be a good idea to go ahead and get them on record while we can, just to make sure nobody tries to jump them."

"You really think that might happen?" Glory asked.

Flint grunted. "I wouldn't put much of anything past some of the varmints around here."

Cord agreed with that. He said, "Why don't you and I go to the land clerk's office, Flint? Steve can stay here with Mr. Olmsted and the girls."

Kat said, "Oh, no, you don't. We're going, too, aren't we, Glory?"

The redhead hesitated, then said, "I'm not sure I want to try to navigate that muddy street. It seems to me like Cord and Flint can handle things for us."

"I'm willin' to go along with that," Olmsted said. "You record whichever o' them claims you want to in my name, son. It'll be fine."

"Well, I'm coming along," Kat insisted. "Somebody's got to watch out for the best interests of this family."

Flint shrugged and said, "That's all right with me."

"It's settled, then," Kat declared as she linked arms with him. "Let's go stake our claim to a fortune."

Chapter 27

When Cord, Flint, and Kat reached the settlement, the main street of Rio Oro City was much busier than it had been that morning. Men on horseback rode up and down the street as wagons rolled through the mud. There were even quite a few pedestrians slogging along. The thick brown muck sucked at their boots with every step, but that didn't stop them from going on about their business.

A lot of that business involved the two large saloons. The Golden Nugget and the Bear Flag both had plenty of customers headed into them. However, not many came out. After a hard day of working their claims, the gold-seekers were ready to do some serious drinking, gambling, and carousing.

Higginbotham's was also doing a brisk business, Cord noted, despite the high prices. The visit to the store to stock up on supplies earlier in the day had eaten up a big chunk of the Bennett brothers' remaining funds.

They would have to find gold pretty quickly in order to afford to continue, Cord thought, or else their dream might come to an end before it ever got started properly.

Flint pointed to a building a few yards past Higginbotham's and asked, "That's where we're going, isn't it?"

The structure was framed in, but it had canvas tacked up in place of walls and roof. It seemed to Cord that there was a lot of construction going on in Rio Oro City, more than there were available carpenters. So to accommodate everybody, they would get a building partially finished, then move on to the next one and circle back to finish up later.

A wide board had been nailed between two posts in front of the canvas-walled building. On it was painted RIO ORO CITY LAND OFFICE AND ASSAYER. In smaller letters below that was CLYDE CASTERLINE, PROP.

"That would be it," Cord agreed.

"Who is this Casterline fellow?" Kat asked. "What authority does he have?"

"I don't know, but we can ask him," Flint replied. "Anybody can set themselves up as an assayer, but if he's the land clerk around here, too, he's got to be working for the state or the county."

They went inside and found that a counter ran from one wall of the building to the other. A gate opened into the area behind the counter that actually took up most of the room. A couple of large tables were back there, along with a paper-littered desk and a pair of filing cabinets. Maps were unrolled and spread out on the tables, their corners held down by chunks of rock.

A man sat at the desk, glaring at several pieces of paper he held in his hand. With an exasperated sigh, he shook his head, tossed the papers back onto the desk, and looked up at the three people who had just come in.

"Something I can do for you folks?" he asked. He was very thin, with dark, wavy hair and muttonchop whiskers. Cord could tell by looking at him that he was the nervous type, but his eyes seemed intelligent.

"You're the land clerk hereabouts, correct?" Flint asked.

The man hooked his thumbs in his vest and nodded. He smiled smugly and sounded mighty proud of himself as he said, "Duly appointed and employed by the State of California to register and locate land claims."

"Well, that answers the next question I was going to ask," Flint said with a smile. "We need to register some claims, but it all needs to be done official-like, so they'll stand up if anybody questions them."

"Nobody's ever questioned any claim I've recorded," the man said. "If they did, it wouldn't work. I don't stand for any foolishness when it comes to land." He came to his feet. "Whereabouts are these pieces of ground? One of you can come back here and show me on the map, but I'll need the other two to stay on that side of the counter."

"I'd better do it," Flint said, "since I'm the one who knows right where they are."

Cord waved a hand for his brother to proceed. He was more than happy to let Flint handle the details of this.

Flint opened the gate in the counter and joined Casterline at one of the tables. Casterline tapped the map in front of them with a bony forefinger and went on, "This covers the upper reaches of the canyon, so I assume that's where your claim will be located. Unless you bought an established claim closer to the mouth of the canyon . . . ?"

"No, it's about three quarters of a mile up in there," Flint said. He leaned over to study the map. After a minute or so, he pointed to a spot. "That's the stretch right there, going by the landmarks that are here on the map. We're claiming four sections along the creek, one each for my brothers and myself and one for this young lady's father."

"Where is the gentleman in question?"

Kat said, "He stayed back at our camp, but he sent me to represent him."

Casterline shook his head. "Afraid I can't do that, young lady. Claims have to be filed in person."

"But I'm here in person."

"And you're a female," Casterline pointed out in a condescending manner. "Females are not allowed to own property or make legal claims."

"Well, that's just —"

"That's the rule," Casterline broke in. "And rules are rules, young lady. Why, without some way to regulate human behavior, our society would soon fall into anarchy —"

"No need for a sermon," Flint broke in. "Can you register these three sections for me and my brothers?"

"Why, certainly. Let me get my book."

For the next few minutes, Casterline dutifully recorded the registration of the three sections, writing down the names of the Bennett brothers in his book and neatly printing beside them a bunch of numbers and letters that Cord supposed denoted locations on the map.

When Casterline was finished with that, Flint asked, "So these sections are now legally claimed by my brothers and myself?"

"That is correct."

"My brother Steve's not here. You said they had to be claimed in person."

"I'll accept you acting as your brother's representative, seeing as how you and he are members of the same immediate family."

Flint pointed to Kat. "But a parent and child aren't members of the same immediate family?"

"It's different. I told you, this young lady is a female —"

Flint held up a hand to stop him. "Never mind. I'm not going to argue with you."

"Well, I might," Kat declared. She stepped forward with her hands clenched into fists at her side, but Flint held up a hand to stop her from advancing on the land clerk.

"Once a fellow's registered a claim, he can sell it, though, right?" Flint went on.

"Certainly."

Flint pointed to one of the spots on the map, the one closest to the mouth of the canyon. "Then I'm selling my claim to Abraham Olmsted, and I *do* accept his daughter acting as his representative."

Casterline frowned. "That's somewhat irregular —"

"But not against the rules, is it? I mean, you said this is my claim, and I can sell it if I want to."

"Well, yes, but —"

"Kat, do you have a coin in your pocket?" Flint asked.

She shook her head. "No, I don't."

Chuckling, Cord said, "I'll loan you a silver dollar. I know you're good for it."

He handed the coin to Kat, who then tossed it to Flint. He caught it deftly.

"There," he said to Casterline. "Money has changed hands, and I'm satisfied with the deal. Are you satisfied, Miss Olmsted?"

"I am," Kat said, smiling. With a twinkle in her eyes, she added, "We can even draw up a bill of sale later, just to make sure everything's legal."

"So, Mr. Casterline, you do whatever you need to do in order to put that claim in Mr. Olmsted's name, and then register this one" — Flint tapped the map to indicate the piece of ground just above the other two —

"in my name."

Casterline glared and muttered, "This is irregular. *Highly* irregular!"

"But legal enough, from the sound of what you said earlier."

Casterline sighed. "Very well." He sniffed and added, "You may think you've out-smarted me this time, young man, but there may come a time when things will be differ-ent."

"I just think it's better not to worry about a bunch of unnecessary rules."

"Rules are necessary —"

"Yeah, I know. Without them, chaos."

Casterline had a point about that, Cord thought, although it was possible to be too much of a stickler for rules and regulations. Common sense had to factor in there somewhere, and in this case, Cord thought it was only common sense to allow Kat to register the claim in her father's name. Flint shouldn't have had to take such a round-about way of doing that.

But it was done, and a few minutes later, when the three of them left the land office, Kat took with her a document signed by Casterline making her father's ownership of the claim legal. Cord and Flint had their papers, as well, and Flint had the one for Steve.

As they walked along the street in the gathering dusk, Kat pointed at the Bear Flag Saloon and said, "Why don't we stop in there? Mr. Elam invited us, remember, Cord?"

"I don't think your father would want you visiting a saloon," Cord said.

"But he told Mr. Elam he'd drop by to say hello sometime."

"That was your father saying that. I don't believe you and your sister were included in that intention."

"Well, he's not here to say one way or the other, is he?"

With that, Kat turned and headed toward the Bear Flag Saloon, moving quickly along the boardwalk.

Flint grinned and said, "If you haven't figured it out by now, kid, you're just wasting your time arguing with a woman. Once her mind's made up, she's going to do whatever she wants."

"Even if it's liable to get her in trouble?"

"It's a man's job to go along and make sure the trouble doesn't get too bad."

That made sense — sort of — in a cynical way, Cord thought. He said, "We'd better go after her, then."

"Yeah, I suppose." Flint added, "I'd kind of like to meet this Elam fella for myself, after hearing Kat talk about him. She seemed pretty impressed."

Cord sensed a chink in his brother's devil-may-care armor. Flint might be just a little bit jealous of Kat's reaction to Patrick Elam.

They walked through the tied-back canvas flaps into the big tent and had to step up slightly to do so, because the floor was made from rough-hewn planks laid across beams to raise it several inches. Mismatched tables and chairs were scattered haphazardly throughout the center of the room. There were bars made from planks and whiskey barrels along both side walls to accommodate the large number of drinkers.

Toward the rear of the room was an honest-to-goodness piano, its wooden surfaces polished and gleaming. Cord wondered where it had come from, how they'd gotten it in here, and how they kept it looking so good.

It sounded good, too, as a man in a black swallowtail coat played a sprightly tune, his fingers flashing over the keys with practiced ease and speed.

Half a dozen young women in skirts short enough to show off their dimpled knees and muscular calves danced to that music in the open area. Cord didn't think any of them were particularly attractive, but that opinion didn't seem to be shared by the miners sitting at the tables closest to the dancing girls. They hooted and hollered encouragement to the dancers, in between guzzling beer and whiskey.

Kat had stopped to stare at the women, allowing Cord and Flint to catch up to her. She glanced back over her shoulder at them, grinned, and said, "Do you think I could get a job here?"

"Doing that?" Flint said. "You'd be wasted here, Kat. You're twice as pretty as any of those heifers."

A new voice said over the music, "I agree with you, my friend. Miss Olmsted is meant for much finer things than tromping around and being leered at in some mining camp saloon."

Cord looked over and saw that Patrick Elam had come up to them. The man moved quietly, although there was enough racket in here, Elam probably could have stomped his feet and they wouldn't have noticed.

Elam went on, "You must be Flint Bennett. I see the resemblance between you and your brother."

"That's right." Flint's eyes narrowed. "You're Elam?"

The saloonkeeper put out his hand. "Patrick Elam. It's a pleasure to meet you."

Elam had changed to a different suit since earlier in the day. This one was a light brown and looked as elegant as the other suit. The stickpin in his cravat glittered. Cord wondered if that was a real gemstone of some sort, or just colored glass. He didn't know much about such things.

Flint shook hands with Elam, who went on, "If you gentlemen care to step over to the bar, the first drink is on the house." He held up a hand. "Wait. I have a better idea. Why don't the two of you, and the lady, of course, join me at my private table?"

"That sounds exciting," Kat replied before Cord or Flint could say anything. "Thank you, Mr. Elam."

Holding out his hand, Elam ushered them to a round table set in an alcove at one of the saloon's rear corners. The fact that the walls around them were canvas instead of wood made it seem a little less private, but it was still quieter than the rest of the saloon.

On the way, Elam had signaled to one of the bartenders on that side of the room. A minute later, the man brought over a tray containing three glasses and a china cup.

"I had him bring tea for you, Miss Olmsted," Elam explained as the bartender set out the drinks. "I don't want to inflict our whiskey on you. It's rather raw, even the highest quality we have. Now, if I'd had a decent sherry or port on hand . . ."

"Cord would probably rather have the tea," Kat said as she pushed the cup over in front of him and pulled back the glass of whiskey. "He's not much of a drinker." She lifted the glass and smiled. "What's the saying? Bottoms up?"

"Are you sure about this, Kat?" Flint asked.

She regarded him coolly and said, "I never do anything I'm not sure about."

Flint shrugged and lifted his own glass. "Then let's just say good fortune to us all."

"I'll drink to that," Elam said.

And they would have, except at that moment, a loud, angry shout came from one of the men in the saloon, and a table went over with a crash.

CHAPTER 28

A poker game had been going on at the overturned table. The man who had leaped across the table and upset it had sent everything flying — cards, coins, paper money, glasses of beer and whiskey.

The other men at the table tried to get out of the way so hastily that one of them knocked his chair over, stumbled on it, and went crashing down to the floor, too.

The object of the attack was driven backward in his chair. When he landed, the man who had jumped across the table was on top of him, trying to lock hands around his throat. The attacker bellowed curses as he attempted to get his choke hold.

Before he could accomplish that violent goal, a man who must have been a friend of the one being attacked grabbed the aggressor by the back of his coat and hauled him off the man on the floor. The rescuer turned and practically flung the attacker away from him.

Unable to control that wild plunge, the man flew right at Kat Olmsted as she sat at Patrick Elam's private table.

Cord came out of his chair in a blur of motion to intercept the man. He lowered his shoulder so that it rammed into the man's stomach. The out-of-control momentum folded the man double over Cord's back.

Cord wrapped both arms around the man's thighs. He could have put that momentum to work and heaved the man up and over, but that would have resulted in him crashing down on his back in the middle of Elam's table.

Not wanting that, Cord set his feet and, with a grunt of effort, lifted the man and then toppled him backward. The man still landed hard on his back, but it was on the sawdust-littered floor, not where he could hurt somebody else.

Flint was on his feet, too, but he headed for the spot where the ruckus had broken out and demanded of the first man's rescuer, "What the hell do you think you're doing? You could've hurt that lady, throwing people around like that!"

The man was several inches taller than Flint but probably weighed about the same.

Muscles bulged the sleeves and shoulders of his flannel shirt. He had a bullet-shaped head and an angular jaw.

With a sneer, he told Flint, "Stay out of this, mister. It ain't any of your business."

"I'm making it my business," Flint said as he thrust his chin out belligerently.

Cord straightened from throwing the other man down in time to see the blow that smashed into Flint's chin and knocked him backward.

"Hey!" Cord yelled. "You can't do that to my brother!"

A split second later, his hurriedly thrown punch wiped the sneer off the man's face. Cord put all his weight behind the blow, and while it staggered the man and drove him back a step, it didn't knock him off his feet.

It didn't hold him back for long, either. He charged at Cord, slugging with both fists.

Cord had to retreat as he tried desperately to block that flurry of punches. Flint, who had gone to one knee as a result of the blow that had landed on his chin, recovered with a quick shake of his head and launched himself forward in a diving tackle that caught the man around the knees. With a wild yell, he went down.

Cord was ready to charge in and give his brother a hand, but before he could do that, somebody leaped on him from behind, wrapped both arms around his neck, and rode him to the floor.

The impact as his face bounced off the rough planks stunned Cord. All he could do was lie there as the man on top of him dug a knee into the small of his back and pounded the back of his head with both fists.

Then it soaked in on his dazed brain that he might not ever get up again if he didn't fight back, and soon. With a roar, he forced his muscles to work. He heaved himself up from the floor and bucked his assailant off to the side. As the man landed and rolled, Cord dived after him.

Now that his head was up again, he became aware that the fight had spread out across the saloon. Men yelled curses and flailed away at each other. The brawl had no real rhyme or reason to it; men were just blowing off steam that had built up during the days, weeks, even months of hard, intensive labor in the gold field.

Cord hoped Kat was staying out of harm's way. He didn't have time to check on her. He came down on top of the man who'd tackled him and rammed his knee into the man's belly. Then he sledged a right and a left into the man's face. The fellow's eyes rolled up in their sockets, and he went limp. Cord had knocked all the fight out of him.

Cord struggled to his feet and shook his head to clear some of the cobwebs from his brain. He looked around and spotted Flint a few yards away. His oldest brother was up again, standing with his feet braced apart as he traded punches with two men who were crowding him.

One man's head jerked back, and blood spurted from his nostrils as his nose crunched and flattened under Flint's fist. He lifted both hands to his suddenly gory face, reeled to the side, and collapsed.

That left Flint free to hook a left into the belly of his other opponent and then, when the man bent forward from the blow, lift an uppercut that caught him perfectly under the chin. The man's feet left the floor for a split second before he crashed down, out cold.

Flint saw Cord watching him and grinned. "We've got 'em on the run, kid!"

Cord didn't know if that was true or not, and they weren't going to find out, because several loud pops suddenly sounded. Cord thought at first they were gunshots.

The rest of the brawlers must have

thought so, too, because hostilities abruptly ceased as men froze in their tracks and looked around to see what was happening.

The sharp noises weren't gunshots, Cord realized. Three burly men strode through the crowd, brandishing bullwhips. The former combatants shrank back from them. Whips like that, in the hands of men who knew how to use them, could flay the flesh from a man's body or put out an eye.

Clearly, nobody wanted to mess with these three.

"That's enough, boys. I believe this fight is over."

That voice belonged to Patrick Elam. When Cord looked in the direction of Elam's private table, he saw the saloon-keeper standing on the other side of it. Kat was beside him, and Elam's arm was around the girl's shoulders in a protective pose.

Elam dropped that arm and stepped forward. He raised his voice so that it filled the tent as he went on, "There'll be no more brawling in here tonight. I know nothing takes the edge off like a good, old-fashioned fracas, but that's enough. Pick yourselves up, tend to your friends, and clean up this mess you've made. Any damages will be paid for. Otherwise, my men will be taking it out of your hides."

He nodded meaningfully toward the three men with the bullwhips.

Cord realized they were there to take care of any troublemakers. Some saloons had guards armed with shotguns, but that wouldn't work in the Bear Flag. A load of buckshot fired into the air would rip a big hole in the top of the tent, rendering it much less effective as a shelter. And a bullwhip gave a man a longer reach than a club. That was a pretty smart move on Elam's part, Cord thought.

None of the brawlers protested or even muttered under their breaths. They just got to work straightening up.

Surprisingly little damage had been done to the saloon's furnishings. Tables and chairs had been turned over, but once they were set upright again, they were perfectly usable. A couple of glasses had been broken, but that seemed to be the extent of the damage.

Cord and Flint turned back to Elam's table. "Sorry for what happened," Flint said.

"We didn't plan to get mixed up in a fight," Cord added. He reached for his pocket. "We'll chip in our fair share . . ."

Elam held up a hand to stop him. He smiled as he said, "I appreciate the gesture, but it's not necessary. I'd say you weren't given much choice in the matter, gentlemen. Please, don't worry about it. Everything's fine."

Flint said, "Are you all right, Kat?"

"Of course," she replied, apparently as cool and undisturbed as ever. "None of the violence ever came near me. Mr. Elam saw to that."

Cord recalled that protective arm around Kat's shoulders. Judging by the sudden frown on Flint's face, he must have noticed that, too.

"We're obliged to you," he said to Elam, a little curtly, "but Kat's a gal who can take care of herself."

"I don't doubt that for a moment," Elam replied with a slight edge in his own voice, "but since she's my guest, I took it upon myself to personally ensure her safety."

Cord didn't want that touchiness between Flint and Elam to escalate into anything stronger, so he said, "We probably should be getting back to camp. Night's fallen, and I'm sure the others are wondering where we are."

"More than likely," Flint said. "Come on, Kat."

She hesitated, instead of stepping around the table instantly, but then she turned and said, "Thank you for your kindness, Mr. Elam."

"You're perfectly welcome, my dear. And you're welcome back here at the Bear Flag any time." Elam glanced at Cord and Flint, then added, "And bring your friends with you if you want."

Making it clear that she could come back by herself if she wanted to, Cord thought. He didn't have to look over to know that Flint had stiffened even more beside him.

But with a smile, Kat came around the table and joined them. Most of the men in the saloon were sitting down at the tables again or leaning on the bars. A few were propped up in chairs, groggy and only half-conscious, including the men Cord and Flint had knocked out. Here and there, angry, shaggy-browed glares were cast in their direction as they walked through the tent with Kat between them.

They stepped out into the night air. It was cool, and even with an underlying scent of dung from the muck and mire of the street, it smelled good compared to the mixture of smoke, beer, and unwashed human flesh inside the saloon. An evergreen tang from the surrounding hills drifted on the breeze.

Flint suddenly slapped his pockets and then blew out his breath in a sigh of relief.

331

"What's wrong?" Cord asked.

"Thought for a second I'd lost those claim papers in that scuffle," Flint said. "But I didn't. They're still right here."

That prompted Cord to check his own pockets, and he experienced the same relief when he felt paper crackle under his touch.

Kat said, "You don't think those men would have started that fight just to steal your claims, do you?"

"No, that was just a saloon brawl, the sort that probably breaks out all the time in a place like this," Flint said. "They wouldn't have had any way of knowing we'd just filed those claims, as far as I can tell."

"What's important is that nobody was hurt," Cord said.

Kat turned to Flint and said, with a teasing note in her voice, "You don't think I should go back there, do you?"

"To that saloon?" Flint snorted. "A young girl's got no call to visit a place like that alone. We probably shouldn't have taken you there this evening."

"But you'll go back, won't you?" Kat laughed. "You want to see those dancing girls again."

"None of them can hold a candle to you," Flint said.

"My, how romantic you are, Mr. Bennett."

Kat linked her arm with Flint's and leaned her head against his shoulder for a second as they walked along. She seemed to be saying that even though she enjoyed teasing him, she didn't have any real interest in Patrick Elam.

Cord hoped that were true.

But he had seen the look in Kat's eyes when Elam had his arm around her, and he wasn't so sure.

CHAPTER 29

Before reaching the camp, the three of them mutually agreed that there was no point in saying anything about what had happened at the Bear Flag. Cord thought there was a good chance Kat might tell Glory about it later, since the two girls were close and didn't keep many secrets from each other, but they didn't need to worry Abraham Olmsted for no reason.

No harm had been done, after all.

Olmsted and Glory had been worried when they didn't get back until after dark, all right, but Steve claimed not to be.

"I always know you can handle any trouble you run into, Flint," he declared.

Those concerns were forgotten when Cord, Flint, and Kat brought out the claim deeds. Those documents were concrete evidence that they were one step closer to the dream that had brought them all to California.

Olmsted held his deed up and gazed at it in the firelight. "For a long time, it seemed like we were never gonna get here," he said. "Now we're here, and we got a piece of land that maybe has a fortune on it. All we got to do is find it."

"We can't count on getting rich," Kat warned.

"But at least there's a chance we will," Glory said. "With no chance, there's no hope, and with no hope, what good is life?"

Cord looked at her standing there with her long red hair shining brightly, and he saw hope, all right. He didn't want to feel that way. After what Caroline had done, he had sworn to himself that he would never fully trust a woman again.

But somehow, when he looked at Glory, he couldn't help it.

"I can give you a hand working your claim, if you want," he said to Abraham Olmsted.

The old-timer shook his head. "Nope. You got your own claim to take care of, son. Don't worry about us. We'll be fine. Ain't that right, girls?"

"Of course it is," Kat answered without hesitation. "I'll admit, I'm not looking forward to standing in a cold creek all day and panning for gold, but we'll do whatever we have to."

"All right," Cord said, "but we'll all be close by, in case you need any help."

"Like if those outlaws come around?" Glory said. "What did Mr. Spooner say they're called? The Reapers?"

"That's right." Glory's question was a grim reminder that dangers lurked here in the gold field, and most of them walked on two legs, Cord thought.

The next day, all six of them went up the creek to examine the new claims, loading down one of the Bennett brothers' pack mules with picks, shovels, and gold pans, as well as some food so they wouldn't have to return to camp until nightfall.

Along the way, they passed the claim being worked by Lou Spooner and Ham Erskine. The two men shook hands and gave them hearty wishes for good luck.

"Just leave a little gold dust in the creek for us," Spooner said.

"If we found a little color, it'd be more than we've come up with so far," Erskine said dourly. "I'm just about ready to give up and call it quits."

"Don't say that," Olmsted told him. "We're just about to get started. You fellas don't need to be givin' up."

Spooner said, "Don't worry, we'll stick it out a while longer. Ham just likes to complain, that's all." He grinned. "You know how to tell for sure when Ham's feelin' crotchety?"

"No, how?" Glory asked.

"He's awake!" Spooner guffawed and slapped his thigh, then added, "For that matter, I've heard him mutterin' complaints in his sleep."

"That's because there ain't enough time in the day to get 'em all out," Erskine said. "I got to get back to work."

He put his pickax over his shoulder and headed for the crude tunnel he was gouging out of the canyon wall.

The Bennetts and the Olmsteds went on and left the two men to their work. A short time later, they reached the claims that had been filed the day before.

Flint pointed out the rock cairns he and Steve had erected to mark the claims. "This first one is yours, Mr. Olmsted," he said. "We're just right up the creek." He looked at his brothers. "I don't care which stretch each of you boys wants to work. It's all the same to me."

"I'll take the first one, if that's all right," Cord said. That would put him closer to the Olmsteds if they needed help with anything.

Flint took the middle section, and Steve, the farthest claim up the creek. Before leaving to check it out, Steve said, "If one of us finds gold, then all of us find gold, right? Share and share alike?"

"That's the plan," Flint said with a nod.

"Been that way from the first," Cord confirmed. "We're in it together."

Satisfied, Steve took one of the pans and a pickax and started up the creek.

Because of the way the stream meandered back and forth in the canyon and the irregular walls, they might not be able to see each other at all times, depending on exactly where they were working. But they would be within earshot, so Cord wasn't worried. Anyway, they weren't likely to run into trouble they couldn't handle.

Unless claim jumpers or outlaws like the Reapers showed up. As long as that was a possibility, Cord intended to keep the Colt Dragoon holstered on his hip.

That was the first day of many filled with grueling labor. All three Bennett brothers began by panning for gold, the same as the Olmsteds were doing downstream. There had been some cold winters back in the Ozarks, but Cord didn't think his feet had ever been as cold as they were after a day of standing in the creek. Even though he wore high-topped boots that should have kept the water out, enough always seeped in so that his feet were soaked in what seemed like no time.

On top of that was the pain in his back and legs from stooping and straightening, over and over again, countless times each day. It was as bad as plowing and hoeing. Maybe worse.

Of course, while plowing and hoeing, he hadn't had the chance of looking down and seeing the glitter of gold in the sun. Just because it hadn't happened yet didn't mean that it was impossible.

But eventually, when they had no luck panning, they turned to other methods. Steve decided he was going to dig gold nuggets out of the canyon wall. He pockmarked it with holes along the whole length of his claim and peered hopefully at countless chunks of rock, to no avail.

While he was doing that, Cord and Flint built a sluice. The principle was the same as panning — gold was heavier and would sink through the mix of water, sand, and gravel and catch on the riffles along the bottom — but once the sluice was finished, they could run a lot more water through it than they could by washing one pan at a time.

Even though he spent most of his time

working, Cord found a few minutes here and there to check on the Olmsteds. The girls panned in the creek while their father chipped out holes in the canyon wall.

Cord was surprised the first time he saw Glory and Kat wearing pairs of Olmsted's canvas overalls and flannel shirts. Olmsted wasn't a big man, so the clothes didn't fit too badly. The girls had to roll the shirt sleeves up. They had thrown themselves into the work with enthusiasm, but after a few days, that began to wear off.

"I thought we'd have found some color by now," Kat complained one day when Cord was visiting.

"Some men work for weeks or even months before they find anything," Glory said.

"Yes, and Mr. Spooner and Mr. Erskine have already been at it for months and haven't found more than a few dollars' worth of gold. How long can we keep that up? We have to eat." Kat raked sweat-limp black hair back away from her face. "I swear, if there was anything else I could do to make money, I'd be tempted to take up another line of work."

"Don't even joke about things like that," Glory scolded.

"Who said I was joking?" Kat looked

defiantly at her sister. "I'll bet Patrick Elam would hire me to work in his saloon."

Glory leaned closer to her and said, "You'd better not let Pa hear you talking like that. He'd say that you aren't too old to get your hind end blistered!"

"Anybody who tries that will be sorry. Even Pa."

Glory just shook her head, clearly frustrated. Then she said, "I'm getting tired, too, but we have to keep working. We came all this way to California, and really, we've just barely gotten started. Isn't that right, Cord?"

Cord didn't particularly want to be dragged into the argument between the sisters, so he said as diplomatically as possible, "Good luck usually follows hard work. But sometimes it follows a pretty good ways behind."

More days went by. Cord dumped buckets of water, sand, and gravel into the sluice until it seemed as if his arms were going to fall off. But he and Flint kept going.

Men came and went, walking up the creek to and from other claims. Sometimes they stopped to talk and ask if the Bennetts had found any color, but most of the time they passed by in wary, sullen silence. Nobody trusted anybody all that much. But now and

341

then, they passed on news from the settlement.

"Only been two killin's in the past week," one man reported. "Rio Oro City's really settlin' down. 'Cept for the trouble between the Nugget and the B'ar Flag."

"What trouble?" Cord asked.

"Oh, Teddy Harville claims that Elam over at the B'ar Flag sent some fellas into his place one night with orders to start a ruckus. The Nugget got busted up some, and the fellas who started the fight got clean away before anybody could see who they were."

"You mean they were strangers in town?" Flint asked.

"That's what I heard. Don't know the truth of it myself. I wasn't there. But Harville was sure they was workin' for Elam, and when word got back to Elam about what Harville was sayin', there was harsh words between 'em. And then a couple o' nights later, there was a fire at the new, permanent saloon Harville's buildin'."

"That's terrible," Cord said. "Was it destroyed?"

"No, somebody come along and spotted it in time to raise the alarm, and folks got the flames put out before they did more than burn up one wall. But Harville's gonna have to rebuild that wall."

Flint grunted. "Did he accuse Elam of starting the fire?"

"Naw, not that I know of. But there's talk around the settlement about that. Harville's friends believe it and Elam's don't, and there's about the same number of each. Reckon as long as that's the case, it won't go no further."

Once the man was gone, Flint said to Cord, "I wouldn't put it past Elam to try to burn down a competitor's business. Wouldn't put it past him at all."

"He's been nothing but friendly to us," Cord pointed out. "And maybe that's why you don't like or trust him, because he was friendly to Kat."

"That's got nothing to do with it," Flint said. "I've seen fellas like Elam before, that's all. He won't stop at much of anything to get what he wants."

Which was a pretty accurate description of Flint himself, Cord mused, but he kept the thought to himself.

What went on in Rio Oro City wasn't really any of their business, anyway. They were out here to find gold.

Which was exactly what happened a couple of days later.

CHAPTER 30

Cord and Flint heard the shout from up the creek and recognized immediately that it came from Steve.

Cord set down the bucket he was about to dump over the trough's side into the sluice and asked his brother, "Do you think something's wrong? Steve could have hit himself in the foot with a pickax or something."

"He didn't sound hurt," Flint said, "and he didn't sound scared. That leaves . . ."

"He's excited about something."

Another loud whoop from upstream confirmed that.

Cord and Flint looked at each other and then broke into a run at the same time.

They pounded around a small bend in the canyon at the spot where Steve's claim started. Instantly, they spotted him over by the canyon wall, holding something above his head as he danced around in what appeared to be sheer exuberance.

"Steve, what is it?" Flint called as he and Cord trotted toward their brother. "What have you found?"

"Gold!" Steve yelled. "It's gold, Flint! Gold, at last!"

Cord's heart slugged heavily in his chest, partly from running and partly from excitement. He didn't care which of them had struck gold first. That didn't matter.

What was important was that if Steve was right, this was the start of a dream come true. A dream that had brought them hundreds of miles and consumed months of their lives . . .

"Let me see," Flint said as he and Cord hurried up to Steve.

The middle brother held out his hand. On his palm rested a jagged chunk of rock about half the size of a normal man's fist. The rock's rough surface was streaked black and brown and gray. But something gleamed through the black.

"I scraped it with my thumbnail, and it was there," Steve said. "See it?"

"Let me take a closer look." Flint took the rock from him. For a second, Steve looked like he didn't want to let go of it, but he was used to Flint doing whatever he wanted, so he didn't object.

Flint brought the rock closer and squinted at it. Then he took his knife from its sheath at his waist and began using the blade to scrape at the chunk's surface. The gleam began to spread and grow brighter as he did so.

Flint turned so that the sun's rays stuck the rock directly. As they were reflected back, he said softly, "Would you look at that, boys? Would you just look at that?"

"Is it gold?" Cord asked.

"Well, of course it's gold!" Steve said. "What else could it be?"

"I've heard men talking about something they call fool's gold, something that looks just like it but actually isn't. I don't know how you tell them apart."

"Neither do I," Flint said, "but that assayer in town will. What was his name? Casterline?"

"That's it. Are we going to take this to him?"

"Damn right we are." Flint looked over at Steve. "Where did you find this? Are there any more of them?"

"Right over here," Steve said, pointing to a small depression he had gouged out of the canyon wall. "I just hit it with the pick, and that rock fell out. Something about it made me pick it up and look closer at it." He peered around on the ground. "I don't see any more that look like it."

Cord leaned closer to the wall and studied the depression, searching for streaks of yellow or even the black that had covered the gold on the nugget Steve had found. He didn't see anything that looked promising.

But he knew from listening to other prospectors talk that it happened that way sometimes. You might find a whole vein of gold, or just one isolated nugget. Either was possible.

"Anything?" Flint asked.

"Nope. But there could be more, right under the surface."

"That's right." Flint clapped a hand on Steve's shoulder. "You stay here and keep digging, boy. Cord and I will take this nugget to town and have the assayer check it out."

"I found it," Steve protested. "Shouldn't I get to take it in?"

"We're better at things like that, and you're better at digging," Flint said. "You trust me, don't you, Steve?"

"Well, sure I trust you. You're my big brother, and you wouldn't ever do me wrong."

"I sure wouldn't. Come on, Cord."

Cord felt a little bad for Steve, but Flint

was right. Dealing with officials like Clyde Casterline was something the two of them were better suited for.

They left Steve there, his pickax *thunk*ing into the canyon wall as he continued to dig. Without even stopping at their sluice, they hurried on downstream.

"Howdy, Bennetts," Abraham Olmsted hailed them as they approached. "Where-abouts are you headed? Thought I heard some yellin' up your way a little bit ago. I hope ever'thing's all right."

"We're going to find out," Flint said as he held up the chunk of rock for the old-timer to see.

"Lord have mercy!" Olmsted exclaimed as he dropped his pick and hurried toward them. "Is that what I think it is?"

"I sure as blazes hope so," Flint said. He held out the rock. "Take a look and see what you think."

Olmsted took the rock with something approaching reverence. He lifted it close to his face and studied it intently. When he looked up at Cord and Flint, his eyes were wide.

"It looks a whole heap like gold," he said. "It surely does. A whole heap."

Cord said, "We're taking it to the land office so Mr. Casterline, the assayer, can tell us for sure."

An alarmed expression appeared on Olmsted's bearded, weathered face. "You better be careful," he said. "You take a nugget like that to town, and somebody's liable to try to steal it from you."

"We have to do something with it," Flint said. "It doesn't do us any good if we just hoard it. We need food and other supplies. I figured to trade it at Higginbotham's, once Casterline's told us what it's worth."

Olmsted sighed. "Yeah, I know. Well, stick it in your pocket and don't take it out until you get to the assayer's office. That's what I'd do. Don't let anybody know you've got it unless you have to."

"That's just common sense, all right," Cord said.

Flint shook his head. "That might be the smart thing to do, but I want to shout it to the rooftops and wave this nugget around so everybody can see the Bennett brothers found gold. That's what we came here to do, and we've done it." He sighed. "No sense asking for trouble, though. We'll be discreet."

Glory and Kat, who had been panning in the creek a ways downstream when Cord and Flint came up, reached them now, having been attracted by the commotion. They arrived in time to hear what Flint said, which prompted Kat to exclaim, "You found gold?"

"Well, Steve did," Cord said.

"It's share and share alike," Flint responded. "Cord and I are taking it to the assayer."

He held out the nugget for the girls to examine it. They leaned over it and gushed about how pretty it was. Kat looked up and said, "I'm going to the settlement with you."

"No, you ain't," Olmsted told her. "Just because these boys may have got lucky don't mean we have. We've still got work to do and plenty of daylight to do it in."

"But Pa —"

"Nope. You girls get back to your pannin'."

Kat scowled but didn't argue. Glory came up to Cord and put a hand on his arm.

"Congratulations," she said.

"Thanks, but it could still be fool's gold. That's what we're going to find out."

"It's not. It's the real thing. I can feel it in my bones."

To tell the truth, so could Cord. He was completely convinced the nugget actually was gold.

It took the brothers half an hour to reach the camp, where they saddled their horses and rode the rest of the way to Rio Oro

City. It was early afternoon when they got there, so while the street and the boardwalks were fairly busy, the settlement wasn't thronged with men like it would be later that evening.

As they passed the saloons, Flint glanced at the Golden Nugget and said, "Maybe we'll stop in there for a drink in a little while, if Casterline has good news for us."

"You don't want to go back to the Bear Flag?"

Flint grunted. "Not particularly. I've had my fill of that Elam fella."

Cord felt pretty much the same way, so he was fine with the idea of stopping at Harville's saloon. He'd felt an instinctive liking for Harville, even though the man was a little bombastic.

They reached Clyde Casterline's office and dismounted, tying their horses at the hitch rack. They stomped some mud off their boots on the boardwalk as they went in, only to stop short as they saw that Casterline already had some customers.

A man stood at the counter with two more roughly dressed men behind him and brought his fist down hard as he said, "What the hell do you mean you're not gonna accept this claim?"

Even though the angry man's back was

turned, Cord recognized the harsh voice and the lean shape.

Rip Jordan.

Chapter 31

With Jordan's demanding question still hanging in the air, Flint drawled, "Looks like you're busy, Mr. Casterline. My brother and I will come back later."

Wide-eyed, looking a little like a spooked rabbit, Casterline leaned over to gaze imploringly past Jordan and the gunman's two cronies.

"No, that's all right," he said hastily. "I'm sure my business with . . . with these gentlemen will be concluded shortly."

Jordan looked over his shoulder to see who had come in. His two companions moved aside so that he could see Cord and Flint. His lip curled in a sneer as he recognized them.

"The Bennett brothers," he said. "What are you doing here? Don't tell me a couple of lunkhead farm boys like you actually found gold."

"As a matter of fact —" Flint began.

Cord stopped him with a hand on his shoulder. "As a matter of fact, we're here to talk to Mr. Casterline about our claim. But you fellas can finish your business with him first."

Casterline said, "They, uh, don't have any business with me, Mr. Bennett."

Jordan jerked around toward him again. "You need to register our claim!"

"That claim is registered to Will McCormick," Casterline said. "I can show you on the map and in my records."

His voice was a little stronger now, and his expression more determined. When Cord and Flint had come in, he had been frightened, that was obvious, but with witnesses on hand, he wasn't as scared.

"I told you, McCormick sold it to us," Jordan said.

"But you don't have a bill of sale or any other kind of documentation," Casterline insisted. "I can't transfer a claim just on the say-so of somebody who comes in here off the street."

"I'm not just somebody who came in off the street," Jordan said. "You know who I am, Casterline. I'm one of Rio Oro City's leading citizens."

Flint grunted and managed to make it sound scornful of that statement.

"Bring me a signed document, or better yet, bring in McCormick himself to confirm the transfer, and I'll be glad to record it." Casterline spread his hands. "Until then, there's nothing I can do."

The upper and lower halves of Jordan's lantern-shaped jaw ground together as he gritted his teeth. Then he lifted a hand, pointed a finger at Casterline, and said, "You ain't heard the last of this."

With that, he turned and stalked out past Cord and Flint, who moved aside to let him leave. The two bruisers who seemed to accompany Jordan everywhere followed him. They cast hate-filled stares at the Bennett brothers as they left the office.

Cord wondered briefly which one it was he had clouted with the water bucket. Enough time had passed that any goose eggs on the man's noggin were long gone.

When the door slammed closed, Casterline rested both hands flat on the counter and drew in a deep breath.

"Thank heavens you boys came along when you did," he said. "There's no telling what Rip Jordan might have done when he found out he wasn't going to get his way. The man's a killer!"

"So we've heard," Flint said. "Are he and his friends taking up prospecting? I thought they just hung around the settlement look-ing scary."

"Oh, Jordan has half a dozen claims already. He doesn't work any of them, though. He has men doing that for him. He's found enough gold that he can afford to hire workers." Casterline shook his head. "He came here with nothing but a gun, though. I'm not sure how he ever managed to make such a successful start." He leaned over the counter and lowered his voice. "I think he's got somebody backing him, but I don't have any idea who it is."

That was interesting, Cord thought. He could have speculated on the question. But that wasn't why he and Flint were here. Instead he said, "Show Mr. Casterline what Steve found."

Flint reached in his pocket and brought out the chunk of rock. He set it on the counter and said, "Our brother dug this out of the canyon wall this morning."

Casterline leaned forward, avidly studying the rock. He gestured toward it and asked, "May I pick it up?"

"Go ahead," Cord told him. "We want to find out if it's the real thing."

"Or fool's gold, you mean?" Casterline rested the rock on the palm of his right hand and moved the hand up and down, as if gauging the weight. He reached under the counter and brought up a small knife, which he used to scrape at the rock's surface. Then he used the point and prodded at the gleaming surface.

"What's that for?" Flint asked.

Casterline turned the rock so that Cord and Flint could see where the blade had made a small indentation in the yellow metal.

"See that? It's soft. That's because gold is a metal. Fool's gold is actually a crystalline substance. It's a lot harder."

"You mean this is gold, for sure?" Flint asked. Cord heard the excitement in his brother's voice.

Instead of answering directly, Casterline moved his hand so that it was below the level of the counter.

"Lean over and look back here," he said. "See how it still shines a little, even though it's not in direct light? Fool's gold shines in the sun, or in lamplight, but not in shadow." Casterline set the rock on the counter again. "Yes, sir, gentlemen, that is a gold nugget. No doubt about it."

"How much is it worth?" Cord asked. His voice practically trembled with a mixture of exhilaration and relief.

"I couldn't say without knowing how

much the gold itself actually weighs. I'd have to get rid of the rest of the rock it's embedded in." Casterline traced a fingertip over the stone. "You see, you can't tell how deeply into the rock it goes. It may just be a thin layer on the surface, or it could be a nugget that weighs several ounces. I have the chemicals here to refine it, if you'd like."

"How long would that take?" Flint asked.

Casterline shrugged narrow shoulders. "An hour, perhaps. Possibly less."

Flint jerked his head in a nod and said, "Go ahead. Can't do anything with it until we know what it's worth, right?"

"That's true. There will be a small fee involved . . ."

"I figure you won't try to cheat us. Not after we came along at just the right time to keep Jordan from causing trouble."

"I don't try to cheat anybody," Casterline replied, with a note of indignation in his voice. "I'm an honest assayer."

"We know that, sir," Cord said, trying to smooth things over. "Why don't we come back in an hour and see what you've found out?"

"That'll be fine." Casterline seemed mollified now. "You say your brother dug this out of the canyon wall?"

"That's right."

"There's liable to be more. The way this runs through the rock, there could be an actual vein there . . . but we'll know more shortly."

Cord thanked the assayer, and he and Flint left the office. Once they were outside, Flint said, "He seemed a mite touchy."

"You almost accused him of being a crook," Cord pointed out.

Flint waved a hand. "Ah, I didn't mean it like that. It bothers me a little, leaving that nugget in his care, but I reckon that's the way the system works."

Cord nodded down the street and suggested, "Why don't we go to the Golden Nugget while we're waiting? Seems appropriate, don't you think?"

Flint grinned. "I suppose so. I'm not sure we have enough money to buy some beers, but maybe Harville would let us have a couple on the cuff if we told him Casterline's working on that nugget for us."

"I thought we were going to trade the gold for supplies."

"We can't sit in a saloon for an hour without buying a drink," Flint said.

Cord supposed he had a good point there. "I have a little money left. I'll buy the beers."

Flint clapped a hand on his shoulder and

359

said, "Come on, kid."

As they walked up to the big tent, they looked at the building under construction next to it. Cord could see where the framework of the far wall had burned. Most of the charred debris had been cleared away, but a few pieces of blackened board remained here and there. Work had already begun on rebuilding the wall. The sharp tang of freshly sawn pine boards hung in the air.

The Golden Nugget was set up differently from the Bear Flag. A long bar was in the back of the room, with tables in front of it. To the right, Cord was surprised to see a roulette wheel and a faro layout, along with several tables covered with green felt, where poker games were underway. The gambling equipment must have been brought out here from San Francisco, he thought.

To the left, a crude stage had been erected. It was empty at the moment. Cord wondered if Teddy Harville had a troupe of dancing girls working for him, too.

The saloon was reasonably busy for this time of day. Some men stood at the bar drinking, while others sat at tables and talked and laughed with the soiled doves who worked for Harville. Those women were sedately dressed, but there was no doubt about their profession. They wouldn't have been in a place like this if they weren't prostitutes.

Cord's jaw tightened for a moment as he thought about Caroline. At least the women in this saloon were more honest and straightforward about their nature, he told himself, not deceptive like Caroline had been.

Then he took a deep breath and tried to force those memories out of his mind. He had no business being judgmental about her. What was it the Good Book said? *Let he who is without sin cast the first stone . . .*

"Why, hello, boys!" Teddy Harville's booming voice greeted them. "Haven't seen you around much since you hit town."

He came toward them with his hand extended. Today he wore dark green trousers, a yellow coat, and a white shirt with a bright red cravat. An equally bright rose was stuck in a buttonhole on his lapel. His thinning hair was slicked down.

Cord and Flint shook hands with him. Cord said, "We've been pretty busy."

"Working your claim, I expect. Having any luck?"

The brothers glanced at each other. "Maybe," Cord said, not wanting to give away too much information.

Harville chuckled. "Discretion," he said. "I like that. You might not think so to look at me, but I know there's a time not to draw attention to yourself. You boys want some beers?"

Cord reached for his pocket and said, "I think we have enough —"

"Oh, no, don't worry about that," Harville interrupted him. "This is your first time in here. Drinks are on me. Come on over and sit down."

He led them to a table and sat down with them, signaling to a bartender to bring beers. Cord wondered if Harville had heard about how Patrick Elam had welcomed them to the Bear Flag. If he had, the competitiveness between the two saloonkeepers might have prompted Harville to match Elam's hospitality.

It would be rude to inquire about that, however, and it didn't matter, anyway. When one of the women carried over a tray with three mugs of beer on it, Harville took his, lifted it, and said, "Here's to Rio Oro City, boys. The best way for it to grow is with fine, upstanding fellows such as yourselves being part of the community."

They drank. The beer was good, and cool enough that it went down smoothly.

"You're really interested in seeing the

town grow, aren't you, Mr. Harville?" Cord said.

Harville wrapped both big hands around the half-empty mug and leaned forward.

"Indeed I am, lad. I don't see any reason why it can't someday be as big and fine a place as Boston or Philadelphia. I'm from Boston, you know."

Cord shook his head. "Nope. Didn't know that."

"From a fine old family involved in the shipping industry. I was never fond of ships, though. Never quite got my sea legs, for some reason." Harville guffawed. "Which means the trip around the cape to San Francisco was a mighty unpleasant few weeks for me! Worth it, though, since I eventually made my way here."

"Why didn't you stay in San Francisco?" Flint asked. "From what I hear, it's really growing."

"By leaps and bounds, as they say. The discovery of gold last year turned it from a sleepy little fishing village into a bustling seaport. But it seemed to me that a man with ambition could make an even better start in a place like this, where he could really mold the community as it grows up."

"Most of these mining camps don't last, do they? They dry up and blow away once the gold peters out."

Harville frowned. "That's not going to happen to Rio Oro City. Just look around you, boys. Did you ever see such beautiful country?"

"It's pretty nice, with the mountains and the forests and the streams," Cord allowed.

"Exactly! Even without gold, there are other natural resources to be had, and you'll never find a more pleasant place to live. That's why I think people will still want to come here, even after the Gold Rush is over. Especially if there's a town like Rio Oro City to serve their needs."

"So you want to build something to last," Cord observed.

"Indeed I do, Mr. Bennett."

"Call me Cord."

"I can think of no finer legacy, Cord, than to be one of the founding fathers of this community."

Cord saw a smirk lurking around the corners of Flint's mouth. Flint probably thought Harville was a pompous old fool. He had never been one to care about much of anything beyond the moment.

Cord liked what he heard from Harville, though. The idea of building a lasting settlement that would be a good place to live appealed to him. And Harville was right: he could see himself settling down here permanently, especially if he had a good woman at his side. A beautiful woman with long red hair . . .

A sudden outburst of angry curses behind him made Cord jerk around. At a nearby table, two men on opposite sides bolted to their feet, and as they came up out of their chairs, their hands dropped to the guns on their hips.

Not again, Cord thought.

CHAPTER 32

Without pausing to consider what he was doing, Cord followed his instincts. He leaped to his feet, lunged at the closest of the men about to draw on each other, and rammed his left shoulder against the man's right shoulder.

That collision took the man completely by surprise and knocked him to the side. He lost his balance and sprawled on the plank floor. His half-drawn gun fell the rest of the way out of its holster and clattered beside him, thankfully not going off.

At the same time as he'd made his move, Cord had pulled his own gun. He saw the man on the other side of the table clear leather and start to bring his revolver up.

Instead of firing, Cord used the added reach the Dragoon gave him and thrust the gun across the table. He struck the barrel of the other man's gun from below with the Colt's barrel. The man fired, but Cord had already knocked the barrel up at an angle, so the bullet ripped harmlessly through the tent roof above them.

Then Cord leveled the gun in his hand, eared back the hammer, and ordered, "Put it down! Try to cock it again and I'll fire."

The man Cord had knocked down pushed himself up on an elbow and yelled, "Shoot him! Shoot the son of a buck! He's a cheater!"

"You're the one who had a card up your sleeve, you damn tinhorn!" the other man accused. "You're just trying to shift the blame onto me."

The gun in his hand trembled a little from the fury that gripped him.

But staring down the barrel of an already cocked weapon was a mighty sobering sight. Without making a move to pull back the hammer, he slowly lowered the revolver and placed it on the table in front of him.

The other man scooped his gun from the floor and scrambled to his feet.

"Much obliged, friend," he said to Cord. "I'll take care of this now —"

Cord turned and covered the second man. "Put that back in its holster," he said. "Neither of you fools need to be shooting in a place like this."

"What the devil gives you the right —"

the man began hotly.

"This Colt Dragoon does," Cord interrupted him, "and the fact that I was sitting right there peacefully, enjoying a beer with my brother and Mr. Harville. I'm not going to let a stupid argument over a card game ruin that."

"But he cheated!"

Cord motioned with the Colt and said again, "Holster it."

Muttering under his breath, the man did so. Cord glanced over at the other one. His gun was still on the table. Cord had worried that he might make a grab for it.

From the corner of his eye, he saw why that hadn't happened. Flint was on his feet, too, his hand resting on the butt of his Dragoon.

"Pick that iron up and pouch it," Cord snapped at the other man. "And then both of you can get out of here until you cool off. That all right with you, Mr. Harville?"

"It's more than all right," Teddy Harville declared. "You fellas get out, and don't come back until you can act like civilized human beings. And if either of you *did* cheat, you can just stay out of the Golden Nugget from now on. All the games in here are clean and honest, you understand?"

More muttering came from the two men,

but they shuffled out of the tent, staying well clear of each other as they did so. Cord thought gunfire might erupt as soon as they were outside, but that wasn't his lookout.

Nothing happened, though. The men must have decided that whatever their argument might be, it wasn't worth killing — or dying — over.

Cord carefully let down the hammer of his Colt. As he did so, he became aware of the hushed silence that filled the saloon. He'd been concentrating so much on stopping the trouble between the two men that the surroundings had faded from his awareness for a moment.

Now he looked around, saw the prospectors and the gamblers and the soiled doves staring at him. He summoned up a brief smile, slid the Colt back in its holster, and turned to the table, where Flint and Harville were still standing. Behind him, the saloon's normal hubbub began to rise again.

"Well, that was a damned fool stunt you just pulled, mixing into somebody else's fight like that," Flint said as he glared at Cord. "You could've gotten us both shot."

"I figured it would be even more dangerous if those two started blazing away at each other only a few feet from us."

"Oh, you figured that, did you? Did you

369

really stop to think about it that much? Didn't look like it to me."

Cord shrugged. "Maybe not, but it still seemed like the thing to do at the time."

Harville said, "As far as I'm concerned, it was the right thing. And mighty impressive, too, the way you acted so quickly and kept those two from shooting the place up. Yes, sir, I'm in your debt, Cord."

"Forget it," Cord said.

"Not likely. You boys are welcome here any time, and your money's no good . . . within reason."

Flint said, "Well, something worthwhile might come out of you being so reckless, after all, kid."

The three of them sat down again. Cord asked, "Have there been many shootings in here, Mr. Harville?"

"A few," Harville admitted. He scowled as he went on, "That fellow Rip Jordan killed a man in here one night. Prodded him into drawing, and the other man never had a chance. I told Jordan he wasn't welcome in here anymore after that, but it didn't seem to bother him. He spends most of his time over at the Bear Flag, anyway."

Cord rubbed his chin. "He does, does he?"

"Elam can have his business. That's one

customer I don't begrudge him." Harville drank the rest of his beer, then licked his lips and said, "That's been the only killing in here. The other fights, the fellows either managed to miss each other completely, or they were just wounded."

Flint said, "Elam has some men with bullwhips to keep the peace."

"I've heard about them. Seems like something Elam would do. My bartenders are tough enough to take care of any difficulty by grabbing bungstarters. The troublemakers usually back away and settle down when they see that."

Cord and Flint finished their beers, as well. Flint shoved back his chair and said, "I reckon we'd better get on about our business."

"Come back any time," Harville said. "Always be glad to see you. Say, Cord . . . if you ever get tired of breaking your back hunting gold, I might have an idea of something else you could do."

Cord shook his head. "Thanks, Mr. Harville, but I don't reckon I came all this way to be a saloon guard."

"Not exactly what I had in mind, but I understand the sentiment. Good luck in your efforts up the canyon."

The Bennett brothers left the saloon.

When they were outside, Cord said, "I wonder what Mr. Harville was talking about."

"I don't know, but whatever it was, you'd never get rich working for him, and that's why we came to California, isn't it?" Flint snorted. "Anyway, you don't want to get too mixed up with him. That idea of turning this place into a respectable town is crazy. It's a gold camp, and that's all it'll ever be."

Cord didn't waste time arguing with his brother, but to tell the truth, he had been impressed by what Harville said. He liked the colorful saloonkeeper's plans, whether they were actually feasible or not.

They headed for Casterline's office, and a few moments later, stepped into the makeshift building. Cord looked past the counter to the desk, but he didn't see the land recorder and assayer.

"Wonder where Mr. Casterline's gone," he said.

"He'd better not have taken off with that nugget of ours," Flint growled.

Cord laughed. "I doubt if it's worth enough to tempt anybody to steal it and run away. It's not that big —"

A low moan interrupted him.

Flint heard it, too, and exclaimed, "What

the hell?"

Cord reached the gate in the counter first and threw it open. As he rushed behind the counter, he saw Clyde Casterline lying on the floor with blood on his head.

Casterline moaned again and moved a little, demonstrating that he was still alive. At first glance, Cord had thought the man was dead.

Quickly, Cord dropped to a knee beside Casterline. Flint looked around the counter and asked, "What's wrong with him?"

Cord took hold of Casterline's shoulders and gently, carefully, turned him onto his back. The blood leaked from a gash at the left side of Casterline's forehead.

"Looks like somebody hit him," Cord said. He looked over the rest of Casterline's body, searching for bloodstains on the man's clothing. Not seeing any, he went on, "I don't think he's been shot or stabbed. Just walloped with something."

"A gun barrel would be my guess," Flint said. "That would open up a cut like that."

Cord agreed it was likely Casterline had been pistol-whipped. The injury had bled quite a bit, as head wounds had a tendency to do. It was hard to tell how serious it was, otherwise.

"Mr. Casterline! Mr. Casterline, can you

hear me?"

Casterline responded to Cord's urgent voice. His eyelids fluttered, and he groaned louder. Cord slid an arm under the man's shoulders and lifted him a little. Casterline opened his eyes.

"B-Bennett . . ." he said. "I . . . I'm sorry . . ."

"What happened?" Cord asked. "Who attacked you?"

"D-Don't . . . know . . . they came in . . . wearing masks . . . Reapers!"

The Reapers, right here in town? The outlaws were getting awfully bold, Cord thought.

"They . . . had guns," Casterline went on. "Pushed me around . . . made me give them . . ." His voice trailed off in an unintelligible mutter before strengthening again. "Then one of them . . . hit me with . . . his gun . . ."

"Wait a minute," Flint said. "They stole something from you? What was it?"

Cord glanced up at his brother and could tell from the look on Flint's face that the same terrible thought had occurred to him.

"I'm sorry," Casterline mumbled.

"You said that before. What did they take? Did they get that nugget of ours?"

"Sorry . . . It was on the counter . . . They

374

took it . . ."

Flint reached past Cord, grasped Casterline's shoulder, and shook him. "Damn you, where did they go?"

"Take it easy, Flint," Cord said. "The man's hurt —"

"He's liable to be hurt worse if he doesn't answer my questions. Casterline! How long ago was this? Where did they go?"

Casterline's eyes opened wider. Cord didn't care for Flint's methods, but the rough handling seemed to have forced some coherence back into Casterline's brain.

"Couldn't have been more than . . . a few minutes. They went out . . . the back."

Cord glanced that way and saw a door standing open in the building's rear.

"How can we find them?" Flint demanded. "What do we look for?"

"Dunno . . . They had masks on . . . One fella . . . had a feather in his hatband . . . like an Indian . . ."

Casterline had forced out all the answers he could. His eyes rolled up in their sockets, and his head sagged back. Once again, Cord thought he was dead, but then he heard the steady rasp of breath in Casterline's throat.

"Come on," Flint said. "We have to get after them."

"He needs help —"

"He'll keep, blast it. Our chances of finding those thieves won't."

Flint was right. There wasn't much anybody could do for Caster line except clean that gash on his head, and that would wait. Cord eased the unconscious man to the floor and stood up.

Flint was already heading out the back door. Cord hurried after him. There was nothing behind the building except a few tents, the closest being a good twenty yards away. Trees were just beyond the tents.

"They could have gotten away into the woods," Cord said.

"Or they could have gone along behind the buildings and tents and ducked into any of them," Flint said. "You're a tracker. Pretend you're hunting game back home."

Cord was about to protest that this was nothing like his hunting trips into the Ozarks, but then he realized that the ground wasn't as muddy back here. In the street, the ooze filled in tracks almost as fast as a man could make them. But here, he might be able to see some sign . . .

Scuff marks led away from the back of Casterline's office. Cord pointed to them and said, "Those might be footprints."

"Well, follow them!" Flint drew his gun. "Find those damn thieves."

That was still going to be almost impossible, Cord thought. The men who had attacked Casterline and stolen the Bennett brothers' gold nugget had a lead of several minutes, if not more. Casterline had been so addled he might not have been right about how long it had been since the theft. The men could be almost anywhere in Rio Oro City by now.

But Cord was just as troubled by the loss of the nugget as Flint was, so he had to try to find the robbers, anyway. He began following the faint marks on the ground.

The trail led behind half a dozen tents and then turned toward the street. Cord bit back a groan of dismay. Just as he expected, the tracks disappeared into the morass of Rio Oro City's main thoroughfare.

"They're gone," he said. "No way to follow them. No telling where they might be by now."

Flint was seething. He asked, "Could you tell how many there were?"

Cord shook his head. "No, the marks weren't clear enough for that. Mr. Casterline can probably tell us, once he's recovered a little. But I'm not sure knowing how many there were will help us any."

"If he says three, then I have a pretty good idea who they were: Rip Jordan and his two partners."

"Jordan," Cord repeated. "You think he's one of the Reapers?"

"From what we've seen and heard about him, would you put it past him?"

"No, I don't guess I would," Cord admitted. He thought back to the earlier encounter. "But when we saw them in Mr. Casterline's office, none of them was wearing a hat with a feather in the band. I don't recall seeing anybody like that around here."

"A man can change hats," Flint snapped. "In fact, wearing something distinctive like that while you're pulling a robbery and then changing out of it would be a good way of throwing folks off the scent."

That made sense, Cord supposed.

Although it made a bitter pill to swallow, he said, "I don't reckon there's anything we can do now except go back to the claim and tell Steve what happened —"

Flint suddenly gripped his arm and said in a low voice, "Look there! Going into the Bear Flag!"

Cord looked and saw three men pushing through the saloon's entrance flap.

One of them wore a buckskin jacket and a black hat with a tall, rounded crown.

A bird's feather was tucked into the band

on the hat's left side and stuck up in plain view.

CHAPTER 33

"That's got to be them," Flint said. "Like you said, nobody else around here has a feather in his hat."

They didn't know that for sure, but Cord had to admit it was likely the three men were the thieves. In addition to the feather in one man's hat, each of them had a bandanna looped around his neck that would be easy enough to pull up as a mask over the lower half of his face.

"Come on," Flint continued. He stalked across the street with the mud sucking at his boots.

Cord's slightly longer legs allowed him to catch up easily. "What are you going to do?"

"I'm going to get that gold nugget back," Flint said. "They'll either give it up, or I'll take it out of them in blood."

"There are three of them," Cord reminded his brother. "We're outnumbered."

"I'm not going to wait until you go back

out to the camp and fetch Steve. The odds are close enough to even. I'm not afraid of them."

Cord wasn't afraid, either, but his nature was to be careful and wary. Still, those men probably *were* the thieves, and he wanted that nugget back, too.

He sure didn't want to have to tell Steve that they had lost it. That would break his heart.

As they reached the boardwalk in front of the Bear Flag, Flint paused long enough to look over and ask, "Are you going to back my play, kid?"

"I'll back your play," Cord replied grimly. He meant every word of it, too.

Shoulder to shoulder, they pushed through the entrance. The canvas sides brushed against them. Cord's eyes went instantly to the bar on the right-hand side of the big chamber. The man in the feathered hat and buckskin jacket stood there with his friends, throwing back shots of whiskey.

Flint headed for them. Some of the men in the saloon must have noticed the fire burning in Flint's eyes, because they got out of his way. Others who weren't paying that much attention got shouldered aside. Several of them reacted angrily, only to subside when they turned around and saw Flint's face.

On the other side of the saloon, one of the bullwhip-carrying guards must have realized trouble was brewing, because he started to cross the room. He had taken only a single step, though, when Patrick Elam stepped up and motioned for him to wait. Elam gazed across the room and watched intently as Cord and Flint strode toward the trio at the bar.

As the patrons on that side of the saloon began to spread out so they wouldn't be in any line of fire, Flint and Cord came to a stop behind the three men at the bar. Unlike in permanent saloons, there was no mirror hanging behind the bar, so the men wouldn't have been able to see the Bennett brothers approach.

"Mister!" Flint's voice ripped out, blunting the remaining hub bub in the room. "You there, in the buckskin jacket and feather hat!"

The man set his empty whiskey glass on the bar and turned slowly. Cord noticed that he kept his hand well away from the gun on his hip. That told him the man didn't want to provoke a fight unless and until he was ready for one.

"Are you talkin' to me, friend?" the man asked.

He had long brown hair and a clean-shaven, heavy-featured, rather dull face. He didn't look too smart, but he might still be dangerous. The same was true of his roughly dressed, beard-stubbled companions.

"Where were you just now, before you came in here?" Flint demanded.

"I don't reckon that's any of your business," Feather Hat said.

"You were down at the land office, weren't you?"

Feather Hat shook his head. "My friends and I just rode into town. We wouldn't have any reason to visit the land office."

"The clerk is the local assayer, too. You pistol-whipped him and stole a gold nugget from him."

The man stiffened. "That's a mighty serious accusation. This land clerk, did he describe us?"

"He couldn't see your faces because you pulled up those bandannas and used them as masks. But he saw that feather in your hat!"

"Could be more than one fella in this town with a feather in his hat," the man replied with a shrug.

Cord thought he saw worry in Feather

Hat's eyes, though. He might be thinking that Casterline could identify them. Why would the man have left something as distinctive as that feather in his hat band? Unless . . .

"You thought he was dead, didn't you?" Cord said. "You thought you stove in his head when you hit him with your gun. But he's alive, and he'll point the finger at you —"

"Damn it, you said you killed that little fella, Doyle!" one of the other men burst out.

Seeing that he couldn't bluff his way through this confrontation, Feather Hat cursed and clawed at the gun on his hip — doubtless the same gun he'd used to clout Clyde Casterline.

The men beside him started to draw, as well.

The bystanders who hadn't already gotten out of the way yelled and dived for cover. Flint pulled his gun with breathtaking speed. It seemed to Cord as if it took him forever to haul his own Colt out of its holster, but then the grip was in his hand, smooth against his palm, and the barrel came up steadily.

The man to Feather Hat's left fired first, but he rushed his shot. Cord heard the lead ball hum past his head. His thumb was around the hammer. It came back to full cock, and a fraction of a second later, he squeezed the trigger.

Other guns were booming already, so when Cord's Dragoon went off, it just blended in with the gun-thunder filling the saloon. He felt the strong recoil against his hand, though, and knew he had fired. Dust puffed from the shirtfront of the man he'd aimed at as the ball struck it. The man fell against the bar and bent backward so far over it that the pose looked unnatural. His feet went out from under him, and he toppled to the floor in an ungainly heap.

Cord didn't know how many shots Flint had fired by now, but Feather Hat and the third man were both hit. The other man reeled to the side and pitched forward on his face. Feather Hat was still on his feet and got another shot off.

Flint jerked from the bullet's impact.

Cord couldn't tell how badly his brother was hit, but he knew Flint was wounded, and that filled him with rage. He yelled as he thumbed back the Colt's hammer. The Colt blasted again at the same time as Flint's gun went off. Both rounds smashed into Feather Hat's chest and knocked him sprawling. His booted feet drummed briefly on the planks and then went still.

An acrid cloud of powdersmoke hung in the air on this side of the room. Cord waved a hand through it and coughed quietly as the stuff stung his nose and throat and eyes. He could see well enough to know that all three of the thieves were down, and he and Flint were still on their feet.

"How bad are you hurt?" Cord asked as he slowly lowered his gun.

"Don't do that," Flint said sharply. "Don't ever relax until you know for sure the other fella is out of the fight."

He kept his gun pointed at the fallen men. Cord followed suit.

"I'm all right," Flint went on. "That shot just nicked my left arm. Stings some, and it'll bleed a little, but it's nothing to worry about."

Cord was relieved to hear that. He hoped nobody else in the Bear Flag had been struck by any of the wild shots.

Heavy footsteps sounded behind them. Cord started to turn, but then Patrick Elam's familiar voice said, "Take it easy, gentlemen. My boys are just going to check on those three."

A couple of Elam's guards stepped around Cord and Flint and started toward the bodies. Flint said, "Hold on a minute!"

The guards stopped and looked back, past the Bennett brothers. Elam moved up alongside them and motioned for the guards to wait.

"Is there a problem, Flint?" he asked quietly. "Other than the fact that your arm is bleeding, that is?"

"This arm is nothing," Flint said again. "I want to search those varmints myself. They stole something of ours."

"Very well. It appears that they're dead, so if you're willing to risk it . . ."

Elam waved a hand, signaling the guards to back off.

"Cover me, Cord," Flint said. He holstered his gun and went to Feather Hat's side. Bending over, he ran his hands over the buckskin jacket, then reached inside it.

When he straightened, he had the gold nugget in his palm. Casterline had gotten the rest of the rock off of it somehow, leaving only the dully gleaming chunk of metal.

"That's a nice specimen," Elam said. "Two or three ounces, I'd estimate. Worth fifty dollars or so. You say these men stole it from you?"

"They actually took it from Mr. Casterline," Cord said. "He was figuring out how much it's worth. They attacked him, too. That one there" — Cord pointed at Feather

Hat — "hit him with a gun and thought he'd killed him."

"You did the right thing by pursuing them," Elam said. "There are enough murderers and thieves around here to start with. We don't need any more."

The saloonkeeper nodded curtly to his men and went on, "Haul those carcasses out of here, then somebody go check on Casterline. He's an important man in these parts." He smiled at Cord and Flint. "Come on back to my table and have a drink. On the house, in appreciation for the service you've done the community by ridding it of those three."

Flint stuck the nugget in his pocket and said, "I ought to get this scratch patched up, I suppose."

"One of my girls can do that for you." Elam turned his head. "Nellie, get a basin and a clean cloth and tend to Mr. Bennett's injury."

The young dove, a washed-out blonde, nodded and went to fetch the items.

"A little whiskey will clean a bullet hole better than anything from a doctor's bag," Elam went on as he led them to his table.

Another young woman brought them drinks, and then Nellie came back with the basin and cloth and told Flint to take off his shirt. Grinning, he did so. Cord expected his brother to make some off-color comment, but thankfully, Flint resisted the impulse.

However, while she was tending to him, Flint did ask Elam, "Do you know those men we shot?"

"Never saw them before," Elam answered. "I guess that one with the feather in his hat was telling the truth about one thing, anyway, when he said they just rode in."

It didn't take long for Nellie to swab the blood away, then drench the shallow gash with whiskey from a bottle. Flint grunted quietly when the fiery stuff washed over the wound, but that was his only reaction. Nellie bound up the wound with another piece of clean cloth.

One of Elam's men came up to the table and said, "Casterline's all right, boss. If Nellie's done here, she might go up there and bandage his head."

"An excellent idea," Elam agreed. "See to it, Nellie. And if Mr. Casterline needs reinvigorating in any other way, you can tend to that, too."

"Sure, Mr. Elam," the girl said. "The few times I've been around that fella, though, he didn't seem too interested."

"Perhaps a brush with death will have

changed his attitude," Elam suggested.

"We appreciate all your help, Mr. Elam, but we need to get back to our claim," Cord said. "Our brother will be waiting to see how things turned out with that nugget."

"Is he the one who found it?"

"That's right," Flint said, "but it doesn't matter. We're all sharing whatever gold we find."

Elam nodded. "That's the best way to keep peace in the family, I suppose. Well, congratulations on the find, fellows. May it be the first of many."

"Thanks," Cord said. He supposed it had been inevitable that word would spread about the discovery Steve had made, but now there was no doubt about it. Throw in the garish details about the robbery and the gunfight in the Bear Flag, and the story would be all over Rio Oro City by nightfall.

He just hoped it wouldn't attract too much unwanted attention.

CHAPTER 34

They stopped at Higginbotham's on the way out of town, where the storekeeper weighed the nugget on a pair of scales he took from underneath the counter. Declaring it to be worth $47.50, he deducted the cost of the supplies Cord and Flint picked out from that total, then gave them the balance in cash.

"Happy to deal with you any time, boys," Higginbotham said as he smiled at the nugget lying on his palm. "I'll put this with the rest of my cache."

"What do you do with the gold you take in, Mr. Higginbotham?" Cord asked, then realized that wasn't a very appropriate question. "Sorry, that's none of my business —"

"No, no, I trust you fellas. Anyway, it's no real secret. When I have enough nuggets and dust on hand to make it worthwhile, I send a shipment back to my bank in San Francisco. Several of the businessmen here in town have gone in together to hire a wagon and some armed guards, and they transport the stuff for us."

"And the Reapers haven't hit the wagon?" Flint asked.

"Not so far," Higginbotham said. "Those guards are plenty tough, and like I said, they're well-armed. We keep it pretty quiet as to when the shipment is going out, too, so that no-good bunch doesn't have any time to prepare an ambush."

From Rio Oro City, Cord and Flint returned to the camp near the mouth of the canyon and left the supplies there in the Olmsted wagon. Then they headed up the canyon to the claims. There was still enough of the afternoon left that they would get there well before dark.

"I hope Steve doesn't mind that we went ahead and used the nugget to pay for those things," Cord commented.

"Gold is like any other kind of money," Flint said. "It's no good if you don't use it. What was he going to do, just sit around and look at it?"

"Maybe he's found some more while we were gone." Cord laughed. "Maybe we're rich by now."

Flint chuckled, too. "I won't hold my breath waiting for that . . . but it's worth hoping for, isn't it?"

When they reached the claim Lou Spooner and Ham Erskine had been working, they found that neither of the older men were there. That was unusual, so Cord hoped that nothing had happened to them.

They walked on up the canyon. When they reached the Olmsted claim, Cord saw that it was empty, too. Alarm welled up inside him.

"Something's wrong," he said to Flint. "First Lou and Ham are gone, and now Mr. Olmsted and the girls."

"I hear what sounds like Steve's pick hitting rock up ahead," Flint said. "Maybe he knows what's going on."

As they rounded the bend so they could see where Steve was enlarging a hole in the canyon wall, a wave of relief went through Cord. Not only were Abraham Olmsted, Glory, and Kat there, so were Spooner and Erskine. The men were working at the rock with picks and shovels, too.

"What's going on here?" Flint asked.

Steve lowered his pickax and looked around. He had a big grin on his face.

"I found more nuggets, Flint! They're smaller than that first one, but they're here. Mr. Olmsted heard me whoopin' and came to see what was goin' on."

"I thought Steve might've been hurt and figured it would be a good idea to check on him," Olmsted said. "Lou and Ham happened to be visitin' at the time, and they come along, too."

"And we didn't want to get left behind," Kat added.

Lou Spooner said, "When we saw that Steve had made a nice find, we decided it wouldn't hurt anything to help him out. You know, just being neighborly."

"This is our claim," Flint said. "We're only sharing among the three of us."

Erskine drawled, "We know that, son. Like Lou said, we're just bein' neighborly. We can go on back to our claim, if you want."

"So can we," Olmsted said.

"No, that's not necessary," Cord assured them, ignoring the narrow-eyed glance Flint gave him. "We're all friends here, and we appreciate your help. Don't we, Flint?"

"Sure," Flint said, not sounding completely sincere about it.

Steve said, "What did you find out about my nugget? Where is it? It's real gold, ain't it?"

Cord nodded. "It's real gold. Mr. Casterline confirmed that. It was, uh, worth forty-seven dollars. We traded it to Mr. Higginbotham for some supplies and got cash back from him, too."

Steve's eyes widened. "You don't have it anymore?"

"Of course not," Flint said. "We put it to good use. *After* we had to burn some powder to get it back."

"What are you talking about?" Kat asked.

"Was there trouble in town?" Glory put in with a worried expression on her face.

They were all going to hear about it eventually, Cord knew, so he supposed it was best that they hear the facts instead of lurid gossip.

"Some men attacked Mr. Casterline and stole the nugget from him," Cord said. "But we found them in the Bear Flag and got it back. We had to, uh, shoot them . . ."

"A gunfight!" Lou Spooner exclaimed. "And we missed it!"

For the next few minutes, Cord gave them the details about the violent outbreak in Rio Oro City. Abraham Olmsted looked concerned and shook his head solemnly as he listened. Glory seemed worried, too. Kat's eyes shone with excitement as Cord described the gunfight.

"So that's how you got the blood on your shirt sleeve," she said to Flint when Cord was finished. "How bad are you hurt?"

He shrugged. "It's nothing."

"I'm going to make a fuss over it anyway."

"Fine with me," Flint said with a chuckle. "I'll let a pretty girl fuss over me as much as she wants to."

"Was that saloon girl pretty? The one who doctored you?"

"It didn't really amount to doctoring. She just cleaned off the blood, splashed some whiskey on the wound, and tied a bandage around it. And no, she wasn't anywhere near as pretty as you are, Kat."

"Well, I'm glad to hear *that,* anyway. You need to be more careful."

"And not get shot again, you mean?"

"And not associate too much with those saloon wenches is more like it!"

Ham Erskine rubbed his jaw and said, "Those fellas wearin' masks like that makes it sound like they were part of the Reaper gang. They claimed to be new in town, though."

"Both of those things could be true," Spooner said. "Maybe the Reapers are growin'. Recruitin' more members."

"That doesn't bode well," Cord said. "They're already causing enough trouble around here. If the gang gets bigger, they might try to just take over everything."

"They're not gonna steal our gold!" Steve said. "And if they try, we'll stop 'em, won't we, Flint, just like you and Cord did today?"

"That's right, Steve. Nobody steals from the Bennett brothers."

The efforts of Steve, Abraham Olmsted, Lou Spooner, and Ham Erskine while Cord and Flint were in the settlement had uncovered more nuggets, but only a few. They were considerably smaller than the first nugget Steve had found, too. The vein of gold, if there was one, appeared to be buried deeper in the canyon wall.

But the discoveries they'd made so far were enough to raise their spirits and enthusiasm, and all three brothers worked with pick and shovel for the next week, letting the sluice sit unused for the time being.

As time passed with disappointing results — some days they found one or two tiny chunks of gold, some they didn't find any — Cord went back to work on the sluice, but that didn't pay off, either.

The disappointment was enough to make a man want to give up, but Cord wasn't going to do that. Determination — sheer, downright stubbornness — was the best thing they had going for them, he told himself.

Flint took to disappearing for long spells. He had done the same thing back in Arkansas before the family left the farm, Cord recalled. When Cord asked him about it, Flint answered, "I've been scouting around for something better."

"A different claim, you mean?"

"Yeah," Flint said off-handedly. "I'll find something that pays off more than this Godforsaken piece of ground."

Cord thought it was a mistake to give up on the claim so quickly. They were finding color, just not much of it and not very often. But the mother lode could be close . . .

Downstream, the Olmsteds had even less luck. Other than a few flecks of gold dust that Glory and Kat had turned up by panning in the creek, they hadn't found anything. One day, Kat stomped out of the stream, threw her pan down on the ground with great force, and said, "I give up! There's no gold here! We came all this way for a fool's dream!"

"Kat, don't talk like that," Glory said. "It sounds like you're calling Pa a fool."

"Well —" Kat began, then stopped short. She took a deep breath and went on, "You do what you want, Glory, but I'm finished with this." Then, unknowingly echoing what Flint Bennett had said, she added, "I'm going to find something better to do."

Glory waved a hand to take in their surroundings. "Out here?"

"I never said anything about staying out here."

Glory stared at her. "What are you talking about?"

"There's a settlement nearby, isn't there? I can find work there."

"What sort of work?" Glory drew in a sharp breath and held a hand to her mouth. "Kat, you aren't talking about —"

"Take it easy. That's not what I mean. There's got to be something else I can do. In fact, I have an idea where to start looking . . ."

She wouldn't say anything else, and she wouldn't go back to panning in the creek. Instead, she stalked downstream, heading out of the canyon toward the camp.

Glory watched her go and felt her heart sink. She didn't know what Kat had in mind, but she was almost certain that it wouldn't end well.

When Kat reached the camp, she went into the wagon and practically tore off the overalls and flannel shirt she wore while panning for gold. She changed into a clean, dark blue dress and then took her hair loose, brushing it vigorously for several minutes. Satisfied that she looked at least halfway decent, she set out for Rio Oro City.

She was only halfway there when some instinct warned her to look over her shoulder. A gasp escaped her lips as she spotted three men slouching along on horseback behind her, maybe fifty yards back. They didn't appear to be trying to catch up to her, but they kept coming at a steady, deliberate pace.

She recognized the man riding a little out in front of the other two: Rip Jordan. Although it was difficult to be sure at this distance, she thought he was grinning . . . and it wasn't a pleasant expression.

Kat picked up her pace. She didn't break into a run, but she didn't waste any time, either.

Another glance over her shoulder told her that Jordan had heeled his mount to a faster gait, as well.

But again, he didn't seem to be trying to catch up.

He just wanted to scare her, that was all, Kat realized. That angered her, and her natural pride and stubbornness made her slow down. She wasn't going to let the gunman and his cronies get away with frightening her. She walked toward the settlement as if she didn't have a care in the world.

A few moments later, the swift rataplan of

hoofbeats reached her ears. She stopped and spun around, seeing to her horror that Jordan and his friends were galloping directly toward her.

That jolted a shocked cry from Kat's lips. Her first impulse was to turn and run, but then she realized she couldn't get away from them by doing that. She couldn't outrun the horses.

So she did the only thing she could. She stood there, trembling slightly, and waited with her chin thrust out defiantly. The three men on horseback swept toward her, closing the gap between them with what seemed like breathtaking speed. Rip Jordan yanked the hat from his head, waved it in the air, and whooped exuberantly.

Then the riders parted abruptly, the other two men going to Kat's left while Jordan galloped past her on the right. He came so close that it seemed like the horse was on top of her. She could smell it, feel the sweat flying from its flanks.

Then the horses and riders were past her, racing toward Rio Oro City. Jordan didn't look back. None of them did.

Jordan had tried to terrify her, Kat thought, but she had stood firm and defied him. He had seen for himself that she didn't scare easily.

She told herself that, despite having felt her knees shaking when the horses were almost on top of her.

Jordan and the other two disappeared into the settlement.

Kat reached Rio Oro City a few minutes later and carefully navigated the muddy street until she made it to the boardwalk and went along it toward the Bear Flag. She entered the saloon and looked around for Patrick Elam.

She had a proposition for him, and it didn't involve her working as a dancing girl or a prostitute. She spotted him at his private table, took a step in that direction, and then stopped short.

Elam wasn't alone at his table. Flint Bennett sat across from the saloonkeeper.

And Flint had spotted her, too. He was already rising to his feet with a surprised scowl on his face.

CHAPTER 35

Kat didn't stand there looking across the saloon for more than a second. Then she resumed her confident stride toward the table. She was surprised to see Flint here, especially after he had made it clear that he didn't much like Patrick Elam, but that was Flint's business and none of hers.

She had her own business in the Bear Flag Saloon.

Elam stood up to greet her, too, but unlike Flint, he was smiling. "Welcome to the Bear Flag, Miss Olmsted," he said before Flint could get a word out. "I didn't expect to see you here, but your presence certainly improves any room."

"What are you doing here, Kat?" Flint asked. "Why aren't you out at your father's claim?"

"Because there's no gold on that claim, or not enough to count, anyway," she said. "Glory and Pa can keep digging for nonexistent riches if they want to, but I've had enough of it." She looked at Elam and smiled. "And thank you for that kind welcome, Mr. Elam."

"To be honest, this isn't the sort of place where a respectable young lady usually finds herself," Elam said. "What brings you here today?"

Kat drew in a deep breath, well aware that accentuated the curves of her body. "I came to ask you for a job."

"A job!" Flint repeated. "You can't mean —"

Kat ignored him and gestured gracefully with one hand. "What this place needs," she said, "is a touch of class. Not that there's anything wrong with it the way it is . . ."

"No, I agree completely," Elam said as he came around the table, still smiling. "For a mining camp saloon, it's all right, I suppose, but class is something that's in short supply around here. At least . . . it was until you came in, Miss Olmsted."

"Please, call me Kat."

"Damn it," Flint said, almost sputtering. Kat had never seen him this obviously flustered before.

"What did you have in mind . . . Kat?" Elam asked. He slid a cigar out of his vest pocket and clamped the end of it between

404

his teeth.

"I have some nice dresses. I could wear them and serve as a hostess, I suppose you'd call it. Circulate around the room, welcome the customers, maybe even sing a song now and then. I have a decent voice."

"I'm sure you do," Elam said around the cheroot.

"But I'm not going to dance around in some sort of vulgar display," she went on. "And I'm certainly not going to do anything else improper."

"And I'd never ask you to." Elam took the cigar out of his mouth and used it to gesture emphatically. "As for your attire, I'll have some even nicer outfits sent out here from San Francisco. You'll be the belle of the Sierra Nevadas, Miss Olmsted . . . I mean, Kat. I think this is an excellent idea." He laughed. "And Teddy Harville won't have anything to match it, I assure you."

Kat smiled and said, "Unless my sister decides to go to work for him."

"Your sister is a lovely young woman, but she's not your equal, Kat."

"Anyway, she'd never do that." Kat laughed. "She still believes she's going to find a fortune in gold out there on that claim."

"There are different kinds of fortunes,"

Elam said, "and different ways to find them."

Kat had been watching Flint from the corner of her eye as his face darkened with angry blood. She hadn't expected to find him here, and she wished he hadn't been. It would have been easier to present him with an arrangement that had already been made.

But that wasn't the way things had turned out, and honestly, she didn't care. She liked Flint Bennett. She was drawn to his determined, almost ruthless nature.

But he had to understand that she shared that same sort of nature. She knew what she wanted, and she was prepared to do whatever was necessary to get it.

"We haven't discussed your compensation," Elam murmured.

"I'm sure you'll settle on something fair. If I believed you'd try to take advantage of me, I'd never have come here."

"Of course I won't. When can you start?"

"How about tomorrow?" Kat asked with a smile. "But I can give you a little sample now, if you'd like."

Without waiting for him to answer, she turned and sauntered toward the entrance, pausing to smile and say hello to the miners at the tables she passed. The dirty, roughly dressed men all looked shocked that a young, beautiful woman would even speak to them, let alone smile as if she were happy to see them. Most of them grinned happily at the unexpected development, especially when she laughed and briefly rested a hand on their shoulders.

She glanced back at the private table in the corner. Flint still stood there, staring at her, and it was hard to tell if he was more upset or confused. He was always so sure of himself. It was nice having him a little off-balance around her for a change. She didn't want him ever taking her for granted, she thought as she left the tent.

This whole thing had been nothing more than her giving in to a frustrated impulse, a feeling that she was wasting her time standing in a cold creek, breaking her back to pan for gold that just wasn't there.

But even though she hadn't really taken time to plan it all out, she had a feeling that this new situation was going to work out very well for her.

Very well indeed.

At the table, when Kat was gone and Elam had resumed his seat, Flint muttered, "If you hurt that girl, I'll —"

"Don't waste my time and your breath on

idle threats, Bennett," Elam interrupted him.

"There's nothing idle about it. I always mean what I say. You need to know that."

Elam put the cigar back in his mouth and chewed on the end. "And why do I need to know that?" he asked with a trace of mockery in his voice.

"Because if we're going to work together, we both need to know where we stand."

"Work together?" Elam echoed. "I wondered what brought you here today. You hadn't gotten around to explaining that before Kat came in. I'll admit, though, I was glad when you asked to talk to me. I have some questions for *you,* in fact."

Elam dropped his right hand under the level of the table.

"Go ahead and ask them, then," Flint said.

"First . . ." Elam paused so that a faint sound was audible. "Did you hear that? It was me cocking a derringer that's pointed right at your belly, Bennett. If you try any tricks, I'll put a hole in your guts."

If the threat bothered Flint, he didn't show it. His face remained stony and tightly controlled.

"You've been poking around for more than a week now," Elam continued, "riding all over these hills, asking questions, sticking your nose in where it's not wanted. You're up to something, and I want to know what it is."

Flint smiled thinly. "I just wanted to make sure who I was going to be dealing with. Every man who's been targeted by the Reapers has been friendly with Teddy Harville. Most are regular customers in his saloon. That told me something."

"What did it tell you?" Elam asked around the cigar clenched between his teeth.

"That *you're* the boss of the Reapers. They work for you."

Elam clamped down harder on the cigar, making it jump a little. Then he shook his head and said, "You're insane."

"I don't think so. I knew as soon as I laid eyes on you, Elam, that you're the sort of man who's always working an angle. Looking for a payoff. You have only one real rival in this town, and that's Harville. You put together a gang to whittle down his support, and you not only get to reap the benefits of those robberies — no pun intended — but you also hurt him and profit from that. The Reapers aren't just some haphazard bunch of killers and thieves. Somebody's guiding them. It makes sense that somebody is you."

Elam took the cigar out of his mouth and leaned back in his chair as he regarded Flint with an intent stare. Finally, he said, "What if I am?"

Flint shrugged. "Then we're two of a kind, and I want in."

"Why would I want to work with you? You've made it pretty clear that you don't like me . . . and with Kat Olmsted working here, I suspect you like me even less."

Anger flared in Flint's eyes. Then he controlled it with a visible effort and drew in a breath before saying, "You should want to work with me because I know something that could make us a considerable amount of money."

"And that is?" Elam prodded.

"How to find out when Higginbotham and the other merchants are going to send their next shipment of gold to San Francisco."

Elam frowned. "I already know they ship their gold to San Francisco by wagon."

"But they keep the schedule a secret until the last minute. I can find out ahead of time, so that you can have your men ready for them."

"Keep going," Flint said after a moment.

"All the men in that little group drink at the Golden Nugget. I'm friends with both

410

Harville and Higginbotham. They trust me because *I* drink at the Golden Nugget, too, and I've been cultivating their friendship. Plus, it's known around town that you and I don't get along that well."

Elam's eyes narrowed. "You might be ruining that impression by coming in here today and seeking me out."

"We'll get to that," Flint said. "Hear me out, there's more. It'll be a lot easier to hold up that gold wagon if you have an inside man."

Understanding dawned on Elam's face. "You're going to get Higginbotham and his friends to hire you as one of the guards."

"I need a job," Flint said, as his shoulders rose and fell. "Our claims aren't paying off. It'll seem reasonable enough when I approach them about a job."

Elam stroked his chin with his fingertips and slowly nodded. "That makes sense, I suppose."

"Of course it does. I've given this a lot of thought and spent some time setting it up."

"Again, though, you risk ruining that once word gets around town that you were in here being friendly with me." Elam frowned. "You should have approached me privately."

"No," Flint said, "this way is better. I would have come up with some excuse, but

411

Kat just gave us a perfect one."

He shoved to his feet, grabbed hold of the table, and with a heave of his powerful shoulders, he turned it over and sent it crashing into Elam, who spilled backward out of his chair.

CHAPTER 36

Elam jerked the derringer's trigger as he fell, but the little weapon was pointed up by then, and the bullet went through the tent's roof.

The derringer had a second barrel, Flint saw, as he lunged toward the saloonkeeper. He lashed out with a kick and didn't give Elam a chance to fire it. The toe of his boot struck the wrist of Elam's gun hand. The derringer flew out of the man's grasp.

Flint reached down, grabbed the front of Elam's coat, and hauled him to his feet. Cocking back his right fist, Flint threw a punch that landed cleanly on Elam's jaw and snapped his head to the side. Elam slumped to the floor again as Flint let go of him.

Pointing a finger at the fallen man, Flint yelled, "And worse than that will happen to you if you hurt Miss Olmsted!" He added a few choice obscenities.

Elam just groaned as he struggled to push himself up but failed, sagging back to the floor.

Flint started to turn away from him, grinning triumphantly, but he stopped and yelled in pain as a line of fiery agony ripped across his back, tearing his shirt and drawing blood from his skin. One of Elam's bullwhip-wielding guards had just laid the lash on him.

Another of the guards came at Flint from the front. The whip in his hand snaked out. Flint knew it was headed toward his face and might pluck an eye out if the stroke landed.

He flung up a hand with the same deadly speed he used in drawing a gun. The whip wrapped around his forearm. Before the guard had time to jerk it back, Flint grabbed the whip farther up and pulled as hard as he could. The guard didn't let go of it, but he was yanked forward sharply and stumbled, falling to his knees.

The first guard struck again at Flint's back. Flint was already moving away, so this time, the lash didn't land with full force. Flint already knew that the third regular guard wasn't in the saloon at the moment; he had checked on that while he was talking to Elam. But he was still outnumbered, and

414

his back hurt like blazes.

He lowered his shoulder and bulled into the first guard while the man drew his arm back to try again with the whip. The impact knocked the guard off his feet before he could strike. He went down on a table with Flint on top of him.

The table's legs broke under their combined weight. It collapsed, and both of them crashed to the floor amidst the debris.

Flint rammed his knee into the guard's groin with enough force to make the man let out a high, thin scream. Flint pushed up with his left hand and hammered his right fist into the man's pain-contorted face. The guard went limp underneath him.

A rush of footsteps told Flint the second guard was coming after him. He threw himself to the side and rolled, but he couldn't completely avoid the chair the man had picked up and swung at him.

The chair clipped Flint's head with enough force that rockets seemed to explode behind his eyes. He was stunned and couldn't make his muscles work for a moment.

That was long enough for a couple of men to grab his arms. They weren't Elam's guards, but they drank here in the Bear Flag and obviously weren't going to stand by and do nothing when the place's proprietor was attacked. They lifted Flint to his feet, wrenched his arms behind his back, and held him tightly.

Elam was upright again, standing beside the overturned table while he rubbed his jaw where Flint had punched him. He lowered his hand, glared at Flint, and stalked toward him.

Elam drew back his right fist and used his momentum to drive a vicious blow into Flint's belly. His hand sunk almost to the wrist. Flint jerked under the impact and would have doubled over in reaction to it, but his captors held him upright. Elam swung a left that smashed into Flint's jaw, then a right to the face that left his lips swollen and bleeding.

Elam finished with another blow to the belly, and as he stepped back, he nodded to the men holding Flint. They let go of him. He collapsed into a heap on the sawdust-littered floor.

Kneeling next to Flint, Elam leaned over close to him and whispered, "I figured out what you were doing and thought I should make it look good. Do you think I succeeded?"

Flint groaned and lifted his head enough to spew several curses at Elam. But at the same time, the eyes of the two men met for a split second. That was long enough for understanding to pass between them.

Elam straightened and stepped back. He gestured curtly to his guards, who were both back on their feet by now, and said, "Get him out of here."

Each man took hold of one of Flint's legs and started dragging him toward the door.

"Don't let me see your face in here again, Bennett," Elam called after them.

Even in his stunned, pain-wracked state, Flint understood what Elam meant by that.

The next time they met, it would need to be in secret.

As the guards reached the entrance, one of them asked, "Can we give him a little farewell of our own, boss?"

"No, he's had enough," Elam said. "Just toss him in the street and let him go."

The guards looked disappointed by that decision, but Flint wasn't. He knew the brutal pair might have gotten carried away and stomped him to death, once they began trying to even the score with him. Elam must have known that, too.

Instead, hands lifted him and tossed him off the boardwalk into the stinking muck of the street. Flint landed face down, then forced himself up. He didn't want to drown in the stuff . . . especially not after taking the first steps in an alliance that might prove to be very lucrative.

And if it did, then once things were set up properly, he could deal with Patrick Elam — permanently — and make sure the man never tried anything with Kat.

There was a considerable amount of tension in the camp that evening. Abraham Olmsted and Glory were upset when Kat announced that she was going to work for Patrick Elam as a hostess in his saloon. Kat was upset when Flint showed up, bloody, battered, and bruised from the fight he'd had with Elam and his guards. She accused Flint of starting the ruckus over her, and he didn't deny it. In fact, he seemed to wear his injuries as a badge of pride, even the stripe of the whip across his back, which made both girls gasp in horror when they saw it.

Cord just wished things would settle down so everybody could concentrate on trying to find gold.

Flint seemed to have abandoned that goal, however. He said that he had a line on some other work and offered to split his claim between Cord and Steve.

"No thanks," Cord replied without hesita-

418

tion. "We're partners, and more than that, we're brothers. Your share in whatever we find will always be waiting for you, Flint."

With a scowl, Flint said, "You don't have to do that."

"Sure we do, Flint," Steve said. "You'd do that same for us."

Cord wasn't as sure of that as Steve seemed to be, but he didn't say anything. He just hoped Flint would get whatever plans he had out of his system and come back to work the claims again.

Glory was in a similar position with Kat. She tried to talk her sister out of going to work at the Bear Flag Saloon, but to no avail. That situation grew even more distressing when, after several days of walking back and forth to the settlement, Kat announced that she was going to be staying in town.

"It doesn't make sense to waste all that time and energy traipsing into town and back out here every day," she insisted. "I've got a room at Widow Flinders' boarding house. Well, it's not a room so much as it is a cot in a space partitioned off with blankets, but at least it provides some privacy and a place to keep the dresses Patrick is getting for me."

"He's buying you dresses now?" Glory asked.

"They're on their way from San Francisco. It's so I'll look nice while I'm working in the saloon."

"And he doesn't expect anything in return?"

"Patrick is too much of a gentleman to act like that," Kat said. "Anyway . . . I'm not sure I'd mind so much if he *didn't* act like a gentleman."

"Kat, you don't mean that!"

"Maybe I don't, and maybe I do." She patted Glory's shoulder and added with infuriating smugness, "You just go on squatting in that creek all day and let me worry about what I'm doing."

Abraham Olmsted was worried about his daughter's move to town, but he had to admit there was nothing he could do about it. Kat was a grown woman and was going to make her own decisions, whether he liked it or not.

As time passed, things settled down into a new routine. Cord, Glory, and Olmsted might not like or agree with the turn things had taken, but there was still work to be done every day when the sun rose, so they set about it with continued determination . . . but not much success.

420

After a day in which Cord and Steve found not even a hint of color, they were sitting beside the campfire that night with an equally frustrated Olmsted and Glory, when Steve suddenly dashed the grounds from his coffee cup into the flames, rose to his feet, and said, "That's it. I'm done."

"You mean you're finished with supper?" Cord asked, although he had a sudden disheartening feeling that Steve was talking about something else.

"No, I mean I'm done lookin' for gold where there ain't any." Steve held out his hands in the firelight and spread his fingers. "Look at these. Blisters on top o' blisters. About the time they start healin' up, swingin' that pick causes new ones. And all for a few nuggets that don't even add up to a hundred dollars' worth of gold yet."

"But we know the color's there," Cord argued. "It's just a matter of finding a vein —"

"What if there ain't no vein? What if there's just the few specks here and there that we've found so far? Can you promise me it'll get better, Cord?"

"You know I can't, but you were always the one who was so determined that we were going to find a fortune. You said there was just no chance of anything else, like you figured you could *will* it into existence."

"I guess I figured wrong," Steve said heavily, "because now I can feel it in my bones that there ain't no gold. Not enough to make it worth lookin' for, anyway."

Glory said, "Other people have found goodly amounts on their claims, Steve. Several have even gotten rich."

"Yeah, that's always the way, ain't it? A few get rich, and the rest of us are left out in the cold."

Something about what Steve was saying struck Cord as familiar, and suddenly he realized why.

"Flint's been talking to you, hasn't he? He was saying things like that before he went off and got involved in whatever he's mixed up in now. Whatever it is that keeps him away from here most of the time."

Steve scowled and managed to look angry and a little guilty at the same time.

"Flint says there's work waitin' for me if I want it. Real, payin' work."

"Doing what?"

Steve opened his mouth to answer, then shook his head. "I can't tell you. Flint told me not to."

"Then it's probably something shady, maybe even illegal."

Steve's hands clenched into fists as he

took a step toward Cord. "You take that back!"

Cord came to his feet. The last thing he wanted was to fight one of his own brothers. But he wasn't going to back down, either.

"Flint's never cared that much about staying on the right side of the law," he said. "If you're not careful, he'll get you in trouble, Steve."

"Flint never steered me wrong! Not ever!"

Abraham Olmsted stood up, too, and moved quickly to get between them, which probably wasn't a good place for a relatively small man to be. But he lifted his hands as if he intended to hold them apart physically, if need be, and said in a stern voice, "You boys just settle down, blast it. If you ain't careful, you'll wind up sayin' and doin' some things you're liable to regret."

Glory got between them, too. "My pa's right," she said with a stubborn look on her face. "You don't need to fight."

"That's right, because you ain't stoppin' me, Cord," Steve said. "I'm plumb sorry it ain't worked out, but I'm done."

With that, he turned and walked away.

"Where are you going?" Cord called after him.

"To find Flint." Steve didn't look back as

he answered. A moment later, the darkness swallowed him.

Cord stared at the shadows where his brother had disappeared. Finally, he sighed and shook his head.

Glory put her hand on his arm. "What are you going to do, Cord?"

"Reckon I'll keep on working the claim. There's not much else I can do, is there?"

"You'll work it by yourself?"

He laughed, but there wasn't much humor in the sound. "Well, I can't be in more than one place at a time, so I'll just work on whichever claim looks the most promising at the time."

"And give your brothers a share if you find anything, even though they ain't worked for it," Olmsted said.

"Both of them have worked the claims in the past, whether they continue to do so or not. Steve's worked mighty hard, too, and he's found more gold than either Flint or me."

"Or us," the old-timer muttered.

"But not enough to suit him, I guess," Cord continued.

Glory said, "Do you really think Flint's been talking to him, trying to convince him to give up prospecting?"

"I'm sure of it," Cord said. "Those two

424

have always been close. I was always kind of the outsider in the family."

"But yet you'll still look out for them and try to do right by them."

"Of course," Cord said without hesitation. "They're my brothers."

Olmsted scratched at his beard and said, "Maybe we can give you a hand, son. It ain't like we're finding any color, either."

"And you wouldn't have to give us a share if we found anything, either," Glory said.

Cord shook his head. "I wouldn't accept your help on that basis. If you were working on one of our claims and found something, you'd be entitled to an equal share, as far as I'm concerned."

"Flint and Steve might not feel the same way."

"Well . . . they're not here, are they? So it's not really their decision to make. Let's sleep on it," Cord suggested, "and see how things look in the morning."

CHAPTER 37

When morning rolled around, it brought yet another unexpected development with it. Cord, Glory, and Olmsted were sitting around the fire, finishing the bacon and biscuits Glory had cooked, when Lou Spooner and Ham Erskine walked up.

"Howdy," Spooner greeted them with his usual friendly smile. Erskine just nodded.

"Kinda early to be visitin'," Olmsted said, "but you fellas are always welcome, you know that."

"We're not actually here on a visit," Erskine said. "We got a proposition for you, Cord."

"I'm listening," Cord said, curious what had brought the two older men to their camp.

"Plenty of folks back home will tell you there aren't many men more stubborn than me and Ham," Spooner began. "But even we know that when you're just banging your

head against a stone wall, after a while it makes sense to stop."

"What Lou's sayin' in his roundabout way is that we've figured out there ain't no gold on our claim," Erskine said. "None in the ground, that is, and precious little dust in the creek. I reckon we could pan out a speck now and then from now until doomsday, and it wouldn't add up to more'n a pittance."

Cord said, "I'm sorry to hear you feel that way. Does that mean you're giving up and going back east? If you're thinking that my brothers and I might buy your claim, I don't see how we could —"

Spooner held up a hand to stop him. "Hold on. We're not tryin' to sell the claim. Shoot, we'd *give* it away if there was somebody who wanted to bust his back and his neck on it. But we're not interested in goin' back east, either."

Erskine grunted and said, "Nothin' back there to go back to."

"No," Spooner went on, "we were wonderin' if you might be interested in us helpin' you work *your* claim. You've been finding color, haven't you?"

"Not much. A few nuggets, some dust from the creek . . ."

"That's more than us," Erskine said.

"Listen, Cord, we ain't askin' you to pay us. We'd work for a little grub."

"And the companionship," Spooner added. "Plus a better chance for the excitement of seein' some actual gold now and then!"

Cord shook his head and said, "I don't know. Those claims belong as much to my brothers as they do to me, so I'm not sure I've got any right to make a decision like that."

Spooner looked around. "I can't help but notice that Flint and Steve ain't here this morning."

It was true. Steve had never returned to the camp after departing in anger the night before, and Flint hadn't put in an appearance, either. Cord hoped that wherever they might be, they were all right.

"From the talk we've heard," Erskine said, "Flint's pretty much given up on prospectin' and taken to hanging around town and riding in the hills."

Cord shrugged, not admitting that the older man was right but not denying it, either.

"Has Steve gone off to join him?" Spooner asked.

"Whether they're here or not doesn't matter," Cord said without actually answering the question. "They still have an equal share and an equal say in how our outfit is run."

"You can ask 'em about it later," Erskine suggested, "and if they turn thumbs-down on the idea, then we'll clear out, and you haven't lost anything. But if Lou and I are already helpin' you with the claim, seems to me your brothers would be less likely to say no."

That was true, Cord knew, and to be honest, he liked the idea of Spooner and Erskine working with him. With Flint and Steve having gone off to do whatever it was they were doing, he couldn't handle the load alone. He would do his best, of course, but it was no way to go about searching for gold.

"I suppose we could give it a try," he said after a moment. "I'll be glad to have you fellas around, to be honest."

Glory spoke up, saying, "Besides, the way they've treated Cord and run out on him, I don't think Flint and Steve will have any right to complain."

"I wouldn't go so far as to say that —"

"Because they're your brothers and you love them," she said. "But they've turned their backs on you, just like . . . just like Kat . . ."

"Here now," Olmsted said. "Don't go

talkin' about your sister like that. She didn't turn her back on us. She just wanted to find somethin' she's happier doin', that's all."

"Isn't that what Flint and Steve are doing?" Glory asked.

"Well . . . we don't rightly know just what they're doin'." Olmsted sighed. "I reckon we don't know what Kat's doin', neither, when you come right down to it."

"Miss Kat?" Spooner said. "Why, she's workin' at the Bear Flag Saloon, singin' songs and jokin' with the fellas who go in there to drink. I hear tell she's mighty popular."

"Dadgummit, Lou, you're makin' that sound a lot worse'n it is," Erskine said. He added to Olmsted and Glory, "There ain't nothin' improper goin' on, is what *I've* heard. Miss Kat ain't like the other girls who work there, so you don't have to worry about that."

To ease the awkwardness that had developed since the subject of Kat came up, Spooner said, "So how about it, Cord? You'll let me and Ham work with you?"

"For now," Cord said. "I'll take the responsibility for it, until I get a chance to ask Flint and Steve what they think about the idea."

And it would be a lot easier to do that, he

added to himself, if he had any idea where his brothers were and what they were doing.

Flint rocked along easily in the saddle as he rode behind the wagon. A man named Brimley rode alongside him. Each had a rifle across the saddle in front of him, and Brimley was packing a revolver like Flint.

The wagon loaded with canvas bags full of nuggets and dust was about fifty feet in front of them. Three armed men were in the back of the wagon with the gold, a flanker rode on either side, and three more men led the way along the trail. A shotgun guard sat on the seat next to the driver.

That made eleven armed guards, a dozen if the driver was counted, and he was packing iron, too. A formidable force, and one that would require planning and preparation to deal with. So far, the Reapers had never had enough advance warning of a gold shipment to get ready for a holdup against those odds.

Not until now.

Flint's hard-planed face was expressionless as he rode. Brimley wasn't the talkative sort, and Flint was grateful for that. The two men hadn't exchanged more than a dozen words since leaving Rio Oro City.

Despite his stolid exterior, Flint's brain

was whirling. Mostly he was going over the plan he and Patrick Elam had worked out during their clandestine meeting the night before in a grove of trees near the settlement.

Flint hadn't been back inside the Bear Flag since the fight with Elam more than a week earlier. He had spent considerable time in Teddy Harville's Golden Nugget Saloon, however, talking about how much he despised Elam and drinking with men who shared that sentiment, including Harville and Orvie Higginbotham.

Because of that, and because of hints he had dropped about needing to find a job after giving up on his prospecting claim, Flint had been able to manuever Higginbotham into asking him to sign on as one of the guards for this gold shipment.

"We can always use another good man to keep those damn Reapers away," Higginbotham had said.

Flint had hesitated before accepting the offer, but just long enough to make it look real. And so he had found out the previous evening that the wagon carrying the gold was going to be leaving this morning. There had been just enough time to alert Patrick Elam to that . . .

But then a surprise had been waiting for

Flint after the rendezvous with Elam, when he got back to the tent where he rented a cot.

Steve was there, having stomped out of camp angrily.

Flint would have been mighty glad to see his brother under other circumstances. More than likely, he could have gotten Steve a job as one of the guards.

But there wasn't time for that, and to tell the truth, Flint wasn't completely convinced Steve would go along with the plan. Steve knew what had happened back there in Arkansas, knew the things Flint had done in order to make it possible for them to head west, but he hadn't taken part in the worst of it.

Better to ease him into the setup here, Flint had told himself. And it would be easier to do that once Steve saw the money that Flint was going to make from this job.

Steve was waiting for him back in town. He hadn't been happy that Flint was supposed to be gone for several days with the gold shipment, but nothing could be done about that.

Anyway, it wouldn't actually be several days.

If all went according to plan, Flint would be back in Rio Oro City by nightfall.

Up ahead, the guards leading the way called a halt to rest the horses and the mule team pulling the wagon. Flint and Brimley reined in and dismounted where they were, keeping the same gap behind the vehicle.

Flint put his hands in the small of his back and stretched, easing muscles stiff from riding. Making what was apparently idle conversation, he said to his companion, "You've been over this trail before, haven't you?"

"Several times," Brimley confirmed.

"I've heard about some place up ahead called Devil's Hill . . . ?"

Brimley smiled. "*El Cerro del Diablo*. The Hill of the Devil. That's what folks called the place when California was still part of Mexico, and Spain before that. But don't get the wrong idea. It ain't haunted or anything like that. It's just a steep hill where the trail takes a sharp turn at the bottom. That's all."

"Oh." Flint shrugged. "Well, it sounds tricky, anyway. The driver probably has to be careful heading down. Sounds like it'd be a good place for a runaway."

"Yeah, but Ben Hooper has been over this trail plenty of times. He knows how to handle the slope."

Flint nodded. Brimley had confirmed what Patrick Elam had told him.

The group pushed on a few minutes later. The trail wound through rugged, heavily wooded country. As far as Flint could see, there were plenty of places where the Reapers could have sprung an ambush, but there was cover close to the trail, and any guards who survived the first volley would be able to hustle into shelter and put up a fight.

The plan they were going to use today would be more devastating, if it worked.

The wagon reached a flat stretch about a hundred yards wide. On the far side of that bench was the top of the trail descending Devil's Hill. As the men approached, Flint could see the landscape dropping down and opening up into an impressive vista of wooded hills and deep valleys. From this angle, the trail appeared to end in a sheer cliff. A man wouldn't be able to see down the slope until he was almost on top of it.

Flint watched the three riders in the lead suddenly vanish from sight. They had started down the trail. The driver, Ben Hooper, reached for the brake lever as the wagon drew near the edge. He would have to lean frequently on the brake to slow the wagon's speed and keep it from running away with itself during the descent.

It was time for Flint to make his move.

435

A subtle jerk on the reins made his horse break stride. "Damn it," he said. "I think this nag's gone lame."

"Might've just picked up a rock in one of its shoes," Brimley suggested. "Want me to take a look?"

"No, I can do it. You go on ahead. I'll catch up in a minute."

"You sure?"

"Yeah, don't worry about it." Flint fought not to reveal in his voice or on his face the impatience he felt.

"Well, all right." Brimley nudged his horse on ahead.

Flint checked the wagon. The team was on the slope now, and the vehicle itself was right at the brink. The flankers had drawn in close, because the trail was narrower there. The guards in the back of the wagon were all turned to the front so they could watch as they started down the steep slope.

That left nobody watching Flint. He drew his revolver, cocked and aimed it, and shouted, "Brimley, look out!"

Then he pulled the trigger.

CHAPTER 38

The bullet slammed into the back of Brimley's right shoulder and drove him forward in the saddle. Flint fired a second shot as quickly as he could, this one directed into the air. He threw himself face down on the ground but kept his head turned so that he could see what was going on as more shots rang out from the slope up ahead. Gunthunder filled the air.

Brimley had stayed mounted so far, but his horse, spooked by the sudden, unholy racket, started crow-hopping around. With one arm bloody and useless from the wound, Brimley couldn't hang on. He pitched off the horse's back and crashed to the ground.

But not before he'd seen Flint lying motionless in the trail, apparently gunned down, maybe even dead.

It sounded like a war on the hill. Cover there was sparse, according to Patrick Elam, but there were just enough hiding places to stage an effective ambush. The driver and the shotgun guard would be the first targets. With Hooper dead, the team would bolt . . . and gravity would do the rest.

While that was going on, Flint took out the razor he had hidden in his pocket. With slow, small, hard-to-see movements, he opened the razor and brought it to his head. Carefully, he used the keen edge to scrape a bloody wound just below his temple. He clenched his teeth against the fiery pain of the self-inflicted injury. He couldn't just make a straight cut. That would have hurt, too, but not as much.

No, this injury had to look like a bullet had grazed him.

He couldn't see it to make sure he'd done a good job, but that couldn't be helped. Groaning for real, he closed the razor and put it away, then pushed himself to hands and knees and started crawling toward the fallen man.

"Brimley!" he called. "Brimley! Damn it, man, how bad are you hit?"

Brimley writhed on the ground, clutching his bloody, bullet-ventilated shoulder. His head jerked around at the sound of Flint's voice. He gasped curses, then managed to say, "Bennett, you're shot in the head!"

438

"I think . . . it just creased me," Flint said. He forced himself to his feet and staggered up to Brimley.

At the bottom of Devil's Hill, the shooting had stopped.

Flint leaned down and grasped Brimley's uninjured arm. "Can you get up?" he asked. "We need to get off the trail."

"Those damn . . . Reapers! It must've been them . . . who ambushed us."

"I know. That's why we need to get off the trail and into some cover. They may not want to leave any witnesses behind."

Brimley cursed some more and struggled to his feet. The two men weaved toward some nearby brush.

Flint's urgency wasn't entirely feigned. He knew that Rip Jordan was among the men who'd ambushed the gold shipment. Jordan was in charge of the group, in fact. Even though the plan called for Flint to survive this violent encounter, along with Brimley, that didn't mean Jordan would follow orders. He might decide this was too good a chance to pass up.

They pushed through the brush and into a grove of trees, where Flint helped Brimley sit down with his back propped against one of the trunks.

"Wha . . . wha . . . happened?" Brimley asked.

"When I dismounted to check my horse's hooves, I spotted a man hidden in the brush on the other side of the trail. He had a gun and was aiming at you. That's why I yelled. But he shot you and then turned and took a shot at me. Felt like a sledgehammer hit me in the head, and I went down. That's all I knew for a couple of minutes."

Brimley nodded weakly. "I . . . I saw you layin' there . . . figured you were dead."

Flint touched the sticky blood that had run down his face and said, "I came mighty close to it."

Brimley was silent for a moment, then said, "Wonder why they didn't make sure we were both done for?"

Flint didn't want him thinking too much about that. He said, "We were both so bloody, I reckon they figured there wasn't any need. I'll take that stroke of luck."

Brimley rested his head on the tree trunk and said, "Yeah, so will I."

A few minutes of silence went by, broken only by occasional snatches of men's voices coming from a distance, calling to each other down at the bottom of Devil's Hill. Then Flint heard the swift rataplan of hoofbeats from that direction and called it to Brimley's attention.

"Sounds like they're pulling out. We'd better go see if anybody's still alive. We might be able to help them."

But there wouldn't be anyone left alive, Flint thought. Not if Jordan and the others had done their jobs.

With Flint's help, Brimley struggled to his feet. They made their way back to the trail. Their horses stood at the edge of the path, grazing contentedly. Flint was able to catch them both. He had to give Brimley a hand climbing into the saddle.

Then they rode down the steep hill, leaning back to keep their balance as the horses picked their way along carefully.

"Doesn't look like your horse is lame anymore," Brimley observed.

Why in blazes is he paying attention to things like that? Flint asked himself.

"He must've kicked that rock out of his shoe when he was jumping around."

Brimley nodded and said, "More than likely."

Several bodies were sprawled where they had ended up when bullets knocked them off their horses and then gravity had sent them rolling down the slope. Flint recognized the men he'd been riding with earlier, but their deaths meant nothing to him. He had come out here to get rich, and one way or another, that's what he was going to do.

If a few men had to die for that to happen, that was just too damned bad.

The terrain at the bottom of the hill was just as Elam had described it. The reason the trail made such a sharp turn was because of the thirty-foot-deep gully that ran alongside it.

The wagon lay on its side in that gully, wrecked beyond repair. The mules, twisted and broken and dead, were tangled in their traces. The bodies of the driver and more dead guards lay here and there like discarded toys.

Once the Reapers shot the driver and the shotgun guard, the wagon had turned into a runaway. Flint hadn't seen it happen, but he could imagine how the vehicle had tangled up with the team, overturned, and rolled the rest of the way down, taking the mules with it as it crashed into the gully.

Already, flies were starting to gather, and buzzards circled overhead.

Brimley cursed again when he saw the catastrophic results of the ambush, but this time he uttered the obscenities in a low, hushed voice that made it sound almost as if he were praying, instead.

"All those men dead," he said. "And for

what? Gold?"

That was right. The bags of nuggets and dust that had been in the back of the wagon were nowhere to be seen. The Reapers had harvested them.

"There's nothing we can do for these fellas," Flint said harshly. "We'd better head back to Rio Oro City so we can let folks know what happened. And get that shoulder of yours patched up before you get blood poisoning."

"Some of these men could still be alive," Brimley protested.

Flint shook his head and said, "Look at 'em! They're all shot to pieces."

That was true, too. The Reapers hadn't left anyone behind to tell the story of the ambush except Flint and Brimley.

Which was exactly according to plan, Flint thought, as the two men turned their horses to ride back up Devil's Hill. Now nobody in the settlement would suspect that he was one of the gang, and he could keep his eyes open for the next opportunity for the Reapers to get even richer.

The bloody ambush and robbery was a sensation, of course. Nobody in Rio Oro City talked about much of anything else for days afterward. Men sat in the saloons and eagerly rehashed the gruesome details brought back by the only two survivors, Flint Bennett and Tom Brimley.

Flint was in the Golden Nugget when Kat came in and paused to look around. Her gaze fell on him where he sat at a table with Steve. When she started toward him, the eyes of most of the men in the saloon followed her with avid interest.

In a blue, lace-trimmed dress that left her shoulders mostly bare and revealed the creamy upper slopes of her breasts, she was well worth looking at. Her midnight-dark hair fell in wings around her lovely face, which was painted but not as garishly as those of the soiled doves in the settlement.

Flint and Steve stood as she came up to the table. Steve took his hat off and said, "Howdy, Miss Kat. You look pretty enough today to plumb take a fella's breath away."

Kat ignored the compliment and gestured toward the white bandage fastened around Flint's head, under his cocked-back hat.

"How bad are you hurt?" she asked.

He smiled. "You're just hearing about it?"

"I haven't been able to get away until now. The Bear Flag is a pretty busy place."

That was true, Flint knew. Patrick Elam could have made a good living just from operating the saloon, if he had been the sort to be satisfied with that.

But like Flint, Elam craved riches, and so he had formed and directed the Reapers. He planned to own Rio Oro City in its entirety before he was through.

That sounded like a good idea to Flint . . . only he figured to be the boss, not Elam.

Such ambitious plans were for another day. Today, he gestured idly toward his head and assured Kat, "It's nothing. The bullet just grazed me and knocked me out for a minute."

"In other words, you came within inches of dying."

Flint shrugged. "I suppose that's true, if you want to look at it that way . . ."

"Were you going to come see me and let me know that you're all right?"

"I'm not really welcome in the Bear Flag," Flint reminded her. "Remember? Your boss ordered me to stay out. His men took their whips to me that time, and they might do worse if I went in there again."

Kat held out a hand. "I could talk to Patrick —"

"No," Flint said, and he didn't try to keep the harsh note out of his voice, even though Kat took a sharp breath and a mixture of anger and hurt showed in her eyes. "I'll be damned if I have some girl pleading my case

445

to the likes of Elam."

"Some girl?" Kat repeated. "That's what I am to you, Flint? Some girl?"

He didn't really want to hurt her, but she would understand later on, when she found out what was actually going on. She'd come around and get over being offended. He didn't say anything, just stood there and regarded her coolly.

"At least you didn't call me a floozy or a whore," she snapped. "I suppose I should be grateful for that."

With that, she turned, lifted her chin defiantly, and stalked toward the entrance, again drawing the attention of most of the men in the Golden Nugget.

A man was coming into the saloon just as Kat reached the entrance. He stopped short and smiled at her.

"Hello, Kat," Cord said. "I thought you'd be over at the Bear Flag. It's sure good to see you —"

"That's where I'm headed," she interrupted him. "Goodbye, Cord."

Out of habit, he moved aside to let her go by. Cord would always be polite that way, Flint thought as he watched the encounter. The youngest Bennett brother just couldn't help himself when it came to acting like a gentleman around the ladies.

Even when the lady was dressed as daringly as Kat was.

Cord turned his head to watch her depart, then headed for the table where Flint and Steve were slumping back into their seats. Neither of them had been back out to the camp since Flint's return to Rio Oro City following the ambush and holdup.

"Hello, boys," Cord greeted them as he came up to the table. "It's mighty good to see you again. I was hoping I'd find you here."

Steve said, "If you figure on asking me to come back and work the claims again, I ain't gonna do it, Cord. Flint says he can get me better work."

"Getting shot at by the Reapers, you mean?"

"I'm still drawing breath," Flint reminded him.

"By the skin of your teeth, looks like." Cord shrugged. "But I didn't come here to argue with either of you. Flint, I'm glad you're all right and weren't hurt too bad. I mean that."

"I know you do. But why are you here, Cord?"

"I wanted to show you this." Cord reached into the pocket of his canvas trousers, pulled out something, and set it on the table in

447

front of his brothers.

Flint and Steve stared at it, both of them recognizing a gold nugget a good inch in diameter.

CHAPTER 39

Cord knew it was a little petty of him, but he took considerable pleasure in the looks of stupefied surprise on his brothers' faces.

"That's gold!" Steve exclaimed after a moment.

"It sure is," Cord agreed. "I don't need Mr. Casterline to tell me that anymore. I can recognize the real thing now."

"How much is it worth?"

Cord shook his head. "Haven't had it weighed yet. I'm guessing at least a hundred dollars, though. Maybe a hundred and fifty."

Flint said, with what seemed like deliberate casualness, "That's a pretty nice find. Is it the only one?"

"So far," Cord admitted.

"Which claim did you find it on?"

"That don't matter," Steve said. "Share and share alike, right?"

Flint leaned back in his chair. "Our little brother might not feel that way anymore,

449

Steve, since we're not out there working right alongside him."

"No, a deal's a deal, and I don't begrudge you fellas a single cent of your share in what this brings," Cord said. "We came out here together, and we stick together, at least as far as I'm concerned."

"I'd still like to know where you found it."

"It was on my claim, but to tell you the truth, it wasn't me who found it. It was Ham Erskine."

Flint sat up straighter and frowned. "Erskine? What the hell was he doing rooting around on our claims? I didn't take the old coot for a claim-jumper —"

"He's not," Cord broke in. "He and Lou Spooner are working for us now. They've abandoned their claim. It never paid off enough to keep going." Cord gestured toward the nugget. "They offered to work for grub, but I've promised them a ten percent share in whatever they find."

"What gives you the right to do that? Those claims belong to all of us. You just said so yourself."

"And like you just said, you and Steve aren't out there working on them anymore," Cord returned. "I am. I figure that gives me more of a say in how we do things."

450

"It doesn't give you the right to take money out of our pockets!"

Cord shrugged. "Fine. I'll take Ham's share out of my third, if that's the way you feel."

"Now, that don't hardly seem fair to you, Cord," Steve said. "If that's what you promised him, I reckon you can take some of what you owe Mr. Erskine outta my share, too. Like you said, a deal's a deal."

Flint let out a disgusted-sounding sigh. "Oh, all right," he said. "Share and share alike cuts both ways, I suppose. There's something more important to consider. Do you think you've finally found a vein, Cord?"

"There's no way to know. I left Ham and Lou out there digging. Could be, by the time I get back to the claims, we'll all be millionaires."

Flint grunted. "That'll be the day."

"You know, I thought that maybe when you saw this, you might be interested in coming back."

Steve looked quickly at Flint, as if he were indeed interested in the possibility, but Flint shook his head without hesitating even for a second.

"You go ahead with what you're doing," he said. "Steve and I have our irons in a different fire."

"Oh? What fire is that?"

"One that's our business. You'll hear about it one of these days, you can count on that."

Steve said, "You know, Flint, since Cord's sharin' the profits from the claims with us, maybe it'd be fair if we was to share —"

"No, Steve, that's all right," Cord said before Flint could interrupt. He saw the annoyance in Flint's eyes and knew he was about to snap at Steve for even leading up to such an offer. "Whatever it is you're doing, that's between you and Flint. I never had anything to do with it."

"Damn right," Flint growled.

"I'll just wish you fellas good luck with whatever it is."

He didn't add that whatever it was Flint was mixed up in, he didn't want any part of it.

Because there was a good chance any money coming from it would be ill-gotten gains . . .

The nugget Ham Erskine had found turned out to be worth $130, according to Orvie Higginbotham's scales, which was enough to stock up on supplies for Cord, the two old-timers, and also Abraham and Glory Olmsted, who accepted Cord's generosity with gratitude and reluctance at the same time.

Cord considered the Olmsteds to be good friends of the Bennetts, and one of these days, Glory might be more than that, although he was still wary of putting all his trust in a woman.

Sooner or later, though, he needed to get over Caroline's betrayal. He knew that. But at the moment, he was more concerned with continuing the search for gold, and over the next two weeks, he and Spooner and Erskine unearthed half a dozen more nuggets of roughly the same size.

The finds were sporadic, though, and none of them came from the same area, which meant they hadn't found an actual vein. It was maddening, knowing that there could be a fabulous fortune just a few inches away under the surface . . . but it was equally possible that every nugget they found could be the last one on all four claims.

And unlike a coin spinning in the air that had to land on either heads or tails, knowing the odds on which alternative was most likely was impossible.

While Cord, Spooner, and Erskine continued working, the lawlessness in Rio Oro City and on up the canyon became more dire. Masked outlaws raided claims, holding up prospectors and stealing valuables and any gold they might have found. Men who came to town and were too careless about showing pokes full of dust found themselves beaten, robbed, and left in alleys . . . and those were the lucky ones who didn't have their throats cut. Teddy Harville, Orvie Higginbotham, and other merchants who used to ship their gold to San Francisco were leery of trying that again after the murderous ambush on Devil's Hill, but as the caches of nuggets and dust began to accumulate, the Reapers struck again, stealing the gold from various businesses at gunpoint.

It was a reign of terror, and no one knew what to do about it.

On a dark night when the moon had not yet risen, a group of ten riders moved through the trees on the northern bluff that loomed over Rio Oro Canyon. The terrain was rugged up here, but the men knew it well and had little trouble finding their way. They reined in when they saw the orange glow of a campfire below. The light illuminated a crude, hastily thrown-together shack.

"You're sure this is the right camp?" Rip

Jordan asked as he leaned forward in the saddle.

"Of course I'm sure," Flint replied from where he sat his horse next to Jordan's mount. "That's Hal Talmadge's shack. I've stopped there for coffee and to pass the time of day with him. And it was Talmadge who was in the Golden Nugget this afternoon talking about how he'd made a good strike and had quite a cache."

"Damned fool," Jordan muttered. "You'd think that by now, all these prospectors would know to keep their stupid mouths shut."

"It goes against human nature for a man not to brag about his good fortune. And that's good for us, isn't it?"

Jordan was to Flint's right. Steve rode at Flint's left. There had been a lot of tension when first Flint joined the Reapers and then brought Steve into the gang, since they had clashed with Jordan and his friends in the past. But Patrick Elam had made it clear that the factions had to get along, for the good of everyone. After the job Flint had done in helping to ambush the gold wagon, that edict was even stronger.

"Talmadge is a good fella," Steve said now. "I like him. He ain't gonna get hurt, is he?"

"All he's got to do is give up his gold,"

Jordan snapped. "Nobody gets hurt."

"Well, I hope he goes along with it. He can always dig more gold outta the ground."

One of the Reapers snickered. "And then we can steal that, too."

"You just do what you're told, Steve," Jordan said. "I don't want you fouling things up, you big ox."

Flint said, "Watch your mouth, Jordan. Steve's been a good member of the gang so far, hasn't he?"

"He hasn't been called on to do anything except rough up a few prospectors, and they weren't his friends. We'll see how he does tonight."

Steve said, "Don't worry, Flint. I'll do whatever you say. I always do, don't I?"

"Yeah," Flint said quietly. "You're a good brother, Steve."

Jordan muttered a curse and said, "Come on," then nudged his horse into motion.

A faint trail led down the bluff into the canyon. The outlaws followed it slowly and carefully, and when they reached the bottom, Jordan ordered them to pull up the bandannas around their necks.

"All right, keep quiet and I'll do the talkin'," he said in a low voice. He led the men around to the front of the shack and motioned for them to stop. Then he called,

"Talmadge! Hal Talmadge! Get out here!"

The shack didn't have an actual door, just an opening with a piece of canvas hung over it. That canvas twitched a little, almost as if the wind had stirred it, but there was no wind moving in the canyon tonight.

"Who's out there? What are you —"

The man inside broke off his questioning with a startled curse as a shaft of moonlight penetrated the canyon and revealed the masked figures on horseback gathered in front of the shack.

Jordan jumped his horse out in front of the others, drew his revolver, and fired three shots into the opening as fast as he could thumb them off.

A cry of agony came from the shack, and then a second later, a man pushed past the canvas, clinging to it with one hand to hold himself up while he struggled to lift a shotgun with the other hand.

He probably wouldn't have been able to lift the heavy, double-barreled weapon anyway, but Jordan made sure of that by shooting him again, this time in the head.

Hal Talmadge jerked under the bullet's impact and collapsed, still holding to the canvas in a death grip that caused it to rip and flutter down on top of him like a shroud.

"What the hell!" Steve exclaimed as the echoes of the gunshots leaped back and forth between the canyon walls. "You said you weren't gonna shoot him if he gave up his gold!"

"You saw him," Jordan replied coldly. "He had a shotgun. He was going to put up a fight."

"You didn't know that when you started shootin'!"

Flint said, "Take it easy, Steve. We'll talk about this later."

"Nothing to talk about," Jordan said. "I'm the boss, and what I say goes. Same for what I do." He jerked his head toward the shack. "A couple of you get in there and clean out everything worth taking."

Two of the Reapers stepped over Talmadge's sprawled body and disappeared into the ramshackle building. They emerged a few minutes later, carrying burlap sacks containing the things they had looted.

One of the outlaws held up a sack and shook it. "Full of nuggets!" he crowed. "We got us a good payoff here, boys!"

"Let's get out of here," Jordan ordered. "Those shots will draw attention."

The outlaws took the trail back to the top of the canyon wall and then rode away hurriedly, following the bluff west for a mile or so and then heading north along a narrow ridge. The landscape fell away steeply on both sides of them to create dark, looming, ominous gulfs. Any rider who strayed too close to the edge risked a bad fall.

The ridge played out at a sheer rock wall, but a narrow cleft opened in that wall, and the Reapers followed it. Inside the passage, it was almost pitch-black, but these men knew where they were going and after a while emerged into a cup in the hills enclosed by more cliffs. A waterfall plummeted from one of those cliffs and formed a pool that provided water. They couldn't see it in the darkness, but they could hear it.

This was the Reapers' hideout, complete with several log and stone cabins and a pole corral. An old road agent named Houk cooked and looked after the place.

He came out of one of the cabins now to meet them, a stocky figure carrying a torch. The light from it shone on his head, which was bald except for a couple of tufts of white hair that stuck out above his ears.

"Howdy, boys," he called. "How'd it go tonight?"

Before anyone could answer, Steve was off his horse and charging toward Jordan.

"You killed Hal!" Steve bellowed. "Gunned him down for no reason!"

"Steve!" Flint yelled. "Stop that!"

For once, though, Steve ignored what his older brother told him. From the looks of it, he intended to pull Jordan off his horse and tear him apart with his bare hands.

Jordan wasn't going to sit still for that. He twisted in the saddle, jerked his gun from its holster, and warned, "Stay away from me, you son of a —"

Flint saw the barrel swinging toward Steve and didn't think about what he was doing. He just reacted. His gun came out, too, and flashed up. The torchlight wasn't very good for shooting, but Flint's instincts guided the bullet as he pulled the trigger and the Colt boomed and bucked in his hand.

Jordan rocked back in the saddle and cried out in pain. He tried to switch his aim to Flint but failed to get a shot off before Flint's gun roared again. This time the bullet drove Jordan off his horse. He crashed to the ground with a final-sounding thud.

"He killed Rip!" one of Jordan's cronies shouted. "Get him!"

Both of the big men who tagged along after Jordan everywhere he went clawed at their guns. Steve didn't give them a chance to draw. For a big man himself, he changed direction quickly and grabbed the closest one, then jerked him out of the saddle.

Steve threw him against the horse the other man was riding, causing the animal to snort in alarm and rear up. The rider wasn't ready for that and was dumped backward onto the ground.

Both men were too stunned to put up a fight as Steve grabbed their collars, hauled them upright, and crashed their heads together. Bone crunched and splintered. When Steve let go of the men, they dropped like puppets with their strings cut.

Flint, who was covering the other five Reapers who were still mounted, saw that and knew that both men were dead, their skulls crushed by the ferocious impact of the collision.

Steve stepped back, panting more from anger than exertion.

Houk let out a low whistle of amazement. With almost no warning, three men had died in a handful of seconds before the startled eyes of the gang.

"I, uh, didn't mean to start a ruckus . . ." the old outlaw began.

"You didn't," Flint told him. He regarded the other men coolly in the flickering torchlight, then addressed them directly. "All of you know that Jordan's been spoiling for a fight ever since my brother and I threw in with you. It doesn't matter what happened

461

earlier, whether he was right to shoot Talmadge or not. He would have killed Steve just now and then gunned me next, and you all know it. Any one of you would have defended yourself, and your brother, too, if he was here."

All five men appeared calm, and nobody was going to reach for a Colt when Flint's gun was already in his hand. He had demonstrated already that he was too quick and accurate with it.

One of the Reapers said, "Take it easy, Bennett. We saw what happened, and yeah, Jordan's been looking for a chance to even the score with you. He even bragged to some of us that he was gonna do that the first opportunity he got. I don't reckon any of us are going to hold what happened against you."

The others muttered agreement. One added, "That don't mean the boss will see things the same way, though, when he finds out that Rip and Holton and Cramer are dead."

"I'll deal with Elam when the time comes," Flint declared. "Until then, Steve and I don't have to be looking over our shoulders at any of you, do we?"

Houk said, "Shoot, it ain't like Jordan or them other two were kin to any of us. Hell, far as that goes, I never even liked Jordan much. He was too damn snakey for me. Lookin' in his eyes was like lookin' at a rattler. You ain't been ridin' the dark trails as long as the rest of us, Bennett. It ain't a life where you make a lot of friends. One fella's just as good as the next, as long as you can depend on him to do his job . . . and I reckon so far you've been pretty dependable." A grin wreathed the old-timer's round face. "So you boys get on down from them horses. I got a potful o' stew simmerin', and it's gonna taste mighty good after this night's work!"

CHAPTER 40

The brutal murder of Hal Talmadge and the looting of his shack was shocking news as word of the crime made its way up and down Rio Oro Canyon and into the settlement.

It was in Rio Oro City, in fact, where Cord first heard about it. He went into Higginbotham's to cash in another nugget and found the storekeeper talking to Clyde Casterline. Both men wore bleak, worried expressions.

"What's wrong?" Cord asked after he'd greeted them. "You fellas look like somebody died."

"Somebody did," Casterline said. "Hal Talmadge."

"Hal! I just saw him two or three days ago. What happened?"

Before either of the other men could answer, realization dawned on Cord, and a frown put deep creases in his forehead.

"It was the Reapers, wasn't it?" he asked.

"Must've been," Higginbotham said. "Nobody saw what happened, but several men heard the shots last night. Somebody drilled Talmadge four times, three in the body and one in the head. Then they cleaned out his shack, including the gold he mentioned having when he was in the Golden Nugget yesterday."

Cord bit back a curse and said instead, "I wish he'd kept quiet about that."

"Hal probably wound up wishing the same thing," Casterline said.

"Somebody needs to do something about those blasted outlaws."

Higginbotham eyed Cord intently and said, "Yeah, we've been talking about that, some of us here in town. You been to see Teddy yet?"

"Not today," Cord replied. "I thought I'd stop in there and say hello once I've finished my business with you."

He was tempted to stop at the Bear Flag, too, and see if he could find out how Kat was doing. But it might be too early in the day for her to be up and about, he reminded himself. It wasn't quite noon yet. From what he'd heard, Kat often entertained in Elam's saloon until well after midnight.

Putting his mind back on what had

465

brought him into the settlement this morning, he reached in his pocket, pulled out a nice-sized nugget, and placed it on the counter in front of Higginbotham. Casterline, in front of the counter like Cord, leaned closer to take a better look at the nugget.

"That's the business I was talking about," Cord went on. "I want to go ahead and trade it in with you. We don't need any supplies right now, but you can put whatever it's worth on our account, can't you?"

Higginbotham looked at the nugget, and Cord could tell that part of him wanted to pick it up and weigh it in the palm of his hand.

Instead, the storekeeper shook his head and used a forefinger to push the nugget back closer to Cord.

"Sorry, Cord," Higginbotham muttered. "I can't do it."

"What do you mean you can't do it? I'm not asking you for credit or anything like that. Actually, it's more like the opposite."

"I know that, but I can't take in any more gold." Higginbotham lowered his voice. "I've got too much in my safe already. I'm surprised those damn Reapers haven't robbed it before now, like they've hit some of the other places in town. I don't want

466

them tempted any more than they already must be."

"But what are fellas supposed to do with their gold if they can't spend it with you?" Cord looked at the land recorder and assayer. "Mr. Casterline, you've got a safe —"

Casterline shook his head and interrupted, "They held me up once before, remember? I'm not asking for any more trouble, Cord."

"What about the other stores and the saloons?" Cord asked with a grim note in his voice.

Higginbotham shrugged. "Elam's still taking gold in the Bear Flag and will hold it for a man in return for a percentage, I've heard. Teddy will take it in the Golden Nugget, but only enough to pay for what the customers spend. He won't hold any on account. The other businesses in town are the same way."

"So any man fortunate enough to find gold will have to protect it himself and hope it doesn't put a target on his back." Cord mulled that over for a moment and then went on, "I suppose that's fair enough, but it's not the way things have been operating around here."

"Things won't get back to normal," Casterline said, "as long as the Reapers are running loose. Like you said, somebody's got

467

to do something about them."

"Go talk to Teddy Harville," Higgin-botham urged Cord. "You might be inter-ested in what he's got to say."

Cord frowned again. "What's going on here, Orvie?"

"Just put that nugget away" — Higgin-botham gestured at the chunk of gleaming metal — "and go see Teddy."

Cord could tell he wasn't going to get anything more out of the two men, so he did as Higginbotham suggested. He put the nugget back in his pocket, nodded to them, and left the general store.

He paused on the boardwalk next to the muddy street and looked around Rio Oro City. The place wasn't as busy as it normally was. That was the Reapers' doing, Cord reflected. The gang had caused an atmo-sphere charged with fright to descend over the settlement. The raucous, optimistic feel-ing that had filled the air when the Bennetts and the Olmsteds and the other gold-seekers first arrived had evaporated in the constant apprehension of violence.

Cord looked across the street at the Bear Flag. The saloon appeared to be doing a brisker trade than any other establishment in Rio Oro City. A speculative expression appeared on Cord's face as he considered why that might be.

He pondered that only for a moment, then headed along the boardwalk to the Golden Nugget.

The sound of hammering banged through the air as Cord approached the saloon. Men were working on the framework of the permanent structure next door. Most of the damage done by the suspicious fire had been repaired. The place was starting to shape up, Cord thought, and looked more and more like the business it was intended to be.

When he went into the tent currently housing the Golden Nugget, he spotted Teddy Harville standing at the bar, talking to one of the bartenders. Today the saloon-keeper wore a frock coat of a bright, sky-blue color over darker blue trousers with a yellow stripe embroidered down the sides that made the garment look like part of a military uniform. Maybe it had been, at one time, before Harville sent off for it. A frilly white shirt and a bright red cravat completed the outfit.

Harville saw Cord and waved to him, then pointed to an empty table in a corner. He spoke to the bartender, who drew a couple of mugs of beer. Harville took them and carried them to the table, where he met Cord.

"Most of the girls are still asleep," Harville said as he placed the mugs on the table. "They don't usually start stirring until noon."

"That's all right," Cord assured him.

Harville chuckled. "Yeah, with a lady friend like Miss Gloriana, you don't exactly have to rely on saloon girls for female company, do you?"

"I'm not sure I'd say Glory is my lady friend —"

"Well, I'll bet you a brand-new hat *she* would say so, and so would most of the other folks around here. Have a seat, Cord." Harville's jovial expression vanished. "I want to have a talk with you."

"That's what Mr. Higginbotham said. He made it sound like it was something kind of important, too."

"I think it's mighty important. Let me just lubricate the old speech box here . . ." Harville took a healthy swallow of his beer, then set the mug on the table again. "Cord, I've got a proposition for you."

"I hope you're not thinking about offering to buy our claims." Cord took the nugget from his pocket and held it so that Harville could see it, but he didn't set it on the table

470

where it would be in full view of everyone in the saloon. "I hope we'll be finding more like this little beauty soon."

Harville studied the nugget and slowly nodded. "Normally, I'd agree with you, son, but I think you have more important things to do."

"More important than finding gold?"

"That's right. Cord, Rio Oro City will never be the place that I know it can be as long as those outlaws are running loose around here. Nobody here or in the camp out by the canyon or in the canyon itself will be safe, not a single man, woman, or child, until the Reapers are dealt with. We need law and order, Cord. We need it mighty bad."

Cord frowned and leaned back in his chair, not disagreeing with what Harville was saying but not much liking the direction this conversation was taking, either.

"Why are you telling me this?"

"Because I think you're the man we need to set things right. I've been talkin' to Orvie Higginbotham and Clyde Casterline and some of the other leading citizens in our community, and they agree with me." Harville reached inside his coat, took something from a pocket, and laid it on the table between him and Cord. "We want you to be the marshal of Rio Oro City."

The item on the table was a battered but polished and shining lawman's badge.

Cord stared at it for a long moment. Even though he had suspected where Harville's talk might be leading, the actual offer still took him by surprise. He had to struggle to find a response.

He began by shaking his head. "I'm no lawman —"

"You may not have worn a star," Harville broke in, "but what about when those fellas attacked and robbed Clyde? You tracked them down and brought them to justice."

"You mean Flint and I did. And it was mostly Flint, to be honest."

"You're being too modest, son."

Cord pushed the badge away. "Maybe it's Flint you should be talking to —"

Again, the saloonkeeper interrupted him. "Be honest, Cord. Can you really see that brother of yours pinning on a badge and swearing to uphold the law?"

Anger flared inside Cord. Harville's question sounded like an insult.

But it didn't sound *wrong.* Try as he might, Cord actually couldn't imagine Flint ever wearing a lawman's badge.

"I have claims to work."

"From what I've heard, you have help out

472

there. Lou Spooner and Ham Erskine have been working on those claims with you, haven't they?"

"They have," Cord admitted.

"And I'm sure Abe Olmsted would be happy to pitch in any time. Shoot, it might not be very long before he's your father-in-law, after all."

"Blast it," Cord said, "does everybody in Rio Oro City have it in their heads that Glory and I are getting hitched?"

"We've got eyes to see, don't we?" Harville waved a hand. "But that's something for you young folks to think about later on. The way things are now, I'm not sure anybody would want to get married in this settlement. Not until we get some real law and order in these parts."

"And you honestly think I could do that? Track down the Reapers and bust up the gang once and for all?"

"I don't think anybody else around here is capable of that," Harville said. "Look, Cord, I know you don't have any experience as a lawman. But you can handle a gun, you're strong and tough and know how to fight, and you're honest as the day is long. Take it from me, son, I know everybody in this settlement, and there's no better choice for the job of marshal."

"Then maybe you shouldn't have a marshal," Cord muttered, still somewhat flabbergasted by the whole idea.

"You wouldn't have to do it by yourself, either. We'd pay you, and we'd include some wages for a deputy, too."

"Where would I find a deputy around here?"

"We were thinking maybe your other brother might want the job."

Cord drew in a breath. That was an intriguing thought. With Steve's size, he would be good at breaking up any trouble in town. He could ride and shoot, too, but nobody was better at bare-knuckles roughhousing.

And if Steve was working with him, Cord mused, he would be too busy to get up to whatever trouble he might be getting into with Flint.

Steve idolized Flint, though. Getting him away from the oldest Bennett brother might not be easy . . . assuming, of course, that Cord was crazy enough to take the marshal's job in the first place.

"Well?" Harville prompted. "What do you say, Cord?"

"I can't give you an answer right now," Cord said. "I need to talk to Steve and see if he's willing to work with me. And I need to talk to Lou and Ham, too, and make sure they're all right with carrying on the work out at the claims."

"I think there's a mighty good chance they will be."

Cord thought that was likely, too, and he also knew he could count on Olmsted and Glory for any help he needed, too.

"So you're not saying no?" Harville asked.

"No," Cord replied heavily, hoping he wasn't making a mistake. "I'm not saying no."

Harville tapped his finger on the badge and said, "Then take this with you, so that when you're ready to make up your mind, you'll have it with you and can go ahead and pin it right on."

Cord started to refuse and push the badge again, but then he realized it didn't really matter. He still wasn't committing himself to anything.

He picked up the shiny badge and slipped it into his shirt pocket.

CHAPTER 41

Flint and Steve actually showed up at the camp that evening, obviously intent on sharing supper and visiting with Cord, Glory, Olmsted, and the two old-timers. They hadn't been around much for a good long while, and Cord took their presence as an omen of sorts.

Cord had planned on breaking the news of Teddy Harville's offer at supper, and now with Flint and Steve there, he knew he would never get a better time. He waited until they were all nursing cups of coffee after finishing off bowls of the stew Glory had put together, then said, "I had a talk with Mayor Harville in town today."

"Mayor," Lou Spooner repeated, then chuckled. "Teddy Harville's what you call a self-made man. He made himself mayor!"

"Well, in this case, he wasn't speaking just for himself, but for a group of the leading citizens. He made me a very interesting offer. A job offer."

"But you have a job," Glory said. "Looking for gold."

"Speakin' of which," Ham Erskine said, "how much did that nugget you found turn out to be worth, Cord?"

"I don't know," Cord replied with a shake of his head. He took the nugget from his pocket. "I still have it. Mr. Higginbotham wasn't willing to take it and give us credit for supplies we'll need in the future."

"Why not? That's a good deal for him. If prices go up — and prices always go up — he makes even more."

"Because he's like all the other honest citizens in these parts. He's afraid of the Reapers. And that's connected with what he asked me."

With the abruptness of sudden realization, Flint said, "Good Lord! He wants you to take on the job of marshal, doesn't he?"

"No!" Glory exclaimed, but Cord nodded as he reached into his pocket again and took out the badge.

"That's what he wants, all right."

"But you can't do that," Glory insisted. "You're not a lawman. Besides, it would be dangerous."

Flint looked like the wheels of his brain were turning over rapidly at what Cord had just revealed. He said, "Just being out here so far from civilization is dangerous. We've been surrounded by danger ever since we left Fort Kearny. After a while, you just stop thinking about it all the time."

"That's true, when you come down to it," Cord agreed. "If I took the job, I might be able to make things better around here for everybody, not just for myself."

Abraham Olmsted said, "I don't reckon you've ever been worried just about yourself, son. That ain't the type of fella you are. You're always lookin' out for other folks, whether you want to or not."

Cord just shrugged at that praise.

Erskine drawled, "I didn't figure on anything like this happenin', but now that I think on it, I reckon you'd make a fine lawman, Cord. You're smart, and you don't back down from a fight."

"And you've got us to work the claims for you," Spooner put in. "We'd be glad to handle that for you while you're busy in town. Wouldn't we, Ham?"

"Sure would," Erskine said with a solemn nod.

Glory said, "This is crazy. You'll get yourself killed."

She was only reacting like this because she cared about him, Cord told himself.

That made him feel warm inside. But he couldn't allow that to sway him from doing the right thing.

"It wouldn't be near as dangerous with a good deputy to back me up," he said. He looked over at the middle Bennett brother. "That's where you come in, Steve."

Steve had been following the conversation with some interest but hadn't chimed in yet. Now his eyes widened in surprise as he said, "Me? You want me to be a deputy lawman?"

"Deputy marshal. It's a paying job, too. I don't know exactly what the wages will be, but you'll make something."

Flint slapped his thigh and said, "By grab! That's a great idea. You'll make a fine deputy marshal, Steve."

"I will?" Steve said, as if he couldn't believe they were even talking about such a thing.

"Of course you will. As big as you are, any prospector who gets drunk and tries to start a fight will think twice once you show up. You'll bring law and order to Rio Oro City, that's for sure."

"But . . . but Cord said Mr. Harville and those other folks want him to go after the Reapers!"

"And you can help him with that, too," Flint said, nodding emphatically. "I tell you,

479

Steve, this is the perfect job for you."

"Well, I, uh . . . I guess . . . I guess if you say so, Flint."

"I'm glad to hear you say that, Steve," Cord told him. "I don't think I would have taken the job if you hadn't agreed to help me."

"Then you *are* taking the job," Glory said.

"I think I ought to," Cord said, even though he didn't like the way she was looking at him.

She would get used to it and get over being upset with him, though. She had to.

But she didn't sound much like it as she said coolly, "I wish you luck, then." She paused, then added, "I'm afraid you're likely to need it."

In more ways than one, Cord thought.

But he said, "Steve, why don't you stay here tonight, and in the morning, we'll ride into town and let Mayor Harville know he's got himself a couple of peace officers."

Steve glanced at Flint, then nodded and said, "Sure, I reckon we can do that."

Lou Spooner lifted his coffee cup and said, "Here's to law and order."

"To law and order," the rest of them echoed, even Flint, who had a bit of a mocking smile playing around his lips.

Except for Glory, who said nothing.

■ ■ ■ ■

Later, when Flint went to saddle his horse for the ride back to where he was staying, Steve trailed after him. Keeping his voice pitched to a low rumble that couldn't be understood back at the campfire, he asked, "Flint, what in blazes is goin' on? I can't be a deputy!"

"Sure you can," Flint answered.

"But I'm a —"

"You're a loyal brother," Flint cut in, "and by doing this, you can help Cord . . . and me."

"Help you? How in the world do you figure that?"

"Cord's going to be the law in these parts, right? If you're his deputy, you'll know everything he's doing." Flint leaned closer, his voice intense as he went on, "And if you know everything the law is doing, you can pass that along to me so that *I'll* know, too." He clapped a hand on Steve's brawny shoulder. "Like I said, this is the perfect job for you, Steve. Perfect for you . . . and perfect for me."

"Oh," Steve said. Flint could tell from his tone that he understood at least partially, although he might not grasp all the ramifications of this development. "Yeah, I guess that could come in handy, couldn't it?"

"You'll see," Flint assured him. "You just do whatever Cord asks of you, and we'll figure out a way for you to get word to me when you need to let me know anything. I'll be counting on you, boy."

"And I won't let you down," Steve said heartily.

Flint squeezed his shoulder again. "You never have."

Then he climbed on his horse and rode away into the night.

The news that Rio Oro City now had a couple of lawmen was greeted with acclaim and a genuine sense of relief among the citizens.

For a time, that relief appeared to be justified. The Reapers seemed to have crawled back under whatever rocks they had come from. No robberies took place in town, and no more claim-jumping went on in the canyon. In their new jobs as marshal and deputy, Cord and Steve didn't have anything to do other than break up a few fights when men got too liquored up and clashed over cards or women.

Cord spent part of the time roaming around the hills and canyons in the area and asking questions of everyone he encountered. He wanted to know if anyone had seen anything suspicious. The Reapers had to have a hideout somewhere not too far from Rio Oro City, and he did his best to find it.

But it seemed as if the outlaws had dropped off the face of the earth. He was frustrated at his lack of success, but at the same time, he told himself he ought to be glad that the Reapers were no longer running rampant, at least for the moment.

The problem was his hunch that the gang wasn't through with Rio Oro City just yet. They were planning something, his instincts told him . . .

And when it came about, it would be worse than anything that had happened so far.

Flint waited in the shadows under the trees. He had seen the signal earlier in the day, the bit of red cloth tied to the pole from which the Bear Flag flew, letting him know that Patrick Elam wanted to meet tonight. It was a simple system, but it had worked so far.

Just like the system Flint and Steve had set up for passing messages had worked. Each of the brothers checked daily at a tree on the other side of the settlement where a hole in the trunk made a handy place to leave notes. They were like little kids playing pirates, Steve had commented once, and Flint could see that. What they were doing was a lot more serious than a kids' game, though.

A soft footstep nearby made Flint straighten from his casual pose leaning against a tree trunk. He put his hand on his gun butt and waited. A moment later, a quiet whistle sounded.

"Here," he said in response.

Elam loomed out of the shadows. "You're alone?" he asked.

"Who else would be with me?"

"That brother of yours, maybe."

"Steve?" Flint shook his head, even though it was so dark in the thick shadows, it was unlikely Elam could see him. "He steers clear of me unless there's a reason for us to get together. We don't want Cord to suspect anything."

"Well, it won't matter much longer."

Flint stiffened. "What does that mean?"

Elam's words could easily be taken as a threat against Cord's life. Flint hoped it would never come down to deciding between his brother — either of his brothers — and what he wanted. He didn't know what he would do in that case.

But he was damned if he would let anybody else try to hurt Steve or Cord, including Patrick Elam.

Elam must have heard the tension in Flint's voice. He said, "Take it easy, Bennett. I just meant that we're going to be leaving Rio Oro City soon."

"Leaving?" Flint repeated. "Again, what in blazes are you talking about?"

"It's simple," Elam said. "The gold in this region is playing out. There hasn't been a good strike in more than a month."

"My brother's been finding nuggets."

"Nuggets. Not a vein. I've seen it all before, and we might as well face facts: there's no bonanza to be found in Rio Oro Canyon. It's not a river of gold after all."

"So you're going to just abandon your saloon and pull up stakes?"

"Why do you think I never tried to build anything permanent? Like I said, this isn't my first time in a situation like this. I've set up saloons in other mining camps and made them pay for as long as I could, but I know when to leave and start over somewhere else, too."

Flint thought about it for a moment, then said, "I'll bet the Reapers aren't the first gang you've put together, either."

"That's always been part of it," Elam admitted. "I've always set out to get the biggest payoff possible, no matter what methods have to be used. Some of the men have been with me through several mining camps. Rip Jordan was one. And before you start getting proddy again, I don't care that you killed him. Sentimentality doesn't enter into this. Jordan was wild starting out and getting wilder. He was too hot-headed. I'd rather work with a man who's capable of cool detachment. Like you, Bennett."

"You want me to come with you?"

"You'd be welcome. You and Steve."

"What about Cord?"

Elam's tone was mocking. "You don't truly believe that Cord would ever throw in with us, do you?"

"No," Flint had to say. "No, he never would." He drew in a breath. "All right, when are we leaving?"

"Not just yet. There's one more thing to do. Get all the boys together. Tomorrow night, we're hitting the town."

"What do you mean, hitting the town?"

"You're having trouble understanding things tonight, aren't you? I mean just what I say! There may not be much gold in the canyon anymore, but there's still quite a bit being held in the businesses in the settlement, and I want it. We're going to loot everything that's worth taking and leave the place in flames."

"You mean to burn Rio Oro City?"

"To the ground," Elam grated.

Flint felt and heard the pulse hammering in his head like a drumbeat. He hadn't expected any of this, but when he thought about it, the whole thing made sense from Elam's perspective. He was going to wring the last nugget, the last flake of gold dust, out of the settlement and then head for parts unknown to start the operation over again. The apparently respectable saloon-keeper who was really the mastermind behind a gang of vicious outlaws . . . It had worked before for Patrick Elam and no doubt would again.

"What do you say?" Elam snapped when Flint didn't say anything. "Are you with me?"

"Tomorrow night?"

"That's right."

"Then I guess I'm with you," Flint said.

"Good. I'll ride out to join you and the rest of the gang, along with the men I have in town. We'll all be masked, so nobody will recognize us."

"Do we burn down the Bear Flag, too?"

"Of course. To spare it would throw

suspicion on me, suspicion that might follow me to wherever I set up next. With the loot we'll have, I can easily afford another tent." Elam chuckled. "I've been letting my liquor supply dwindle instead of trying to replace it, so I won't even lose that much when it goes up in flames."

"You've got it all figured out, don't you?"

"Of course I do. Now, I need to get back —"

"Wait a minute," Flint said as Elam started to turn away. "What about Kat?"

"What about her? She'll be coming with us. As it turns out, she's a fine entertainer. Quite the draw for business. Don't worry, she'll be well taken care of."

"What happens to her father and sister?"

"If they're not in town tomorrow night, I assume they'll be fine," Elam said carelessly. "They'll still have a near-worthless claim, but that'll be true no matter what we do, won't it?"

"I suppose so. And Cord?"

Elam's voice hardened. "I can't provide the same assurances where he's concerned. He can't fight us alone, not as outnumbered as he'd be. If he has sense enough to step aside, he ought to be all right." Elam paused. "Is that going to make a difference?"

Flint thought about everything he had done, all the lines he had crossed, and as he did, a chill settled inside him. He had come too far, risked too much, to throw away all his ambitions now.

"No," he said. "It won't make a difference."

Everything was quiet in the trees after Flint and Elam were gone, heading out in separate directions. Several minutes passed, and then a shape emerged from the thickest, deepest shadows.

Kat Olmsted stood there, breathing hard, heart pounding in her chest, wishing she hadn't followed Elam out here . . .

Wishing she had never found out the things she knew now.

Wishing she knew what to do about them.

CHAPTER 42

The ringing sound of pickaxes striking rock filled the canyon and bounced back from the other side. Lou Spooner and Ham Erskine worked about twenty feet apart from each other, swinging the tools in a steady, relentless rhythm.

Each man had a good-sized hole gouged out of the canyon wall. They stopped from time to time to bend over and paw through the chunks of rock and dirt that gathered at their feet.

Now and then, one of them would take a particular interest in one of the chunks, lifting it closer to study it intently for a moment before tossing it aside disgustedly.

Hearing a clear, musical voice call, "Mr. Spooner! Mr. Erskine!", the two old-timers turned to see Glory Olmsted walking toward them. Even though she wore work boots, canvas overalls, and a flannel shirt, she looked quite fetching, and both men leaned on their pickaxes and smiled as they watched her approaching.

"I swear, Miss Glory, the sight of you warms an old man's heart," Spooner greeted her. "I surely do appreciate the chance to look at a pretty girl."

"And appreciatin's all he can do," Erskine added.

Glory blushed but laughed. She wasn't offended by the mild teasing.

"My pa and I are heading to the settlement in a little while," she said. "Is there anything we can bring you?"

Spooner dragged his sleeve across his face to wipe away some of the beads of sweat that came from swinging the pick.

"I can't think of anything," he said. "How about you, Ham?"

"Nope," Erskine said. "Thank you kindly for thinkin' of us, though."

"Actually . . . if you go into Higginbotham's . . . he's got some penny candy that I'm a mite fond of," Spooner said. "I'd take a piece of that, if you don't mind loanin' me the price of it."

Glory laughed. "You don't have to worry about that. We have credit at Mr. Higginbotham's store, thanks to Cord, and to you two for all the help you've given him. So I'll be glad to get a piece of candy for you, Mr.

Spooner."

Erskine said, "The old coot's got a sweet tooth, I swear."

"When you get to be our age, you take your pleasures wherever you can find 'em," Spooner said. "I'm much obliged to you, Miss Glory."

She gestured toward the holes in the canyon wall. "Are you having any luck?"

"Not today," Erskine replied, with a gloomy shake of his head.

"But you never know when your luck will turn around," Spooner added.

Glory said goodbye and headed back down the creek. Spooner and Erskine resumed digging at the rock wall.

They had been working for several minutes when Spooner paused and leaned down to pick up a chunk he had just knocked loose. He gripped it in one hand while holding the pickax in the other, but after a moment, he let go of the pick's handle and wrapped both hands around the rock. His feet started to move in excitement, almost as if he were dancing.

"What's wrong with you?" Erskine asked. "Are you havin' a fit?"

Spooner ran over to him and thrust out the rock. "Look at this, Ham! Look at it!"

"What are you . . . hold still, blast it . . ."

Erskine suddenly dropped his pick, too, and snatched the rock out of his old friend's hands. "Is that . . . it can't be . . ."

"It is! Gold!" Spooner whooped. "And look at the way it runs all the way through there." He turned and dashed back to the spot where he'd been working. He pawed at the rock and pried loose a piece that was broken but hadn't fallen out yet. He waved it in the face of Erskine, who had followed him. "There's more! Look at it! It's a vein!"

Erskine stared at the canyon wall and then said in a solemn, awed voice, "You're right. It's a vein of gold, sure enough, and there ain't no tellin' how wide it is or how far it runs."

"Like I said to Miss Glory, there's no way of knowin' when your luck will turn around! Well, ours had done turned around, Ham!"

The sound of horses approaching from up the canyon made them look back over their shoulders. Flint and Steve Bennett were riding toward them.

The night before, Flint had left a note in the hollow tree telling Steve to meet him this morning where the narrow ridge turned off from the bluff and led to the Reapers' hideout.

"What's goin' on?" Steve asked when he

rode up and found Flint waiting for him. "Cord thought it was kinda strange when I told him I was ridin' up the canyon this mornin'."

"Did he have something he wanted you to do?"

"No, not really, but I usually hang around town and make sure everything stays peaceful. I told him I wanted to come out and take a look at the claim and visit with Lou and Ham, since I hadn't seen 'em for a while. He said that was all right, but I could tell he was curious."

"He didn't follow you, did he?" Flint asked sharply.

Steve shook his head. "No, I kept a good eye out behind me."

"Well, after we're done talking, you can stop by the claim, just in case he happens to ask those old codgers about it later." Flint grunted. "Not that we'll have to worry about that for long."

"Why not?"

"Because after tonight, you and I are leaving Rio Oro City and the canyon behind us."

Steve stared at him for a second before asking, "What? We're leavin'?"

As quickly and simply as possible, Flint told his brother what the plan was. Steve listened intently but still seemed to have trouble grasping what he was hearing. When Flint was finished, Steve said, "But I kinda like bein' a deputy, Flint. I like it more than I ever figured I would. Folks . . . well, folks almost seem to look up to me."

"They'll look up to you even more wherever Elam sets up his operation next, because you'll have money. That'll be better, won't it?"

"But you said you were gonna take over from Elam sooner or later. You were gonna run things in the settlement."

Flint made a face. "That was a good plan when it looked like Rio Oro City might survive. But if Elam is right, and the gold strike is playing out, there won't be anything to take over."

"Mayor Harville says it's gonna be a real town, even when the gold is all gone."

Flint shook his head. "Teddy Harville's just a dreamer."

Steve frowned for a long moment, then said, "I thought that was why we all come out here, Flint. Because we were dreamers."

"Dreams aren't real," Flint rasped. "Just when you think you're about to grasp one, it turns to mist in your hands. The only things that count are money and power. Have enough of those, and you can get anything else you want."

When Steve didn't say anything, Flint added, "Have I ever steered you wrong?"

"No," Steve said with a certain amount of grudging acceptance. "No, I don't reckon you have, Flint. If you say this is how things are gonna be, then that's how they'll be."

Flint clapped a hand on his shoulder. "That's good. You'll see, it'll all work out fine." He grinned. "Now, let's go see Spooner and Erskine, so Cord won't have any reason to worry. I wouldn't mind seeing those two old pelicans myself."

"Flint." Steve's voice was urgent. "Cord's not gonna get hurt when the gang raids the town tonight, right?"

"Of course not, and it's going to be your job to make sure of that."

"How do I do that?"

"Stick close to him, and when the attack starts, rap him on the head and knock him out. Then you can tie him up and stash him somewhere safe."

"But you said the gang's gonna burn down the town. That won't be safe."

"Take him out in the trees and leave him there."

Steve nodded. "All right. What about Kat?"

"Don't worry about her. I'll make sure

she's safe. She's coming with us."

"You think she'll do that? Leave Glory and her pa?"

"Kat likes money," Flint said. "She'll co-operate."

They mounted up and rode down one of the narrow trails to the bottom of the canyon. As they started toward the stretch of the creek where the Bennett claims were located, Steve said, "I sure hope you're right about all this, Flint."

"I always am," Flint said confidently.

A short time later, they reached the claims. As they approached, they saw that both Spooner and Erskine seemed excited about something.

Steve leaned forward in his saddle and asked, "You reckon they made a good strike?"

"I don't know," Flint said. Elam claimed there weren't any more good strikes to be made around here. If that wasn't the case . . . if the two old-timers actually had found something worthwhile . . . that could complicate things.

Spooner and Erskine turned to look at them. Spooner trotted toward them, waving a chunk of rock over his head.

"Look at this, boys!" he called. "Feast your eyes on a sure-enough vein of gold!"

Flint and Steve urged their horses ahead faster. They reined in as Spooner came up to them. Flint swung down from the saddle and took the chunk of rock from the older man's hand. His heart slugged hard in his chest as he saw the line of gleaming metal that ran through the heart of the rock.

Erskine ambled up and pointed at the canyon wall. "There's more of it back there," he said. "Hard to say for sure until we do more diggin', but it looks like there might be a good-sized vein running through the wall. If it is, we ought to be able to follow it."

"And there's no tellin' how far it might go," Spooner said. "This is what we've been lookin' for, fellas."

"This is on our claim, you know," Flint said as his hand clenched around the rock. His brain was whirling as he tried to figure out what to do about this unexpected discovery.

"Sure, sure," Erskine drawled. "Lou and me aren't claim-jumpers. Cord said he would give us ten percent of whatever we found, which seems mighty fair."

Flint nodded and asked, "You just found this?"

"Yeah, just a few minutes ago," Spooner said.

"And nobody else knows about it yet? Cord doesn't know?"

"Nope." Spooner grinned. "He's gonna be mighty happy when he hears about it, though."

That would be true . . . if Cord ever found out about it.

Images whirled through Flint's brain. Rio Oro City in flames . . . the survivors leaving, hoping to make a new start elsewhere . . . the prospectors who still had claims in the canyon following them. With no settlement to serve their needs, and with the general feeling that the Gold Rush in this area was over, Rio Oro Canyon would empty out in a hurry.

Leaving this strike for whoever knew about it.

Those thoughts flashed across Flint's mind in an instant, and it took him no longer than that to decide what must be done.

He half-turned, drew his gun, raised it as he eared the hammer back, and fired a round through Lou Spooner's head.

Ham Erskine barely had time to widen his eyes in shock as his old friend's blood and brains splattered on his face before Flint shot him, too. He flew backward, arms outflung, and crashed to the ground on his back, where he lay with a worm of blood crawling from the hole in his forehead.

Steve looked only mildly puzzled, as if something had just happened that confused him. "Flint?" he said. "Flint, what did you do?"

"I made us rich men, Steve, that's what I did. Now nobody knows about that vein of gold except us. We'll come back here later, after Elam and the rest of the Reapers are gone. They can do whatever they want. It won't matter to us, because we'll own one of the richest gold mines in these parts!" Flint holstered his gun and grabbed Steve by the upper arms to shake him. "We're going to be rich, boy! Filthy rich!"

"But . . . but you killed Mr. Spooner and Mr. Erskine." Steve pulled away from Flint's grip.

"I had to. They would have told Cord about the gold. Now we're the only ones who know. I didn't have any choice!"

"It's part Cord's claim, too."

Flint shook his head. "Not anymore." A harsh note entered his voice. "He had his chances. He could have come in with us and gotten a good payoff, but he couldn't be trusted. And now he's a lawman! He puts everybody else above us, his own brothers." Flint's lips curled in a snarl. "Whatever happens to him, he's got it coming."

Steve backed away. "No," he said in a half-moan. "No, this ain't right, Flint. You . . . you sound like you're gonna hurt Cord."

"He'll never let it rest once he finds out these two old coots are dead. He'll want to keep digging at it. Cord shouldn't have thrown in with those respectable citizens. It's like he never even paid any attention to all the things I tried to teach him!"

Steve shook his head as a stubborn expression that Flint knew all too well came over his face.

"You shouldn't have done that, Flint," he said. "Those old fellas never did you any harm. They were our friends."

"We don't have friends! We don't need friends! We're brothers, that's all we need."

"And you're gonna hurt Cord," Steve went on. "I know you are. But I'm not gonna let you. I'm gonna tell him —"

Steve stopped short with what he was saying, jerked around, and ran toward the horses.

He had taken only two steps when Flint's gun came up and roared again. The shot struck Steve in the back and threw him forward. He landed face down, groaned, jerked a little, and then lay still.

A thread of powdersmoke curled from the

muzzle of Flint's Colt as he lowered the weapon and said, "Steve . . . oh, hell, Steve . . . Why . . . why did you make me do that?"

No answer came from the man on the ground.

It was all changed now, Flint thought. All the carefully laid plans gone.

But they didn't have to be, he realized. The Reapers could still make their raid on Rio Oro City tonight. Cord would die in that battle. It was a foregone conclusion. And with both of his brothers dead . . .

Flint's eyes went to the hole gouged in the canyon wall, drawn there like iron filings to a magnet.

With his brothers gone, all that gold belonged to him now. He would hide the nuggets the old-timers had found. Get mud from the creek and daub it on the rocks so that no tell-tale yellow gleam showed. No one would know the gold was there until he was ready to come back and take it for himself.

And he would take Kat for himself, too, even if it meant killing Patrick Elam. That could happen tonight, as well. It was all falling together in Flint's head now, all the luck turning his way.

He was going to have everything he

wanted at last.

All he had to do was hide the bodies, he thought, as his gaze dropped to the bloody, fallen men. Easy enough to drag them into the trees, he told himself. He wouldn't even have to hide them all that well, just enough so that nobody would stumble over them before the raid that night. After that, nothing would matter.

Disposing of Spooner and Erskine would mean nothing to him. Less than nothing.

As for Steve . . . well, that was a shame. A damned shame. And later, when the urgency had worn off and he had time to think about it, to feel the loss, he was sure it would hurt. But if Steve hadn't been such a fool, Flint would have taken him along for the ride. He would have been rich, too.

And being rich cured everything.

After all, it was why the Bennetts had come to California in the first place, wasn't it?

CHAPTER 43

Glory and her father had just reached the camp near the mouth of Rio Oro Canyon when Abraham Olmsted said, "Ain't that your sister comin' this way?"

Glory shielded her eyes with her hand and peered toward the settlement. She saw the familiar figure walking toward them. Kat had lifted her skirts a little so she could move faster.

"Looks like she's in an all-fired hurry," Olmsted said, having noticed the same thing.

"I hope nothing's wrong," Glory said. Worry stirred inside her, though. It wasn't like Kat to get worked up about anything.

They had been on their way to town, but since Kat was heading in this direction, they stopped at the wagon to wait for her. She came up to them a few minutes later, breathing hard from her efforts.

"I was going . . . up the creek to find

you . . . but I'm glad you're here," Kat said.

She drew in several deep breaths as she pressed her hand to her chest above the swell of her breasts in the low-cut dress she wore. At that, it wasn't as brazen as some of the outfits Patrick Elam had had brought from San Francisco for her to wear in the saloon.

"Tarnation, girl, what are you so het up about?" Olmsted asked. Unknowingly echoing what Glory had just thought, he went on, "It ain't like you to get carried away about anything."

That was true. Kat was the closest thing to imperturbable that Glory had ever seen.

Kat had caught her breath, but she still looked upset. "I found out something last night," she said. "Something terrible. And I don't know what to do about it. I . . . I was hoping you could help me figure it out."

"You want us to tell you what to do?" The question was startled out of Glory. That was really unlike Kat. She was the most self-assured person Glory had ever known.

"What is it, girl?" Olmsted asked. "We'll help you if we can, won't we, Gloriana?"

"Of course," Glory replied. She put a hand on Kat's arm. "Just tell us."

"It's Flint."

"Something's happened to him?" Glory

felt a surge of anxiety. She was closest to Cord, of course. She thought there was a very good chance she was in love with him. But she was fond of the other two Bennett brothers, although to be honest, sometimes Flint frightened her a little with the cold ruthlessness she sensed inside him.

"No, he's all right. But I found out that he and Patrick . . . that they . . ."

"Are they gonna have a fight?" Olmsted asked. "I know those two don't like each other."

"It's worse than that," Kat said. "They're working together. They're the leaders of the Reapers."

For a long moment, Glory and her father could only stare at her in confusion and disbelief. Then Olmsted burst out, "Flint's mixed up with that bunch o' skunks? Worse'n that? Ramroddin' 'em?"

"Kat, you've got to be mistaken," Glory said. "The Bennetts have been good friends to us —"

"Cord, maybe," Kat broke in with a bitter note in her voice. "And I guess maybe Flint was at one time, but now he's fallen in with that gang of outlaws, and as usual, he's dragged Steve into it with him."

Olmsted sighed and said, "You'd best tell us whatever it is you know, I reckon."

For the next quarter hour, Kat did so, starting with how she had seen Patrick Elam slipping out of the settlement the night before and decided to follow him.

"I'd noticed a few times before that he was gone with no explanation, but I figured he didn't owe me one," Kat said with a shrug. "He's not the sort to go tramping through the woods at night, though, so when I saw that was where he was headed, I was curious enough to try to see what he was doing." She drew in a ragged breath. "Then I wished I hadn't."

She told them about sneaking up on the rendezvous between Elam and Flint and eavesdropping on their conversation. Glory could tell that she was having to force the words out as she explained about the raid on Rio Oro City the two men had planned.

"I just can't believe it," Glory murmured when Kat was finished. "I can't believe Flint and Steve would be mixed up in such a thing."

"Steve probably don't know just how bad things are," Olmsted said. "He always goes along with whatever his big brother tells him to do, and Flint can make him believe just about anything. Flint's probably twisted things around in Steve's mind until the poor

507

fella don't hardly realize that he's an outlaw."

Glory looked at her father and asked,
"Then you believe Flint is capable of such
things?"

Olmsted sighed. "I hate to say it, girl, for
Cord's sake, but I do. I reckon if Flint had
his eye on a big enough payoff, he'd do just
about anything to get his hands on it."

In a voice hollow with emotion, Glory
said, "This is going to break Cord's heart."

"Then you think I should tell him?" Kat
asked.

"Ain't nothin' else you can do," Olmsted
said. "You got to tell Cord so he can put a
stop to this. Otherwise, there ain't no tellin'
how many folks would be hurt when those
blasted Reapers attack the settlement."

Kat looked at her sister. "Glory?"

"You have to tell him," Glory said.

Kat laughed, but there was no humor in
the sound. "The two men I thought I cared
for," she said. "And now I have to turn them
both in to the law, with no way of knowing
what's going to happen to them." She drew
in a breath and squared her shoulders as a
bleak determination came into her eyes.
"But you're right, of course, both of you. I
can't stand by and let them get away with
widespread murder and destruction. The

Reapers have to be stopped."

"And if there's any fella who can do it," Olmsted said, "it's Cord Bennett."

Cord didn't have an office in Rio Oro City, although Harville had promised him that eventually, the town would be building a proper jail and marshal's office.

In the meantime, when he wasn't out circulating around the settlement, making sure things were peaceful, he could usually be found in Clyde Casterline's office. The land recorder and assayer had agreed to let Cord use it as his headquarters and had even tacked a hand-lettered sign reading TOWN MARSHAL onto the board above the entrance.

Cord was sitting in a chair next to one of the canvas walls while Casterline leaned on the counter as the two of them talked. Earlier this morning, Cord had made the rounds of the settlement, and everything was tranquil.

"Where's that deputy of yours today?" Casterline asked. "He's usually around, but I haven't seen him."

"Steve's gone out to the canyon to check on our claims and pay a visit to Lou and Ham."

"I like those two old-timers," Casterline

said. "It's a shame they never had much luck finding color."

"Yeah, but I was lucky getting them to take care of the claims for me." Cord tapped the badge pinned to his shirt. "I wouldn't have been able to take the marshal's job if they hadn't volunteered to help out."

He might have said more, but at that moment, Glory Olmsted appeared in the opening where the canvas of the front wall had been tied back to form the entrance. Cord stood up as she hurried in with Kat and their father behind her.

Cord was surprised to see all the Olmsteds, but especially Kat. Because of her job at the Bear Flag, she didn't usually start stirring until the middle of the day. As he came to his feet, he immediately sensed that something was wrong.

"Glory, what is it?"

She didn't reply. Kat stepped around her and said, "Cord, I have something to tell you, and it isn't good."

He wondered if the news concerned Patrick Elam. Since Kat spent nearly all her time at the saloon, Cord didn't see how it could be about anything else.

"All right," he said calmly. "Go ahead."

"Flint is one of the Reapers," Kat stated. "He and Elam are running the gang."

Hearing that the saloonkeeper was tied in with the outlaws came as no real surprise to Cord; he had suspected that Elam was involved somehow with the Reapers for quite a while now. That explained why the Bear Flag hadn't really suffered from the gang's depredations.

But the blunt statement that Flint was part of the gang, too, was like a hard slap across the face. He had thought he was prepared for anything, but clearly, that wasn't the case.

Cord caught his breath and then shook his head, saying, "No, that's not possible."

"Just listen to her, Cord," Glory urged. "It's a terrible story, but I believe she's telling the truth."

As Cord and Casterline stood there staring in amazement, the details poured out of Kat. Cord struggled to grasp everything she was saying. She was obviously sincere, though, and given the way she felt about Flint — and possibly about Patrick Elam — he couldn't see how she would benefit from telling such a lie about them.

It had to be true . . . even though admitting that his brothers were outlaws left Cord feeling sick and hollow inside.

"You have to stop them," Glory said when Kat had finished. "You can't let them attack the town tonight."

"I don't plan to," Cord said. "But the first thing to do is arrest Elam."

"Where are you going to lock him up?" Casterline asked. "We don't have a jail."

Cord rubbed his jaw and frowned in thought. "I reckon what we'll have to do is tie him to a tree and put guards on him, until I figure out what else to do."

Casterline reached under the counter and brought out a pistol. "You can't go marching into the Bear Flag alone and expect to arrest Elam. He'll sic his men on you. They'll cut you to ribbons with those bullwhips. You'll need help."

"Mr. Casterline, I can't ask —"

"You're not asking, I'm volunteering."

"And so am I," Abraham Olmsted put in. The old-timer lifted the rifle he carried. "I'll back your play, son."

"We can stop at the Golden Nugget and recruit more men to help you, too," Casterline suggested. He sniffed. "Sounds to me like the Bear Flag is a den of thieves, and it's past time the good citizens of this town cleaned it out. Um, no offense, Miss Kat. I know you work there."

She smiled sadly. "I guess Patrick fooled me," she said, "but at least I wasn't the only one."

She turned and moved toward the entrance. Her father stepped aside to get out of her way, saying, "You and Glory best go on back out to camp until all this trouble is over —"

That was as far as he got, because at that moment, a gun roared outside, just as Kat stepped through the opening, and she rocked back with a cry of pain.

CHAPTER 44

A few minutes earlier, one of Patrick Elam's bullwhip-wielding guards, a man called Lemmon, had hurried into the Bear Flag and looked around for his boss. When he spotted Elam at his boss's private table, he strode across the room toward him. The bullwhip was coiled and hung from a loop at his belt.

Elam barely glanced up at the man as he asked, "Where are those cigars I sent you for?"

"I didn't make it all the way to Higgin-botham's, boss," Lemmon replied. "I saw Miss Kat going into Casterline's office and figured I ought to come tell you."

That caused a frown to crease Elam's forehead. "What are you talking about? Kat's never up and around this early."

"Well, she is today," Lemmon insisted. "It ain't like I'd mistake any other gal in this town for her. Besides, she had that red-headed sister o' hers with her, along with their pa."

Elam's frown deepened. "And they went into Casterline's office, you say?"

"Yeah. I didn't get too close, but I was curious enough to take a peek inside. They were talkin' to Cord Bennett. He's been usin' the place as his office, too, since he pinned on that marshal's badge. Miss Kat seemed pretty worked up about something. They all did."

Elam suddenly felt as if the bottom had dropped out of his stomach. He didn't know why Kat would have sought out the new marshal, but it wasn't likely to be anything good.

Was it possible she had found out the truth about his activities? Elam didn't see how she could have. And even if she had, would she go scurrying to Bennett to spill the truth? That didn't seem like Kat. She was out for the main chance, the big payoff, just like he was.

Unless he had misjudged her . . .

Elam made up his mind abruptly. He had to find out what was going on. He came to his feet and said to Lemmon, "Come with me."

He didn't think he would need any help, but it never hurt to be sure.

Without bothering to put on a hat, Elam left the Bear Flag and strode along the boardwalk until he came to a place where he could navigate across the muddy street without too much trouble. That put him fairly close to the entrance into Clyde Casterline's office. Close enough that when he stopped, with Lemmon halting behind him, he could hear what Kat and the others were saying in there.

An icy chill descended on Elam as he listened. A giant fist clenched on his guts and turned them watery. Clearly, his estimation of Kat Olmsted and her morals — or lack of same — had been completely wrong. She was ambitious, true, and ruthless enough to play him and Flint against each other. Actually, Elam had rather admired that about her.

But in the end, she was honest. She had ruined his plans by revealing them to Cord. Ruined *him.*

And the rage that welled up inside him washed all reason away with it, like a flood-tide sweeping through his brain.

As Kat stepped out of Casterline's office, that same insane, white-hot rage made Elam jerk a pistol from under his coat, thrust it at her, and pull the trigger.

Kat fell backward, but her father was there to catch her and keep her from toppling to the floor. Glory cried out in alarm and leaped forward to take hold of Kat, as well.

Cord saw a red smear of blood on the creamy skin above her dress, but he just caught a glimpse of it from the corner of his eye as he charged past the Olmsteds and through the opening onto the boardwalk.

Another shot blasted. Muzzle flame came from his right. He twisted in that direction and crouched. He didn't know where the second shot had gone, but he wasn't hit.

The Dragoon was in his hand. He didn't know how that had happened, either, but it didn't matter. Patrick Elam stood there, no more than ten feet away, gun in hand, ready to fire again.

Cord triggered first.

The Colt boomed. The bullet driving into Elam's chest jarred him, knocking him back against the big man looming behind him. Cord recognized that man as one of Elam's guards. He had a bullwhip hung at his waist, but he ignored it and tried to claw out a gun stuck in the waistband of his trousers.

Elam was in his way, though, making the

517

man's effort to draw the gun awkward and slow. Cord had plenty of time to cock the Dragoon again and yelled, "Don't do it!"

The man gave Elam a hard shove with one hand and finally pulled the gun free with the other. As Elam pitched off the board-walk to land face down in the muddy street, the guard tried to raise the gun.

Cord squeezed the trigger again. The shot caught the man high in the belly and dou-bled him over. He dropped his gun without firing it and reeled to the side as he crossed both arms over the wound. After spinning in a circle, he collapsed on the planks and lay there writhing in agony for a moment before a final breath rattled in his throat and he grew still.

No more than a double handful of seconds had passed since the first shot struck Kat.

Cord wanted to see how badly she was hurt, but at the same time, he knew he couldn't turn his back on the two men he had gunned down. He hurried forward, keeping the Colt ready to fire again.

The guard was dead, no doubt about that. Unseeing eyes stared across the boardwalk.

Cord stepped down into the street, ignor-ing the mud that sucked at his boots, and bent to grasp the collar of Patrick Elam's coat. He hauled the saloonkeeper up and then let him fall on his back. The brown muck coated Elam's face, and Cord could tell that he wasn't breathing, either.

"Hold it right there, mister!"

The shrill shout from Clyde Casterline made Cord look up. Another of Elam's men had run from the Bear Flag into the street to see what was going on, but he lifted his hands in the air and backed away as Casterline pointed his pistol at him.

"Hold your fire," the man said. "Is . . . is the boss dead?"

"He is," Cord said flatly.

"Then there's nobody to pay me to hold a grudge against you, Bennett. I'm gonna get on my horse and ride out of here —"

Cord pointed his gun at the man, too, and said, "No, you're not. You're under arrest for being a member of the Reapers."

People had begun to gather in response to the shooting, and startled exclamations burst from several of them as they heard that accusation. Elam's man looked for a second like he might put up a fight, but then resignation washed over his face. He was caught, pure and simple.

Cord said, "Some of you men get his gun and then hang on to him. Can I get some volunteers to go over to the Bear Flag and take the rest of Elam's men into custody?"

The bystanders hesitated until Casterline raised his voice and announced, "Elam was the leader of the Reapers. Now's our chance to clean them out, boys!"

That sent a near-mob hurrying toward the Bear Flag.

Cord turned to the land recorder and said, "Go after them, Mr. Casterline, and see that they don't kill anybody. We're going to handle things legal-like. No lynch mob justice."

"I do represent the State of California, I suppose. I'll take care of it, Cord. We'll do things by the book!"

Casterline headed for the Bear Flag, while Cord turned back toward the office.

He came in to find Kat sitting on the floor and leaning back against Glory, who was sitting behind her, propped against the counter. Glory had a cloth pad pressed against Kat's chest, high up under the right shoulder. Cord recognized the fabric as having been torn from the hem of Glory's dress.

Kat's eyes were open, and she seemed reasonably alert, although her face was pale and drawn from pain. She looked up at Cord and asked, "Patrick . . . ?"

"He's dead," Cord replied. "He didn't give me a chance to do anything else."

Kat closed her eyes for a second, then looked up at him again and said, "I'm sorry, Cord. I . . . I didn't know about the Reapers . . . I swear I didn't."

Olmsted was hovering over his daughters with an anxious expression on his bearded face. He said, "Shoot, honey, nobody thinks you did. If you'd knowed about it all along, you wouldn't have told nobody today."

That was true, Cord thought. He looked at Glory and asked, "How bad is it?"

"I don't know. I wish we had a doctor here in town." Glory swallowed hard. "I think the bullet is still in there. Somebody's going to have to get it out —"

"You can do it," Kat interrupted her. "I trust you, Glory."

"But I'm no doctor!"

"You've got a good keen eye and a steady hand," Cord told her. "Those may be the most important things right now."

"I suppose I can try . . ."

Cord would have encouraged her some more, but he heard a lot of shouting from the street and knew he ought to be out there, doing his job as marshal. He said, "Abe, help me lift Kat onto the counter so Glory can get to that wound."

The commotion was even louder by the time Cord and Olmsted got Kat stretched

521

out on Casterline's counter. Cord found a jug of whiskey, splashed it liberally over the blade of the knife he handed to Glory, and then left them there to step out and see what was going on.

He wasn't surprised to see that several dozen prospectors had dragged Elam's two remaining guards out of the Bear Flag and now surrounded the three men, who'd had their guns and whips taken away from them. But at least they weren't decorating any tree limbs, and Cord was grateful for that.

Clyde Casterline had put himself in charge of the vigilantes. Hitching up his trousers, he said proudly to Cord, "We've got things under control here, Marshal. We'll tie these fellows up and make sure they don't get away; then we'll find out just how much they knew about Elam's connection with the Reapers."

"Thanks, Mr. Casterline. I reckon you're my new deputy, since Steve's not here —"

Teddy Harville rushed up to Cord and caught hold of his sleeve. "Your brother's riding into town, Cord!"

Cord turned around hurriedly to look toward Rio Oro Canyon. His hand dropped to the butt of his gun, which he had reloaded as soon as he got the chance. Flint and the rest of the Reapers weren't supposed to attack until tonight . . .

Another of those sick feelings went through Cord as he wondered what he would do if he found his own brother in his gun-sights. Could he pull the trigger, no matter what Flint had done?

But it wasn't Flint riding into the settlement, he realized with a shock. The size of the man swaying back and forth in the saddle was unmistakable.

Steve Bennett had returned to Rio Oro City.

Chapter 45

Cord ran to meet the horse. He could tell by the way Steve sat in the saddle that something was wrong with him.

Steve must have seen him coming, because he reined in and waited for Cord to reach him, gripping the saddle tightly as he did so.

"Steve!" Cord said as he came up to his brother. "What happened to you? Where's Flint?"

"Don't know. He shot . . . he shot me —"

With that, Steve swayed again and started to topple off the horse.

As big as Steve was, Cord couldn't have caught him and held him up by himself. But several other men had gathered around, and they were there to lend a hand. They kept Steve from sprawling in the mud, and as they did, Cord saw the bloodstain on the back of Steve's shirt.

Steve had said that Flint shot him. Cord

could hardly believe that, but Steve was wounded, there was no doubt about that.

They were close to the Golden Nugget. Teddy Harville had followed Cord along the street. He waved toward the saloon and said in his booming voice, "Take him inside, boys! We need to lay him down and see how bad he's hurt!"

Harville and the others didn't know that Steve was a member of the Reapers, Cord reminded himself. But that couldn't have been the case all along, he thought. The Reapers had already been carrying out their crimes before the Bennetts even arrived in Rio Oro City. Flint and Steve must have joined the gang after they'd been here for a while.

And Flint was likely to blame for that. Cord hated to think so badly of his brother, but he knew Steve never would have gotten mixed up with a band of outlaws on his own.

The men lifted Steve and carried him into the Golden Nugget. Harville grabbed a couple of tables and shoved them together to make a platform big enough for Steve to be lowered onto. As the men did so, they turned him on his belly so Cord could reach his back. Cord had given his knife to Glory, so he borrowed a blade from one of the other men to cut away Steve's shirt and reveal the bloody bullet hole in his back.

Steve's breath rasped in his throat. He seemed to have lost consciousness. Cord could tell that the wound had bled a lot, but he wasn't sure how bad it was.

There hadn't been any blood on the front of Steve's shirt, so that meant the bullet hadn't gone all the way through. Like the bullet that had struck Kat, the deadly pellet of lead was still inside him somewhere.

"I need a wet rag to clean some of this blood away," Cord said. "Somebody soak one in whiskey for me."

He worked over his brother for the next quarter hour, cleaning the wound and pouring whiskey in it. The sting of the fiery liquor made Steve jerk but didn't rouse him from his stupor. Cord probed for the bullet with a finger but couldn't find it.

He was surprised when the crowd around the tables parted, and Glory stepped up next to him.

"How's Kat?" he asked her.

"I think she's going to be all right. I was able to get the bullet out without doing too much more damage, I hope. She's resting now."

Glory was haggard from the strain. Cord didn't want to ask anything more of her, but he didn't have any choice.

"Think you can get a bullet out of Steve?"

"I . . . I can try."

Steve shocked them all by rearing up off the table. Cord had been sure he was out cold. But he pushed himself up on his hands and gasped, "No! No, we . . . we gotta stop . . . F-Flint . . . The Reapers . . . are gonna . . . attack the t-town . . ."

"Take it easy," Cord told him. "We know about the Reapers' plan."

Steve twisted so that he could stretch out a hand toward Cord. "I . . . I'm sorry . . . Never should'a listened . . . to Flint . . ."

"It's all right," Cord started to reassure him, but Steve shook his head.

"You don't know . . . the worst of it . . . before he . . . shot me . . . he killed . . . Lou and Ham . . ."

Cord stared at him in horror.

"Somebody . . . gimme a drink."

A prospector pressed a bottle of whiskey into Steve's hand. He sat up straighter, lifted the bottle to his mouth, and took a long swallow from it, his neck working as the booze glugged down his throat. When he finally lowered the bottle, he looked stronger, more clear-headed.

"I'm not hurt . . . that bad," he said. "Just got knocked out . . . for a while. Flint must've figured . . . I was dead. I woke up . . . in the trees along the creek . . . not far from where they found . . . the gold."

"What gold?" Cord asked.

Over the next few minutes, the whole terrible story came out of Steve's mouth in fits and starts. After all this time, all the disappointments, it was difficult for Cord to comprehend that there was an actual vein of gold on the Bennett claim, but it was even harder to believe that Flint would murder the two old men in cold blood and then gun down his own brother rather than let his villainy be revealed.

After Kat's earlier revelations about Flint, though, Cord knew Steve had to be telling the truth. You could know someone your entire life, Cord reflected, could grow up with them and think that you knew everything about them, and still there could be unknown depths within them. They could be capable of things you would never expect, both good . . . and bad.

Steve took another drink from the bottle, and his voice was steady this time as he said, "We got to stop 'em, Cord. We can't let them attack the settlement."

"We'll be ready for them —" Cord stopped as Steve shook his head.

"I know where the hideout is. I can take

you there. There's a way into the place . . . not even Flint knows. But I found it one day, when I was pokin' around. We'll take the gang . . . by surprise."

"Not you, Steve," Glory said. "You're hurt. There's a bullet somewhere inside you."

He smiled at her. "Well, if it's inside me . . . it ain't goin' anywhere, is it? You can dig it outta me, Glory . . . when we get back."

"Steve, that's crazy," Cord began.

"I could never tell you how to get there," Steve insisted. "You know me, Cord. I . . . I ain't too good with words. But I can show you. I can lead you and a bunch of men out there. I swear I can." He looked intently at his brother. "Let me . . . make it right . . . for Lou and Ham."

At that moment, as their gazes met, Cord knew that Steve was dying. The massive frame, the iron constitution, allowed him to fight off some of the effects of being shot, and the whiskey had braced him up even more, but nobody could lose that much blood and have a bullet bouncing around inside them, doing who knew how much damage, and hope to survive. Yes, Steve was dying . . . and asking one final favor of his brother before he crossed the divide.

As they looked at each other, it was like they were the only two people in the crowded saloon. Cord even forgot that Glory was standing next to him. He said to Steve, "You're sure that's what you want?"

"Yeah. It is."

"Then we'll do it. We'll stop Flint."

Steve smiled and said, "Thanks, little brother."

The sun was lowering toward the western horizon as the group of twenty riders approached their destination. It had taken quite a while to organize the posse of vigilantes, round up horses and guns for all of them, and then ride a big circle through the hills so that they could approach the Reapers' hideout from the direction of the hidden entrance Steve had found.

It was a long, twisting gully choked with brush, Steve had explained. They wouldn't be able to take the horses through it but could push their way through on foot.

"This gully comes out next to the waterfall," Steve had told Cord, "but the brush looks just like the stuff that grows along the wall on both sides. You can't tell anything's behind it when you're lookin' at it."

For the tiniest fraction of a second, Cord had worried that Steve might be leading them into a trap, but then he had put that thought away. Whatever devotion Steve had felt toward Flint had vanished when that bullet smashed into his back.

"We can get in there without them knowin' we're anywhere around, and then if we hit 'em hard and fast enough, we can beat 'em. But we'll need to take them by surprise, because they'll outnumber us. I reckon there's thirty men there, gettin' ready to raid the settlement tonight."

"They won't get the chance," Cord had promised.

Before they left, he had checked on Kat, who had been carried carefully to the cot in the space she rented in one of the rooming tents. Her father was sitting on a three-legged stool, watching over her as she slept.

Glory was there, too, and she had walked outside with Cord to assure him that Kat was doing as well as could be expected.

"She woke up for a little while and said again she never should have gotten mixed up with Elam," Glory had told him. "I think she'll recover from the wound, but she's really upset that she let him charm her like that."

"No need for her to feel like that," Cord had said. "I don't reckon anybody will hold it against her. It's not like she knew about the Reapers. As soon as she did, she tried to set things straight."

Glory laid a hand on Cord's arm. "You're going to be all right, aren't you?"

He smiled. "Of course I will."

"You won't take any foolish chances?"

"Well, now . . . I can't really promise that . . ."

"You had better come back to me, Cord Bennett," she told him fiercely. "That's all I've got to say. You'd better come back in one piece."

"I'll do my best," Cord promised.

"Steve really shouldn't be doing this, you know. He's wounded. He should have let me try to patch him up and then gotten some rest."

"Steve will be all right. You know he's strong as an ox. And this is how he wants things to go."

"Well, he's liable to be laid up for quite a while after he gets back, so he'll just have to get used to it."

"Sure," Cord had said. "Sure he will."

But now he looked over at his brother as they rode together at the head of the posse and was more certain than ever that Steve wouldn't be going back to Rio Oro City. Steve was able to sit fairly straight in the saddle because he had bandages wrapped

tightly around his torso, but his face was gray, and his eyes seemed to have sunk deeper into his head.

"I like our claim there in the canyon," Steve said out of the blue. "It's a mighty pretty place."

Cord thought he knew what Steve was getting at. "Yeah," he said. "It sure is."

"I'll be glad to get back there. Shouldn't be too much longer now."

"No." Cord swallowed. "But not yet."

"No," Steve agreed. "Not yet." His breath rattled a little as he drew in air. "Still have some things to do."

They reached the gully a short time later. Steve estimated it ran about half a mile between high walls before opening again into the cup where the Reapers' hideout was located. He had explained about the other way in and how it could be easily defended against an army by even a small number of men. But by coming in this way, they ought to have the advantage of surprise on their side.

The brush was as thick as Steve had warned them it would be. They dismounted and left the horses with Teddy Harville and Orvie Higginbotham, who had insisted on coming along to help, even though they were too old and heavy to be wiggling through the brush.

Clyde Casterline was in the forefront of the group with Cord and Steve. The land recorder had said, "I'm skinny enough to squeeze through anywhere I need to," and declared that he was coming along. He still looked as nervous as a long-tailed cat on a porch full of rocking chairs, but Cord had seen that he could be cool-headed under pressure during the shootout back in Rio Oro City.

The other men were mostly prospectors, with a few bartenders and store clerks mixed in. Cord knew that individually, none of them were a match for the sort of hardened killers who made up the Reapers. He was counting on the element of surprise helping a great deal in the coming battle.

But even though they might be at a disadvantage, this was their only chance to strike back at the gang, Cord knew. The only chance to restore law and order to the area. They had to seize it.

Branches clawed at them, hung on their clothes, tried to hold them back. The men forced their way through the natural barrier. Their clothes were ripped, and blood from numerous scratches almost made them look like they'd already been in a fight.

But eventually, they reached the end of

the narrow, brush-choked passage. The smell of woodsmoke drifted to Cord. He heard the waterfall splashing nearby. As he bent forward to part the brush and peer through a small gap, Steve groaned softly beside him.

"Can you make it?" Cord asked in a whisper. "You don't have to. You got us here, just like you said you would."

"No, I'm . . . I'm all right. I'm comin' with you. I ain't gonna . . . let my brother down."

He said that as if Cord were his only brother. In a way, that was true, Cord supposed. Flint had severed the family connection between them. That thought put a bitter, sour taste in Cord's mouth, but there was no denying the facts.

"We can use the corral . . . to hide us . . . while we're sneakin' up on them," Steve went on. "There'll be men . . . standin' guard . . . where the other trail comes out . . . on the far side. Don't forget about them."

"We won't," Cord said. From where they were, he could see the cabins and tents and the horses in the corral. Smoke from a cooking fire rose on the other side of the cabins. Spray from the waterfall hung in the air and gave everything a bit of a hazy look. Cord felt the water's cool caress on his face as he leaned forward.

He turned his head, ordered quietly, "Let's go," and pushed out into the open.

CHAPTER 46

Crouching to make himself less noticeable, Cord ran toward the corral. Beside him, Steve loped along, too, grunting in pain with each step. Steve tried to bend down, but he was so big, it was difficult for him to make himself smaller. Casterline and the other men followed close behind them.

The horses in the corral began to whinny and stir around as the men approached. Cord grimaced; that reaction was liable to alert the men inside that something was going on.

But it couldn't be helped. He waved his arm in a signal for the vigilantes to spread out. They didn't want to cluster together and make themselves better targets.

They might have been able to get into position where they could lay siege to the cabins, but luck suddenly turned on them as one of the Reapers stepped out of some nearby trees, where he must have been answering the call of nature. In fact, he was still pulling his trousers up as he spotted the men and let out a startled yell.

The outlaw jerked a gun from its holster and fired a hasty shot that flew well over Cord's head.

Cord's Colt thundered the next instant. His bullet punched into the outlaw's chest and drove him backward, causing the man to drop both his gun and his trousers as he fell in a loose sprawl.

His death had alerted his fellow Reapers, though, several of whom charged out of the cabins, guns in hand, and looked around for the source of the shot.

Cord and the rest of the posse didn't give them a chance to put up much of a defense. A volley roared out from the vigilantes' guns. Lead scythed most of the outlaws off their feet. A few of them managed to get off some shots in return, though, causing Cord and his men to duck for cover.

"Wish we could have gotten a few more of them before they knew we were here," Cord said, as he knelt with the spooked, milling horses between him and the cabins. Steve and Casterline were with him.

The other men from Rio Oro City had scattered, hunting cover wherever they could find it. A couple of them stretched out behind a wooden watering trough and raked the cabins with rifle fire.

"Look out!" Casterline suddenly exclaimed. "They're flanking us to the right!"

That was true. Half a dozen outlaws had gotten out of the cabins and were charging around where they had clear shots at Cord, Steve, and Casterline. The three of them threw themselves to the ground on their bellies and fired from there. Two of the Reapers tumbled off their feet and rolled forward loosely. Two more staggered and would have fallen if their companions hadn't grabbed their arms to steady them. Cord drew a bead, fired again, and saw the head of one of the previously unwounded men jerk as his bullet drilled through the outlaw's brain.

A deafening storm of gun-thunder filled the cup in the hills. Clouds of powdersmoke rolled from both sides, stinging the eyes and making it hard to see. Outlaws charged from the cabins, carrying the fight to the vigilantes, and several times Cord had to hesitate before pulling the trigger to make sure whether he was about to fire at friend or foe.

Three outlaws loomed out of the smoke, almost on top of Cord, Steve, and Casterline. Cord was about to twist around and try to bring his gun to bear, but before he could, Casterline leaped to his feet and charged the Reapers, yelling at the top of his lungs as he triggered shot after shot. They fired back at him, and Cord didn't see how in the world Casterline avoided the swarm of bullets around him.

But one by one, the outlaws fell, and Casterline was left standing there among the bodies with a smoking iron in his hand, seeming amazed not only that he was still alive but also that he had downed the three men. He looked at Cord and Steve and grinned.

A second later, another gun blasted nearby, and Casterline jerked halfway around as the bullet struck him. When he collapsed, it revealed Flint standing behind him, smoke curling from the muzzle of the revolver in his hand.

With a roar of fury, prompted perhaps by the sight of another man being shot in the back by Flint, Steve surged to his feet and charged toward his older brother. Cord saw Flint's eyes widen in shock. Flint had believed Steve to be dead, but instead here he was, barreling toward him like a runaway freight wagon.

That shock didn't stop Flint from reacting almost instantly. His gun came up and belched flame again and again.

Cord couldn't return the fire, because Steve was between him and Flint. He saw Steve shudder as Flint's bullets pounded into his body. Momentum carried Steve forward, though, despite being shot again, and an instant later, his massive frame smashed into Flint and drove him backward off his feet.

Cord scrambled up and ran toward his brothers as they writhed on the ground. A thick gout of smoke blew across his face, blinding him for a moment. He waved a hand at the smoke and stumbled; then his vision cleared, and he could tell that both men had grown still.

When he stepped closer, he saw that Steve was lying on top of Flint. Both hands were locked around Flint's throat, with the thumbs dug in so deeply that Cord could barely see them. Flint's eyes were still open wide, but they weren't seeing anything anymore. Between Steve's iron grip on his throat and the odd angle at which Flint's head was cocked, signifying a broken neck, he'd had no chance to escape from his brother's vengeance.

Cord dropped to a knee beside them and rested a hand on Steve's back. It no longer rose and fell. Death had caught up to him, too.

In the end, Flint *had* steered him wrong, and it had cost both their lives.

Even knowing everything he knew about Flint, grief for both of his brothers welled up inside Cord. A sob shook him as memories flooded through his brain. Childhood memories, growing-up memories, sunny days when the three Bennett brothers had been inseparable and had always loved and defended each other . . .

And to have it all come to such a bitter end as this, because of nothing more than greed and ambition, lust for treasure and riches that were fleeting in comparison to what they'd had . . . For a moment, it was almost too much for Cord to bear.

Then he became aware that the guns had fallen silent, and a groan from behind him made him look around. Clyde Casterline was propped up on one arm, his shirt and coat bloody, but apparently not wounded fatally. He looked at Cord and said, "Is it over? Did we win?"

Cord looked around, saw many of the vigilantes from Rio Oro City still on their feet, holding smoking guns, but none of the Reapers.

"We survived," he told Casterline. "Reckon for today, that'll have to be enough."

■ ■ ■ ■

Rio Oro City, three weeks later

Down the street, workmen were raising the rafters into place on the new, soon-to-be-permanent home of the Golden Nugget Saloon. Quite a few people had gathered in the street to watch the construction.

From where Cord stood in front of the temporary marshal's office, the land recorder's office, and the assayer's office, he could see the crowd and was mildly interested, but not enough to walk down there. The saloon would get built whether he was there looking on or not.

Hammering and sawing sounded from a number of other places in the settlement. With the new strikes up and down Rio Oro Canyon — the one at the Bennett claim had been only the first of several to uncover a vein — it looked like the chances were good there would be a real town here, and sooner rather than later, too.

Casterline came out of the office to stand beside Cord. His right arm was still in a sling. Flint's bullet had bounced off one of Casterline's ribs and torn a gash on the inside of his arm. The wounds had been enough to have Casterline laid up for a week or so, but he was getting back to normal now.

"Lot of commotion in town today," he commented as he looked up and down the street. "New people coming in all the time since word got around about the new strikes."

"Yeah, the town's booming, all right," Cord agreed.

"Of course, it's not all prospectors coming in. I've had several families come in and claim land to use for farming, and one fella said he was going to build a sawmill and start logging."

"The mayor will be glad to hear that." Cord chuckled. "You can't build a town completely around a bunch of grizzled old-timers who want to pan or dig for gold."

"Even so, if you wanted to sell that claim of yours, you could get a mighty good price for it," Casterline said.

Cord shook his head. "I won't be selling it," he said.

For the time being, Abraham Olmsted was working the claim on shares, along with several other men Cord had hired for wages. A little farther up the canyon, though, past where the vein of gold was located, there were four graves. Lou Spooner and Ham Erskine were laid to rest there, along with

Flint and Steve.

And someday, he would be, too, Cord had decided. The Bennett brothers would be together in death, even though fate had taken them down different trails in life.

Casterline sniffed and said, "Well, suit yourself. I'm just glad we've got ourselves a good lawman here. We'll need one if the place grows into a real city." He started to turn and go back into the office, then stopped and added, "By the way, one of the fellows who came in yesterday while you weren't here said he's a preacher. Figures on building a church here. I reckon you might find that a mite interesting."

Cord looked along the street, and a smile spread across his face as he saw two young women emerge from Higginbotham's store and start toward him. Both were beautiful, but one had hair that shone like fire in the sun.

"Yeah, that's pretty interesting, all right," he said; then, still smiling, he headed along the boardwalk to meet the woman who was going to be his wife.

545

ABOUT THE AUTHORS

William W. Johnstone is the #1 bestselling Western writer in America and the *New York Times* and *USA Today* bestselling author of hundreds of books, with over 50 million copies sold. Born in southern Missouri, he was raised with strong moral and family values by his minister father, and tutored by his schoolteacher mother. He left school at fifteen to work in a carnival and then as a deputy sheriff before serving in the army. He went on to become known as "the Greatest Western writer of the 21st Century." Visit him online at WilliamJohnstone.net.

J.A. Johnstone learned to write from the master himself, Uncle William W. Johnstone, who began tutoring J.A. at an early age. After-school hours were often spent retyping manuscripts or researching his massive American Western History library as well as the more modern wars and conflicts. J.A. worked hard and learned, later going on to become the co-author of William W. Johnstone's many bestselling westerns and thrillers. J.A. Johnstone lives on a ranch in Tennessee and more information is at WilliamJohnstone.net.

The employees of Thorndike Press hope you have enjoyed this Large Print book. All our Thorndike Large Print titles are designed for easy reading, and all our books are made to last. Other Thorndike Press Large Print books are available at your library, through selected bookstores, or directly from us.

For information about titles, please call:
   (800) 223-1244

or visit our website at:
   gale.com/thorndike

Printed in the USA
CPSIA information can be obtained
at www.ICGtesting.com
JSHW022241090824
67802JS00001B/2

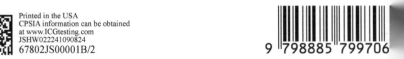